**The Bronze Rod**
a  novel

Edwin Ahearn

## Thea

I was not always maker of magics, but a sad disappointment to my father. At thirteen, I killed a bloke, and did not enjoy it. No one of any standing, and the killing was not meant.

Much of my remembered youth has rain in it, rain and wet clothes, muddy paths and the steaming sides of horses flecked with mud. Caer, where I grew up, seems a wetter sort of spot than others, not set on high ground like some other royal places, but in a deep fold of the land, frowned over by a ruddy great hill — the very one, so said, where an ancient king of All Brittan lies sleeping with all his warriors, some day to waken and come forth to save us. As a child it properly gave me the willies, when the rain-clouds hung down over its dark dome.

Yet the day I killed Barr was warm and sunny, and his rich blood creeping across the courtyard dust is always there in a chap's head; we were practicing with swords, and I slashed his throat. His face had less expression than a pudding bowl; he was a farm-boy with thoughts of soldiering, and I was a prince, so there would be no punishment. As I think of it now, it seems likely my martial father bragged it, and if so the boast soon went sour for him. I gave up use of all weapons, and no threat or beating could change me.

For my seventeenth birthday my cousin Worrel decided time had come to make me into a man. Of his manhood were no questions; he was born brawny, or so I was always told, as if I was at fault for my own spare frame, and at five (the year I was born) had seemed eight. He loomed over me, even when,

with a late spurt, I reached height not more than two inches
less than his (but that was later than the time we consider
now).

He had been the one who tried, before the murder, to
teach me the beginnings of weaponry.  He bullied me
somewhat then, I small for my age, he already full-grown.
Perhaps a touch overfull, a broad, dark-eyed, shock-headed
warrior with fists like turnips, whose contempt soon gave
place to a watchful indulgence for my lesserness, and he stuck
up for my farewell to arms, saying I was meant to be learned,
no fighter.  Like a black bull, like Tom Rhinocerous (in old
myth, a creature to give fits even to a tyger), Worrel was
seldom crossed or even queried, so good nature was normal
with him.  Yet he had, too, the obstinacy of his blood, and
carried about an underlying danger, and it was always luxury
to be on the same side with him.

So too in larger sense.  Our fathers were brothers,
Worrel Heir in Marchlen, Gwyn's ally in all time, or so we
liked to trumpet: it was true while any difference between
neighbours was less than shared threats.  During my years at
Caer the Lords of March were our oftenest guests, as we
theirs, so Worrel's riding in a few days before my birthday was
nothing out of the regular.  Rather than invitation he brought
orders for me (that was his way); I was to ride with him back
to Pormarch.  Gwynis my sister, haunting within earshot,
asked if the roads were safe, not always a reasonless question
even if she was just trying for a part in a do not hers.  Worrel
tipped back his shaggy head to roar laughter; he was bound for
home from skirmishes on the borders, and the Nettle-Greens
(from the colour of the skaufs they wore) were with him, a
dozen young toughs, well-armed and war-blooded, a match, so
Worrel had his boast, for any hundred ordinary fighters.  He
might be right; ten well-trained warriors with trust in each
other can easily beat off or even rout a rabble of fifty, though
one can't take on five, unless in a doorway or some such

narrow place.  As Worrel said, this was different once, and would be again if we could get back the Viztas' gift of guns.  Lots of the old machines are forgotten or doubted, but guns are not.

We set out when the sun had scarce risen, the heavy dew not at all.  Worrel brooked not to be delayed, and now, after so long years and too many dyings, I still envy the smiling ease he handled to turn aside further hospitality of my parents, giving no offence because it never came into his noggin he might offend.  Gwynis, however, let disappointing show.  My sister, now fifteen, had taken to clothing herself in linen instead of plain girlish stuff, dressing her hair like a woman's, but her wheedling of Worrel was really not more than training herself for the chump she might someday wish to chain to her eyes.  Worrel was no quarry for her, too near in blood, not only first cousin through our fathers, but cousin again, like half those I knew, by way of our grandmothers.  They were two among the several daughters of Edlin I, through whose schemed matings that southern king had laboured and failed to knit this island into one.

Wet to the thighs from long grasses and the caress of leafing branches, we were at first a straggle of horsemen on winding paths.  Later we would reach the broad, open way, sometimes channel, sometimes causeway, where if tales were not kidding had sped of old wheeled machines driven by means now forgotten, able to gulp down in an hour what was for our toiling horses a day's steady chewing.  It was hard to know how much to believe.  The hawthorn was still a little from bloom, but oak and ash together had begun to spray fresh green, and there were banks of daffodil going past their prime.  As we jogged under silvered sun Worrel told me what lark he had planned; we would not bide at Pormarch, but would be ferried across the wide river to the tiny kingdom of Sevenin, so as to see the big May-fair at Bris.

I was a long way from delight.  Ages before (told in

those cumbrous slabs of time that are the years of childhood) I had been taken to that gathering, and had mostly had fun of what neither frighted nor tired me, but such dos, as I said to Worrel, are most for boys, and those whose japes will be the same at forty as at four. Speaking, I faltered, seeing at midpoint I could well be describing the easy-lounging giant I rode beside.

Strange how a chap can be wrongest where nearest right. Grinning, Worrel reminded these fairs were never without one pleasing at least not for small boys. Believing (quite rightly) I was not started on mannish games, he meant to bring me to the star players, the famed Dauwas of Thea.

He himself was all appetite at the notion, and Worrel was no beginner. He had, I believe, fathered his first farm-lad-to-be at fifteen, and I may run ahead a little to record that by the time of his wedding, now some years to come, he had sown a dozen scatterlings in five or more different realms. His wiving, matter of fact, was in part caused by his father, my Uncle Bryan, who grew shirty over the cost with not a sausage to show: being a lord with honour in his sport Worrel saw to it none of his sons was at risk of starving, and later on gave small dowries for the earliest among his many-dammed daughters. I've seen Worrel take a ripe apple and in swift snaps of his square white teeth fill his mouth with flesh and juice, leaving the slenderest wisp of core. All living was his apple.

And I? It would be a silly imposing of niceties that came later to deny Worrel's scheme started stirrings in me. If at seventeen I was a complete dud in the lore of bedding it was not for lack of interest. Some birthdays had gone by since first a chap was startled, perceiving the glee felt when a serving-girl reached across the table, soft skirts betraying with loyalty the twinned young roundness. Unwarned glimpse of a girl's bare leg or bared shoulder could check my breath, and soft hair nestling where neck and shoulder met was the start of feelings more muddled, flame and fondness and folly all at once.  All this was ready, and I knew the ripeness of my equipments; as with much else it was the beginning that daunted.

None of this got protested to Worrel.  I stammered, and he said I must take heart; the battle, once joined, was less dangerous, leaving no wounds to linger.  He was, as I can now say, a lucky blighter.

There would be a day, he told further, when a woman, much to be pitied, would become my wife, and she, if not I, would be grateful for my learning what Thea's Dauwas had to teach.  To that effect.

Worrel was no seer.  She never was, but at the time there was sense to it.  It seemed sooner or later in this, I was dead sure to make a blithering ass of myself.  How much better, then, with some unmeaning and soon-farewelled hireling, than when starting out with a wife, whose rue — whose scorn, it might be (even then, I had heard of such), would be the longer to endure.  Then, a chap could not know how scorn can find the form it needs, nor all the different ways there were to be a nincompoop, in bed or out of it.

It was taken as settled, and at Pormarch I spent no longer than Worrel had at Caer, just time for nicety to his parents and to my lovely cousin Cara, as small and fair as her brother was large and dark.  We went to Sevenin not as lordlings but cloaked in roughweave, unrecognised, or so we hoped.  Worrel was armed beneath, while for safety some half-dozen of the Nettle-Greens dogged us.  We were not as windy, so Worrel instructed me, for death or wounding, so much as capture and the price we might fetch in ransom; even in those days, so mild in memory, no place was safe from the unscrupled, and there was everlasting wrangle over the proper borders between the realms.

No doubt, ages ago, Old Bris was a teeming and

prosperous place. I write knowing as much as any alive, likeliest more, about those lost times, and yet with Bris, as even more with the vast barren of Lunn (which I now know was called London), it fair makes a chap's head swim to try guessing what riches lay in bringing together so many, or how, for the big part, they made their livings. As is true of machines, of books, of so much that made up that world, it is the variousness that does in our lessened minds, yet can it be there were tasks for such uncountable numbers? There were shoemakers then, and a ruddy crowd of feet to be shod, but how were the shoes earnt? Alone, the notion of feeding numbs the old noggin: how could all that grub be grown and carried to these anthills, and how could such a lot more have the eating than the growing?

Now, to us, these hard places are chiefly where no farm can prosper, soil spare and barren with grit of crumbled brick and mortar, poisoned with sour stuffs which on a time may have had a purpose. All right, within these deserts are patches that flourish with growth, but they grow wild, since no one would farm in the midst of the untamed Mynas, and where cities were the Mynas always are. The northern clans have a song in their own uncouth speech (harsh to our rotten ears, then how would it have seemed to Keats or Tulsingham?) where they boast to be something like "Free in the sunlight, owning the dark." That's a bit thick, but not much. The Mynas could never challenge for overlordship of any realm, but still, no overlord had been able to bring them to heel. Coming it too uppity with some ruler, clans had met reverses, but they were safe from final defeat in their command of the undercities, bafflingest of all relics from our lost past.

Marvels at second hand make tedious tales, but I (like any outside the Clans) have had no more than a glimpse of than world below the cities, main of all beneath Lunn, where even a Myna will admit he can never know all the layers and layers of passages and tunnels, where every fresh clearing of

rubble finds yet more halls and branches, shafts and buried
stairs.  It is guessed there were drains, and ways for travellers
on foot or by wheeled machines; some places no doubt were
used for storage, but as with the cities themselves the very
muchness makes puny our guesses at purpose.  Clearly a city
was not then a crowd of buildings, shops and places of work
brought together for safety and so as to be near each other, but
had become a single thing, like a giant machine itself, stone
joining stone joining stone, road meeting road and tunnel
tunnel, so setting foot at the outmost rim of that great waste
then London was at once to be linked to all the other feet, to
all roads and buildings, to become part of a man-carved realm
where trees and grass were ruddy gate-crashers.

So too at Old Bris and elsewhere, though lesserly;
Lunn is all by itself for size and the huge tangle of its
undercity, but all these places have somewhat the same,
encampments of Mynas where not a bean can grow, and where
they can readily vanish into the tunnels, their safety and their
living.  I should say not all their mining is under ground; they
also find orts in the shells and rubbles of great buildings.  Still,
though they spend a lot of their time where there is no sun, the
Mynas, and surely their women, do not make their dwellings
there, except when in danger (the days just before and after
childbearing are so considered, and many if not most Mynas
have been born below ground).  They live mainly in what's left
of of old buildings, having hidden access to their tunnels.  But
night-visioned from generations of their calling, and of mating
Myna's son to Myna's daughter, they are abashed by sunlight,
and in the open wear low-brimmed hats, or else deep hoods.
Their habit of keeping eyes lowered and neck bowed beneath
the strong sun may be why we think of them as short, which
may not be true, though they are generally narrow of shoulder,
hazel-tough rather than oaken.  They seldom travelled far from
home except in tight, wary companies, and plenty of lords had
tried to put a stop to that lark.  Quite decent chappies can

practically froth at the mouth, talking on the ways of the
Mynas.

I've said they lack power to rule, but if they ever
dreamt of such they might have had a better shot if, for more
than a fortnight at a time, they could have stilled their
differences; Myna clans fought over their boundaries, or the
spoils from a newly-pierced hill of rubble, sometimes over a
wife desired, or nabbed by stealth.  For a year the Brown Hares
and the Badgers, strongest of the northern Myna clans, were in
cahoots, and a counter-alliance of realms was needed before
they were subdued — but that tale brings in my kin, and
comes at a time later than the subject from which I have
astrayed, my birthday and Worrel's plan.

Before putting aside this account of the Mynas,
however, I should add they had no use for farming or herding,
and not a farting for service and rote obedience.  You would
not find Mynas riding in ordered ranks, acting together upon
an agreed plan of battle.  Though he answers to chieftains and
to leaders of bands, each Myna keeps his own tally of goods
and dealings, of his family and feats.  Many were to be seen at
the Bris fair; such gatherings are above all a selling of wares,
and aside from foodstuffs it is always the Mynas who have
bulk of what can be sold, and the greatest need for money to
get them their bread and meat.  On the steep hill above where
the ferry landed were stalls and booths, some given to sweets
or more earnest eatables, more to clothes, trinkets and tools or
might-be tools.  Of what the Mynas unearth some things have
with us an agreed use, not always the purpose, perhaps, for
which they were made an age ago, others are given a use,
could be with some reshaping or sharpening, but well-made,
unspeaking shapes of metal or the smooth, tough material we
call plass are simply put out for sale in hopes the buyer may
invent an employment.  Ago, or so I believe, miners who were
not our scavengers delved ore which was brought to those who
could refine it, for others who forged the thousand things

needed: our smiths have made scarcely anything new, and for the big part only hammer and rebend what already is. The Mynas often bring up strange rods and plates and tubes of hard metal, still lustrous, with which the heat of our little forges has no power, and these we must either make use of as they are, or leave idle, unmoved by fire or hammer. At Bris, as always, what they could not name the Mynas tried hardest to sell; some, both men and women, are crafted at exchanging quips with those who might buy. It may be I've made too much of their darker side; though they always kept in the shadow of their covered booths, the afternoon bright but not sunny, these could be affable, their pals never far.

I looked out for books, but they were getting scarce. My father used to speak of his grandfather's boyhood when books were, he said, everywhere, cheaper than firewood, so even the poor would use them. Those made of the yellowish, rough, breakable paper were thought best; heavier books with smooth, white paper a bloke had to feed to the flames a few leaves at a time, and burnt grumpily.

The slope once breasted, there were more booths on the broad level
beyond, going towards Old Bris, and packed campings. Here, too, were the rings where cows or sheep, sometimes poor horses, were sold, or where games and tricks were shown, jugglers and simple conjurers and so forth. Worrel, after dismounting near a cooking-fire to buy and stuff down a smoking chop of mutton with a brick of coarse bread (he used the bone to make friends with, then leave, a fanged black dog I wouldn't have gone near), challenged and quickly threw a young giant from Stanglin, who was offering to wrestle any. Winning, Worrel helped the big easterner to his feet, and refused both the prize he had won, a shrill piglet, and return of the coin given for the bout. With a grin he explained to me no one not flat broke would make such a long journey for such a purpose; I admired the thought and still do, but remain

divided.  A bargain is after all a bargain, and even the very
poor must not risk what they may not lose; I could see the
young wrestler knew himself lessened by his gratitude to
Worrel.  The gesture, you may imagine, made rubbish of our
roughspun disguise, common people drawing back in respect,
some bowing, as we pushed through the crowd drawn there by
the bout.

It surprised me a lot the Dauwas of Thea could lodge
themselves in the best building still standing; they must, I
guessed, have paid off the Mynas well.  A thick-walled, massy
place with heavy pillars at the front, and few signs of scorch or
crumble.  There was a rough new roof and, inside, rougher
new ceilings.  The large halls had been screened into lots of
rooms, too little for much more than a bed apiece.  Some
square windows, partly blocked, had thick slabs of our murky
glass to let in a dribble of light, and where the window-holes
were completely stopped with boards or rubble, good candles
burned clean.  These, with the skins and weaves that softened
the chilly stones of this ancient place, told me the Dauwas
were in the dibs.

After a challenge at the entrance, we were taken to
Thea herself, who greeted Worrel as a fellow she knew.  It was
not that the Dauwas took their name from her, but the other
way; this guild came from time beyond memory, and its
captain, as we might call her, always rising from the ranks
(and the couches) got the name of Thea.  This one was slim, of
middle height, not yet forty, with a clean-boned face that,
never beautiful, was still — and a chap fails finding word to
say she drew eyes to her, and would in a place thronged with
women younger and more beautiful.  Judged so by most
chappies, I mean to say.  Thea's eyes were large with lights
deep in their darks, and her body was in blue, close-fitting up
to the throat, but leaving her pale, slender arms bare.

A woman of gifts, yes, but it was with Thea a chap first

recognised himself as out-of-the-ordinary by reckoning larger than a family's. We sat with her at a table and cool drinks were pertly brought, while Thea matched ease of manner with Worrel. She seemed truthfully glad to see him again, laughing at his jokes, teasing him with the names of women that might fit his needs. Worrel was not shy to list what he desired to do and have done, and it was soon fixed he would have two women, one the girl, no more than sixteen, who had brought our drinks. I felt my mouth go dry at the thought of her restless young bum, but was bothered without real reason to find we would spend all the night there. No difference made that mattered, but in those days I liked plans settled in advance, not made or unmade all at once. I still do.

Quite right Thea should make a fuss of Worrel, who would have been a lord among men if born without a bob to his name, and whose warmth was always the cause of warmth in others — and yet when for the first lingering time she turned eyes to me, we understood each other in ways Worrel could never reach. The notion was daffy enough to bowl a chappie over; I came humbly to let Worrel have a man made of me, and now Thea without a word was telling she and I were the grownup ones, and would speak of proper doings so soon as my cousin was happy with his toys. Neither this reading of glance and manner, nor knowing old Worrel was blind to our silent treaty, changed, then or ever, my admiration of him. While a room was being made to his liking, he tried to talk to Thea re what would be best for me, but his wishing her to know and take care of my needs was at odds with his own mounting eagerness, and he was glad enough to leave faith in Thea's judgement when the changed drinks girl came to lead him away.

Thea, smiling a trade smile, drank from her cup, and murmured to me that I too could be served. The way she spoke made plain she did not expect a chap to hasten off to be womaned and so manned, and then came family talk. Oh, I

was a young lord, full of haught, not much tickled she knew
my fathering and my place of birth, and why I might never rule
a realm (the last not said).  No mystery: the Dauwas travelled
the realm following fairs, treaty gatherings, rumours of brief
prosperities, musterings for war, their wares sought by every
kind.  It was verily their blooming business to know who ruled
and who served, who wed, who rose and fell.  At first a chap
might have called Thea's familiar talk presumptive — no,
presumptuous — but I made myself holiday-minded.  In public
a chappie sometimes has to keep a position, but I soon learnt
in private not to stickle.  Some I know without youth for
excuse whose need for dignity makes them preposterous asses.

Now Thea spoke knowingly of the realms and rulers
jostling, as ever, for power.  It tells a lot about her presence
that at the time I didn't see anything odd, hearing of such stuff
from a housekeeper to dauwas.  In short memory, a day or so
later, when Thea's flattering gaze had stopped bemusing a
chap, I approached doubting she'd talked as she had, but in
long afterview I see she was trying to tip me off about my own
power, to tell me words and strategies of shrewd thought can
outmow swords.

She had even the nerve to warn me about Suvram's
weakness.  This was no news, and so I told her.  At that time
Suvram was still largest and richest of the realms, but any nit
knew it had fallen off in the years since the death of Edlin I,
King of Suvram *and* Stanglin.  He, making all he could of his
descendance from the House of Regions (the Colinid branch),
had used forty years advancing his claim to rule all Brittan,
failing at last by the thinness of his own patience, that was the
tale.  He left treaty talks, it was said, with it all going his way,
to look over some brood mares he might wish to buy.  Dying,
he left good horses but only his own realm among a dozen to
his one son (there were six daughters).  Stanglin, the
easternmost bulge of Brittan, had already gone as dowry for
his firstborn girl.

Very well, Thea said, we might agree Suvram was no longer what it used to be, but the long reign of Edlin I had so usened us to its largeness we were blinded to how much had been lost under his dull son, Edlin II, now past fifty. He had a great love of shellfish.

What of it? was my answer. If the southern realm no more had armies to awe us all, then neither had anyone else. Border squabbles cost a few lives, a dozen heads of cattle, yards rather than miles of disagreed ground, but these petty wars gave a pastime to young lords like Worrel, and we did not seem at brink of return to general unlawfulness.

Here, as I now believe, Thea checked herself; later in our friendship she might have jawed at me, like Cassius with Brutus in a story of old Rome, over my not doing anything about trying to change the world. At this time, she kept to her path, asking or challenging me about the ambitions of Raug — of the Vandene Kingdom of Raug, as she was careful but sourly unglad to name it. She and the Dauwas came just then from a gathering in the Midlen, on the borders of Raug, and had heard and observed signs of a warlike mood in the Vandene Kingdom, of arming and drilling, captained largely by a bloke whose name I knew, but hitherto as kinsman to the king and a priest by his own right, Forn of Raug.

Thea asked suddenly whether I believed in the Viztas and I laughed, not able to think her earnest. How could I not believe — and see now what I've done. More than once, more than twice with my tale so new, I've spoken of our riddled past, not as I would have then, but out of present knowledge and opinion; it's very hard, I learn, to conduct one's mind back to a former ignorance. Ago, like everyone else, I was not baffled. Not to mean I or anyone else could explain the steps of how plass was made or the hard metals, how cities and their undercities came to be, how books or glass bottles or swift machines numerously created. But we had — all but a few still have — a single, embracive explanation for the shebang;

the Viztas. A lulling view it was, not easily forsaken, and a chap would still believe in it, if he could. It holds that what is beyond our understanding, beyond the skill or knowledge we've got now, was brought to our world by the Viztas, beings who came from the sky in fiery, gleaming craft. Not air-craft, though they had those also; the Viztas came from nowhere on this Earth, but from the unmeasurably far stars. Where they had now returned, but with a promise to come again.

So far what I've said is generally agreed, and hardly anyone fights with the time given for the Year of Leaving since our present age dates from that: I am writing this in YL 754. (Whenever, dealing in such matters, a chap writes *anyone*, what is meant is any of those who give it smallest thought: for common blokes make it enough to count the weeks till spring, and they neither know nor mind where they are or when, in any grander sense.) Nor is there much questioning of the tale that to rule in their absence the leaving Viztas appointed the Regions, the first being Colin I, ruler of All Brittan. But beyond those, there are strong differences as to (for instance) whether the Viztas came once or often, how long they stayed, when was their first coming, and whether they were like giants, or, clad as men and women, could go among us unknown. Differences, I say, but these unmatches of belief as held by various sects, various rulers, have often been passioned matters of death, too often cause for war. Or an excuse for war; blighters who care not at all about adding a river-bank, a narrow strip of land to their realm will grab weapons joyfully when the cry is Death to the False Believers.

Largest and bitterest of all disputes concerns teaching and learning: some — and these are also the ones who think the Viztas came often, though for only brief remainings — say they taught skills to us and then withdrew, coming again when men (by which I mean both men and women) were ready for a new learning; the making itself, the building, the printing, the very many arts we can do no longer was done by taught men.

Others hold a middle view that we worked long under the guidance of the Viztas, in time having skills of our own, which chappies could teach other fellows. But the purest, least yielding creed, whose followers call themselves the Vandenes, is certain men and women, being as they now are, a clumsy lot, could never have been master of the knowledge needed for the world as was before the Leaving and at best were tools plied by the Viztas, to whose powers alone was owed all that was ingenious, lovely, and marvellable.

While, as I have just said, wars have been fought over differences of belief, it must also be said in more parts you could and can find reasonable types, even among rulers, those who can have one belief and let others have others. But not among the Vandenes, who are certain there can be only one truth, and who've held it their duty to put kibosh on what they call falsehood. Always, the Vandenes have held the Kingdom of Raug, where the ruler was always named Vandis, and all subjects must be of the Vandene sect. Alone of the realms Raug kept a cumny armed with the task of seeking out and putting end to other beliefs. Seeing in the snake's skin-shedding way an emblem of the Viztas, who do not die but are to return ever-youthful, these Vandene enforcers of creed call themselves the Adda-Priests — and now it can be seen why Thea's question was not the orphan it might seem: the Forn she had spoken of was a leading Adda-Priest, and now it appeared also a captain of fighters.

I told her I was no Vandene, nor any of my kin, and she said to believe in the Viztas, as the Vandenes did, made all the world like weather. Recording chinwag, when the people or the matter is more couth than our present language, a chap is going to pretend sometimes we used words we could not have. I also leave aside interruptions. Evening was coming on and trade briskening; several of those coming to spend coin had been said important enough to have Thea guide their choices. This talk all occurred, mind you, years before a chappie knew

any of the wonder of how words once were; then I believed, as
still, that no one, not even Marten, was more skilled than Thea
in using the poor language of our time to say hard things.

Seeing my puzzlement, she explained: we cannot
change weather, not now, not next year, not in any time.
Saying we never learnt is to say we never can, yet there were
Vandenes everywhere, not only in Raug.  This time I
understood at once and rebuked her; loyalty to their lords came
first.  She smiled, as if at one far off, and reminded a chap the
Adda-Priest Forn did not believe so; there was rumour among
the Mynas of Midlen, she said, Raug meant to claim the
jackpot inheritance of the Regions, when time was thought
ripe.

This I negatived.  They would never dare.  Thea kept
up her grin, saying people who desired rule found ways of
retelling old tales; what was known about the Viztas was not
told by Viztas, but by men.  There were, she darkled, some
nasty times to come, and we must find joyment where we
could; so she meant to say we would leave this talk of powers
and power, and now, to a chap's utter deprivement of breath,
she asked whether I would wish to pass the night with her.
There were younger, she allowed, but a chap would find few
men to say better.  I must not disappoint the Lord Worrel, after
the trouble taken.

While a chappie tried to mutter it was myself I should
not disappoint, she called a girl to her, and told her any further
customers who came should be clasped with whatever dauwa
was free (by *free* I mean to say, idle, not buckshee).

In the morning as we rode for the ferry after a poor
breakfast by one of the cooking-fires, Worrel, blurred himself
but grinning at my dazement, asked which of the girls had
shown me how it was done.  I did enjoy his unbelieving gape

when I told him who.  Thea, he alleged, was not on offer, not
ever, not for the five years he had known the Dauwas, not for
years before that.

My not trying to answer this was doubtless better
convincement than any insisting.  Worrel went on to say he
had heard that before she became the Thea, she could crazy a
man with joy and leave him emptied like a skin bottle, and it
was a waste she would take me (instead of him, that was to
hint), who could not know how extra she was.

How, indeed, could I know?  But as child I was given a
fine linen shirt for some birthday, the first linen I ever wore,
and yet I knew without telling it was uncommon for fit and
softness.  Besides, full many a time I had heard oafs telling —
or braying — of long, hot nights with women, and even
allowing for their unskill with words nothing they boasted
came near the dog's share of the feast we had gorged, Thea and
I, past middle night and at last trying to fend off sleep because
sleep would be a thief.  (But in the end a chap dozed, and so
learnt yet another joy, waking to nail down night with
morning's last hammering.)

In the newness of envying me Worrel asked whether
she or we had done this or this.  A chappie gave the least
answers he could without ruding; Thea counted as dauwa, so it
would not have been shame to spill beans about all she did.
Worrel, besides, was kinsman and friend; when the time came,
a few years after, he relished long describing of his first
married night.  Still I wished to be private of Thea's varied
skills, not because those delights would wither at the frost of
words, but because the sum was not a jot like any describing.
Once, if I'm not completely off the beam, people used to talk
about *making love*, but Thea and I had been making trust.  One
more of Worrel's questions I dodged; Thea in fact had warded
away any payment, but was pleased to accept what would have
been hard to refuse, a jewelled clasp off my shoulder, long in
the family.  All these years later a much older chap can still

feel the awkward hope Worrel would not take notice it was gone.

He, without malice, got into his noggin my slowness to boast must mean little to boast of. I let him think such, and did not answer his sidelong jibes about Thea's great sacrifice. If a chappie can say so without too much conceit, the truth was, in the long reaches of night she, looking all at once no more than my own age (or less, perhaps), dark hair stranded damply, knelt beside me in dying candlelight, face both blazing and tender, and said hushed words I can render as, "You'll do very well, Master Evan."

That, though top-hole, nor even memory of the doing, treasure as that has stayed, was not the grand prize. From that first meeting with Thea a chap carried away notions, yet only dimly espied, there might be ways to alter time by means neither swords nor royal marriages. Not alone her warnings of the threat from Raug. No, it was the way she used words to probe and test: things any mug was sure of might after all be a house of only words, a breath in the sky. What we did with the world would never again be like the weather, good or bad beyond my power to do aught but put up with. To become so, as another well-loved and gifted woman says, is not without loss.

### Seeyow

In my childhood he was Uncle Marten, although not in fact my uncle; our kinship is a remote one. When I was small he came bringing me sometimes strange presents; one is beside me now as I write, a block I can hold in my hand, shaped like giant tombs in a very old place called Egypt; Tulsingham names them Pyramids (William Shakespeare has one in a play, too, but he makes things up; Tulsingham has a picture. In his day they were still standing, and we might find them still so, if we could discover where Egypt is again). My toy is of solid plass, once deep red, but the outside is now much pitted and pinked. In the square bottom there is a piece can be slid out, and then the whole block will come apart into a dozen odd-shaped parts, to be put back together only in a certain order. The first piece out is also the last in, working as a sort of lock. I, after such years, could do the putting-together in the dark, but it took me an age to learn the trick of it, and it has baffled lots who boast their cleverness.

Young, it was of such matters I thought hearing Marten's name, and I was always tickled pink when he came, though his shaggy hair and loud laugh, his unusurped beard made me a little fearful. He told roaring jokes, and there was a time when, unjustly, I was beaten for retelling at table one I could not understand, only knowing Uncle Marten had made himself hoot with laughter. It was after that time he ceased to

visit Caer, and not till years after did it enter my old noggin his
exile and his jokes were connected. He had taken to calling the
Viztas, for example, the Goatherds, and demanded to know
whether they ate man-meat; for what other reason, he asked,
would beings so masterly make so hard a journey to be with the
dullards we are? It was repeating this question in all innocence
which caused me to be birched raw.

     Though I had seen him seldom since there were famed
stories of his strange doings on the lonely island of Seeyow,
and I never lost memory of the joy his visits used to bring. In
the summer to which Thea had been my spring, my Uncle Yew,
the king, wished to send someone of rank to question Marten
about taxes, and I greedily offered to be messenger. I was
wishing to take part in greater matters than Caer had to offer,
and I was heeding Thea's advice. On our single morning, in
between the made and the spoken farewell, she said lots of
advices, some rather riddling, others plain, and one that might
have been laughable, except it was Thea, and not joking Thea:
she said I should become better friend with Marten, if my life
allowed it. She had not used the name that was usual; Mad
Marten.

     Yew, a weathered geezer with a face like my mother's
as a baked apple is like one sun-bathed on the bough,
swallowed doubts but freighted me with exact orders fitter for a
simpleton. For the journey he gave me six of his own gawd,
the Red Hounds. Lydd my servant, wholly mine since my
birthday, went with me on the journey, and it is a nice question
whether I was given less respect by him or by Rann, the officer
of my scawt. Eight-fingered and scarred from his fights, Rann

was younger than would be guessed, but trusty. I was safe with him and the Hounds, though he had no opinion of me, or of anyone whose chief amusement was other than war. These are points that once gave me much hurt I kept private; how (or whether) one is served is chief, yet I was thirty at the least before I ceased to desire the admiration of those I had no reason to admire.

But because Yew said I could not go without, I did wear a sword on this journey, and on my travels thereafter. You see how easily that is told? the solemnest vows of youth have more give than Pyramids.

Seeyow lays off the northwestern corner of Farragwyn. A goodish trip from Caer, even in summer, the roads mainly dry. The easier way, if not the shorter, was going due north from Caer in easy country by Marchlen, turning westward only when the sea was glimpsed from hill crests near where three realms came together, a district of often dispute. Here, the last tongue of territory claimed by March, dark and tumbled between Gwyn and the southern borders of Raug, was where Worrel with his Nettle-Greens had his spring skirmishings, but with lots to be done on farms the land was peaceful now.

At evening in a cool valley we came to a gathering of poor houses, smoky and tumbledown; what little livestock I saw was a ribby lot. This was still within our own realm of Niragwyn, yet there was a sunset rite led by a man of Raug. An Adda-priest of the Vandenes, known at once by the Myke, an emblem which properly belongs to all believers, but which (as I had heard another priest, not one of the Addas, complain) we've allowed the Vandenes to usurp. A short rod, a little thicker at one end, through the power of which (believers say) the far-off Viztas know about us, and by which the chants of those who worship are heard. These chants — and now a chap sees for the first time (or I might say my ear tells) there are things for which I fetch no echo in this Print English, where the roughness of the tongue we speak is needed. It would be painting a dove black to pass him off as a rook to try forcing this smooth music to the harshness of ours. There were also that time and spot, dank valley under failing light, smoke of foul cooking hung blue in the air, and the gormless bleat of a tethered goat.

As for the words, they are not so much, especially those of the gathered, who bleat answers to questions the priest chants. Most, being about who made that world that was? from who comes wisdom? who knew the tall buildings and the swift machines? and who will return to make it all new again? — have the same answer; the Viztas (blokes in my own cumny, sitting in saddle, let their mouths shape the word). But a few questions, demanding of a sudden such as who should obey them? always caused to me tickling disarray, some starting to say the same once more whilst others after a pause gave the proper answer. A chap writes lightly now. At the time I gave the rite respect, though not without recalling Thea's thoughts, and now to agree; Vandene beliefs made failure into no one's fault; how could a chap honour Viztas not wishing us to do all we could unaided? Perhaps (this was the brainwave I had), that was the test their absence gave, and when they came back and saw what a doomy mess we had let the world become we would be judged unworthy of their help.

At that age I was, a new thought could be crystal dawns, and send mind soaring miles, like an early falcon in silent flight, though in the mean time not considering some necessary question, such as where I would best spend that night. A chappie can't say even now he has reformed that altogether, though as I pass more years I find my flights more tethered; what for one bright moment seems new soon finds rings oft-circled to move in. Perhaps it's better... but here my tale is standing still again, as I did then, wondering whether these Vandenes, more than a just a blooming nuisance, were betraying us all.

As skill may be judged apartly from what it makes happen, the Addapriest of that twilight gathering was about the best I had heard, and I wondered if he might not be the famous Forn of Raug. But this was an older blighter; when I had him brought to me, he knew (and I thought feared) Forn, and even admitted it was at Forn's orders he had taken to journeying from place to place, one of several who were crossing all realms to renew (quoth he) the worships of all the Vandenes they found. As if showing me his warrant to do so, he held up his Myke of smoothed wood, quite plain. The True Myke, of which all others are mere memories, was said to have come from the Viztas, and was of polished metal, but it had turned up missing long ago. The Vandenes, however (not other believers) say in a priest's hand these little toy copies work just like the True Myke: I remember Marten once giving scandal to a whole gathering, shouting *Allo, Viztas!* into an Adda-priest's Myke.

Before this priest could say more I suggested it would

be not less than courtesy to visit Caer and let the king know what he was up to. The priest's smooth agreement, making no promise, irked me inwardly. Calling Rann to me I told him two of our six men must be spared to escort this bozo forthwith to Caer, not as prisoner, but with no choice.

Rann baulked, saying his orders were to see to my safety. He had the nerves also to say we were not at war with Raug. That was true, and the priest was going against no law and breaking no treaty; in the long run perhaps there was no preventing what he was doing, but in the first place, though I might be overruled in time, I was the only nephew to two kings in this mouldy corner of the realm, and not willing to debate matters with a junior (if war-scarred) officer.

The second place was the coming-home of Thea's hints; renewing Vandene worships this and other priests were advancing Vandis of Raug as the proper lord for Vandenes everywhere. In these border parts which had so often changed hands the people themselves must often be dizzied to know what ruler was owed their taxes and their loyalties.

It was a struggle which, we may say, had already begun with Rann's questioning of my orders, because Rann eyed the priest with respect he withheld from me; I guessed he was Vandene himself. He was among those who had silently made mouth with the chants, and at the end, unseen as he thought, had made the Sign of the Return with his hand.

Now the shrewd priest, supposing division, tried to agree he could quite well make his own way to Caer. In this one instance whether he went under escort, went alone, or only feigned to go would not be life or death of realms, but for me, on my first outing as king's emissary, it was, I knew on instinct, a tide that must be taken at the flood. A burly warrior like Worrel could be seen to waver, but not I. Strange to ponder had I then let any doubt be known, a chap might now have no tale to tell.

With Rann, to give reasons for what I was bally well going to have done would have been as fatal. Instead I repeated my orders, slowly and coldly, and when Rann, after blinking, turned to choose the two who would go with the priest in the morning I was cagy to show no satisfaction, which would have admitted relief, hence doubt.

To furnish some sort of end to that tale, Yew, when I saw him again, asked for what I had sent the priest to him, and could not understand my reasons. Early on, the best ally a Raug could have was always the pride, not to say conceit, of other rulers, who could not admit the chance of their subjects changing or wobbling in allegiance, never asking what of they had ever done to earn the loyalty of a poor bloke living in a wretched border hamlet. (Here, a chap sounds more like Thea than I would have then.)

Meantime, I lodged for the night in the least filthy of the hovels, and in the morning when I was just dressed there was a disturbance, six
or eight oafs shoving and cudgelling a shabby, shirtless traveller in what they called the street, a muddy bend of the road from the south. The victim was angry as he ducked and dodged, but did not draw the knife, near long enough for sword,

he was wearing.  I suppose he was windy if once he bared steel, though he might wound some of the villagers, they would in the end kill instead of merely bruise him.

Shouting for my gawd, I put an end to the brawl, more of a bullying.  The villagers, I found, were upset because the man, whose name was Donal, had been given a bed for the night as a travelling Tela.  Washing by the brook in the morning he had been seen for what he was, a Myna.  His shoulder was marked with the two-eared tattoo, emblem of the Brown Hare Clan of the north.

It was all most strange.  Mynas made their journeys oftenest in bands, and if they seek lodging it is with others of their kind, when they find a clan with which they have no quarrel.  Householders do not take in a Myna because, so they say, Mynas bring disease or bring vermin, or steal; the real reason is flat dislike with fear at its root.

Still, to charge this Donal with falsely passing himself off as a Tela was silly.  Though I had never heard of a Myna being a Tela as well, there was no law or reason why not.  These Telas travel carrying news from place to place, and when there is not enough news to pay for their keep they recite made-up tales or sing songs.  Bulk of Mynas, I guessed, would think Tela an unmanly calling, like sowing or reaping, but if one had the needed skill with words (skill by our poor measure) he was as much a Tela as any other poor blighter who wished to put on the black cap by which they were known, and put up with the hardships.

This I told the villagers, and the one who had taken

Donal in, and been first to point finger at his tattoo, I ordered to return the rest of his clothes and belongings, and also to spare him a cup of milk for a breakfast, for which I would supply the bread. This was all done, even if my servant Lydd was surely one with the cudgellers (when he could speak privately the fathead reminded me Donal was a *Myna*, and a Myna of the north, what was more).

Discovering Donal was going west I told him he could hang along with our cumny, if he could ride a pack-animal, which the consuming of our supplies left free. It is not uncommon, I should add, for Telas to wait at towns and villagers for a chance to go with a riding that passes in their direction, though their poverty is a proverb, and robbers do not waste minutes or arrows on them. Yet again, as Lydd tried to urge, it was unknown for a Myna to be given such a courtesy, and Rann too muttered about the packhorse. But my firmness about the priest (who had already been started south for Caer) had done its work; it might be a chap would end this adventure with a name for madness as famed as Marten's, but I was going to be obeyed.

At the question whether he could ride Donal's face had flashed a quick pride. It was a keen-boned face with a good brow; though his dark eyes were set deep he was less inclined than lots of his people to keep them to the ground. He was lean and clean-muscled, and I thought he must be of the leaders in his clan, though his age was hard to guess, except he was above twenty and surely not forty (he was at this time twenty-six).

As for me, I was very young, as now can be seen, and like the young divided between myself and the thoughts of others.  It was a beano to give long faces to Rann and to Lydd, but after time a chappie began to wonder whether he had not made a bally ass of himself.  Easily begun, to let a shabby Myna ride beside me on a drooping pack-animal, but to end was another matter.  Donal had brains, and could tell me tidings about the north I had not known, and jolly little tales about the doings of northerners, but there was a darkness about him, not only in his eyes, aye, and a closeness, too.  No Myna will ever say more than he wishes about his people's ways; they've learnt not to trust, and while Donal was grateful I rescued him, he was not ready with the secrets and customs of his clan.  But beyond that was a dark I have no name for.  Knowing his later story I do not wish to put myself forward as a seer, but even then, surely, I found tautness and ominousness, like the straining threat of a bent bow; his travelling alone was reckless, but he had the face of one who would dare much more, of one, perhaps, who could know himself alive only when face-to-face with death.  There I've gone too far; not possible I could have had such thoughts then, struggling between my own daring and the embarrassment it was beginning to bring me.  Yet I could see Donal was unordinary, not least in how little he deferred.

When I told him where we were going he laughed suddenly; he too was bound for Seeyow, and for meeting with Marten, whom he knew well.  Like others of the Mynas, he said, he had standing orders from Marten to bring odd bits that might be found, mainly things that could not be sold elsewhere; Marten, it seemed, gave good money and needed supplies in exchange for what others refused, and the less a chap could imagine a use for some device the better Marten seemed pleased. His collected trophies, according to Donal, had overflowed a large storehouse and were piled against walls, but he still bought. With him now Donal had parts, it might be, of machines, and some tiny tiles, samples, only, of what could be brought by the hundred if Marten wished to buy. There were also one or two fairly well-kept books, which Marten sometimes bought, though not to burn.

It was some relief to my — the word, I think, is discomfit, not discomfort — to know I was not first among lords to befriend this Donal, though I was not sure I was wishing people to bracket me with Mad Marten.

For a loony Seeyow would certainly be the place, a wild, windswept island where the trees grow crooked, parted from the coast of Gwyn by a narrow, often little more than a moat, in old times crossed by at least two bridges: one was still in use well into the time after the Leaving, the strong piers and pillars still to be seen. It broke at last not to be mended only after the fall of the House of Regions. Some time after, I mean, not that it fell down in omen. Yet a narrow strip of water it takes a fellow no more than minutes to cross by a ferry does to make Seeyow a realm all its own, more so in the weakness of Farragwyn.

Perhaps one reason Marten chose Seeyow for home is that old learnings were kept there for generations after the Fall of the Regions. That was a time when things fell apart and none of the centres held; from warring kings Brittan went to no kings at all, only rude war-captains, with the rule of any

particular place almost always in doubt.  Before, the two
centuries under rule of the Regions, it is said (not by the
Vandenes) there were still learned and clever types, in Stanglin,
on the upper parts of the River Tem, and in other spots (the
religious other than Vandene say they were taught by Viztas).
But after, these were chased by war from their old homes, and
the last of them in the end found edgy safety across the straits
in Seeyow.  They became known as the Counters, being great
reckoners of time and distance, and but for their keeping of
records, we would have no true count of the years today.  But
there were other secrets the old geezers guarded.  Could be they
still knew, or again learnt, how to read in the old books, but any
writings they may have made using the old signs have never
turned up; Marten and I both did more than a bit of ransacking.
The Counters themselves vanished, never heard of after Brittan
began settling into the separate kingdoms, like Raug and
Suvram and Wezram — that is, the time of my grandfather's
great grandfather.  No one can say who it was at last invaded
Seeyow and put out that last little light (pretty obviously, it
must have been the Vandenes, because they would have had it
in for the Counters), but chaps feel some of what the Counters
knew must have been left behind there, in the air, as it were, or
the stones of where they lived.

     By luck, the old road leading straight as a fallen ash
from where the bridge once was (now the ferry's landing), is
still fit to be used, kept clear with its lower-lying parts filled
with broken stone.  I called the island a little kingdom, but
really not so little, in size not much lesser than the Kingdom of
Sevenin, though Sevenin with its red soil and watered valleys is

heaps better farming.  Seeyow rises to no great heights, but
north and east are desolate tumblings, and the whole island is as
if tilted, with much of the western side low and boggy.
Marten's stronghold, near middle of the island, is a bruised old
stone building, much patched, perched on a ridge away to the
right of the road, looking out south and west upon marshlands
which stretch to the grey sea five miles beyond.

It was the evening of a cool and rain-flecked day when
we came to the village lying beneath Marten's house.  Soldiers
of his bright-clad gawd had met us at the ferry, but one at least
must have cantered ahead, since the rest of the Peacocks with
their captain were waiting to greet us where the road divided,
and to lead us on the long upward curve where the trees all lean
as if digging in heels so as not to slide down into the marshes.
Marten, shaggy, drest in what looked like chance-found
oddments, was by the gate to shout his hello, and I was
bemused he was no older.  He was younger: at twelve I had
thought him a hundred or more, with his bushy eyebrows and
craggy nose, but now, windburn and all, he was not much more
than forty.  Though short and waistless, Maire his wife was
younger still.  There was little to choose between Marten's
greetings to me and to the Myna, Donal, and I recollected one
more proclaiming of his madness was his blindness to rank.  He
had chosen for wife the daughter of a mere tanner.  But Maire
was both able and shrewd, and devoted to Marten, even to his
ways that lots of chaps find strange.
　　　　With jumbles of what looked like building stone and
piled metal, and stuff I could not name filling much of the

stable court, with tattered weave on the walls and bits of carpet
even more threadbare on the floors, Marten's hall would dismay
anyone who arrived at evening, yet its hospitality was less
countrified as the place seemed; there was warmed water for a
chap to wash, and dinner was a good roast of lamb with heaps
of supporting dishes and fine beer, served on stainless linen by
servants well-trained.  My bed, when I got there, was clean and
easeful, in a room with a hearty fire.  But I did not sleep well
(nor the next night, for differing reasons), my head racing with
thought; my host might be cuckoo but was not tedious.  A
chappie wonders now whether, if I had gone to Marten without
that May-fair romp with Thea, I might have verdicted he was
not much else but bonkers, and so have failed to find the profit
in his oddness?  This would have been a different story, except
I would never have learnt to write it — nor been allowed to.

He'd had no interest in what brought me there, bundling
away my beginnings of talk about taxes, and pretending (or
pretending to pretend) I had come all that way for a good
chinwag, for old times' sake.  Over and again he asked Maire if
it wasn't spiffing of me to ride so far, explaining hardly a chap
he could fully talk with ever came here (Donal, I should say,
was not at table; Marten's shockingness knew some bounds).

He was not so keen on debate; in my time there majority
of what I did was listening, and I was mostly content to, though
at times wishing Marten could be seven yards farther off; his
voice gets loud when his interest kindles.  Or where he has
strong opinion, as where does he not? but custom is to lower
the voice when chewing over beliefs, even when no one of
consequence can overhear, and on that first evening I was less

embarrassed by Marten's disbelief, scornfuller than ever, than by his seeming wish to tell everyone on Seeyow the Viztas were frauds.  Too, he was smelly, with the sharp staleness of a badger at the end of winter's sleep.

It would be dopey now, after so long a time, to pretend I remember just when what wisdoms were said on that first time in Seeyow.  It must have been next day, when Marten showed me the tower room from which he watches the skies, that he suggested, just like his long-ago joke, the Viztas would never have made such a journey as was said unless we were the only food they could eat.  With him, perhaps alone in Brittan, "such a journey" was more than words; he could tell me how far the moon was, and was almost angry about even the nearest of stars being many times more far.  He shoved sheets of parchment at a chappie, covered with signs that meant bugger all, and when I said so tried to show me how easy it  was to learn the ancient numbers, bringing forth a fat book, better kept than most, and telling how the numbers at corners of pages had given away the secret (there were scattered others, it seems, who had found out the same, though only Marten did as much with the signs, once understood).

We come now to a humour I've often seen and struggled against in others, harder to see in oneself.  We have, of course, our own number signs, simple for doing small sums, and quite doable for all numbers an ordinary bloke's going to meet with in a whole life of buying and selling.  Now, I was particularly proud of my skill with our own way, and got quite shirty about not needing any other; I said this ancient
manner of using the same few signs over and over again made

counting harder, not easier. Marten, becoming louder, waving his arms, tried to make a chap see how, where the signs fell into ranks like drilling soldiers, sums could be done in an instant that with our way would take an hour, if they could be done at all. Well, true telling. a distance like Marten's reckoning for the moon is not to be written or said with the numbers we use. For large numbers we have no names for Marten had made up his own, and still clings to them, although years after I was able to give him the words used of old; thousand, million, billion, and what they stood for.

Without the old numbers, he told me (truly, as I now know) he could scarce have kept record of the sky-gazing that had led to his measurings; this was never a study of mine, and was not then, surely, but I took his word length of shadows, changing places of the stars, and eclipses the mortal moon endured all came into it; the sun, he said, was a near star, yet greatly more distant, four hundred times more distant, than the moon. He had much to say, about three-sided shapes, and how, knowing two sides a chap can tell what the third is, and how the way round a circle is always the same number of times the distance across; a bit more than three times.

It would not be fact to say purposes such as building, making, having our own machines were behind Marten's learning of numbers and patient watching of the skies. Yet he liked to rant on about the bettering to all we did knowledge like his could give.

I remember he said (not with these words), giving centre to his unbelief, that the Viztas were never needed. Men before were no marvels of thought and knowing; they must've been like us, bulk of them thick, and slow to teach. But they had writings, and numbers were a part of that, they had books, where last answer from heaped years of labours and mistakes could be written down. Once right and there, it was learnt in an instant by all but the very dullest. So there was no need to keep making the same mistakes over and again, as we did, not knowing someone, somewhere, had done that work. No matter how stupid, one who could read had the profit from before.

A chap's face must have doubted. Not that I said a dicky, but Marten broke in on himself to ask whether I had liked a dish at dinner last night, a sort of forcemeat pasty in a sharp and tasty sauce. I had praised it at the time, and now did so again. Marten sillily asked whether I could cook it, knowing the kitchen (as I answered) was no domain of mine.

But Marten said the girl who made that pasty from start to finish had no letters, meaning, of course, our own clumsy signs, and if asked whereaway Caer might lie, would never know which way to point.

A chappie was hanged if he could catch this drift. Like a sword-fighter crowding in on a vantage Marten next asked, with a tweak at my woollen wristers, whether I could knit.

Now thinking I saw what he was about, I said no, but my sister, in most doings less clever than I, had learnt knitting from our mother — or to be truer, from Jinny, a servant woman who looked after us. Then Marten asked, if I came to be in a place where there were no women who knew knitting or the other spider-tasks, could I, given yarn and thread, work out from my own brain how cloth and knit were made? Having, moreover, both weave and made wool to copy from? Or, when my clothes wore out, would I have to go naked, or bump off rabbits for their skins?

While I went on scorning those women's tasks, Marten came to his point; my sister, like others of far lesser brain, like the kitchen-maid with the pasty, were taught by others who had been taught; no one would have a clue where to begin once the chain of learning was broken. So also with the smiths' helpers who in time became smiths, and with makers of harness and thatchers and the rest. But in kitchen and forge, one person learnt at best, all just one knew. How, then, would it be if without journeying one chap could learn what all the smiths knew, all the carpenters, all the makers and dyers of cloth? not only what was known now, but all that had ever been known? We lack language for this, and even in his telling Marten was hobbled by the language we have. Still, the meaning came clear; knowledge written down was there for any who could read, not vanishing on the air like speech, and could be added to, changed with experience, talked about by everyone, put to use. Nor was it needful for all to know all; words too could be used to bring together different skills, just as our own carpenters and stone-cutters might club together their crafts in putting up a new house, or mending an old one. Those are simple arts which by former judgement we do badly, but Marten's heat was starting to persuade a chap far harder jobs could be done far better if we could still learn from the triumphs and no less from the botches of the past.

Not all at once could I come to Marten's opinion.

Writing this, I now agree, in those old times that to us were
made by giants, the swift machines and swifter weapons were
worked, mostly, by stupid blokes who could never have made
them, and even the cleverest that then were could have only
parts of the skill needed to make the whole. But as yet there
was no answer, Marten had none, to the question: what, then,
had happened? If the Viztas were a made-up tale, and our
forebears by themselves had made their world, how had the
inheritance been lost? No tale answered as well as the Leaving;
if a dark place has works that could have been done only by
daylight, then sun must once have shone there. This and other
talks on that first visit may have turned a chap into a
questioner, but not more, not yet an unbeliever.

For my second night Marten found a girl for my bed, if I
wished it, daughter of a stableman. A common courtesy to a
young bachelor of my standing, and a chap (thanks to Worrel's
thought and Thea's lessons) made good use of her. Now
Worrel, in his knowing way, had foretold it would be hard for
me to be without something in my bed, once having wrestled
away a night; true, I was (and still am) easily roused, not the
least staunch. But I am not Worrel, and after Thea, with a girl
no more than pretty and willing, I found greed soon slaked;
even with the fierce blood of seventeen I got impatient to move
on. Abed, three things guard against tedium (there can be
tedium of the heart, I discovered, even when the prick stands up
for renewal), and two were there with Thea; she was dashed
clever with her body, and good for talk. It was a long time
before I knew the third.

I did talk with my stable-girl. Well, she was only a servant, but it is not my way to behave to one who bares and gives her body as if she has done no more than fill a drinking-cup. She was not much of one for talk — she was a girl of few words, they used to say in old books, and with her that was exactly it; the number of words she knew was not a crowd. Enough, however, to tell she was windy of Donal the Myna. He had not, as a chappie first thought, tried to force her (another of the tales about his people we are always ready to believe), but had frighted her with his hungry looks. She was flaxen-haired, that girl, with bright blue eyes, and folk like to say the dark Mynas would sell their own mothers to possess a fair woman; I made up mind to blow the gaff to Marten. Even he could not allow this.

As turned out, by morning Donal was gone, having had his jaws with Marten. That was the day I decided it was useless trying to discuss with him the business I had come on, and went instead to Maire. Taxes are not what we think of as women's affairs, but any moron could see Marten had not a jot to do with the even running of his household, and I soon found my guess was bang on. Maire knew the exact amounts owed — taxes are always spoken in hides, bushels and fleeces, though it can all be changed to money. In those old days she was very respectful to me (to my rank, to be truer), but she would not be shifted from her firmness these taxes were owed not to King Yew but to Jon VII.

Of course she was right, if in this world it made not a farting's difference. Seeyow, you see, belongs to Farragwyn, not to Niragwyn, though whether the former was a true realm or a vassal province was a matter of debate. Years ago Jon VI who then ruled Farragwyn had been killed in a fight, leaving behind a nine-year-old (also Jon) as heir. My grandfather, Tavy, king then of Niragwyn, had taken on the rule of both kingdoms, till Jon, so said Tavy, was old enough to rule for himself. That time was now long arrived, but Jon was a rather timid blighter, and hedged by gawds whose chief loyalty was to Tavy heir, my Uncle Yew. No one, bar perhaps Marten, whose sister Jon had married, called his a proper kingdom. The weakness of Farragwyn was another reason why Marten could get away with ruling Seeyow like his own realm; Caer is more distant than Landin where Jon was.

In those days of innocence I was a big fan of the law and thought it worked or ought to work without regard to the power to make it do so. I was Yew's man, but could not dispute with Maire. Nor could a chap return sheeplike to Caer with such answer, so we settled I could collect the owings on Jon's behalf, and carry them to Landin, where I was sure Jon would agree they should go to Yew. It only took me a bit out of my way, the road from Landin to Caer being easy. Still, I can see now this was another sort of beginning for a chap; by putting myself out a little, still gaining what was aimed, I let all maintain their pride; Seeyow could hardly refuse to cough up the taxes. It tipped me off for other, larger matters, courteous rites might betimes do what unbending stubbornness could not.

There was no hurry with summer still young, and I made good stay at Seeyow. To this day there is much about

Marten I have to guess.  He is often walled off in his own thoughts, and while I could not discover about his friendship with Thea that's not that he was bent on guarding secrets. Certainly he was not one with her when I brought up her view of Raug and the Vandenes as a threat that loomed; waving at his work with numbers and the stars, he said all that would be at an end when they triumphed, but he was being sarky.  In Vandene belief reaching for knowledge as Marten did (or the old Counters had) was all evil.  Laughing, he allowed it might be other if they could lay hand on the True Myke of the Viztas.

That was to put in another but joking way what Thea had said, the heritance of the Regions.  The Myke had been given to the first Colin at the Leaving, and a chap supposed somebody who found it and could rightfully claim it would have a good go at ruling All Brittan.  But it had been lost, I reminded Marten, more than five hundred years ago.  He only smiled the larger.

Yet like Thea, and surprisingly, he seemed to think I should take part in the doings of realms, though it was not till the warm morning of my leaving, with the men from the Red Hounds already mounted, that Marten asked if I did have the income, now, for a following of my own.

The thought had never come to me; my parents, rulers of no realm, kept a good household and enough armed men for our safety and the pride of our rank, and whilst other lords of about my age who were not heirs had their own cumnies of fighters, I couldn't take part in the warring they followed. Marten, for once low of voice, told me I could not go on my travels, speaking with rulers, in the care of borrowed soldiery.

Not properly seeing what he was getting at, I laughed a bit, and said one with the repute in weapons I had might end with a strange following. His reply was the shrewdest and worldliest I yet heard from him. I should choose good fighters, he said, and when I picked, ask them, not what their beliefs are, but what they thought of the beliefs of others. Then I should take only the ones who shrugged.

I cannot be done with this tale of my first manly journeys without the bit about Landin. There my business was soon settled when Jon lambly agreed the taxes I had wrung belonged by right to Yew. Marten's untalkative sister Elen made no comments.

They live in what is left of what was once, but long ages ago, a castle. These were not as cleverly made as the buildings that came later, but their massiveness has helped keep them standing, as too with the churches. For those we have another name, but they can only be the churches Tulsingham mentions. They are in all parts of Brittan, some altogether tumbled, others with whole walls still standing, made with the carven look things had before the machines made everything smooth. Not places we trust: a traveller caught in bad rain might use a church for shelter, and still we go nowhere near these places unless we need to, but only watch their slow crumbling. (Later, perhaps, if a place arrives, I can write down some of the stories, all fake, told to explain churches.)

Great stone buildings, not like stored fruit, rot from outside in, and at Landin, inside layers and layers of crumble, the heart of the once-huge fastness is still sound. Other rulers I

might name could be grandened by grandeur in decay, but Jon
was smalled by his choice of dwellings, and it was easy not to
remember that as well as third cousin to Edlin of Suvram, he
was descended, or so was said, quite nearly from the House of
Regions. Nearly in blood, not time; that line led back five
centuries to Cara, sister of Maud, last in the Colinid line to rule
all Brittan. Yet Jon, as I've said, was only in name ruler of
Farragwyn, a mouse-coloured mouse with restless eyes, not as
little as the habit of shawling his shoulders made him.

His wife differed from her brother, having fair
colouring, light hair of nameless shade, like the half-bleached
tufts sometimes found under matted shocks of grass. All the
more abacking then was the long, lovely hair of their daughter,
soft gold of no weight but much gleam. Now twelve, she had
been a sickly infant, so for long it was all Billingsgate to a stale
bloater she would not live. Except for that dreamish hair she
was now no beauty, being mainly elbows, neck and knees. At
table she was sullen as porridge, and her pouting was not lifted,
was made worse, when her mother explained she had been kept
from riding that day as a punishment for rudery; the girl's face
filled with lidded anger, and she made eating into defiance. For
one lone instant she kindled to attention, and that was when I
told about the Myna, Donal. The girl looked up quickly to ask
whether, like his kind, he could have put curse on the village
for turning him out. She began a tale of her own, which her
mother soon shushed away, about a fisher whose boat, after he
insulted a Myna, kept starting holes. Later I had heaps of
reason to remember this, and even at the time was struck by the
pattern it made; the dark Myna at Seeyow tranced by the fair

stable-girl, the gold-haired girl at Landin curious about the Myna. Things darken with age, tales as well as cut stone. The girl, not yet budded, was Caif, who lots of blokes, not excepting I, would be in love with, Caif the Golden who would cause a war.

**Tales**

Things read make it quite likely Gridge became our holiest place by goof. We call it the place where time begins, and preponderant guys now say that is because it was from Gridge the Viztas had their Leaving, on the date where we begin to count our years. Also often said is that Gridge, a crowding of buildings which must once have been spiffy indeed (though now mostly ruined) was built by men commanded by the Viztas themselves, and it is not far from the spot shown as where the Viztas first came to Brittan, reaching shore by boat where the River Tem begins to widen to the open sea. But this lump of the tale was, in earlier times, told about a place ages to the south and west. A half-day's ride from that coast is Stonedge, circles of older bloody big stones, lots now fallen, stuck in windswept grassland. Stonedge would really fill the bill much better; the work there was quite botchy, just what you would expect from bozos who were only learning how to build, partly trued stones simply set one on top of two to make arches. Anyone can see the Sign of the Viztas the Vandenes use is copied from one of those arches. They were built carefully in line with the rising and setting sun, to help, so the story went, guide more of the Viztas as they came from the sky. (Later than the time I have to write of, I found Stonedge, with a bit different name, in Tulsingham's book, and what he says about it could have no tittle to do with the Viztas, but seems nearer what some call the Old Beliefs. Of this, more anon.)

So at one time, in my humble, it was at Stonedge all the chiefs and their followings used to hold their get-togethers, as we do now at Gridge, much nearer the wilderness of Lunn. Though within Suvram's borders, Gridge belonged to anyone: the kings in Suvram were pledged to keep it eternally free for the whole lot. On Midsummer's Eve each third year there is a herding, when people from the farthest north, the distant east, Midlen, Gwyn and throughout the south and west come to Gridge to look at the dawn. A place of truce, and no one, even when war was going on, had ever barred travellers from making the midsummer journey to Gridge, where battling kings could set up their campments side by side without fear of any argy-bargy or hugger-mugger. To be sure it has been a time of holiness and prayers, but also of meetings and remeetings, the big guys vying with each other in the splendour of their tents and banners and appointed followings. If not in altogether peace, spats could be discussed with no weapons drawn, agreements and alliances made or remade, and often there were marriages and betrothals. The last ran wild in the year I am now up to, when I was twenty-one.

Already ways were changing, though not as much as they would. The border-warrings of my youth, while they meant death and maiming for some, seem now like a springtime of innocence next to what came after; battles were mainly brief between such forces as were at first brought against each other, and there seemed an unsaid agreement rival realms would not like puffed and reckless gamblers start to double and redouble their stakes, to the utter ruin of one or both. Even Suvram, at the most of its power, aiming to rule all Brittan, had not tried to win the whole shebang in war, taking the elbow of a river-valley here and the crest of a line of hills there, gaining more by treaty than blood. Long ago, after the Regions fell, there were big, ruining wars, and I don't say we have become brainier than then, but the memory of famine had, I thought, helped teach us where small farmers need every son that can be bred to help work the lands is no flesh to be spared for warring the year round; to a ruler there is no profit or flourish about doubling his realm if both his old domains and new are beggared.

The change, already begun, was due altogether to the Vandenes of Raug who, warring for their faith, rewoke an old unforgiving mood, and willed fights to the finish. It does amaze me others were so slow to recognise; how and for how long Raug was able to make use of the old fashion in border-fighting to accomplish what it purposed, beginning battle with the usual bands of fifty or a hundred, luring an enemy and then launching out far mighter forces of well-trained soldiery, keeping to their ranks like a machine that could fight, to rout the enfeared adversary and seize coveted territory. Not once but over and again this was the M.O., and still blokes like Worrel rode out with their little bands searching stardom and renown against enemy who thought of neither, only victory. As soon as midsummer, 729, Raug had pinched a dozen patches of new land, and was peckish for more — concerned, as Vandis spoke it, to afford protection for all of the Vandene faith, whether at present within the borders of Raug, or wherever they might be.

A chap says Vandis, but the voice and in verity maker of his policies was this Adda-priest Forn, who to his skills as holy man and soldier added a dangerous seeming-courtesy.

Perhaps it would have come to pass in any case, but as things are this one blighter, Forn, is father to the change in war. First in memory to raise cumnies of soldiery far beyond the need of bodyguard, and to maintain them year round, he himself fought ruddy seldom, and that made him a new sort of captain. Of his soldiers he demanded some craftiness in weapons, but mainly the discipline to fight together, seeing no blush about using numbers to win. Forn kicked off with small cumnies which, riding or fighting on foot, always kept their ranks, and these soon earnt repute lots beyond their strength in numbers.

I had begun to change, too, and at Gridge that year for the first time was able to forge, for a brief bit, the show of single purpose against the ambition of Raug. At issue was a moiety of Worrel's inheritance, a narrow stripe of Marchlen, which Raug did covet, and which Worrel's father, Bryan, seemed to think not worth the warring for, despite his son's brave aptness to fight (this was the very country where I had met with the Myna, Donal). It plained to me that once having swallowed that slice of March, it would not be long before Raug chewed off, also, the northward finger of Niragwyn, and would be looking hungrily across to the dark hills of Farragwyn, that guarded the way to Seeyow. A chap did what a chap could to put the wind properly up Yew, meanwhile telling Worrel to go again to his father and say if he were minded to put up fight, Yew might well be ready to chip in a bit of help. My four years of journeys were making me known in all courts, and when Tam, the new-succeeded, tough young king of the far northern realm of Cumba, rode in for the rites, I had parley with him, and pointed him out if that bit of Marchlen were lost, he would not make any southward journey without Raug leave; the old coastal way would lie all within the borders of the Vandene Kingdom. It was no giant feat to kindle up the anger of Tam, a raw-faced bullock of a bloke who had killed with his unadorned fists before now. Returning to Uncle Yew I tipped him Cumba would fight beside Worrel to keep March as was, knowing Yew would have to join them, since otherwise those allies, once sword was out of the sheath, might decide to carve off a piece of Gwyn for themselves. With all three kings (a fourth, Jon, would as ever follow Yew), each believing the others more eager to fight, I was ready to inform Vandis of the strong coalition bolstered against his greedy claims.

For this a chap walked, with only Lydd my servant, from our modest family campment between the larger ones of my two uncle-kings to the imposing tents and booths of Raug, nearer the river. A chap was happy not to have to speak to Vandis, a fat, haughty blighter whose pure faith had not purged natural rotten manners. I was sent to the Adda-Priest Forn.

You might've expected him to be peeved when told Raug's demand for the narrow stripe of land would be resisted by my cobbled alliance. If he was, he most warily did not let me see. No doubt believing there would be other time (as there was, and soon) he brushed away the matter with a joke, only somewhat carbolic, about Yew and my warrior-cousin having found a novel champion. Then Forn went on to other and quite abacking topics.

I had been with him before at this or that do, and heard him speak with a Myke in hand, but this was the first time face to face.  It was spoken he could not put ten words together without finding a way to plug and honour the Viztas, but it was not so that day.  Forn is dark-haired but with piercing blue eyes; not statured, he is well-knit with good shoulders and a firm chest.  Standing, he puts his feet strongly, with the mien of one who does not dislike himself.  In some, and rightly, this is called beastly conceit, but Forn it made seem a fellow to be liked, if possible.

His unloud voice, too, is a pleasing one, by our standards (when I sound in my head the poems written of old, I must believe there were voices then more tuneful), not worse because it was plain he practiced to make it so, all without ridding the one fault all noticed.  His front teeth, white and small, fail properly to meet, top to under, so he hisses a bit on words with esses in them.  This habit was cause of multitudinous jokings about the Adda-priest being adder indeed — jokes, be sure, not without shudder in them.

To my startlement he asked after Gwynis, whether she might be turning thought to marriage.  My sister was now at her score, and to my view it seemed she had thought of bally little else for about half her life.  That was not my answer for Forn.  We fenced a little, but politely, and soon I saw he was speaking, not for the Heir in Raug (whose name at that time is of no consequence; if he succeeded he would become Vandis, like all before him) but for himself.  Forn was thirty-three or four, and being also cousin to a king his rank was proper — as a toff known everywhere, whose power still waxed, lots would have said he did honour for my sister.  Not this chappie.  Nothing could make me dislike him there; so few have any skill or grace with our shrunken words I could have chinwagged the morning away with him — but it was a blooming nightmare to dream myself kin-by-marriage to this Vandene of Vandenes, whose minions in Raug sniffed out disbelief like ferrets diving after rabbits. It was battle to keep that feeling absent from my face as I tipped Forn he must first have words with Gwynis self, and then the pater. Forn's reply was to the effect that brothers, as famed, are ever last to see beauty in their sisters. His funk, he said, was that Gwynis, being distantly admired, might already have planted her heart elsewhere.

I bowed and thanked him, but was thinking there are blisters can't speak straight if asked whether it's raining. Quite right, too; Gwynis, as I after twigged, was Forn's third choice (it was thus never true, as Worrel postulated but I no more than wished to believe, that this was altogether because Forn hoped as his brother-in-law I would be less a rub to his plannings). But Forn's first choice, like Worrel's, like mine, like any farm-lad who could but dream, was Caif. It was her golden being, the grand prize of all prizes, that made that into the famous year of troths.

Caif, a chap was always sure, would take Worrel, and with him in the field did not give myself worm's chance. Mine was the nearer friendship with Caif as she blossomed, if it can be called friendship, oafstruck in her company as I became. Twice we had ridden so far as Seeyow together, and more than twenty years after, a chappie's breathing still stumbles at remembrance of her light hair lifted in the wind. But I never made bid for her or to her; she admired warriors, and assuredly knew herself worthy of one like Worrel, who would be a king.

Between Caif and Worrel, however, there barged a misunderstanding I never quite fathomed, but that it engaged Worrel's pride. She, courted now by Forn of Raug, chose in hurry, or so it seemed, to put herself beyond reach of the lesser by favouring the advance of a more northern suitor, Tam, the young king of Cumba, of whose big size and temper I've said above. Forn, meanwhile, had next tried his fortune with my twice-cousin Cara. Not yet free of threatfulness from Raug, Bryan her father was not opposed, but not the sort to make her go against her own choosing. Dear Cara was Worrel's sister indeed and said she would take a slow-worm sooner (this was to cleverly say, sooner than the Adda); not long after she bound herself to the goodhearted albeit somewhat dry Kennet of the little realm, Sevenin.

Thus it was only the dance going on when Forn settled on my sister. I expected she would say much the same as Cara, yet both my uncles were all for it, perhaps believing they could offer to Raug a bit of atonement, both for my schemings and for Cara's naysay. So my father left Gwynis decide for herself, and she, to my stun and irk, okayed Forn. It meant, with other alterings, she would have to become Vandene in her beliefs. Cara could never have done it, and not Caif neither; she was not much bothered with belief, but had been often with her Uncle Marten, and did not call him mad. Belief was not a sausage to Gwynis. For no reason a chap can explain, Gwynis was always of that sort whose religion is only words and words nothing but noises that are made. Any belief that did not pauper her or take off her comforts she would gladly avow, and chuck it away next day, if that suited her. She was soon wearing, as with Vandenes, a little wooden copy of the True Myke, hung about her neck. After one fierce but bootless attempt at causing my father forbid the union, a chap found himself becoming kin-by-marriage to the policies most hated, and schemes most feared.

Worrel was next.  In right mind, which is to say quick-mooded, impatient of obstacles, he might yet have had good shot at making Caif change.  But Worrel was upon his pride; hearing of her betrothal (and to Tam, of all, an old wrestling rival, ill match for her beauty, *like a gem set in mud*, Worrel groused) he dickered with quick success for the hand of Alma, daughter to Tobert, king of Stanglin.  Alma, some held, was a bang-on pairing for Worrel, a tall girl who had been taught swordplay and could shoot awfully well with a man-sized bow.

His own wiving set, Worrel made it his business to persuade me that as for him, it was undignified to be a bachelor when a chap's younger sister has brought down a husband. Though I do not, and even then really did not see why that should be thus, I had more than met Rowan, dark-haired niece to Edlin of Suvram (by blood, to his wife and queen), and was moved to become one more in that coupling year to *speak into the Myke*, as the phrase is.  With all our oaths, if made solemn by a priest, he holds out the wooden Myke he carries, "so the Viztas may hear," but when we say, speak into the Myke, that always is a way of saying *marry*.

This heap of weddings brought forth torrents of talk and several songs, majoritally joky; one which had all the husbands trying to find the right beds was forbidden to be sung in Gwyn, and was therefore sung with the bigger gusto and bawdy detail. Thought of Tam and Caif being bedded still made Worrel clamp his teeth and go glum, but all that was eclipsed by what befell

Caif, whose songs, after more than twenty not-eventless years, can still sometimes be heard.

It was about harvest time when she rode for Cumba and her wedding, but her cumny was waylaid and Caif (only) was abducted by a warlike bunch of Mynas. Both Tam and Jon her father expected a demand for ransom, but it was ages coming. Then it was found out Caif's trappers were from the Brown Hare clan, their boss, Donal. A chap might have guessed as much. Recalling Donal's hungering for that other fair-haired girl when I first went to see Marten, I no longer believed Caif was going to be meekly sold back for ransom. On one of his visits to Seeyow when she too happened to be there Donal must have got a glance, no *glimpse* at Caif, and, like any other bloke, become in love. Understand, damn few of us would permit that a Myna could be that much like any other fellow; our decent would not call his famish by the name of love, and everywhere the news came knives began being whetted for Donal's balls. Ransom, plainly, did not come into it, but with Tam's blood up, lives did, and I hied self to Seeyow to find whether Marten could reach Donal with a nagging message, convince him he had to give up Caif. Not yet counting the threats for Donal self, all sorts of men were saying this went to show all the worst reported re the Mynas must be true. Retribution, as always, was having the innocent suffer, and lots of fruity partnerships between Mynas and those who did deals with them were being unmade in blood.

It was a long ride in the muddiest season to Seeyow, and occurings easily outraced me; there I learnt Tam, the wronged fiance, joined to by fighters from his neighbour, Umba, and with all the fighters of Cumba he could find, was pursuing a dreadful war with the Mynas.

That carried on for most of a year with cruelness and much wanton destroying for both sides. Tam's fury took him to challenge the Mynas in their own elements, darks and the windings of tunnels. The Brown Hares outkilled, but not in ratio to the odds against them; in the end the paltry few dozen who were left fled south. Although declared outlaw in all lands they were hard to catch and hardly easy to kill. Later they made refuge in the wilderness of Lunn (near the Tower), wresting some of the twistingest and branchingest of the underground passages away from other Mynas not desperate enough to withstand. For a good while it was favourite rant to mouth about extinguishing that clan to the last woman and last infant, but rooting them out was more of a bally job than bragging on it; they stayed in Lunn, grew a bit in numbers, and kept their sad, unlikely dreams of returning one time to their old northern haunts.

But Donal, to the mighty ire of Tam, who thirsted to take him live and make dying last as long as might be, had been done in in the last of the big fights up north. Tam had to be content with chopping at the corpse till it was piled gore. Winning his war he won bugger all. Caif, true telling, came off unhurt, but by Tam's reckoning long ways from unspoilt; at rescue she was five months with Donal's child.

As happened, when the war was plainly approaching its end, this was a chance I had guessed. Appointing myself not asked and unconfirmed to voice for her father Jon, I turned up at Cumba to remind Tam he had never gotten to be Caif's husband,

and did not have disposing of her. He was a clumsy big gargoyle for whom thought often came after the act to which it belonged, but whether, without my embassy, he would have killed Caif cannot be said as cinch. As was he only forswore betrothal. Then it was I with my cumny who took Caif back to her father's house.


The way they treated her during captivity had not been harsh, except for what war made it, constant change of place, and huddlings in dank, dark hides, but she was now very melancholic, and spoke seldom during the longish ride back to Landin. Later, after birth of a hale son, she went to live with Marten and Maire at Seeyow. Sheal, a kinswoman of her mother's, one without a bean to her name, came as her companion. Caif had not been welcomed at Landin, where Jon's suspicions and those of people at large were one with my thoughts, Caif's abduction had not been simple rape. But how can any chappie tell what might go on in the head and heart of a worshipped girl, bright and risky as flame? With less to go on than this chap, some songs made out the Myna and the king's daughter as secret claspers before her betrothing. That may outstrip fact, but Donal in lots of ways, rank aside, race aside, was the better bloke, better-spoken, even better-mannered than the raw and gusty Tam, and less handsome only for those (lots) who cannot see good looks in a Myna's.

Assuredly, Caif's chances now of finding a husband of her own rank were a little less than nil. If a chap had not been married, the lady willing, I would've cocked a snook at custom and opinion and taken her with no dowry, and counted myself king of infinite wealth. Without smiles she was still lovely, and

I was yet young enough to nearly believe that could make up for loss of standing and lack of the ready, or property. (Such a match would also have clouded my friendship with Worrel, he having gone on, ever since Caif's saying yes to Tam, and through all since, as if she had ceased to be. Ha ha.)

There were yet stronger miseries a chap escaped by having a prior wife. I cannot flatter self a chap could have changed the tale by making Caif wish for living again. Vanity, it looks like, has counted as a vice among all peoples in all time, but Caif vain had been happy, and I for one would have given a lot to see, like a rip in rainclouds, even half a mo's return of her old bright surety she was loved and would be served by anyone she let her smile shine on. Any guy. When Col, her strong and handsome son, was four, Caif died by drowning, and like the rival songs about it, any bozo is free to choose how that came about, as accident or by fell design, her own or someone else's. But who was there to wish her dead, aside from Caif? One sappy tale that calls her murdered tells that a Myna, Donal's brother, putting blame on her for Donal's death, took revenge — but what Myna could be so foolish? Granted Tam's temper and the abduction itself, it was plain Donal had made his own death. As happens Donal's only near-brother is a bloke I know well, and he sure did not kill Caif, my life on it. With the other choices, a path pierces between: Caif, swimming, might have given herself to a mishap she could have saved herself from, if only she'd had more yen to go on living. All this is waffle; no matter how, she was really dead. It was a rotten waste of youth and the beauty of things perfectly made. She was only twenty-three.

Col her son comes more (lots and lots more) into my story later on. For now I shall say he was always of breadth beyond his years, fair like his mother, but with eyes of dark brown (hers were blue, such blue); part of his proud father was in those and in the set of his chin. A chap saw heaps of him on my often visits to Seeyow, and liked his quickness, the more when I too came to tutor him a bit. He had benefit (not all called it so), of Marten's odd learnings and odder wonderings, but in earliness Maire was the one who knew Col was a child, seeing to his caring, and to his punishment when needed. That was chiefly a waste effort; foolish goofs Col did not repeat, and what for him was important to do, he did, whether or not there would be beating at the end.

Yet before his mother's death, even ere Col's birth, there were happenings a chappie's left out and now has to backtrack for. In Cumba Tam's war with the Mynas had been mainly in what then was the southwest of that northern realm, seaward lands where leavings of sprawled cities had given cover for Donal's followers. Whilst Tam was still combing through ruin after ruin, ferreting after Brown Hares, Vandis of Raug found, so said Adda Forn, my sister's choice, that in the more inland parts of Cumba bordering his own lands were crowds of Vandenes craving his protection (in all the times and places this was spoken, not once was it explained, protection from what?). Vandis so laid claim to a wide swathe of land, up to and in parts northward of where extremely anciently had stood a bloody great wall of no known purpose, worn snaggles of which can still here and there be seen jutting from those windy grasslands like an old fossil's blighted teeth. No danger at that time could have made Tam leave off or cool off his hunt after captive Caif, and as that war sputtered out his damaged and weary forces were not up to regaining the lost lands.

Tam was still untaught for patience. Next spring, with no stronger friend than his neighbouring Umba, traditional ally as it was also usual rival to Cumba, he picked fresh fight with King Vandis. The big palooka ought to have known the fighters of my unwished kinsman, Forn, could not now be resisted by armies near their own numbers. The war kept being reborn for the next three years, each round with the same outcome. Cumba was driven from not only the lands first grabbed by Vandis, but also all the country where the war with the Mynas had mainly been. Their ally Umba was also forced to cede southern territory coming to a third or more of all it had; whilst all other realms just stood gawping Raug had grown grossly, while the two northern kingdoms had become small spots between wildness beyond and the swelling powerfulness of the Vandene Kingdom. Too, Adda-priests came snaking into the added lands to watch on the keeping of the Vandene faith.

Blithering asses like Edlin among the southern lords were not (yet) displeased; Tam had never been loved in the south, and it was sillily believed these plunders would satisfy the hungerings of Raug. To me, but not just me, any sane chap (Worrel was much louder about it), it was obvious the Raug meal would soon be digested, and Vandis would be looking south again. Soon enough war began in the old place, that northerly spike of Marchlen. Again Forn opened with little border raids, and was ready with lots of force when Worrel replied.

For the first time Worrel was fighting as a king, my Uncle Bryan having turned toes up surprisingly in winter. Bulk of us, so I judge, peg out sooner than we ought; not many of us get to seventy, fewer eighty, but what one may achieve might be brought off by all, and as I write Maud, last alive child of Edlin I, is near her ninety and not wholly disgusting to see.

Worrel's fight in all ways was kingworthy. Not taken by surprise, he was still short on soldiers. Lacking allies, too: what had happened in the north made each ruler hope his truly would not be next to face Forn's fighters. Yet Worrel was brave beyond describings, and stubborn to boot; he was wounded, returned to battle only half-healed, and when once more wounded was taken prisoner. The news, which came to me in Seeyow, made a chappie frantic. To keep truth whole, I was that vexed with Worrel, too, for the very valour that had made my anxiety.

My sister was become a perfect rote-Vandene — this is put here because I tried like billy-o to get Worrel's release, and dealt with Forn by way of Gwynis. Terms were spoken, but Worrel, quenchless as a caged cat, spurned any agreement giving Raug lands of his land they were now occupying. Yew, treating with Vandis direct, soon settled matters over all heads. He got the vow that after small redrawings the borders of Gwyn would stay the same, but for Worrel's release he paid price the captive never okayed, and all the northern Marchlen went to Raug. Freed, Worrel said it was no freedom, to be caught in dismemberment he had no way to undo. The very lords he looked to for help, in hopes of saving their own borders, had joined in the moving back of his.

I too now had little left but disgust for the Caer crew, not unhooking my own father, who had been beside Yew for everything. Yet a chap was other from Worrel in more items than prowess. He, like a proper king, thought of honour, and I in my prideless way spoke prudency. In wisdom, no one could stand alone against Raug, and I did all I could to cool Worrel down, so not to let rancour leave him friendless. His largeness of heart let him take this advice, though in private he could burst out in spleen against the caitiff princes. It was parky comfort to point him out in Tam's witless trying for vengeance, Umba had lost far more than Marchlen. But we made an oath, he and I, we would refuse no course that might stop more gains by Raug. Only a bozo blinded with pride or made oafish by hope could not see the Vandene Kingdom aimed at no less than overlordship of all the lot of us, final peace where the Adda-Priests could slither about, dealing death to all beliefs less pure than theirs. By now there were tales from Raug's new-added lands up the north that proper faith in the Viztas now had fire and hot iron on its side; lots of good family (I mean, those with the moolah to) had fled.

My Adda brother-in-law and I had begun a stealthier war, that was going to go on for fifteen years or more. As a chap went from court to court, trying to get into heads they all shared one enemy, Forn, nasty but not stupid, was always a few days before or a few steps behind, harping that Raug did not wish another bean, and anyone who would see how reports of Vandene cruelties were bally great fibs could come and see for selves.

My wife's land Suvram, with its large numbers and rich fields, most needed waking, but Raug had so far been cagy not to give straight threat to its powerfulest possible rival, and Forn (with my sister) was often visiting Edlin at Saffam and elsewhere. Edlin III was turning out no more foresighted or clever than his father, but joyed to hear Forn plugging the glories of Suvram in the days of his grandfather, and was tickled pink when asked to okay the treaties Raug made with (usually, crammed down the mouth of) other kingdoms, as if what Suvram thought still counted. Next to that toxicate brew a chap had none to tip but cold water, doing his best to make Edlin see how loss to Raug of the northern Marchlens left a province of his own half-enclosed, like a ripe apple dangling, where the old southward border of the Vandene kingdom followed a deep bend of the River Tren. Understand, each snatching of land made Raug stronger; the armies sent against Worrel had men of what had been Cumba and Umba riding for Forn. Yet if Suvram with all its people and wealth of goods could have been waked up in time that time — if Worrel had been king there instead of his own littler land — a chap might have a different story to set down.

Because food became scarce there, at time when everywhere else the past two harvests had been bonzer ones, Raug had to take a breather from conquest. This looked like a chance, to make sale of corn and meat to Raug parts of treaties wherein all borders were given the same assurances Gwyn had, and what if Raug agreed to lessen its year-round armies, heaps more than needed for guarding frontiers and keeping the order in a land at peace? By taking hands from the working of farms, it was these soldieries that had made Raug short on the eats.

It was still hard to make the different rulers come together. Hungering Raug was awash with money; in their new-added territories, old landlords (those who had been there, I mean; they were not all ruddy antiques) had been made pay an overtax to hold their acres. Lots elsewhere were greedy for some of that moolah, and anyone with goods to sell was afraid if he failed some other crook would cash in. Not only foretells are made come true by believing.

About this time, I had been with Marten at Seeyow, where Col, his seventh birthday just past, was joying everyone but Maire with his pauselessness; he was riding now on a three-quarter sized horse, had shoulders to manage a sword with skill, and was boastful when next he met his kinswoman, meaning Worrel's wife Alma, he would outshoot her with bow. That, a chap thought, might be a good time distant; Alma was with child for the fourth time.

But in all Col was lots like others his age of family, also in his love for tales, mostly of fighting and wars. But he used to ask, at the end of a story, "Is that true?" Seeyow, you see; it's not a question much heard with the rest of us, child or grown. A windy sprat of four or five might ask it at the end of a Tela's recount with ghosts or itlas in it, but that was only with purpose to be told there were no boggles so nasty that could come for him that night. Col, made odd by Marten's lore, really yearned to divide made-up wonders from true.

When time came to ride back south, I made side-journey to Pormarch, where Worrel told me he heard there were men idle in Wezram. He desired his friend King Follen to let him bring some to March, to train them for war. For this, Worrel's only payment would be that after learning, they would stay for a half a year as his soldiers. He was certain war would come back to Marchlen, though losing the lands in the north had left him only a short border to defend against Raug.

This particular scheme never came to much in the end, but it tells why instead of turning homeward, I agreed to go to Wezram carrying Worrel's proposal to Tawn. A chappie no longer had much todo to do with birthdays, but this was right by my thirtieth, as was put in mind when I took the ferry across to Bris and found the fair going strong. The Dauwas of Thea were there.

A chap had seen Thea a few times across years, but the last had been more than five years ago, and I was abacked to see her so much older, looking worn, mayhap ill, as the cleverness of aftersight can say. She had always coddled her hands and now they were rasping dry, knuckles raw-looking, while down her cheeks went long creases. These made her look sorrowing, but as was she was angry with me, because I had done too little to stop Raug's wickedness, both north and to Worrel my friend. When I began to recount what schemes a chap had tried and was now trying, she stopped me, and said I was a fool.

If Thea was going to foul a chappie with names, and in no whisper, I thought and told we should take our talk somewhere more privy, out of my vassals' hearing; I would not wish to be obliged to have an old friend thrashed for the sake of maintaining dignity. We were in that same old stone building, in the place where Thea could oversee her girls and the choices of her clients; my servant Lydd, who grew no sager, was there, and Shan, captain of my armed cumny.

To my suggestion she wearily smiled, and pretending to misunderstand said I didn't hunger for her; when I answered that I was now a man with wife, she smiled more bently, and vouchsafed there were stories saying I did not burn for *her*, either.

Defending, a chap attacked, asking in a sarky mode how long she had been dealing in gossips. Soppy question: as Thea soon reminded, gossips were the first trade of the Dauwas, and the last; they learnt its worth before they were ready to spread selves. Journeying lots, as they did, they became skilled in listening, and when they came to where no one lusted them on their backs, they still had that.

More than her hands, I thought, were rougher. Again I must explain I cannot give her words, harsher than these.

We went together to the same bed-place of that long manning night of my seventeenth birthday, and a bright-faced, freckly girl (later, Thea sent her to me for good games) brought drink and left us alone in the dimming light by which Thea explicated my folly. Here I can hardly even feign to give her words, but she built her tale in blocks, like a stonemason, one of old times, not living bunglers.

To begin, "Do you believe in the Viztas?"

That had been asked before. Now, and in this place, the answer was easier. "No." I had heard too much from Marten, seen and thought too much for self.

"Yet all your deals are with princes and lords, who have no choice but to believe."

"I am a lord. Marten is a lord."

"Marten is famed to be mad." She went on to say what I

had always known, no ruling lord, nor any who under him held title could ever have doubt. It was from the Viztas all rights to rule came down, bulk of the princes holding they were heirs to the House of Regions, charged by the Viztas with the lordship, others saying only that the Viztas had decreed the idea of kingdom. We must begin somewhere, but to put it all on the Viztas, Thea said, left the other kings armless against Raug. Even those who hardest disputed Raug and the ways of the Adda-priests could not help admitting the Vandenes professed their own faith in its purest form.

"Not armless," I said, and told her of my present errand, and my idea, to put conditions on the selling of food to Raug. Thea had heard of these efforts (there was not much that escaped her deputy ears, customers), and gave them very tiny hope. The shortage of food in Raug, she said, was not just because their armies took men from the farms; that was to speak it back-to-front. My priest-kinsman had plan, she said, bound to go badly before it could go well. Forn had discovered (Oh, I wish there was some describing the scorn of Thea's face and voice) the great Viztas, in their terrific wisdom, had never meant the wide lands held by lords under the king should be cut up, over and again, into little family farms. No, the landlords, proxies of the Viztas, had been meant to overlook, no *see*, the working of much greater farms, where big fields each of but one only crop would need less tending than the small and different plantings that, with a few grains over for taxes and to swap for needed goods, kept a family alive.

I nodded head, having heard in the new Raug lands there had been much rooting up of hedge. As time passed, it might well be these put-together farms could grow more, sparing blokes to carry swords.

"For his armies, and others to be trained for searching out unbelievers. This has been in Forn's brain from the start."

Funny a chap did not ask her how she could know Forn's brain. There was, she went on, nothing not having price; Raug might become stronger in war but might yet be done down by Forn's own cleverness. Ever in beginning his border warrings Vandis had come to aid of believers needing his protection, and in the northern kingdoms and in Marchlen too Vandenes, no doubt, had aided Raug, if not by acts then by the lack of them, their slowness to fight for rightful lords.

"What, now," Thea asked, "when these true Vandenes without the borders of Raug learn that others like them, under Vandis, are now labourers and minions on lands they've named theirs?"

"But those lands really have never been theirs. The families that farm are all tenants of their overlords."

For a moment a chap thought she would choke, or perhaps spit. Then Thea touched my arm. "Poor cousin to kings," she had cheek to say. "Well, lord, you are less dumb than most, but because you can speak with a Myna or share bread with a smith does not make you the gift of seeing by their eyes. Tenants! Through all time you can trace your lineage they've been, lots of them, on the same lands that have given them all owned and worn and eaten. They know those fields like their bodies, which too, in law, their lords own. Who do you think will hang to a belief that is going to lose him all he's ever known, like a puddle lost in a pond?"

Here I saw she was right.  As it is with my sister, lots will claim beliefs that cost nothing, but I've never seen even the blazingest faith go very much against a fellow's best interests. Chaps do die for belief, yes, but that's more often a startle for them; what they meant to do was kill.  For every extra fighter he raised in Raug, Forn, as Thea said, could lose a dozen who might be allies in other lands, once they understood what the Viztas said about the farms.

"Still," Thea warned, "he could vanquish without allies, by strength itself.  They say his men are well-trained, but what makes them better is being all Vandenes together, and knowing."

"Why should Vandenes make better fighters?"

"I say any lot fights better making war together for what all believe.  That is why the ones who go against the Vandenes must also hold fightworthy thoughts.  These lords you spend your days chinwagging with — is that anything a man of sensibleness would fight for?"

Gradually, a chap was not even bothering to pretend offence.  "What, then?"

She murmured "The Old Beliefs."

"Toys," I said.


Keep that on your hand's palm, reader, whilst I expound. So far, except mentioning some foretells, I have not said lots about the Old Beliefs, though a chap left hint when talking about rites at Stonedge.  This is no simple topic, and harder for me, with two reasons.  One we are to come to, but also, because I've never understood how men and women can in one time say they worship the Viztas, and still do customs, credit powers from a

faith that at best sits shiftily beside, at worst goes clean contrary
to priestly beliefs. Sayings in which the Viztas had no part, small
rites to make the fields fertile, healings, and darker doings to do
with love or wealth or revenge; all this, priests said, was bad
memory of before the Viztas came to free us from superstition.
In Raug lots of this could be punished by death, yet even there
(Thea said, but it was no astonishment) the Old Beliefs whispered
on in secret. Otherwhere, pretty much in the open. Lots whose
belief in the Viztas was lesser only by Vandene measure can see
no harm to blooding the seed at planting time or burning harvest
dolls. At any fair you can buy charms against bellyache or pains
of love, have your future said by one of the methods or another.
There are seers for every taste; readers of hands or heads,
fire-gazers, explainers of omens, and those pricey ones who make
maps of the stars and ask to know one's very hour of birth. These
last can still be found, here and there, as part of the followings of
high lords, or their ladies.

"Toys," I said (not twice; this is reminding).

If I thought Thea was shirty with me before I realised now
that had been naught but growl. Her quiet voice became keen like
teeth, and anger, the proper article, was in her eyes. She said to
be done with the Viztas, yet to keep contempt for what that faith
scorned, was to uproot a weed but still to store its poison fruit (in
truth, she did not say just that, but a chap likes to give life to her
meaning). The Old Beliefs, she said, were ill-understood, and
heaps of things done with their name were done wrong, or
remembered dumbly, so what we saw was like a child's aping of
grown-ups, earnest without understanding. But the Beliefs

themselves went on because, much beyond the striding tales of the Viztas, they came from and came back to what was forever, change of seasons, the sun's rising and setting, waxing and shrinking moon, growth, harvest and the long winter sleep, birth and birthing, death and renewing. Beside such everlastings, Thea said, it was the bleeding Viztas with their shiny, fast machines and steel marvels that were the toys.

Very well, I said, a bit knocked off kilter by her fierceness, but as the world now was these beliefs were not in the middle of people's lives. It was more like they learnt off a dream; they just went on with habits their mothers gave them (mothers, I said, because it seemed to me with women the Old Beliefs stay strongest), little doings they had been told would help the crops and at worst did no hurt. But these and all the other witchings were no part of any large tale. The Viztas were strong because their coming and the Leaving told us about the world we saw, and how whole lives should be, and thus brought whopping great crowds together to witness in faith.

"Then what is Gridge?" Thea asked. "Do you think all those gather there at third midsummer to gawp at the spot where the Viztas last touched earth? There is Stonedge, too, and to me it is fact, as you must have guessed, Stonedge and other spots older still were places of power through ages before any tale of comings from other worlds."

This was fine to hear. Another time, a chap might have asked more about it, but I had not lost where we had been. "You were speaking," I jogged, "of beliefs blokes fight for, as the Vandenes do for theirs. People of all differing sorts come to Gridge, but they are one only by coming to Gridge, and why they do they have no foggiest, except it's done. If it wasn't Gridge but somewhere else, Stonedge, still, or a place bang in the heart of the Vandene Kingdom — if the Vandenes made it crime to come there, unless to honour the Viztas — heaps would still turn up, every three years."

"Without moving inch, Gridge may veritably one day be the heart of the Vandene Kingdom," and the grimness of Thea's voice gave a chappie chills. "Yet you're wrong about Stonedge; some still keep its true meaning. Some of the Mynas. The Dauwas of Thea are not forgetting, and other guilds, where old speeches have been kept the best. Though few are left, like us, to make their own fates."

That, I knew, was melancholy truth. In times of trouble, especially, when there were roaming bands of soldiery who might rob or rape, these companies of dauwas would hire selves strong gawds. Again and again it happened that bruisers bought to protect would end by owning, and the women as their vassals. When I considered, it was wonder Thea could remain in charge of the Dauwas with so little guarding that could be seen, even if Mynas, as I twigged, were never far. A chap began wondering how long the Dauwas had been, with how many Theas coming from within their ranks, and whether this guild and other guilds had always kept the Old Beliefs.

"Of Mynas," this with sadness, "the Brown Hares of the north were the truest. They kept lots of lore lost to others."

"A pity lore could not keep Donal from follies."

She made face go hard. "It had to be so. The boy was to be born."

"Was to be?"  A note in her tone was cooling my spine again.

"Foretells go like streams.  If there is no bed for their flow, they make them one.  The boy had to have his descent."

She was speaking of Col, and this went too far.  "His descent?  His lineage is bastard, now orphan.  Caif might have had a son with Tam of Cumba, and he would be heir there." Thea's scorn of princes was, notwithstanding, starting to shake a chappie: thinking of that lug Tam, my words were thin to me even as I said them.

"You know the boy, I hear.  Does he shape worse for being bastard?  But Donal the Myna of the Brown Hare Clan, lack-land as he was, had descent to little Tam of Cumba.  No, wait!  Some old tales I am oathed not to tell, and they would be empty to you if I did, but for beginning, Donal's line was straight from the last kings of All Brittan."

This was barmy.  "A Myna sprung of the Regions?"

"So they are called."  She did not like to give the name, I guessed, because to admit its rightness was to acknowledge the Viztas.  "In the line of Gavin, the last ruler but one was Joan.  Her son came after her, but her other child was Dora, and from Dora does Donal's lineage come."

"Yes?"  I said.  "Then why did one of Donal's Myna forefathers not make claim to rule of all Brittan?"

"Because they were Mynas."  Thea told from my voice I was not buying a dicky-bird of this, but she carried on as if I was lapping it up.  "The lineage was always from mother to daughter, where blood flows just as true as father to son."

After it seemed strange if I doubted so much of what Thea

said, as my brain then was, fixed on Raug and its growing power to make war, I did not do much disputation.  She herself must have made spells.

"Caif was not disgraced," she said.

"Caif died.  She might have been Worrel's wife."

Thea laughed.  "When first I met you, I saw you were unlike other princelets.  The true reason you would like to save us from Raug dominion is that the Vandenes would outlaw your own thoughts, but your thoughts are not about greed and gain.  Your own desire for Caif was a festered illness, so you tell me she might have taken Worrel.  But you were foretold, just like Col."

"Nonsense," I said, not allowing myself to be drawn into her faith.

"Toys, toys again?"  Thea, by heaven, mocked me.  "Well, what will people do for the sake of toys?  You've seen that thing King Tam sometimes has with him, which, so he has it said, is the true belt worn by one of the veritable Viztas?"

I had; a gaudy ort to my eye, with too much bright metal, yet crafted kilometres beyond anything we could do.

"When he has that toy with him," Thea reminded me, "men and women crowd about, shading their eyes from awe.  Fathers lift children on their shoulders to get glimpse of it."

I nodded, but my agreement was not blithe.

"Long ago, I was near tipping you Raug has another toy, which is not a toy.  The Rod, you call the Myke of the Viztas.  Oh, yes, it is true, though not what you believe of its beginnings.  Your kinsman the Adda knows where it lies, but time has not yet run for Vandis to display it.  He can't claim it for his, not while there might still be dispute of his right.  Some would think Edlin the proper one to hold it — for this time. But Forn has it kept safe. He knows if it were to come to one who, much better than Vandis, answered prophecy, that one might be King of All Brittan."

"Who would acclaim him?"

"The Mynas would, to a man, if they knew his descent, even the Mynas not strong in the Old Beliefs."

"A King of All Brittan, proclaimed by Mynas!" We were embroidering dreams, but it seemed Thea was meaning Col, now seven.

"Not yet," she said, reading mind. "When he can show off himself a warrior, too."

"He'll need more than that," I said. Thea, certes, was speaking truth — by which I mean she was neither repeating chance gossip nor making her own fiction; what she said she believed. My memory of Donal, his prideful front, stopped me from saying utter rubbish to the idea of a Myna with lord's blood in his veins. But blood of the Regions, with good records kept over six empty centuries, that was a bit steep. If madly true, we were indeed arriving at points of prophecy; Caif self, as I've mentioned, was descended through her father from the other side of the lost Regions, the line of Colin. If two long bloodlines could be shown, through those score generations, Col then might be named the long-foretold reunion of Colinid and Gavinid, worthy to hold the Rod. Thea let me go on calling that the True Myke; it was years before I heard why that was not its right name. But a chap let his brain make a picture of the little strawhead kid trying to string a bow too big for him, and it was all sillier than words can say, Col taking the True Myke, and by right.

Yet, with or without that awesome emblem, it would still be no easy leap, from saying, well, Col's descent might be such and such, to foreseeing him — or anyone not first a strong king — coming to power.

"The Mynas' acclaim," I told Thea, hardly knowing whether to be amused or made anxious by this sudden dream, "their praise, would not help win over the rest.  Exact the opposite."

"Dirty, thieving Mynas," Thea said.  "But more than you think, people know Mynas can teach them, above all in the Old Beliefs.  Are Myna women not known for charms and foretells?  Farmers might not do so openly, but lots of them ask the Mynas' advice in secret; Mynas know the day for planting, and give words against flood or drought.  Some, not all, respect the Mynas; tons, not all, fear them.  Still, of all the names you've heard given them, have you ever heard *fool*?"

"Not before Donal."

"He was not to be saved," sadly.  "Your Marten tried; he held out safe haven at Seeyow.  Donal would not go there and bring risk."

"Marten has not told me that."  To this day I don't know whether true, or how Thea could have known.

"Do you wonder?  You are Marten's pal, but he knows you have other friends.  Is there one who, after Caif was nabbed, had an idea but death for Donal and any who helped him?"

A chap could see that was true, even for Worrel — and then I saw it was Worrel Thea meant; there were borders even to her plain-speaking.  But, dash it all, Worrel loved Caif — as I had, and even for me, there had been times I would have liked to have been the one to have done in Donal. The time Caif without a warning and without a sound was all at once weeping, then.

"Then Marten," I said, going after a different hare, "must know about this descent you claim for Col."

"Well, Marten, as you know, now has no interest in foretells. What you call toys, he calls history. They are, but that is not their power. He used to look into such, but now it's all his measurings, and the one of all alive who can foretell with surety the next eclipse has no time for our tales from behind the moon."

"If the Vandenes have the True Myke — your Rod, it must be well hidden and guarded well."

She grinned, tickled, I suppose, to see my brain was running on, no matter how ga-ga a chappie told himself it was, to thoughts of making a king. "There is time. The time for the Rod does not come for years, yet, not before Col is a man. But the Rod must find its way to the right grasp when its hour comes."

I shook my head. "Foretells can be a tool the cunning ply, but those who hold them claim right to too many explainings. All comes true if the sayer is allowed to say what true is. Give me foretells that mean one small thing — the next eclipse, mayhap. Here I am not so different from Marten."

"No one calls you Mad Evan," Thea said. "Vandis himself keeps eye on your journeys, and Forn would like to guess your thinkings."

A chap wished she could get hers straight. She goes from insult to flattery, and both seemed unearnt. "You scold me wasting my time with princes, and now you nag me to waste it chasing dreams."

"If it was that or nightmare, who would not chase the

dream?" Thea said, but without much weight, smiling. "Prophecy, you say, can stop being toys and be a tool. Well, it might begin to help blokes stand together against Raug — not lords, men of the land, I mean — if they believed sayings, other than what the Adda-priests speak, might come true. If they came to think that against a Vandene rule that would rob them of their farms, the Old Beliefs might stand, beliefs they already in part share with the Mynas..." Thea paused, and her smile was an askew one. I twigged she was trying to instruct me what to do, even before she added: "There might be a job for one who now jogs from hall to hall, trying to unsay what the easily-flattered are told by his brother-in-law."

## Words

This, now, is a big part of my story, and tells how a chap comes to be able to tell it. But so to do I have to leave whole realms wobbling, as t'were, on cliff's edge, going forward by some years. Yet I would not have a reader lose, among these tales of quieter matters, the worry of Raug's advance, or our anxiousness as we sought ways not to be swallowed whole. No matter what long silences I found, the thoughts of Forn's brute soldiery, the grimness of the Adda-priests, knowledge of how feebly they were opposed never left me.

Having said he is jumping frontward, a chap must start by going back. The morning after my long talk with Thea is the best place for beginning. Then, a peril happened it still shames me to tell, and after all these years I can still hear in my head how Worrel would have chid me for my carelessness. As must be plain, Worrel lived a hundred, a thousand risks to my every one, but never without object; even within war a large helping of prudency was under his quenchless bravery. Outside of war, surely, he would never have done what I unmindedly did. Remember, when we were young and had no realms in our keeping, though he might have come to that place disguised as no one, he made sure to have soldiery within sight and call. Not doing likewise also made me break my childhood oath never again to use a blade.

My lone excuse is, I felt absolutely spiffing. The freckled girl Thea had sent me had been a worthy Dauwa, well-chosen and (I guess) instructed as to my best pleasings. That was a spring had seen more rain than needful, but now all was silver with sun; fed full, so to say, with a good night and a gleaming morning, I went for an amble, telling no one. My gawd was not far but I didn't try to bring them, meaning to come back for a farewell to Thea. To tell the honest I was often irked by being never alone.

The thick-walled place of the Dauwas long ago stood where two ways met; broken steps down from the pillared front came to a stretch of paving that's still there. Up the hill, leftward, this paving soon gives out for muddy ruts, but lining that once street are still buildings, bulk ruinous, a few still whole enough to give lodging, at least at fair time; I never came that way when there was no fair.

From the head of the hill a chap could look south and east against early sun to the low, grassy, spring-bright hills, topped with dark clumps of tree. Near where I stood, a building which kept most of its walls, back and ceiling, though not a lot of its front, was home to a booth where a small, dark woman sat behind a table making her breakfast. By her sign, the painting of a sickle and a scatter of yellow stars, she was a seer. She would be one of those who use tiles scratched with signs, which for a fee are set forth on the table and read, the order they come in being the story, so is said. The tiles are called the roecards, and I have no clue why, unless it has to do with rock; they are often pieces of slate, somewhat squared off. About the whole proceeding I knew (as I still know) next to sweet F.A., and was not shamed by that. On any other day a chappie would likeliest have waltzed by with not more than a glance, but that dazzled morning Thea's urgings of the Old Beliefs were still alive in my ears.

The seer was a Myna woman with eyebrows like a man's, pretending still to be concerned only in her bread and sausage. Yet she glittered an eye at yours truly; as usual I could really not guess her age; she was not young. Others were up and roaming the fair that morning, and at that moment a girl of what might be sixteen, dressed for a farm-lass, came breathless to offer potatoes in exchange for a foretelling. The woman, whose eyes put me in thought of Thea, sniffed as she gazed on the potatoes, starting to bare little fangs, but she took them, putting them aside with her breakfast, and began to lay out tiles. These she dipped from a deep rush basket next the table. Other passers stopped to witness, and the young girl used a halt whisper to speak what she wished to discover. Old potatoes were not enough pay to spare her redness; a chicken, perhaps, might have waged the seer to lower the coarse curtain and speak in private.

One by one the roecards were turned and the girl's question was answered; she should marry this year but not the first bloke who asked. I forget which of the signs told this, being taken up mainly with how the small clump of watchers watched, how they listened as if afraid a breath would spill and spoil the magic. The seer droned her tale with lips hardly moving: what Thea had said was true, and a chap had known it all his life; in questions of lore there was no scorn for the Mynas. Indeed, but perhaps this goes too far and I tell this too soon, before I'd had time for longer mastication, all the scorn may be way of fighting off fear.   I can remember rough words Worrel had for his terrifically adored Caif when she took Tam, and that I know was because, of all, Worrel feared to let be seen he could be wounded. Yet after all it may be far-fetched to think of them as same.

All at once I was rudely knocked and there were loud, angry voices; a young oaf pushed past me, who overturned the seer's table. He was followed by others, all simply clad and harsh in speech. The seer went back in crouch like a cat, and the young girl her client fled with screams. What the young roughs were announcing was, this was bad belief, a sneer to the Viztas. There seemed to be five, and no less than three were provided with staves, two brandishing these at the flabbergasted audiences, bawling they were to go away, and hew, from now on, only to proper beliefs. The young faces were uglied with hate, and the watchers, a farm-lad, three women and a small boy soon obeyed the bullies' command. The first part, I mean; a chap can't say what they believed after. At the same time the third of the armed ones swung a downward blow at the backing seer-woman; she was dodging aside but was hit between neck and shoulder, so one heard, with her cry, the snap of the gable-bone there.

There is too much to recount for the instants this took. I of course had not scarpered with the others, had begun to proclaim my rank; a chap didn't mean to make issue of how he was pushed aside. I was simply dressed, though the stuff of my jacket should've told these bruisers I was not a common fairgoer. I was armed with knife at my belt Worrel had told and told me never to be without. This, as I heard bone break, I drew: times arrive when skill or the lack of it, even words given in childhood, are outside the question. With an order this madness must be halted, I stepped forward.

Seeing steel the closest of the stave-men gave way, but it was the other I was after, the knave still menacing the seer, now on her knees. He was snarling out hating balderdash, calling her witch. A word not much in use, except in Raug where the Adda-priests were making it more common.

In hurry, a chappie stumbled over the basket of slates, and lurched frontward with knife-arm going out as a hand does to prevent a fall, or lessen it. My knife, which might sustain itself upon the thigh of far deadlier than I, is a great bit keener than its guider, slender-bladed and kept bright. Only partly by design I sent a good part of its length in one side of the bully's arse, trampling him further as he went down and I scrabbled to restore my uprightness. After a little doubt my knife had come free and was still in my gripe. The eyes of the woman looked all whites, and I turned to face the balance of toughs, letting them know in a huffing shout I had power, and kin here in Sevenin, to see them all hanged. The blade had abacked them all, but the nastiest-looking bozo, loudest in shouting on the Viztas, had dropped his stave and found a knife of his own, not fine like mine, a fat-bladed, dull, heavy blade. Among evenly-matched the goodness of a weapon counts, but there was no surety I would win against even quite moderate skill, and the ugly guy with his ugly knife had all the allies. Even the varlet squealing and oozing blood on the floor was far from done for.

Before the slightness of my prowess could be bared, help, tons of it, came as if out of the air; Mynas, lots of Mynas. Not actually more than eight or nine, but eight or nine blokes appearing as suddenly as they did seem a great gang. Some were from deeper within the house of the seer's booth, others seemingly out of the ground among the neighbour ruins. They were shrewder than to show any weapons, but quickly hemmed and pinned the pious uglies, leaving me as bystander, my knife held like the wilted gift of a failed courter. The Mynas were swift, silent and dangerous, and all the noise there was came from the bullies. The one who had drawn knife was still bawling on about Viztas and true belief, two of the others crying they had been assailed, whilst the one stabbed wailed like a hurt dog. His victim, whose pain could surely be not less, was starting to ponder gaining back on her feet, but before I could either aid or dissuade, one of those Mynas, their plain boss, was squatted next to her, sharp-boned face so like hers any twit could see they were mother and son. His arm was behind her shoulders, but she gave me a keen look, the pain clearing from her face. Jabbing hand the woman said "This is — " but the rest lost itself in hubbub. When I booted her bag five slates had spilt out, and she leant forward to turn over the two fallen face down. You know how, when two children have been in dispute, and something happens to prove one right, that crow of triumph she then gives? That came now from the seer. "Boy Who will be King," she said (or would have said, granted good words), pointing at a tile. "The Moon. Dark Rival, Light Rival, Rod — all in care, in keeping of him."

By "him" she meant yr. humble servant. Like Thea she had said "Rod," of the one roecard everyone knows, mostly called True Myke.

Her son seemed about to get to his feet to honour me, but before he could do that, or utter, there were more comers, horsemen. Several of my own gawd under Shan, together with six from the royal gawd of Sevenin, the All-Brown, who at fair-times always kept a campment nearby. All had their swords unclad, and seeing how it stood they would it's a cert have tackled the Mynas to free the bullies, if a chap had not been there to prevent it, calling out to Shan. I also knew by sight the All-Brown boss, Kay, a young officer no longer with favour at court because of his way of loosing hot eyes to stray miles above his station, even as high as my cousin queen. Like many of the war not in my pay, Kay I believe thought little of me, but he knew who a fellow was, and that his lord would go with no matter what I ordered. That saved us from a long wrangle. The head lout, the loudest one, was still unabashed, certain wronged faith could make no choice other than his and his companions'. He claimed, as I made out, distant kinship with the Adda-priest Forn, and went with the name of Ermin. Another, perhaps the eldest, was permitted to attend to the stabbed one, and while trying to halt the blood, roughly put forward the wise view that they were not subject to the law of Sevenin, being (as one might have guessed) men of Raug. That argument would set a bounder free to wander doing murder where he chose, so long as he kept from home; this I began to explain for Kay, but in mid-thought found I had heard enough and to spare. Though it was to worsen much, at that time our interest in justice already, in sooth, was not what might have been in former gentler years — well, most always admire justice and are tickled when it is doable, but as we are order comes before, and if that betimes must be bought at the price of unfair judgings, we find a way not to look too long or close.

In this case, any or all of these young fruitcakes could

have been hanged from the nearest suitable tree, at my insistence (which Kay expected), simply for waving weapons at me; formal trial could have taken more time but with the same outcome if I chose to press Kennet. Yet, a chap reflected, Kennet's realm as yet had no special cause of quarrel direct with Raug, and even among Kennet's friends the adder-tongue of Forn could make seem these loonies of Raug had been hanged not for their crimes but because they were true believers.

That thought, I turned to Kay, and told him to keep the youths under guard with the other troublemakers till fair's end, when they should be given a whipping and let go. The wounded one, I said, could be spared the whipping.

Kay asked who gave that wound. His eyes, not hot now, were journeying from one to another of the Mynas, hoping he could add one of those to his bag. To answer him I displayed my bloodied blade. A sec's disbelief, then the officer nodded acceptance of my tale and the sentence I had given. No doubt the story of Evan wielding a knife in hot blood was going to make rounds, not add to a chappie's fame as a fighter; I never heard a tale or a song where a hero stabs his enemy in the bum.

As they were led ungently away the captives were still claiming their imagined rights; it was like the farring after-rumbles when a storm has burst and passed over. Now the leader of the Mynas made me a deep bow, and, calling me *Lord*, offered his thanks. I told him none were needed,
and he smiled telling what a chap knew, that few, of any rank, would draw a blade for the sake of Mynas.

He asked if I was not the Lord Evan, friend to Thea, and

a chap was interested to hear how he spoke her name, but all at once I realised, high lord as a fellow was, I had become like a conspirator. My wary-watching gawd was too near and too nosy. Beckoning Shan I told him to remount the gawd and wait in the street.

Shan's blunt look was at the Mynas, and at last he dared ask whether I saw myself as safe with these. Only two, actually, not counting the leader, were still to be seen; the rest had gone as they came, like weather.

There was reproach here, and a chap hurried to give his burly virtues their due, asking his pardon for being out unguarded, and thanking him for being alert enough to come to my aid. A good sort, Shan, no company for a talk, but his service to me never faltered.

With my orders obeyed, I could ask the Myna whether all Mynas honoured Thea. Last night I had been puzzling how long the Guild had been, but now was trying to guess what it might be, whether the Dauwas were only a little part of its job. Among Mynas at least it seemed Thea was a bit like a priestess.

He grinned in his people's somewhat sidling way, and said there was no one single thought all Mynas shared. A lord as I was had his own strength, as we saw here, but if needed, I could count on help from those clans where Thea was honoured, such as the Badgers, the Grey Cats of Lunn, and the others.

I grabbed at that "others," asking what clan this man was, though a chappie didn't have to be Einstein (an ancient brainy geezer) to guess. The slyness more manifest, he told me his name was Wott, and here at Bris he was a Badger.

The outlawry and sentence of death on all the Brown Hares had never been lifted: Wott was silent when I mentioned that clan, but for me the other resemblance had clicked — besides, I mean, the likeness to his mother — and I sured him he had nothing to fear from me, who had known Donal, his kinsman.

His brother, so said Wott. The seer woman had been helped away between two men into farther depths of the house, but my eyes must have gone to where she had been, because Wott answered what I had not asked, saying he was what I would call Donal's half-brother. Their mothers were different, Donal's having pegged out young, but Mynas counted descent only from their fathers.

Passion had cooled as Caif's rape had faded from news. Still, a chap thought, it must be dangerous here for Wott and his lot. When I asked, he gave a shrug, as if to say his clan still had its duties. But if the horsemen of Sevenin had come to stop the fighting, he went on, it would have gone less blithely for them if I had not been there.

When a chap said I had come by chance, Wott said, "My mother says chance is the skill of dreams." No, he did not, but as near as I can get in better words to what he did say.

We spoke together for a time, and I took to this bloke right off. Wott has some of his brother's same pride of person, but none of Donal's — how can a chap say this? When a child is at the brink of rage outside control, betrayed, maybe, by a broken promise, or disappointed in his plan, there comes to his voice a cracking, a kind of sob unborn. Not in Donal's voice, which he kept mastered, but in his whole self, there had been that feeling of a branch bent to the last before splintering; it was in his hard eyes and tight mouth, the shoulders with readiness of a crouched cat. Wott, a chap thought then, might see less in the world than Donal, but he saw as was, and his laugh was undyed with his brother's riskiness. Later, knowing him more, I could tell how much Wott mourned on the one hand for lost Donal (whom he called best of all the Brown Hares), on the other for what Donal's greed for a woman had brought, the bust-up and exile of their clan. Wott was no coward himself, as could be told in his being there, so far from their den in Lunn, with purpose, I judged, of seeing Thea and the Dauwas properly guarded. He did not seem one who put lives he valued at hazard for the sake of a thing yearned for himself —

My well-loved over-shoulder reader asks if it is right to give later reflections in place of a tale. True, I've gone once again to thoughts a chappie could not have had till years after. But at times I must: with so much story I cannot let fall, scrap after scrap, as old writers could, how this or that man or woman came to seem. Besides, that skill is lost, and if found again it must be by others whose job is other than mine, which is to unwind the true account of years terrible and astonishing. Then again, while a chap may not have known as much about him as later, this Wott was indeed my true ally before we spoke more than minutes. On his side, he could recount more about my past than a chap had thought was largely known, and in all truth it was no end pleasing to be so soon trusted by this bloke, from a people famed for their just suspicion of others.

As well as his own clan, or what of it still breathed, he told me where I could look for friendship, lots of names of blokes in all parts I could safely go to. With bad word for their treason, he warned me the Moorhens, one of the littler Midlen clans, was in alliance with the Adda-priests, and serving them as spies. Yet among all Mynas, Wott said, was now a quickening of belief ancient foretells were to come true. Signs were everywhere, not only seen by those with his mother's craft.

It worried me he spoke next about Seeyow, the way one thought followed the other. What Thea said and thought about Col seemed pretty daft to me, but if, together with their own family matters or the chances for rain, Mynas all over the shop were gossiping codswallop, about the boy's blood and his right to the True — to the Rod, whatever it might be, it was not going to be very long before those who were no Mynas, Vandenes, too, heard about it. But a chap does not need a Vandene to find jealousy. For instance, when I was very little there had been a blighter in Niragwyn, who tried to be king there, saying he was Tavid's lost elder brother, Ben. He was utterly off his crumpet, but a few other gargoyles followed him and waved swords about. Tavid, my grandfather, was a nice buffer who used to find and feed me the sweetest blackberries, but when he caught the rebels he killed them all, and the way he did in poor Ben, as a warning for others, is disgusting just to think of; it took five days, and lots of women (so my mother told) shoved bits of rag in their ears because of the screams. I thought my horse was about as likely as Col ever to be hailed, following some moony prophecy, as Heir to the Regions. But a jealous prince, hearing people oohing and aahing over it, even if he thought it was nothing but cobwebs, could still aim to be on the safe side by killing the boy. Being no more than talked of as a pretender was dangerous for Col.

Wott soothed me; what the clans now rumoured about was

without names or guesses at names, and besides the little remainder of the Brown Hares, only Thea (with me, now) knew a jot about the lineage Col was supposed to have from his father.

Still, you can see how this went well beyond a lark; together with Thea's plans and warnings there was a lot for a chap to chew over, and in my ponderings I almost overlooked what seemed at the time the least of Wott's acts; he gave me a small bundle of books tied up in a strip of rag. He had brought them here hoping at the fair to find someone who could ride safely for Seeyow, or at least start them on their journey to Marten there. Books not mildewed beyond hope or crumbling at a touch were now becoming very scarce, and Marten had let it be known he would pay for whatever could be brought him. Wott would take no money from me, saying again that without me he and his clansmen could have looked for no less than whipping; shirtless their Hare tattoos would have been their death. At the time, as I say, they were less than an afterthought, those books, an afteract on which a chap had no thought to spare.

As I rode with my gawd under quickly clouding skies beside the opening of the river (here like a sea in width), the meadows moss-green with the season, my brain turned back to Wott's mother and her tellings, which I've rendered; Boy Who Will Be King, Moon-Girl, Dark Rival, Light Rival, Rod. Some of this was not to be understood, but reflect: if Wott had heard Thea's prophecies, so had his mother, and if Wott knew me by sight so could she. Yet in the thick of fear and muddle and the pain of a broken gable-bone she still had to have her rite, her wonderful reading of the spilt roecards. It was amusement to see foolery become so strong a habit — I gave Shan a start with my sudden laugh for the hardiness of fraud (with talking to Mynas and laughing to myself, a chappie could soon rival Marten's repute) — or perhaps in time all who traded in mystery became their own best customers.

Likeliest, looking back, it was there a chap first was teased by half a thought: if so it was a long time being born to full day. Yet how could there not have been, somewhere in a chap's head, that to come true, prophecies did not need my belief. Wott's mother had no lack of mugs to swap food or coins for her skimble-skamble stuff: many more could be made to put faith in a foretell with bloodlines in it, the True Myke of the Viztas, a hidden Heir.

Not till after Tawn, and coming back to spend rare time at what was called home (where my wife lived) did I first look at Wott's books, a mixed lot. One was much larger. Not in thickness, quite a thin book (and still is; it has been kept with care since). Not much could be seen on the cover, which had gone through much damp and batter, and inside, lots of pages were stained and broken, some altogether missing. On each of the pages still present and to be read, not much was printed, and what was was large, pictures of a simple kind as well as words. Not even Marten, not even Thea, would have dared guess what this book would mean to us.

Over how the old writing worked there had, it must be understood, been quarrels without end. Not alone between me and Marten, though we were best armed to argue; my cousin Cara and her husband Kennet of Sevenin, Edin, younger son of Edlin of Suvram, even others less noble, all had their say. I've told books had been used mainly for the fire, but all courts, just about, kept unburnt a few of the best-preserved, the more so when there were pictures, or when gilt had been used on the covers. Like other things, small well-made machines or bits of machines, fragments and sometimes whole pieces of old crockery, objects of unguessable purpose but artful crafting, were kept simply to wonder at.

What we call writing signs stand for words, or the sound of words, though with us there is no difference. One, sometimes two, at top three signs stand for a word, and the signs are made in columns down the sheet or the strip of bark or skin, beginning at the right edge. Because of how old books were printed, not many tried to dispute that the former writing went in lines across, though whether the lines began from the right or the left was a question for hotly urged opinion. I was too cagy to be sure, though Marten's discovery of how old numbers worked, adding ones to the left after each order of nine was passed, made right to left seem slightly more likely than it had. At first, Marten was very strong for that, saying the place the number was printed was also in favour, since before reading on a reader would wish to be sure two pages had not been turned. Almost all the books we find have some pages stuck together, often forever.

Just for the dispute I once showed him how, writing right to left, unless with a curled wrist, the hand would keep covering what had just been written. But Marten demanded to know how I could be sure writing and print were done the same, and even so how I knew it was the right hand that had been used for writing. In old times, he said, more fellows might have been left-handed, or else writing been done with the left hand, as our young princes are taught left-handed fighting with the knife, so that will be as strong a knife-hand when the sword is in the right (Worrel was helped to be so good a fighter by a left hand as strong and sure as the right).

Again, I pointed to the way, at the top of each block of printing, a line began (or ended, as I allowed it might be) a little rightward of the rest, and always with one of the bigger signs — in some of the more fancied books, at the top of the page with a very large sign indeed; I had seen them decorated with colours, and others were put in a frame like a picture, or wound with drawn vines. To me it seemed more likely those would come at the very beginning. It could be seen also when the bottom-most in a block of lines was shorter, the space left over was always on the right, never the left, and always had to the left of that space the dot I held must show an ending: when that same dot was within a block of lines it was always to the left of a short space, and to the right of that was always one of the bigger signs. But a chap could not disprove Marten's cunning reply, writing might have gone back and forth across the page, and it was all the idlest of games so long as we had no guess about what the signs themselves stood for. Clumped as they were in small groups, of which bulk seemed to be of from two to eight signs, with some larger clusters and a few standing alone, it was hard to think they could stand for anything but sounds, but that was far from certain. For one objection there were too many signs; Marten made a list of more than fifty, counting as only one those found both big and small; some he could find only large, others only small (I may say, now this puzzle has been solved, large and little letters are still a beastly annoyance to me when it comes to teaching others; any nit can see s and S are the same, or c and C, but such as b, d, e, g, q and r are always hard to understand).  Only four signs, Marten said, could ever stand alone in a space with no dot beside them (he meant a and A, i and I, but we've since decided really those are only two, and we've found another, in William Shakespeare and in other poetry).  But fifty sounds!  While we did not doubt Print English had more to it that what we spoke, nobody could think of so many different noises.  Just as noises, I mean; we've got a lot more than fifty signs, but those are whole words, mostly.

Now, gingerly opening the slender, bashed book, I could not know I was holding the answers to all these questions.  It is next to me now; more than a third of the space on the first page is taken up by a huge black *A*.  Next to it, simply drawn and easy to know, is the picture of an apple.  Underneath that is the line:

*A is for Apple*,

and down at the foot of the page, not as large as before but still black and bold are the letters *A,a*.

This at first meant little.  I turned the pages which are printed only on one side, some breaking as I turned, noting the drawings, often of orts I could easily name, and when I came to "*T is for Table, T,t*," I was struck by how the two signs at one end were the same as in *Apple*, just as the two words end much alike.  Many old words have changed a lot (not as many as have vanished altogether), but as we now know, lots of the simpler words for simple things have scarce altered.  It came to me when I began to hunt with purpose that this ABC book (as I found it was called) had been made for teaching young how to read. Not till long after was a chap able to read Tulsingham's great book, where he tells about a wonder called Rosetta Stone, a device which in his own time had helped them to read grave writings even more ancient. When I could, and came to that Rosetta Stone it was also the story of Wott's ABC Book, the small secret that bares a huge one, the tiny key unlocking a bally huge door.

Not that it came to a chappie in one blinding flash, like the Roman bozo on the road to Whatsit (not a tale I know, but it may some day be found). As I went on, *C is for Cat* shed a faint bit more light, not for the *a*, which at first muddled me, but because I could see that in print as in language one end of Table and the other end of Cat were the same (except breath begins with one and comes up to the other). Then *L is for Lamb* stopped me. The pictured animal was very young and could be naught else than a lamb (or *lam*, as we would write it if we used print letters: I can't make up mind whether the *b* of the ancient spelling could ever have been said — there is to be be more about that in a while), but if, as I began to believe, the "*L,l*" at the foot of the page was meant to show big and small kinds of the same sign ("*C,c*" was a strong ally for that), then the L that began Lamb should be very like the l near the end in Apple and Table, and I could find no such resembling; either the word for a lamb was very much changed, or else I was wrong about what this book did. That question was never easy to answer; it is now my belief our way of saying words like "table" has altered, and once they did have a sound like the beginning of "lamb" in them; if our guesses at the sounds old letters stood for are somewhat near right, we would now write Apple "appuw" and Table either "taybuw" or tybuw," depending on what part of Brittan we come from. As with lots of world, laziness comes into it; the sounds, after all, are much the same, except in one the tongue is like a dog at midsummer, too lazed to raise his head.

In both their big and small forms, *p* and *b* became a red herring that wasted us much time. It was plain the sounds they stood for were (and are) different only in that the one is whispered, the other hummed, so to speak, and once the sound of *d* was settled it was natural to think *q* should be its unhummed counterpart (which is really *t*, of course). In general the search for some order to the old signs was a wild goose chase we took too long to abandon. "We" means Marten and me; I've begun to write about this great solving as it much of it came all at once, but in fact it took months, with big argument and to and fro of suggestion. Soon after the first guess as to what I had in the ABC Book I irked my wife Rowan (no unusual happening) by going back on less than a promise to pass summer on our own lands, and riding best haste to Seeyow, where not only Marten but a larger number of books were to be found.

(A chap went through Pormarch, and there gave Worrel a report of the meeting with Follen of Wezram. I told him, too, of seeing Thea, and it now seems to me most strange, not that bugger all was said about her words concerning Col and his will-o-the-wisp lineage, but that, as a chap remembers it, I never once debated with myself whether my oldest friend should be told. So soon, I had become conspirator indeed. Mark you, short of giving it to every Tela on the roads, there was no better way of spreading news than confiding in Worrel.)

For a beginning I could get Marten het by telling him his list of fifty-odd signs could be shrunk by at least fifteen, more likely twenty; though pages are missing from the book, or missing in important parts, there could now be no doubt about twenty of the signs he had found only large and only small were really, despite slight resemblance, ten pairs, large and small, of the same signs. Equally, since the little curled dot was evidently no more than a divider, I could readily believe other similar marks, like the plain dot, dot over dot, dot over curled dot, were also kinds of pauses, and that went also for the doubled marks above the line I now know were used to mark off talk and the names of things. I may say the sign used to show a question, and the one we at last named the shout mark, as well as brackets, the sign for "and," and the special crossed letters for sums of money, were all for a very long time a muddle for us, and there still may be other rarer signs waiting to pounce on us all unwarned.

Marten deserves honour for ridding a nag that long retarded us. I was always curious to know by how much speech had changed since the days when Print English was the spoken tongue, and over and again, as we tried to use what we were learning to puzzle out harder books, I wondered how really a word had been said, when in shape as well as meaning it was plainly like one we still have. Marten, at last losing patience with a chap, truly enough said (or shouted) that I would never be able to have talk with men and women a thousand years dead, and how they sounded was no right concern; so long as "rat" and "cat" were so much alike, in Print English as in our speech, and so long as the one difference between them was good also for "rock" and "cock," how once they had been spoken did not matter. As a way of working that was and has been fruitful, but I confess the yearning to know for sure has never left me.  The two words once spelt *son* and *sun*, to take one easy instance, are for us one word but with two different meanings; we use the same sign to write either, and if there is a chance of doubt we can add beneath them the sign meaning "man" or the sign meaning "sky."  Now while, in Print English, the letter *o* has usually what seems a different sound, there are other ancient words with an *o* in them that for us are sounded with the sound oftenest given by the sign *u*, and I can never be sure how "son" was said when everyone read and could write Print English.  A chap can see more to it than that, because even if they were said alike, being spelt differently must have made them *seem* quite separate words.

The letter *h* is another question without an answer, or rather an axle about which lots of questions turn.  I made Marten agree it was a real letter, though for a long time we thought it must be a special kind of sign with no set meaning of its own; we could see how it changed the sound of *t* and *s* and *c*, because we still have words like *then* and *shit* and *chase* (as well as *ten* and *sit* and *case*), and they don't seem to have changed much; but to us the words that once were "ear" and "hear" are, again, the same word with different meanings.  But it could (and can) be seen *h* starting a word once had had sound, because while in Print English they wrote *an* apple, *an* oak, *an* eye, they didn't, as we would now saying those words, put *an* hope, *an* hand or *an* hill.  So I maintained, and Marten after searching found some, like *honour*, *heir* and *hour* where it was "an."  But I said that was an argument on my side, if sometimes or for some people *h* was seen not to have had any sound, that made more likely, not less that at other times or for more people it did have one.

What that sound might have been is now beyond any guessing, and the puzzle of *h* when it comes after *g* only makes more puzzle; *light* and *straight*, to show two. They are plainly the forefathers of words we have still, yet we have no sound in the middle to explain the *gh*; and when in a poem I found two lines next to one another ending with *straight* and *gate* (in which we still make the same middle sound) I would have been sure the ancients, for no reason to be guessed, had gone on writing letters that had no sound — except for a word like *laugh*. Lots and lots of the changes, it seems to me, between their language and ours are due to sounds being left out as the years passed (others have changed: bulk of the words I just wrote about, with *th* in them, would have *f* or *v* if we used the old signs), and so it is hard to believe we have put a sound where they had none; *gh*, as I argued with Marten, must stand for a soft sound, or perhaps two, altogether lost to us, which we might guess at if we knew what *h* alone was like. As is, in many places, we seem teased by what stays just out of reach.

No doubt in those times language was rich with a thousand fine hues of both sound and meaning for which we no longer have the ears. A thousand, I write, and that means ten hundreds: in one of the silly magics plays by William Shakespeare (as they are said to be) the treasonous servant Caliban says sometimes he hears a thousand twangling instruments, and somewhere else I have read symphony was played by hundred instruments of twenty different kinds; who can ever imagine what sounds came from such a mixture in such numbers, or the fineness of the hearings that could enjoy such variousness? Though in that play, I do not believe "a thousand" is truly meant; in another, better play, still marred by ghosts and long jawings no one could ever really have said, Prince Hamlet says, ranting, he loved Ophelia more than forty thousand brothers could, and another old poet in a good story about a long sea trip (also with a lot of superstition, but it all takes place far off in the ocean, where strange happenings are less hard to disbelieve) writes of the sea having a thousand, thousand slimy things, and a chappie can't think we are meant to believe the sailor sat there counting them.  So when I write "thousand" it can mean, as then, a very large number.  Marten dislikes my doing this.

I've strayed a little.  What a chap began to say is, no matter where in the past one looks one is bowled over by plenitude and by such variety, and by the thought of people whose senses could make judgements of differences I'm sure we would never notice.

Take wine (as instance, I mean, though would pour you some, if it could be).  We do know somewhat about our nearest neighbour across the sea; from the farthest point of Brittan to the south and east it can even be seen when the weather is clear, or so is said; I've never been there.  But I knew some of our boats had sailed to France, and in the south, not far from where my wife had her lands, boats sometimes came from there, more often in summer.  They brought with them to sell skin or earth bottles of a drink we call "van" (or so I would spell it), after their own name (though I've heard those sailors talk, and they have sounds Print English signs have no true match for).  For lots of us the sounds $v$ and $w$ are easily mucked up, so I believe this drink, a lot stronger than beer, must be the one of old called wine.  It is either red or light yellow, mostly clouded or mudded-looking, not always good to drink.  But every so often a boat brings wine (if this is it), clear and smelling of fresh fruit and almost flowers, and then the well-born bid against each other to have some; between good and bad as between red and yellow we can still tell difference.  But ago, so I read, "wine" was the name of a kin, like "tree," and there were as many different, named kinds of wine as there are of trees, perhaps more: port, champagne, bracer, sack, martinis, Burgundy, double, Hippocrene, hock, Falernian, Rhenish, brandy, chateau and claret are just some of the names they had, and in one or two places the name of the wine has a number which can be no other than the year of its making.  To think of mouths that not only knew the goodness of twenty different kinds of wine, but could tell goodness of one blooming year from another is as flabbergasting as all a chap knows about machines and buildings they had.

Slowly it comes to seem to a chap one and the other are great lots alike in needing words, heaps of words, each with meaning all agree to.  I just made mention of trees, and beyond writing even speech must once have been learnt, and had to be made before it could be taught.  Long ago past thinking, there must have been a time when men and women first made names for what they saw, heard, tasted and felt and smelt, what they chased or bunked from, weather, and what was useful or dangerous or pleasing: they named the world.  Soon there must have been a word for tree, and then as time passed they must have begun to notice how one tree was different from others.  One gave them nuts and another fruit, the wood of one was better for burning, another for arrows or the straight handles of spears or tools for building, another tough, good for walls or boats.  Then they would see how the shape, how the tree grew, colour of bark and the shape of the leaves could help them; the heavy-limbed tree with the loby leaves and the acorns always had the stout wood for building, but it was the one stooping over rivers, with sharp, light leaves, that was good for carving into bowls, and gave also the bending but strong strips they could weave into baskets. So names would come, oak, willow and all the others, ash and apple, beech and hawthorn, birch and elm and maple, each name holding lore about usefulness or beauty. Yet, as still is with kiddies (and with some grown lords and ladies, who learn no learning that has any use, lest they be taken for workers), the general, I believe, would have been content to call them all trees, never seeing how an oak is like oak, a beech like beech, until those names were given. Differences a fellow can see are the only ones that can be for him. So as the words were made, if this is not too much to say, they made the differences.

Much later, the same with wine, and so too for those ruddy machines and all their thousands of clever parts; names and knowing of names let them be born; names for ways of working different sorts of metal, the names for what each machine would do, and each part inside that machine, the names of measurings and powers and jobs that wanted doing. Words have now become few and clumsy of meaning, and that is not only sign of our poverty but warrant poverty must surely go on; no one can think about what has not got a name, nor give a name what cannot be thought.

A chap tried to say part of this to Marten, one day in squall-blown Seeyow, when we had begun to inkle the vastness of what was in old books. Remembering how he had pictured for me the lost heirlooms of learning, a chap thought he would be swift to see how words made knowledge as much as knowledge words. Instead, he took the thought half said, so to blame faith for all our dullness. There what he says is still true, such feeble seedlings of understanding as may start are soon blighted when the Viztas are made the one answer for everything not understood, or, as I would now resay it, multitudinous small things which only patient naming could begin to explain are turned into one dark bafflement called the Works of the Viztas. As if (I said to Marten), far worse than one name for all kinds of trees, a whole wood could be seen only as a mystery indivisible not yet as lots of clustered trees. And Marten was right, is right to blame those who forbid even the asking of questions about that forest. But not by themselves, I say: once there must have been such hunger for knowing and naming that even the Adda-priests could never have stayed it with their stupiding beliefs. As we are now, mostly, so people became their own gaolers, for reasons we cannot now guess.

With this, Marten and I could never quite agree — or he never quite heard what a chappie was saying. It gave me a turn. Oh, we'd had disputes before; a chap had not perfect awe, but Marten was first ever to tell me the world might not be what I had been taught (as Thea was first to show a chap might, notwithstanding, have a special part in it), and I had never before gone to places of thought where Marten could not follow. Not that I am brainier altogether; he knows secrets of movement and measurement that dizzy me, and has never been dismayed by whole armies of numbers. What now was new to me was knowing, for the questioning of the world we had, I had got all

Marten could give me, and was now my own vanguard. To grow, if only in one way, beyond a loved teacher is like an orphaning.

This again is too much said in this place, and like a hound gone wrong I must scoot back to pick up the scent, where Marten and I began to find what they were, the mixed books he had saved from the fire. Now, after so much, it is not easy to remember what we expected from those thick blocks of pages, those forests of even lines. What sorts of thoughts they wished to have printed and kept, those ancient masters of so much, was outside our imagining, and wherever we began, it was bang in the middle of the tale.

By now a chap has read all through more than thirty books, or what of them can still be read, and seen parts of lots more, but still my picture of ago may be quite false: I think of all the thousand thousand books thrown on sightless fires, and not to be supposed is that what we've saved, mainly by chance, are a true sample of what once was. In one way it is certain they are not; ever since mastering the numbers Marten had told his friends the Mynas to watch for books with mainly numbers in them, and in his library (as a marshalling of books was called) were more of that than any other kind. Some greatly disappointed him when we learnt to understand the words telling what the numbers were. Among all the variousness of old there was a thirst, strange to us, for numbers to do with games; score as they were called (though that word also meant twenty). Lots of blokes today, true, will gather to watch the best bowmen or swordsmen go against each other for bet or challenge, and no mystery in former times immense throngs came to see those who best played their games (though the numbers told are surely as wild as the forty thousand brothers Hamlet gave Laertes). What puzzles a chap is that scores and all sorts of other numbers were carefully kept and printed for people to read long after, ranks and columns of numbers filling page after page; what type of temper took pleasure in that? It is, or so it seems, the old passion for counting and measuring brought to perfect unmeaning, as if they became fed up with numbers that did work, and treasured these lists for their very foolishness. Nearly as dull for us are the long lists showing times of high and low tide at hundreds of places not now to be recognised. Among other number books there was (and is) one filled with jesting figures about how much coal there was and how much oil, and how many tons of wheat grown, how much of all manner of stuff made in all parts of the world. This, though there is no smile, must be a joke or a fiction outside our understanding, a bit like those tales of ours, where a whopping great feast is told of, with more roasted sheep eaten, more beer swilled down than could ever really be: with every allowance and more for the size of the old cities, what use could ever have been in a single year for tens of thousands of thousands of tons of coal (a ton was a big measure by itself) just for one country? For oil the numbers are even stupider, though printed down to the last ten barrels; for what could so much oil have been needed? When I found the old poem about the sea voyage and told its gist to Marten, his joke was, it must have been all the oil that made a thousand thousand things slimy.

Even of the kind of number-books he really desired some are simpler than his needs, others beyond his grasp or anyone's; I can still remember how he came in shouting and waving arms the day when he made out the secret of *logarithms*, but there is no unwinding what's called *calculus*; more than once in his ire Marten has called that a book of superstition disguised as the lore of numbers.

With books that are mainly words, more than a chap would have chosen (I mean, of what we have) are stories. We have Telas, and not more than one in a dozen of us can use and read even our simple signs; it had not come to me that in a time when lots could read, not even tales would be left to memory, but printed in books. My hope had been for more true history of large events, perhaps to explain how it was broken, the old learning and mastery of machines. We came now, beyond any eluding, to that question little Col had asked: for a long time I could not say if the very long, ravelled stories that took a whole book to tell were meant as true. Some drivel on about gloryless people who, while making use of marvellous machines (which of them, if any, truly existed a chap can't know), do not a thing with them that seems worth remembering.

That could argue one way or the other: a guy writing history might be expected to choose to write about the great men and women of his time or of other times (as William Shakespeare indeed did, sometimes), but still, who would take trouble to invent the drear lives of such little creatures as these long books have? Our Telas would soon be left to starve if they gave stories about what a chap can see for himself, unheard-of farmers and their wives who eat breakfast in the morning and do their work, or bed with others no more grand than they. At last, because so much time is taken up with reciting, beyond the drab deeds, the

strange joyless thoughts of these caitiffs, and the reasons why they
do what makes no difference to any but themselves, I decided they
must be for the main part made up. Not good to still know doubt,
even in Seeyow where it has come to matter. Our own Telas
often mix their imaginings into what really was, and the past, for
bulk of us, is what the Telas tell; the Seeyowites came to be
loonies even for asking whether a tale is true or invented, and the
best of us can never see other of the past than what words teach.
Yes, words tell us what to see, invent what we must see in our
own time, but yet we are at words' mercy for worlds no longer to
be seen. Then long tales teach me less that a chap had hoped for;
if they were never meant to be true in any part a chap still holds
at a loss to find for what they were written. It can be seen there
was a gain in having the letters; none of our Telas could keep in
the memories tales so long and yet so neat in how all that is
mentioned has a place. Yet I do not think a Tela could keep the
spot won beside a midwinter hearth if he stopped his story so
often for long describings. Our tales are stretched out by a crafty
Tela with lists of jewels or treasures or gorgeous clothes, or the
big feasts I've already spoken of, dish after tasty dish. Such
delight the poor and hungry who can finger and taste in their
brains what they cannot in life. But Telas do not spend their
words on what any ass can see for himself, twilight or a rainy day
or a lime-tree of no special size or more than usual beauty. These
parts of the old books can make a chappie quite shirty, telling me
too much and too little; describing, when there is so much a chap
would like to learn, a sunset or a bird I can see any day: then a
thing I've never heard of is named, and tons about its colour or its
weight and how it caught the light, all without saying what it was

and did; betimes I can't tell whether it might be a machine, a food, a piece of clothe, or an animal.

It might be tales became less tale-like as time went on. We have got not enough books to be sure, but the most we do have come printed at the starts with numbers that can only be dates, and Tulsingham, as in so much else, was very helpful in explaining how time was counted. His own era counted from the birth of their hero-king (God, others say, but Tulsingham says he was only a man) Jesus. As much time and more was held to stretch backwards from the date of that birth, and Tulsingham himself takes us back so far to speak about the Pyramids and the land called Egypt, but of the later era there were about two thousand years. All the books we've got are from the last three hundred of those years, more of all from a quite short lifetime, between 1870 and 1910. Not all dates of printing can be trusted; the book of William Shakespeare says it comes from 1894, but William Shakespeare lived, so it is sure, much sooner: Tulsingham, whose grand book has the date 1878, mentions William Shakespeare more than once, as a guy long reverenced. Besides, William Shakespeare never has any of the speedy machines, not even the famous trains, which are in just about every tale of Tulsingham's time and after; here, if in small else, William Shakespeare's world seems more like ours, with weavers and joiners and boats that need the wind, fighters with swords, so we must be wrong to imagine the spiffing past time, the Age of the Viztas, stretched back, as the priests say, into time beyond time; if the Viztas caused the building of Stonedge so long ago even Tulsingham (who calls it Stonehenge) cannot say when it was done, they sure waited a long time before beginning to teach what else they knew. But it was with the coming of machines the long, adventureless stories began, or so appears, and a chap often wonders whether they were planned as a joke we can't understand now. Of course they did have jokes, ago; I've got some pages and scraps from a printed story with a laugh we still enjoy, the foolish master who can do no single thing right, with his know-all servant. A strange tale, much of it in speech, with what seem to me very lively words, though not in the same way as William Shakespeare's. But the writer takes the jest too far when he has the master trying to remember a line from the older poet, Keats, and the servant knows it better; how could the world be so much changed? To have the servant know more about food and drink and other practical matters is good, but in any time the master would know more of learning than the servant, even if ever so wise. In this, William Shakespeare is truer to life.

William Shakespeare's name comes more often than it should. At times I think he must've been part bonkers, or perhaps only a cause of madness in others. At first a chappie could understand only pieces, and did not see why his tales, so stuffed with annoying words, were so strangely done. After I read more poetry I saw William Shakespeare had been meant to be spoken out loud, and later again, when I could read most of the one about Hamlet, and the very daffy one about Midsummer, I realised that, like the plays there are inside those plays, his had been acted out by people who spoke the lines as they had been pronounced to them, and spoke no more than was set down. They were a little bit like our Telas, having in memory what they had to say; poetry, being easier to remember, must have helped them. We believe they dressed themselves up, too.

William Shakespeare is rich food, but also a kind of trick, like the conjurers at fairs who make a fellow see what is not; naught in his tales goes like any life that ever could have been, yet his cunning makes it nearly seem his kings and soldiers and ladies could be real. He is often filled with misery, and yet not small or snivelling, and it is pity so much of what can be learnt from such powered words is false.

For what is true, I've gone to Tulsingham. To me it seems strange while William Shakespeare is mentioned much by later writers, I've never found a single naming of Tulsingham, whose book, *Revelation, Superstition and Sober Sense*, must have changed the time in which he lived. How much like our own time that was is now hard to guess, but in one big way, surely, it differed. It was filled (as can be judged) with hope. Tulsingham believed the long ages of superstition, the nursery years of Mankind, as he names them, were at last near their end. Whether he was one among lots who wrote so we can not now know, but it is certain he wrote like one who knows a time has come; they had priests then, too, but their power must have been on the wane. Big parts of what he says, which must have been plain to those for whom he wrote, are murky for us, as when he much praises the character and courage of the hero Jesus, but goes on to deplore (a word Tulsingham likes to use) the "fairytale apparatus of shoddy miracles wherein the plain simplicity of his teachings is bartered away in exchange for a specious appeal to ignorant credulity." Some of these words are doubtful in meaning, but here as everywhere in his book Tulsingham, plain to tell, is saying what I meant when I said "Toys" to Thea: he thinks Man has outgrown the need to believe in strange magic. Till this very moment when

I write this, a chap has never seen Tulsingham was, for his time, lots like Marten for ours, though print must have given him a louder voice.

It would be waste to spend more pages describing and praising a book which could be read by any able to read this; someday be we shall once again be able to print, and Tulsingham's book can be famed once again. Not like William Shakespeare, he writes plain and explains himself, and he also does his job without falling in love with words for their own sake; too much in William Shakespeare the clearness of a thought gets lost in a muddle of colours and strange shapes.

With Tulsingham, too, though a chap cannot get lost in him, is a true likeness of Man, as Marten said so long ago, not so greatly different from what we are; Tulsingham does not see or wish to see giants or magicians, still less demons. This, as well as what he teaches about the long history before his time, always stays good lesson, and important for us to understand. William Shakespeare has no reasonable limits, as if words themselves were magical machines. Even in a terrible tale about a mad old king, with cruelty, sadness, greed and misfortune enough to wring the smile off a Cheshire cat, there is wild glory hard to explain, a deceit like belief in the Viztas, but worse in a way; how can this William Shakespeare be bold to tell about men and women cheating, wounding, hating, blinding and killing each other, and still make us take pity as cure? We're safer, surely, with Tulsingham, and soberer, too.

## Loss

It is well to say again, those accomplishments didn't come before but marched together with events, the many years I must now turn into an hour-glass, even if doing so a chap must seem to scant great injuries and heaps of losses.

In three summers one of my warnings came true: Raug, having been quiet, suddenly moved, and for the first time openly violated Suvram lands. Forn's soldiery marched into that province loss of the northern Marchlen had left dangling, so to put a stop, Forn said, to injuries and insults undergone by Vandenes there. The whole territory, with much good grazing and some fine farms, was overrun in a trice, and the bleats of King Edlin were ignored.

Besides signalling Raug's rewaked ambitions, this meant Worrel once again had a long border to defend, made longer when Yew, without fight, ceded a strip of Gwyn land beyond the very frontier Raug had sworn to five years before. It was a spot I knew from childhood, the western side of a shallow valley, between river and hills, and would perhaps have been a bit of a job to defend. But Uncle Yew was now so firm to avoid firmness against Raug he was made loathsome to me. A chap now went to Caer only when he must; my father had yoked himself to Yew's policy of keeping on Raug's good side, and would far rather see my sister there, with her priestly husband and the only grandchildren, my two nieces, perfect Vandenes in the making.

I've not said much about my father. He'd been big warrior
in youth, but about the time I was born a breaking of his left arm
which never properly healed made him unable to fight on
horseback, and ended his warring. He stayed a good swordsman
afoot, but his injury, no doubt, made my unaptness for weapons
the more a disappointment for him. But having scorned me in my
youth as no fighter, in his age he called me fou l names for the
opposite, and was an echo for Yew in charging me with stirring
up hatred of the Vandene kingdom, which would be in peace with
all but for me and others like me (Worrel, he meant, but Worrel
was a king and so not named plain). An echo of Yew, I said, but
it was, truth told, Forn at third hand; not (so far as I can tell) in the
history of all other times has there been a bounder so able to
preach his peaceful intent while letting loose so much war.

Besides bringing new threat to Marchlen, the fresh Raug
conquests laid bare the softness proud Suvram had become. Late,
King Edlin began the raising of some fighters. Though this was
a course long urged, I had little influence and less hope; they were
under captaincy not of his younger son, but of the elder, Erril who
has all the pride of the first Edlin, but the wits only of the last.
The sort which can make boast of uninstructed mistakes, like a
farmer, years ago, who showed me an outbuilding, wretchedly
made, ready to tumble with the first gale, and proudly told me he
had made it all alone, too bally silly to see his first and worst
failure was in not seeking help.

The younger son, Edin, was then at Seeyow, learning to
read. He was far my favourite among the lords of Suvram, having
shown from the start an unusual thirst for knowing. He first
disputed with me over the way of reading Print English when he

was no more than ten or eleven (that was before the finding of the ABC Book); he had been wrong, but in no thickskulled way. He was now seventeen, very tall, and at that time all alone among us in not ceasing to believe in the Viztas. He held the interesting idea the old writers, like William Shakespeare, must have been Viztas themselves, and the people they wrote about who seemed such giants to us were indeed never of our world, but remembered from that other, far place whence the Viztas had come. So too with what seemed like dreams in Tulsingham's book, such as the land where it was day half the year, or Alexander the Great, or America.

When I said, but every word of Tulsingham's book was written against believing what wasn't seen, Edin answered that what our priests taught was superstition about the Viztas, not the beliefs *of* Viztas; there would be no aspect magical to Tulsingham about being a Vizta, or of their race, if he was himself. All the Viztas, Edin said, could've tried to get rid of the old superstitions and teach (as Tulsingham did) that we were makers of our own world. But after they left (Edin was sure the Leaving must be real), our blokes got scared, seeing all the Viztas had taught us to do was falling to bits, and so the priests began, and they made up all about the Viztas still watching us, and coming back and punishing the ones who didn't keep to their ways.

So Edin, for a while, said approaching the same about the Viztas as Tulsingham says about Jesus. This irked Marten, who still asked for a reason why the Viztas ever came. But seeing Edin get stubborner the more he was disputed, I stopped. Belief or disbelief didn't matter for such Viztas, who had come and gone, not even mentioned in sober history, leaving no power behind them.

Seeyow, it must be known, was then becoming a place where clever fellows came. Not lots, but bulk were of the best. On my travels when I met a builder, a carpenter, a worker in iron, a boatwright vexed with questions skill with numbers could solve, I would tell him about Marten. Quite many couldn't afford to leave their trades and their families for so long, but blokes who could came, and a few sent their apprentices. A gaggle of youths of family also made the journey, some, like Edin, able to teach us by questions they had. In old times there were things or places called Universities, not just schools, but where those of learning could gather, some to spend a lifetime. Because no one, no matter how learned, could ever know all there was, and because in all times (or so I suppose) as it is now even the wisest may learn from talk and argument, inventing, betimes, new wheezes to know, such places were greatly honoured. It may be the old Counters were the leftovers from that, and now Seeyow was again a place for learning.

We weren't in honour with the Adda-priests, or any others who held it was wrong to ask a question that could be more simply answered with *The Viztas*: this became the one place, I think, where no thought, no word, almost, was an Island entire of itself; all joined together, so only in Seeyow thinking was the start of journeys without end. I was there myself, to study and to teach, whenever I could be, but Seeyow in that time was always a foreign place for me, riding from there as a chap always was into thoughts of war and preparings for war. It was as if that ribbon of seawater (if this isn't too fanciful) split Seeyow not just from the mainland but from its time.

Now, with invasion of Suvram and Yew's bland surrender of borderland, the Vandene Kingdom was too near Seeyow for my peace. Marten, though he still fronted some, tickled others, with guffawing impieties, never acted as if there could be any danger, so much did he despise varlets who would have all believe as they did. It became my part, with advice from Worrel, to make sure all coasts were watched, especially by the narrows, and to see all those who came were of the sort, as Marten himself had once put it, who, when asked about the beliefs of others, shrugged.

Col came to be ten, reminding those old enough to remember of Worrel's boyhood. Both in muscles and use of his strength he was always beyond his age, and he outfought with staves, outshot with the bow and outdared on the rope-walk sons of the Peacock gawds who were not far short of manhood. Worrel had too much to do keeping his kingdom to pass time at Seeyow, and I was no end bucked when Edin made a friend of Col; Edin, with a strength not to be guessed from his slender shoulders, was admired as rider and swordsman, and liked everywhere for his even temper, generous in winning some game, and courteous in defeat. With all this and in his appetite for learning he turned Col to the good; the boy's boiling fuel had sometimes made him impatient of what needed sitting-still to master, and other fighters he knew and took pattern from had no use for brain. Remember, Col had never known a father, and had lost his mother near his fourth birthday. Too, his bastardy was known, and there were places he wasn't welcome, Caer for one. Even his grandfather, Jon, always windy about offending Yew, hadn't much to do with

Col. Caif had been only child, but now Jon had adopted Neal, the son of a sister, as heir in Farragwyn; such slightings weren't lost on a boy of Col's pride and skills.

Edin soon taught Col to smile more often, treating him in every way like an equal, even though the boy (so far as he knew) was of a base father. Also he came scarcely up to Edin's breastbone. Seen from behind, while Col had broader build, they might have been taken for brothers, with their tousles of straw-coloured hair, but when they turned the contrast was sudden, Edin's light, botherless eyes and high forehead, the boy's hungering, dark gaze under straight brows. Edin was, we may say of boys, having no thought to unnatural ways, Col's first love, and surely the first chap he gave full admiration. Yet still it was Edin who taught Col much more to admire the lore of his great-uncle Marten (there had never been any bitter in their fierce debates about the Viztas). It was a sad morning when Edin, after over a year there, left Seeyow.

He went as I once had, to get himself a cumny of soldiers, though a larger one, and for other purposes. He was proud for Suvram's glory, and at the fall of his father's lost province he rued that apart from his own small following he was unused to captaincy. Even so, not much beyond boy, he would have ridden to war, but I argued the lands were already gone, and if he rode off to death or capture it left Suvram's defence in the hands of his father and his brother Erril. With Edin there was never need to labour such a point. Instead, I said, he should raise fighters, especially amongst blokes driven from his father's lands, and take them to Marchlen to ride and perhaps fight alongside those of Worrel. So he would help against Raug, but also learn the larger strategies of war from the fellow more now agreed was the best captain of our time — some, true to tell, might have chosen Syme, the giant of a blighter who now led for Forn, but while his strength and prowess was no more to be doubted than his famed cruelty (he was gossiped to have chopped at prisoners one finger at a time, one hand, and so on, telling them one live Vandene body was better than two dozen unbelieving parts), Syme had never fought except with the numbers on his side, whilst Worrel, with skill and thought, some cunning, had often won against the odds.

Best, years of battle, wounds and captivity, loss of lands and the need always for more battle had left Worrel hard in body and brain, but not in spirit. When I saw him at Pormarch in the beginning of winter he met me with a chuckling plan. Raug's war-bands, he forecast, would shy from the defended Marchlen, advancing instead deep into butter-soft Suvram. When they did, Worrel would slip behind them and strike for the heart of Raug itself, capture old Vandis, and make him give up all lands conquered in his rotten reign and permit any of his subjects to believe as they chose.

In one way this was founded on fact; cumnies of Forn's soldiery were already riding without opposition well within Suvram, escorting Adda-priests as far south as the headwaters of the Tem and beyond. But Worrel knew with the numbers he had he couldn't carry war to Raug, though help that had come made him confident of holding his own borders, and more seriously he talked about harrying the flanks of the Raug soldiery.

Well, but in spring Worrel was killed. That is now twelve years ago, and still as I write the words there is a feeling of the sun dwindling in the sky, of a sudden gap in nature. With no formal alliance to Edlin, though with Edlin's son for a kind of warrant, he was carrying out his plan of hampering Raug in upper Suvram. His forces did turn back more than one riding of Forn's men, and how he died has mystery about it. It happened at a village, well within Suvram, where Raug, nevertheless, had collected taxes due Edlin. Worrel, who sent his chaps scouting out for enemy, was with only three companions, who all were killed with him. It was said Worrel was killed in single fight with Syme. That at least was Raug's tale. Elsewhere, never count what a bruiser Syme was, it stayed hard for anyone to believe Worrel could lose a fair fight, and Telas soon had a tale with treachery in it. To believe such, if no comfort for me, might have been a mark where to aim my anger over the death itself. This is not now knowable.

Death a fact, Raug acted with correctness, sending to Alma, and also informing King Edlin, telling him the death in his lands had come when fine fellows of Raug on peaceable business had been assailed by rotters from Marchlen. While Vandis didn't think the question of compensation arose, he equally meant no punitive action against Marchlen. With Edin, the brothers from Wezram, Worrel's own fighters, and even Alma herself all mad for a chance to spill some Vandene blood, the last part was more disappointment than promise in Pormarch.

Beyond anger was grief, and beyond that the question of rule; believing it was in doubt brought Uncle Yew to Worrel's funeral at Pormarch (like a piebald raven, Alma rudely said, not only mocking Yew's patched face, but to mean a picker of dead bones). Calm Kennet of Sevenin was the only other king who came, but he of course brought Cara, Worrel's sister, and there were proxies for Wezram and Suvram, and even my own sister Gwynis, for Raug.

The king's house at Portmarch, like others, is part old, part new, rough building of our own time added to a big old house of stone, never in old times part of a city, though now next to the largest town of March. While the others were still gathering for the funeral in one of the older parts of the house, a tall-ceilinged hall used also for feasts, I had a quiet meeting with Alma, who told me Worrel, like anyone of sense who often goes to war, had left a will. In it, in the case of his dying before any of his sons was eighteen, I was named as Guardian.

A chap thought there must be some mistake. What would become of Worrel's kingdom was a tricky business, all right, but for the sake of strength, and to keep Marchlen safe for Worrel's sons I had hoped Alma's younger brother, Frick, might come as Guardian. A bit of a brawler, and not the cleverest bloke in all Brittan, he was enough of a soldier for soldiers to follow, and in due time would've passed the rule to Bryan, Worrel's eldest son, the same age as Col, and now king. Frick himself was heir in Stanglin, and that was separated from Marchlen by the whole width of Brittan (of Raug, as it now was), too much ever to tempt Frick into robbing Bryan by trying to make the two kingdoms one. But just as here in the west Stanglin was under the threat of Raug, so Frick, their best fighter, couldn't be spared by his father, King Tobin.

Even so, Alma herself would be lots better than I. Women who in their youth are a match for lads at riding and running and even weapons often slacken after marriage, or are weakened by childbearing, but Alma, though the fifth (now the last) of Worrel's children, a second daughter, was less than two, as after every birth, had regained her lean strength. Alma and I had always been cordial together, but there was nothing between us to call friendship; we were like two spokes of the same wheel, and now the hub was gone. Smiling at me, she said what a chap could have worked for himself, Worrel had chosen me knowing I would do all I could to keep Marchlen for his son.

I said I was no one for leading fighters in the field, and she indicated it would be no honour to Worrel's memory to think he ever thought I was. More than with most, much more than with Thea, I can give only the sense of Alma's words. She still has the accent and the — *dialectic* is the old word, I believe — of her native place; unlike arrows she doesn't send words straight and exact. But what she said, not flattering, was true; Worrel hadn't made his will thinking I would overnight become a captain of horse. He must have believed I could keep the borders with other men's arms, using what he always called my cattish cunning, comparing himself to a hunting dog. It wasn't fair that if Alma (who could knock spots off me with a weapon in her hand) tried to rule, Vandis of Raug and his lackey friend Yew would soon divide Marchlen between them, but we have lost the habit of ruling queens. Kennet, the only other neighbour king, could've been trusted not to try pinching Bryan's throne, but Worrel (of anyone) knew the coolness there was between his own wife and his sister, Kennet's Cara.  He couldn't have left me aught of his a chap less ambitioned to, but I would have to take the job.

There was another point.  More tactful times might have been found for it, but it couldn't be left for those.  The will, I pointed out, having just read it, didn't say about Bryan's fostering if Alma take another husband before he is come to age.

Alma's look was scorn — for the idea, I believe, not for me; she couldn't believe I could think she would ever have another husband, after Worrel.

Those were feelings right to the time, and a chap could believe the thought had never come to Worrel, but Alma, mind, was only my age, and Worrel's memory wasn't honoured, either, by supposing he had married a woman to bury her life in his grave.  This was important, because if she did take another husband, and more so if she had another child, it would be up to me to see after no supplanting of Bryan as heir.  Marchlen was now Alma's home, and it was plain she still saw herself as queen.  That for now was no hurt, but when her son grew he would be king, and Alma his guest.

My reader chides I make myself seem ice.  Not a bit, and if these cold future chances were considered then, that is a chappie's nature.  Once mentioned, I didn't press them.  When I hugged Alma our tears damped each other's shoulders.

Coming into the large hall I was hailed by Gwynis, who had come roundabout by way of Caer, and had greetings, she said, from our parents.  I was bucked she had left with my mother the two girls.  The elder was a horrid child, at seven a perfect little Adda-ess, who knew by heart the Midsummer Prayer and all of the Evening Answers; as Marten once said of such children, her first word was "Viztas."

Gwynis had ridden in the company of Uncle Yew, to whom, as I soon discovered, she had carried a message from Raug. Wheezing and snuffling as he now did much of the time, blotch-faced Yew led me aside to say King Vandis made objection to the nest of unbelief at Seeyow, where, report was, young guys and others were taught to despise the Viztas, to doubt their greatness and works.

This message was sent to Yew, or so he would have it, yet Seeyow, as I took chance to remind him, was in the Kingdom of Farragwyn, not his.

He peered a bit to see if I was having him on, and counter-reminded me Jon, as was known very well, took guidance from Caer. His tone said Pormarch must, also; this, with small subtlety, was to tell me now Worrel was gone I could be brought to heel. Yew had no children, and no one knew who was to be heir for Niragwyn: it was a cert he wouldn't follow Jon and adopt the son of his sister (me).

I told him a story I just made up, about a wolf who met two dogs, and didn't know what would happen if he fought both at once. (This kind of tale, where animals stand for humans, called a *fable*, was once very common. Only Telas have them now, and general people hear them just as stories, not lessons, as they were meant. No one alive, by the way, has the foggiest what a wolf looked like, but they're still in some of our stories.) So the wolf, I coined, called the bigger dog his friend, and told him the littler dog was going to attack him. Then I asked Yew to guess what he thought the wolf did, after one dog had killed the other.

Yew wasn't a one for parables (another name for the same sort of account; I think they make a good way of saying hard things softly, but mine sounded far rougher than is written here). He couldn't make mind up whether I was mocking him, insulting him, or merely babbling, as a chappie was reputed to do. At last he told me Gwyn made its own choice for friends, and Marchlen would have to choose, too. I told him bluntly Marchlen judged friendship by friendly acts, and our talk stopped there, old Yew frowning (he hadn't heard Worrel's will, and didn't know how much I could speak for Marchlen).

But what he said about Seeyow was a worry. Marten, I thought, would try to fight off even the men of Jon, his lawful king, if they tried to bring his island under rule that would outlaw his studies, but if I had to be long times at Pormarch, and Yew, or Jon told by Yew, stopped the road to Seeyow, my only way there and from there would be a long sea-journey all about the coast of Gwyn. These weren't what should be the first thoughts for a chap with the threated March now in his care, but even so soon I began to know Seeyow had weapons against Adda-priests and the ambitions of Raug better than any found in men's scabbards.

Worrel was buried with priests. He never would dispute with talk doubting the Viztas, but said the beliefs of his father and mother were enough for him. Priests, but not Adda-priests, and my sister remembered to be shocked when an old prayer was used which, among ten titles for the Viztas, calls them "Messjas ovva Sun," a blasphemy (if I have the right old word, an insult to faith) in Vandene belief. Otherwise the rites were much like others, except praise for the dead one, hollow words so often, were for once solid and real.

After, Alma stunned Yew by reading Worrel's simple will, and the reason why I stood at young Bryan's side became clear.

"Evan?" Yew questioned, loud-voiced.  "Evan Tela, to rule this kingdom?"

A nickname heard before, and didn't mind it, given because of my constant travelling.  Yew was trying to give the others his scorn, like a cold or a fit of yawning, but I'd had time for private words with the other lords here, and knew they would honour Worrel's wishes.  It was soon shown any challenge to the will would have to come at sword's point.  A dozen swords were already bared in the big hall, as, following Edin, Kennet of Sevenin, the two brothers of Wezram, and Worrel's chief fighters drew to hail Bryan as king, under my protection.  Yew, taking my sister, left that same day.

Testing for me came at once.  Alma and her brother Frick were very hot for a raid of vengeance against Raug, and made plans a chap knew sod all about, till Powl, Worrel's chief captain (a top-notch fighter, who unjustly blamed himself for being elsewhere — as his orders were — when Worrel was killed), asked if I meant to take part.  Likeliest, this was in hope of hearing *no*.  If so he got more *no* than he asked for, when I said no such raid was to be done.

That caused a strong quarrel; the young brothers of Wezram (King Follen's two nephews) were on Alma's side, and Frick made plain his belief cowardice was to blame for my nixing of the raid.  As to that a chap can't say, but it surely wasn't the only reason.  Raug, I argued, with Worrel gone, would already have tried to swallow up Marchlen, but for the hope their ally Yew could take it with no blood spilt; so soon as news got to Forn about Yew's failure, I expected to hear about the Vandenes in March needing the protection of King Vandis, and then an attack. For that, I said, we must stay on watch, and not waste good fighters on costly revenges.

Edin, the new star amongst young warriors, against whom no one would charge shyness to fight, supported me, and so did Kennet. Yet this wasn't their kingdom (any more than it was Frick's), and my day was won only when Powl asked me, then, what spots I thought should be specially watched against Raug's coming attack. Alma wished she had burnt Worrel's will (another, gladder, time, she told me so), and her brother's angry snort was just like Yew's when the will was read; like Yew, also, he left Pormarch with his following next morning.

As in private I remarked to Kennet after, my lack of battles wasn't counting against me, at least with Worrel's blokes, and Kennet answered, as if surprised there was any question, Worrel's will was lawful.

Edin, who was nearby, said, "Yes, and they've heard Worrel call you the Magician. He often told how you used swords and armies of your own inventing to stop Raug."

This gave a chap a turn; it seemed a short time ago, that Gridge meeting, but Edin talked about it like a tale heard from old history. He would've been a boy of six; thoughts like that remind us better than mirrors about time's endless appetite.

Soon (the news came, I remember, on the same day my wife arrived at Pormarch, with most of our servants) there was the battle expected; a small body of Raug soldiers were found by

Powl picking their way along a remote valley inside the northern borders. They quickly were put to flight, too quickly; but Forn's tactic of keeping hidden a stronger force was becoming old hat, and when more fighters of Raug tried to ambush Powl's cumny, they too were sent packing by our own reserves coming up in strength (the brothers from Wezram, who had stayed on hoping for some war, were with our main force). Nor, once the enemy was beaten, was there any far pursuit; Powl held to our plan of keeping to defence. Except for the disappointment the huge figure of Syme wasn't spotted in the fight, we were no end cheered up by the victory.

Not long after that, Jon's nephew and chosen heir, Neal, came to Pormarch, to pay respect, he said, to the new king. Burly and thicklipped, somewhat older than I, with the touch of dusk on his skin you can see, now and then, in the valleys of Gwyn, his pale little wife had given Neal three sons, the eldest then twelve or so (the youngest, born weak, died soon after).

We had chat in private. He is not the subtlest fellow I know, and it was soon plain he was trying to find what, if anything, I knew about Yew's intentions. Having come by a winding path to be heir in Farragwyn, he found its king less than a king, and aimed (I guessed) to be more than the tail wagged by Yew's tame dog. I tested him, saying, no matter what Yew decided, Jon, as always, could be counted on to agree.

Neal's face flashed a quick anger he was as quick to hide. To be just I believe his kindled ambition was less for himself than for what he would pass on to his sons, but it burnt all the hotter, perhaps, for that, and could be all the more handy for me. You shouldn't take me for a simp, or a teller of tales with chappies all good on one side and evil blighters on the other; there were Vandenes working for what they thought was the general good, who behaved quite well, while lots of of those ranged against Raug had base reasons for what they did, and could match Adda-priests for cruelty.  Closing the door of the room where we were talking, and lowering my voice, I told Neal we of Marchlen wouldn't cry eyes out if Farragwyn came to be freer of Niragwyn, where Yew's friendship for or fear of Raug wasn't what we liked in a neighbour.  But a large difficulty, I pointed out, was the fighters in Farragwyn were as much Yew's men as Jon's, true even for Jon's personal gawd.

Neal barked a laugh.  Quieting his voice to match mine, he said there was a change.  Good men who had been in Neal's following before he was heir were now in trusted jobs at Landin, and amongst others he had found a new mood.  The captain himself of the royal gawd, he said, only the other day, had been asking him about Niragwyn, to know what would happen to those who weren't Vandenes if Yew swallowed Jon and was swallowed by Raug.

I don't know what Neal took me for; a ninny would know no such a talk could ever have been, a mere soldier questioning the heir about the king.  It was plain the talk must've gone, rather, the other way, Neal trying to win over the captain by putting the wind up him about Yew's closeness to Raug.  That sounded like plotting, and while, as Yew now was, a Farragwyn with a king who would act on his own would be in every way better (not just for Seeyow), it was an object I wasn't willing to pursue by sacrificing Jon; he was sixty now, and Neal must be patient.

So I spoke bluntly, telling Neal Farragwyn couldn't be free overnight; the sudden death or unkinging, for instance, of Neal's uncle-king (Jon) would surely cause my uncle-king (Yew) to march on Landin; the two Gwyns would be made one by force, and no other realm would raise so much as a whisper against Yew's actions. Jon living out his reign, and in due time a quiet succession were the best hopes for what we both would wish for.

Neal agreed, so heartily and hastily I was dead certain he had been thinking of an unquiet path to kingship. Jon's safety, the po-faced bounder said, was first. So we were allies. There is no better understanding than one between a rogue by choice and a rogue by need.


It can be seen in this time, myself an unwilling ruler, I was again up to what Thea despised, dealing with lords and princes. A chap had to spend long times at Pormarch, though my understanding with Neal kept the Seeyow road open for me. This became, then, the last time Rowan and I lived together. The mood she brought to Pormarch, glad I had a realm to rule, didn't last, and she soon found the great house there not to her liking, cold when winter came, and damp all seasons. She was never fond of Worrel's children, and bickered with their mother, suspecting Alma of targeting me for her second husband (this was ridiculous). When another midsummer came, Rowan rode back to her own lands, and for me it was like waking to find a toothache gone. Mind, I don't put fault wholely or even mostly on Rowan; as husband I had been no ruddy prize. She complained very often I had time for all the world but her, and in my brain (not aloud) a chap used to protest these were important jobs he was doing.  Across years can now be seen I was glad of having judgements to make, a young king to teach, realms to save, as excuses unanswerable for not being alone in Rowan's cold company.  She had asked for lessons in reading Print English, and they soon came, like lots else, to her fury and tears, the true belief a chap meant to little her.

In Marchlen our fighters were brave and skilled, our policies clever, and all the time we were losing.  That our borders held firm was due in part to courage and cleverness, but mainly because Forn for now was smug to do no more than test us, knowing if Suvram could be conquered and Gwyn brought to its knees by Yew's own folly, Marchlen in the end would fall.  And all the time a chap kept peering for some sign
Thea wasn't talking through her hat (an old saying, to mean talking bosh: I never saw Thea with her hair covered), and wondering how to proceed.  Col a few times came back with me to Pormarch, and I saw him more often in Seeyow; he wouldn't've shamed any parent, and was jolly eager to be old enough to fight Vandenes, but truth told there was nothing the boy did or said to make a chap smite his brow and know Thea must be right.

Not two years after Worrel's death, Edin made open the break with his father, when King Edlin was bullied into what they called a settlement of differences with Raug.  Suvram signed away a further wide band of territory, with some of the best grazing and growing land; Raug's southern borders were now within a day's good riding of Lunn.  Edin's brother Erril, the heir, was in on this redrawing, and sworn to keep it, but Edin now set his home west of Stoneplain, and started gathering to him all the ones who (because of belief, or dispossession) hated Raug and swore they could never make peace with the Vandenes. As Kennet remarked (being always strong on proper law), no one could deny this was plain treason; kings are supposed to help each other in such cases. But it was said with a small smirk: Sevenin, because of Suvram's retreat, was now within reach of Forn's war-bands, and a traitor who meant to resist Raug made a better neighbour than a true king like Edlin: Edin's lot were quite near the borders of Sevenin, between there and Wezram. We all knew if Edlin couldn't defend his borders against Raug, he surely had no means, when words failed, of bringing his younger son to heel.

As often, this treaty was made in autumn; in only brief years we had usened ourselves to fighters who were in the saddle and under arms the year round, but it stayed true that armies were larger when there was neither planting nor harvesting to be done, and a peace that came in time to release blokes for the farm was more readily agreed.

Another treaty that year, drawn by me, had little to do with either war or the ripe corn, swearing Penrid, Prince of Wezram to an oath he would honour young Bryan as true king of March, and defend him against all enemies. This was needed because Alma was about to marry Penrid. He in due time would be king in Wezram, and is honest enough among rulers; I didn't really think he would try to grab Bryan's inheritance.

Alma chose Penrid, I guess, because — well, that's not really any of a chap's business, is it? His, Penrid's, speech is so strong with the thick western accent and so unlike Alma's Stanglin talk, it was wonder they could change a single thought, but they seemed content. Sevenin was among ruling houses that came to witness the treaty and the marriage, and that gave me chance to have quiet words with Cara, about surrendering guardianship of Bryan, ergo of Marchlen, to Penrid and Alma. Cara, like me, thought Worrel would have said yes to that, and thus finished my eighty weeks as ruler of a realm. They were, and would've been, enough to suit me for a lifetime. I put to death only the worst criminals, but even those few hangings gave me nights without sleep.

Being Lord Lackland again made me freer to resume my travels, but the winter that followed was the longest and worst in memory. It cost me both my parents, who died at Caer in a little more than a week. Because of deep snows the news reached me far too late for their funerals. A chap inherited nearly bugger all. Long time after I discovered by chance Yew made a lie in having it known my mother (his sister) had been the earlier to die; in truth she was for nine failing days only owner of all our properties in Gwyn. In her will (which Yew made not to count), I would've fallen heir to bulk of our lands; Gwynis became sole heir in my father's will only after my mother. As was, Forn now had a further foothold, and even a house, his wife's, in Gwyn.

But when the long winter lifted and overdue spring came, his riders, so soon breaching the treaty he had made, were at once ranging in Suvram's remainder, and Edin fought bitterly against them. Oh, it's easy to call them ninnies, those like Edin's father, or like Yew who, made peace with Raug, hoping this time, perhaps, the hungry beast would be fed enough, but what else could they do? All that really kept Raug from complete triumph, so it seemed, was that Forn still needed to take a breath between conquests. Kennet, Edin and warriors of Wezram and Marchlen could still give Raug wounds, and in the east we heard Stanglin was holding its borders whole, but truth told, the advance of Raug towards overlordship of all Brittan was slowed chiefly by themselves, their need to tame and order what they gained, and to see to matters of religion, oftenest with the use of death and torture.

It was all like crumble and decay; Yew in his fawning went so far as to swear himself to the Vandene faith. He didn't yet dare to force his landowners and captains to do the same, but it was clear that would please him. Then, King Edlin, whom I saw again in summer, was suddenly quite dotty with thoughts that strayed, at one moment putting the blame on treason for lost lands, the next carrying on like his own grandfather, planning (as people said that first Edlin had) to take warring across the water, and win new realms in France. When I was there, his heir, Erril, though kitted out for a warrior, had less anger for Forn than for his own brother. Yet at Saffam, always gracious, and least warlike of any place where kings dwelt, with its broad lawns shelving down to the summer-bright sea, they still kept state as if all Brittan was in awe of Suvram, though for my money only the king's aunt, Maud, last alive child of Great Edlin, had any reason left for pride. She was past eighty, but knowing a chap (though he didn't say so) would be riding from Saffam to find Edin, she gave me on the Q.T. jewelled bracelets and rings to buy him food and arms, and a scawt from her own bodyguard. I had men of my own, but it was plain Maud expected hers not to return, but to join with her rebel grand-nephew. She became an emblem to set against despair I otherwise felt at Saffam. All I heard from King Edlin were demands for his recreant son's surrender.

After that, it was restoring to see Edin again, in what was becoming his small separate realm between high moor and sea. His followers, with their families, had taken to the deep green valleys, but good guard was kept on the circling hills. As we had in March, Edin was making strong places in the uplands, with stone walls, and stocked with food and arrows. The idea was, if it came to worst, not to gather everyone who meant to fight on into one last stronghold, which might be surrounded and sieged, and in the end overcome, but to have lots of hill-forts, each with a good captain, so there couldn't be enough enemy to surround them all.

Marten said sourly we were thinking now like Mynas, and that might really have been how the Mynas began, defeated blokes making places to hide. Yet if the strength of all the realms still struggling against Raug could be gathered, we ought to be a good bit farther from defeat than we seemed. It was hope that was scarce. What Thea had said, years ago (and since), was true; fighters with a cause, like the Vandenes, would always outdo those who fought just for themselves.

That got me back to thinking — but before, there's a meeting that happened with me, little in itself. At brink of another winter, I was visiting Pormarch, and at court there now was Ennis, one of those types I've mentioned before, who tell your life from how the stars were in the sky when you were born (but Marten says the clusters, where bounders like Ennis see pictures, aren't any realler than when a sparrow flying past your nose is big enough to blot out the sun). Penrid, Alma's new husband, had made a boasting wager with his brother-in-law there wasn't a horse he couldn't ride, and on my ride there from northward I had heard from a travelling Myna, a pal of Wott's, that in summer he, Frick, had secretly — well, secretly may be too strong; on the Q.T., then — sent a man up to Cumba to buy the fiercest young horse he could find (Cumba, though not so much as ago, was known for spiritous steeds). The scheme was to bring the horse by boat to Farragwyn, so as it could come to Penrid as a present from Neal, who was in on the jape.

Not for the first time, Ennis, a fat little man with squint of the eyes, came bundling to see me before even a chap had washed off the road dirt, much less done a bow to young Bryan and his Guardians. Considering I made jokes about his foretells, it was mystery why he so sought me, and then one day it dawned on a chappie Ennis, under guise of telling me wonders, was trying to get news from my travels, so as to win fresh repute for magic powers. Well, this time, after he told me the three days coming should be good ones for me (he never noticed I kept changing my birthday for him), I let drop Penrid had better be careful what new horse he rode. A chap would've told why, but Ennis made his eyes as round as they would go, and said Penrid was trying a new horse at that moment.

He was thrown off that day, by luck landing on bushes, suffering not more than a sore wrist with some scratches and bruises. What made it wonderful to Ennis (and soon to those he told the tale in the voice he used for marvels) was, the Lord Evan was gazing in his glass when he gave his warning. A small, square mirror I carried with me, an ancient one bought from Mynas, dark now, with lots of the silver inside dulled, flaking away, but still better than the polished metal most guys use, or than the ones made with our dull glass. There aren't many left whole. At the time, with Ennis, a chap was looking to see road dirt on his face, but there are seers at fairs who gaze into such old mirrors, and can tell (so they say) what happens miles away, or in the future. A chap did his best to explain the truth to Alma and the unlucky Penrid, but couldn't tell about the gag pulled by Frick without giving away how Mynas brought me news: anyway, it was easy to see they liked the untruth of Ennis much better. Remember, Worrel's name for me, *Magician*, was no joke for people who don't know a certainty about either submarines or mermaids, but that they were sea-marvels long ago. The tale of Evan's Warning went everywhere, carried by lords as well as Telas.

This, with recalling, as I said before, Thea's words, got me to thinking. To stay the slow death by bleeding (as it appeared) of all realms surrounding Raug, a cause was needed to make them fight as one. Thea told me stuff about Col, and now a chap was wondering if it really mattered he didn't believe a word of it, when he lived in a land that could grant him magical gifts because of what a moron in Pormarch said. That growing repute, indeed, might be used to pull wool over lots of eyes.

There was unease in suspecting Thea would spit like a treed cat if she knew a chappie could think so crookedly about what she (no doubt about this) believed in with passion; I didn't think I would have much luck with her, pretending I had come think it true about Col's ancestry. Still, pleasing Thea wasn't the jackpot, either. I made my main wonderings go to Col himself, whether his gifts would be enough. After all, to put him forward as found heir to the Regions would be like putting salt in soup, not a move a chap could take back if he didn't like the result. And

Col, seeming daily bigger and surer of his strong body, was as good a lad his age as you find, taking the good of good teachers in learning as well as weapons, afraid of no one, and more ready to smile; our little kings might have asked the Viztas for such a son. Yet from that to the rule over them all was still a leap too far for my daylight imaginings. A chap went on brooding through a watchful winter spent at Seeyow — no longer with pretence but for pressing business, I would be with Rowan in softer Suvram.

Then, with everyone trying to guess who Raug would pick on next, Vandis IV quite suddenly died. After a fall, so we heard. Like his kingdom, he had more than doubled in size, and one tale (this might've been made up by some Tela still brave enough to mock Raug) said, when his seat at a feasting broke under his mass.

The son, now Vandis V, was young, only twenty-three, tall and lean where his father had been fat, but it would have been lame-brained to expect his appetite for conquest to be any the less. He began as the purest Vandene of them all, taught from childhood by Forn himself. Kennet, with his habit of looking for good, said he might be less of Forn's pupil now he was king.

His first act sure caught us all on the hop; breaking off all fighting everywhere, he summoned rulers to Raug to see his robing. He declared Noble's Peace.

This Noble is one of only three Viztas ever named, said to have come at a time when vast wars threatened to end Man's life on earth. Noble (a chap's only telling what has been taught) brought a weapon so terrible it could in one flash kibosh a mighty city of old with all its life. Three times, the priestly tale says,

Noble showed the power of his weapon, turning three cities to ash. Then, seeing how it was useless to war on, everyone made peace in his name. Our word *noble* is said to come from the name, but this I know can't be true. Noble's coming was put late in the age of the swift machines, but William Shakespeare, who was before that time, uses the word in both meanings we have, a person of high birth, and the manner of his proper acts. Other writers also use *noble*, and not once have I seen it written as a name.

But with this Peace, Vandis was also near saying Raug was heir to the House of Regions; in the long time, hundreds of years, since the fall of that house, only Suvram in the days of Great Edlin had ever called on the name of Noble. The Peace, or as it might better be called, the Truce, was from new moon to dark of moon, twenty-five days, of which five had slipped away before we heard of it at Seeyow.

It was plain, as Marten said, the hatching king had points to make, bringing all the kings like subjects to Raug. There was even a lesson in his choice of places, Vandennis. When the father of Vandis V began his rule, Vandennis, not then with that name, wasn't much, a few straggled dwellings by a crossing of the Tren, at the edge of where a city had once been, and next to a large ancient castle, only partly in ruins. This was then held by Mynas, that Moorhen clan Wott had told me never to trust. From Wott, too, I knew it was Forn who had pinched the castle, though not by force, by secret treaty with the Moorhens, in which Wott guessed Forn had oathed they wouldn't, like others, be forced into Vandene beliefs. For alliance and a useful dwelling even an Adda might bend.

The best masons and carpenters who could be found then laboured at restoring the castle, and with its new name, Vandennis, it was where Forn lived with my sister, but had also become the centre of Vandene belief and Vandene ambition; the Adda-priests were there, and fighters were trained nearby, and the gathering large and small new houses had made it as near a city as our times had to show. Now Forn, we heard, would give the castle to his new king, as his seat of rule. Such had been the southward reaching of Raug that what once had been a border-hamlet was now at the very heart of that realm. As it was near centre of Brittan itself, if we leave out the wild and farmless north.

My own quiet fear was Forn now meant to bring out the treasure Thea said he had, the True Myke (as he would name it). Oh, Thea was sure there was a right time for that, still years away, but to me it seemed the only rub to make Forn think twice about claiming and proclaiming the new Vandis as King of All Brittan, Heir to the Regions, would be the chance of failing. If he was sure of the armed strength to make it stick, he would do it now. As said before, he wasn't any dope, and give him the brains to see such a claim made too soon would strengthen the will of his foes, yet if indeed he could lay hands on the Myke (whose powers he would believe in), a new kinging might seem the best of times, and this Noble's Peace be the chosen setting.

Marten, stubborn not to go, made half a joke about being asked to dine with wolves, and finding out too late what the dinner was to be. He meant realms, not persons; we both knew no one, not even a Myna to whom the name of Noble meant bugger all, would break the Peace once agreed.

Col had been like a pent cat, striding and stopping. He was near fifteen now and, even before hearing about the gathering, bored with the narrowness of Seeyow. All the young princes, and their sisters, too, would gather at Vandennis, and there wasn't a good reason for keeping Col hidden. We would ride there, a chap suddenly decided, together.

## The Bronze Rod

Closing a chapter called Loss doesn't finish with our losses; some of the painfullest were yet to come. But the coming to rule of Vandis V, and the great gathering at Vandennis need a new chapter. This, at last, is the real beginning of the story I have to tell. To get to this place I've had to scant off much important doing of long years. Twenty-one years almostly to a day; I turned my thirty-eighth birthday as we set out for King Vandis's beano, and I felt no wiser than when Worrel took me to the May-fair at Bris, as told at the beginning.

Spring had now become the time for renewing wars, and it was strange to ride out (with a small armed cumny, as rank prescribed) free from fears of sudden fights. Weather, too, was in on the truce; in deep blue skies the sun was warm, and the fresh fields and spraying trees told the lie everything had been made new. We started somewhat southward, so as to join with the easiest way for Vandennis, one of the old highways of seeming giants, running straight or in lordly curves to the east. Some of the bridges were now unsafe or wholly broken, but its swathe is so broad another thousand years could pass before the bushes and striving trees at its margins, the weeds and seedlings thrusting through and widening its cracks, can altogether reclaim the road for countryside. On this way we soon fell in with other ridings.

For once, I mean to do as Telas do, and list the great names: at Vandennis, you see, the weather soon altered, and there were days of soaking rain, keeping us, lengthily, walled up in the massy built cliff of a castle. Noble's Peace prevents crossing of swords, but can't stop plots and counterplots, questings for alliance, promises and threats, veiled or less so, and confining such a swarm of princes in one big stone hive made the buzzings louder than ever at Gridge. To tell who came may give an idea of the strangeness and strain.

Two reigning rulers were missing, both ailing, Edlin of Suvram, who was cuckoo, Jon from Farragwyn, who hadn't been at best health since that same fierce-toothed winter when both my parents pegged out. The heir was there for Edlin, but his young rebel brother was there, too, and Edin and Erril had hard words for each other. For Jon, Neal came, bringing his wan wife (to be just, Fay's eyes, if naught else, are memorable, of a shade between blue and green I never saw before) and the two living sons, Daf and Osset, both dark and sinewy. In age they straddled Col, being sixteen and thirteen. Their father didn't attach himself to Yew, as Jon would have, but kept mostly with us who still meant to thwart Raug. Yew, weary, face more than ever patched as with unhealing bruises, was anxious to be in with the new Vandene king; years after I still wonder at how thick he was to watch and even help, as his kingdom slipped away from him.

From the north came Urt of Umba and Tam of Cumba, whom I've not mentioned since Caif was alive. Tam was still oaklike, and brought his tall daughter and big-knuckled son. These two kings had been warring in harness to largen their realms into the wilder north; Raug had let them be. No doubt

Forn was smug both could be gathered in when harvest came.

Alma's father, silvering Tobin, came from the east, a king who said little, but bringing with him her brother Frick, no wiser than before, who let anyone hear his father stood with the western realms against Raug's greed. Though flat, Stanglin has fens and long dikes to help in its defence.

Alma herself was not a reed's breadth less slender than when she married Worrel, fifteen years ago; fifteen years and five children. The eldest, Bryan, was losing his boyish plump as he got nearer the age of full kingship over March; his stammer still came from time to time, but, like his father's son, he was quick to mount guard over his next brother, the bright-faced, often giggling Alan, and over May, his sister.

It was Kennet's and Cara's near-grown daughter, Robin of Sevenin, who was for me the swiftest memento of Worrel, having fallen heir to her uncle's honest, untroubled eyes and well-remembered grin; she had Worrel's way of shedding light by herself being truly pleased. Robin was, or soon made, friends with Rina, the plain but gentle-tempered daughter to Follen of Wezram, there also with his eldest son, Trevor, an almost worshipping admirer of Edin, under whose captaining he had fought. Through Alma's second wedding they were now bound closer to realms bordering and more urgently threatened by Raug.

There were dependent lords and second cousins to fatten the company, and from Raug even a few well-off of no family, a weaponsmith, for one, and a brace of the newest merchants, buyers and sellers of the big single crops now grown; as I told Edin, no stauncher Vandenes could be found than those made rich when the true intents of the Viztas were re-read by Forn.

He, Forn was not much changed. At their wedding he had been twelve years older than my sister, so still must be ten more than I, but his thick, smooth hair was still dark, and he held himself well. With all these kings at Vandennis, it might have been flattering he found time to visit me and see I was made comfortable, except a chap was wondering what he was after, behind the soothing smile and polite phrases. After telling me what lots he had to do in this, his last week as owner of the echoing castle, he stayed in the doorway of my room to pass time.

It would interest us of Seeyow, he said, that in the north of this realm there had been found a machine, approaching whole, of the kind that worked by boiling water. It had been buried under tarry stuff, which must have kept it from rusting away.

"A *steam engine*," I said, in best Print English, from which I came down to ask him if it was one of the ones that used to move on steel tracks. This he didn't answer, remarking if a smith could be found who could make copies of the few broken parts, it might be made to work again.

Aha. As he must bloody well know, we had a bloke at Seeyow who had made a special study of just such matters, but I told him there were some of his belief who held it dishonoured the Viztas, to mend such, thus showing impatience for their Return.

Forn made a rocking hand-gesture to mean there was belief on both sides of the question. Yet I had heard Forn himself had once had the hands lopped from a smith, for trying to copy another of the old, wheeled machines, the one called *bike*, I believe. This part of the chat went no further. He had just been showing off how good his spies were, that he knew such a lot about doings at Seeyow.

Less idly, though without forsaking his smiles, he spoke of how valued I might be as friend to the new king, how much it sored my sister to see me among those who wished no good to the Vandene Kingdom. Not openly, but plainly enough for me, he hinted my well-loved Seeyow might be left untampered if a chap showed less unfriendship to Raug. This, don't doubt, contained the contrary threat, and was partly heard by Col and Edin, who, as bachelors, just then came from visits with daughtered families. Edin asked, very sarky, if Forn meant, else a Vandene glee would come to sad Seeyow?

Forn wheeled to him, but the smile never failed, as he asked if Vandennis seemed miserable to Edin, and did he see signs of forced faith or enforced obedience?

Col laughed, and I speechlessly agreed; the question was silly; Vandennis! Where the Adda-priests clustered round Forn, and the king's captains and soldiers had their families. To seek disloyalty here was like looking for revolt in an ants' nest.

Forn stayed smooth, but more hiss came into his speech, as he uttered that Lord Evan himself (i.e., me) was known for championing a Brittan ruled by one, with one law, an end of killing, safety and peace everywhere. That Brittan, he said, was now within our reach, but here was the same Lord Evan with his cronies, doing all to stop it. The kings we had would always be rivals and never agree; one realm could only come when a strong king rose to set himself over all the others.

Having long ago thought this out, I quickly answered his one lovely realm didn't have what I heaviest championed; difference. No bargain, I said, in peace and safety bought at that price. At Seeyow we all spoke minds, and no one was made to bow to what he couldn't believe.

Forn's bafflement seemed real, as he enquired to know what was the good of differences that made falsehood? There was only one truth.

Here again, Col laughed.

Forn faced him direct. Col had sprouted lately, and was nearly of Forn's height. Nor was he put out by the unwavering eyes of Forn, who said, "Your famed kinsman, Marten, and the Lord Evan here can teach you lots of clever wheezes, but they are of great rank, and for those not so high it may be risky to take the Seeyow infection of laughter at what others find serious."

Not wishing to be tedious about words, I must again point out what is written here is what might have been said in Print English, which among ourselves Edin, Col and I, with a few others, now spoke as readily as the language of our own time. But Col, having come youngest to the older tongue, found it all the harder to make our own uncouth words work for his thoughts.

Yet he did spiffingly. Very respecting, he said, "Sir, laughing, I think, must be like those skills of old, but not lost like them, a special gift to us. I've seen cats smile, and dogs rejoicing in the joy of their masters, but only men and women ever laugh. And children, too."

The thought, said a bit differently, was a favourite of Marten's, but Forn changed entirely; he beamed at Col as if inventing him. Though Col, of course, had made no mention of the Viztas, it was easy for Forn to find them in what was said, and he must now see Col as a secret believer. He turned back to me, and had the brass to tell me I had done well to give this lad a lordly upbringing; his poor mother would be proud to see and hear him. Then, with a graciousness which had more loft than can be shown in words, he reminded there were to be games for the young, and Col, whom I had hidden away too long, might wish to take part, with the other princes.

In a passing pleasure Forn may have conceded more than his intent, that though a Myna's bastard, Col might rank with kings' sons. Grabbing the moment I uttered a speaking that became more famous than the light mood of its speaking deserved: "It is time, as you say, for Col to come from the shadda."

I little thought, till I saw the eyes of Edin, even of Edin, widing, that this rusty phrase from the common stock of the Telas still had any weight. Besides the Arfra stories, we have more than one tale of kings and princes not yet known, and in the years when they seem to be simple herdsmen or stableboys they are always told to be waiting in the shaddas — the shadows, as it was in Print English. For a hint of what Col might become, that went far beyond any intent of mine, but it did help (as comes in a moment) my reputation for small prophecies.

Now, to deal quickly with what brought us all there, the rites for the new king were filled with Vandene chanting. If looks made greatness Vandis would have been all the priests said of him, king in the line of kings. But he had less warmth than any man or woman I ever knew, and his handsome young face was dead, like a mask. Once he was robed, Forn, chanting on about the glory and mightiness of Raug, and the special faith granted to Raug, handed the new king a rod, but it was of dark wood, and

Forn said no more than that it was a sign of the True Myke, the Myke of the Viztas.

Thus it seemed Thea had guessed aright; he stopped short of yet claiming the rule of all Brittan, or demanding Vandis be hailed King over kings. Watching the sulky face of Erril, knowing he had agreed to cede Raug another great swathe of his rule, I thought the last fall of Suvram would be sign for that claim and that demand. Then I was all at once calling myself a mug for giving any belief to Thea's tale; she must be wrong, and the Rod still be lost. Why, otherwise, would Forn not bring it out?

It was true there were those there with spine enough left to dispute Vandis's title to it. I was comforted to know that last night, as counterweight to Suvram's weakness, I had brought together four kings, here at Raug's heart, to make a quiet treaty, saying that attack on one was war on all. More, the three in the west had agreed to ignore for purpose of defence their common borders, sending fighters wherever they were needed. Edin, I thought, best of captains, not a king himself, would be keystone if that arch of realms could be made to stand.

Then came the games. With rain soaking down they were held in the great, chill covered court. Col would have tried the lot, but I argued him away from the bow-shooting where the sons of Alma had advantage, and also from the rope-walk. That was a game for the lowborn, and whilst princes with no doubt in their bloodlines could play at being farm-boys, there could be no such holidays for Col.

As they made ready the one who took more eyes wasn't Col, but Daf, Neal's eldest. He was like his father in colouring, but it was as if the pale small woman his mother had pured Neal's dark, lumpy ore into dusked steel; the boy was taut and long of muscle, and in the shirt and the cloth shoes worn for the games moved like a keen hunting-beast.  In some book I've read about panthers, and they seem to have been big, sable cousin to the cat, littler than lions, but sleek and deadly.  Such was Daf at sixteen, and in the bragging wagers among the fathers Neal had to put three horses for one before anyone would bet against the youth. Daf did win the rope-walk with ease, but in bow-shooting he lost at the last arrow to Bryan, who was very serious, glancing over often to where his mother sat.  Again, his brother Alan, nearly youngest in the games, liked by the watchers for his cheeriness, just beat Osset, Daf's brother.

No mood in Daf's face, certainly no particle he said, gave away any upset in defeat.  It came out otherwise.  As the players were readying for the short staves, Daf pointed at Col, and asked, "Who is this?  These games are for us with royal blood."

This was an ugliness I had feared and tried not to.  Col's face clouded, and he jutted his chin.  Before he could speak, I stepped out, saying, "This is your cousin, grandson to your own king, Jon.  He is also my porter."  The last sounds like a servant, and would be for most, but is a title of honour bestowed only on one of good birth, when given by a rank like mine.

Daf wasn't a bit cowed.  My own unskill with weapons was famous, and he didn't take to my jog his father wasn't yet king in Farragwyn.  Also he must know how much concern Jon had for his grandson (none, I mean to say).  But I had given Neal a hard look, and he now barged in, and made his son ask Col's pardon. I still kept a hold over Neal, for knowing his plottings.  He said

Daf must leave the games, till he learnt better courtesy.

Carefully not showing rage, Daf did withdraw, passing in front of where the new king was seated. I saw some life in that cold face, and how the eyes of Vandis followed Daf's light stride.

Yet Daf's slight may have helped in making Col, that day, beyond defeating. For the staves, the youths put on straw-stuffed jackets, but I don't recall Col was ever touched, skilled and nimble as he was. These were best-man fights, pitting winner against winner till two were left, and in short staves Col won over a nephew of King Vandis, then against the King of March, and last, Tam son of Tam, a little shorter than he, but much the more brawny. Whether Col fully realised who he faced I don't know, but guys I saw were aware of how strange this meeting was: if Caif hadn't borne Col, young Tam, too, would never have been.

Wagering quickened when Daf was permitted (as Col's victory demanded, and the king, too, desired) to return for the long staves. Geezers themselves seasoned fighters did their best to measure unlike strengths, while the two commonest chosen and oftenest watched didn't eye each other direct, but did so skewedly. As by luck the draw went Col and Daf didn't meet in the earlier fights, and both, to big shouts from the onlookers, kept winning. At last, and in the last contest of all the games, they came face to face. King Vandis found a merchant to take his murmured wager, but everyone else fell silent, and well-nigh forgot to breathe.

After seven fights, short staves and long, Col might be a little bit tired, but none of it came into his face, which all through had been that of a careful craftsman, adjudging his task. Anyone looking for signs he was hot to avenge insult was disappointed, and I must say Daf, equally, seemed grudgeless. Both young men, when they began, fought with harnessed skill, but while each set seemed a near thing, Col won it, four hits to nil.

When the last hit was called there was a strained moment, before the shouts and clappings began. Col grinned, but with wry rue, as if saying there had been luck in it, too. Letting his stave trail, he put hand on the other's shoulder. Applause began, and Daf now smiled in answer, cuffing Col's shoulder. As the two went arm-in-arm to make bows to Vandis, the court was an uproar of cheering, servants and attendants adding din. Col's blood, I thought, wouldn't soon be questioned again.

There, too, for the first time I noticed, Col had an eye for girls, or, as it is at that age, for a slender wrist, the soft swirl of a gown, fine hair stirred by the breeze. Lots of fine frocks and bright ornaments were to be seen; Col as victor was admired, and had much to admire, not leaving out the elder of my two nieces, Avanda. Thirteen now and supple as willows, she was far less a pain than the dwarf Adda-priestess she was at seven. She had one of those teasing laughs, made with a tilting and circling of the head, that go straight to a young bloke's prick — and yet I was much happier when Col was showing off for a cousin of Alma's from the east, or when he gazed after Robin, as all the youths and not a few grown did, pert as her name and graceful as her mother, with (as I've said) parts of Uncle Worrel's easy way of causing joy. But it was plain Col would soon need a Worrel of his own. One, I mean to say, who would take him, for example, to the May-fair at Bris, not this year, but likeliest next. Edin might, if any of us could live on so long.

The main feast was next day, and it was there my words

with Forn were shoved into prophecy.  The big hall at Vandennis is vastly tall, and crosses the whole width of the castle at its westerly end.  Repaired and in part built new, its plan, a strange one for an indoors, made at the start, long beyond dreaming ago in massive cuts of stone, is little changed.  Coming to the hall from the upper parts of the castle, a chap finds himself on a broad shelf, or so I call it, running high across the inner wall.  To one side, a stone stair descends, first hugging the inward curve of a rounded wall before swooping down a crafted cliff to the broad flagged floor.  Here, long tables were set for the feast, clad in linen and heavy with dishes.

That hall eats light.  At first, there were great windows high on the outward wall, but those holes were now stopped up, except for gaps to let smoke escape.  Sheafs of candles set on the tables made isles of light below, but above, flaring brands dipped in pitch and set in iron wall loops that might have been made for the purpose were not more than bright splashes in the great dim.

Col had made himself so late he came near missing the entry of King Vandis.  Late in morning the rain had dwindled and paused, and Col, with some of the others, had gone riding.  He came back sodden, mostly from brushing against bushes brimming with rainwater.  Always short of patience with clothes, in changing he lost buttons from the red-brown coat meant for the feast.  Not being as rich in suits of clothes as the young princes, not willing to borrow, or to wear the same blue had on at the rites for Vandis, and with his other brown still oozing water, he was forced to a black coat over black breeches, a getup no one would wear to such a do, and especially in that gloomed hall, where everyone, I knew, would dress bright.  By now Col was pettish enough to wear his travelling coat, but I went to where Kennet's family stayed nearby, and from Cara borrowed a nenky of fine bleached linen, which at Col's neck would make him less dreary. Leaving him then to finish dressing, I made my way to the big hall. The guests were gathering within the three-sided ring of tables, waiting for the coming of the king. Forn, with his wife my sister, and young Avanda, were in talk with Kennet, Cara and their Robin, with Edin joined; no apparition made the strangeness of Noble's Peace more strange.

Apart a stride or two, Forn had his stand. At his side, as for most time of the Peace, was a younger, taller man (though not so much of either) who hung with deferring air of a prentice. As I skirted near, our glances tangled, and I knew him; those were the stoat eyes of Ermin, who, back a bit, had made disruption in the roecard booth at the Bris Fair, who had drawn blade against me after I gashed the arse of his hench-youth. He knew me, too, and I doubt there was much love in that, since at my order he had been whipped in consequence. It tickled a chap just a bit to wonder if he knew whose brother I was; that Ermin, by his twisted mouth, was my enemy for life, did not count for much.

Against the westward wall, amongst gawds (whose being there should be mere ceremony), the servants were ranged, ready. One, a stringy young woman, all at once showed failed training by making a sudden gesture upwards. For a mazed moment what she saw (and others now turned to see) had no reason. Shafts of red-gold light had thrust through smoke and dim, one striking the stair where it stooped to its long sweep down to the worn floor. What it was was the sun, going down, had reached the far fringe of the overcast in time to show us this farewell.

Just now Col, but at first only guessed, came onto the wide balcony above. Where the stair began, flaming torches had been meant to spill light, but, due to the bulge of the rounded wall, only made a more deeply shadowed place. There, Col, but for the white at his neck, was almostly invisible. Making the turn, he stepped down, all alone, bringing his upper half into coppery sunlight.

The looking up caused by the servant's gesture had continued to spread like illness, and lots of eyes were on Col. Silence struck as if all breaths were caught at once, and then Edin said, soft but very clear, "As the Lord Evan foretold, he comes from shadda."

That started a murmuring, wind shuffling an autumn wood, and whilst there were chuckles in it, there was no word like mockery. Col, all unknowing, came down the stair, his black now striking, not sombre. He held more eyes, though not those of Forn, who looked at me between wonder and accusing, as if I had power to do this, sunlight and all.

Almost at once, shouts proclaimed the coming of Vandis. There was ceremony about his entry, and he was dressed very spiffingly. His coming was hailed as was only proper, but a timely sunbeam had turned him into a less-happy afterthought.

Whether anyone, then or ever, told Vandis what had happened, I don't know. For me, after a quick sip of enjoyment, everything had begun to taste of worry; some of my object in bringing Col here had been to make him known, and to see what might be made of rumours. Now, helped by his skill with staves and an unguessable chance, I had succeeded too well. As an Adda-priest, Forn knew old foretellings, what could be made of them (by fraud, need be) was part of his trade, and I had read it in the long look he gave me as Col came down the stair. Questioned, near anyone there would call it loony to think a boy known to be half Myna could ever hope to do much better for himself than that day, when he won welcome and a smiled-on place in the company of the great. But that was one side, and the other was the wish to believe that gave me strange powers. Too, Forn, in his scheming desires for Vandene power, could torture and kill his hundreds and thousands without ruffling calm, and on the least off-chance of Col becoming a threat, wouldn't blink to have him put down.

A danger slyer than war was here. It would be great in a few days' time, when Noble's Peace trickled away, but danger to Col would outlast the homeward ride; I saw his life had changed. Knives could be hired in all places. Wherever he went, it must be known to as few as could be; he must go back to the shaddas, and soon.

Before I could work out where the safest might be, my own plans were changed. The feast was wearing down to beer and loudening talk when I went to ease myself at a long trough placed in an inward courtyard for that very job. In the doorway a man made his bow, and asked if I wasn't the Lord Evan. Though taller than some he had the look of a Myna, and by his apron I saw he must be one of the added cooks brought in for this week. A chappie by the kitchens, he said, had a message for me.

I followed the cook down a dim, rough-walled passageway, with the feasting noises littling behind me. My hand found the haft of my hidden knife, Noble's Peace a cobweb thought in this narrow place. This might be a Myna of Forn's allies I had been warned of, the Moorhens.  Killing me could be start of a plot against Col.

We reached a scullery, now choked with the wastage of the feast.  There was a heap of bloody beef-bones, no doubt for sharing between soup and dogs, and I shivered to think how well such a place would suit secret murder and a corpse never found.

In better-lighted kitchens beyond the scullery men and women were taking their rest at last, but my guide turned the other way, to a rough door in need of new hingeing.  Its frayed corner scraped bare earth as it shuddered outwards.  In the courtyard, just outside, was a bloke more certainly a Myna.  Yellow light from the open door touched his face; it was Wott.  Though I had seen him a few times since our first meeting at Bris, the last was more than two years ago.

"Lord," he said, "I come from Thea.  She must see you."

"Is she at Vandennis?"  It seemed likely enough; good trade for the Dauwas.

"She is in Lunn, sir."

But that was five or six long rides away.  "I can see her at Bris in a few weeks' time."

Wott shook his head.  "Not this year, sir.  She is dying.  My mother tends her.  She was nearly gone nine days back, when I left, but swore to keep alive till Lord Evan could come."

This was awful.  When there was time I learnt Wott had set out to find me at Pormarch, or in Seeyow beyond, always afraid he would be too late.  Riding north of Stonedge he'd had word of Noble's Peace and the gathering at Vandennis, and supposing I would be there, had turned northward on his borrowed horse, for the bulk part going by dark, snatching daytime sleeps under bushes.

It was his haggard look, as well as the risks he had taken (there was no assurance even Noble's Peace would keep a Brown Hare safe) that let me believe what I couldn't imagine, Thea was near death. Seldom as meetings had been it came of a sudden to a chap Thea was to my whole mannish life what a sure home is to others, well-loved, known, trusted, always there after long absence. It goes beyond truth to say Thea taught me thinking, but absolutely she got me to see my thinking made me one apart, and that apartness ought to be coddled, not kept dark as a private shame. It was a big debt, and I must go to her now, even if it was a beastly bother.

To find her, I had to have Wott with me, and he needed feeding and sleep; daybreak was the soonest start. And Col couldn't be with me. I didn't like separating from him, but then it came to me by doing so we might be able to make his whereabouts into a hard puzzle for Forn.

I made plans with Edin. To get private talk I had to miff him a bit, he having hoped to take a serving-girl to his bed as a topper to the feast (because he began so soon to take on cares for his kingdom, it easily slipped the brain how young he still was). With this scheme, he had forethoughtedly drunk less beer than majority; he was flushed in the face but sensible when I brought him to my room.

I had already decided to leave quietly at dawn with Wott as guide, and no more than a couple of my gawd. The rest of my small cumny would leave Vandennis about midday to follow me south at their own slower pace. At the same time I desired Follen of Wezram to leave with his band, and Edin to go with them. It shouldn't be too hard to hide Col amongst soldiers or servants, and with farther to go than others, Follen's early leaving would raise no questions. At Tawn in Follen's kingdom seemed to me the best place now for Col; Wezram still had no border with Raug, and the approaches were through country Edin himself guarded.

"And very few," I said, "will know where he is. If thought he left at dawn with me, so much the better."

"Then you smell danger?" Here, for once, as well as I can remember, I can give exact words; we were speaking Seeyow English. So others named it, and not lovingly; it irked many to overhear speech where they could pick out known words, but not understand what was said.

"The Peace," I said, "soon runs out."

"Most true," Edin agreed, a bit grim. "And I would give lots to know why Syme hasn't been seen at these ceremonies, and where he is, with the lion's share of Raug's armies. Still, we can all be back among our own before dark of the moon. The boy, you believe, is in special danger?"

"Forn took to heart your words when Col was on the stair. Even an imagined rival to Vandis is one too many for him."

Edin nodded, but he was no fool, and his face thought more. In time he said, "Col, you must know, would join my fight."

"Later," I said, knowing it would have to come. "When he gets his man's shoulders. Not now. But I'll have chinwag with him."

"Is any royal court the place for him, if not circled with friends of tried assurance? Vandis is not the only king who can smell a rival."

A chappie was dumb a sec, stunned a change could be so swift — and that Edin felt it.  Then I began, "If he is with you — "

"He can learn war."

Once more, I barred any thought of Col riding in battle till he was older, and Edin reminded me he had lots of youths in training.  Col, he said, would be safe in so-called rebel country, even when he, Edin, went warring.  There were made plans for hiding and escape of survivors, if Edin should meet with defeat, capture, or worse.  He spoke about such chances with a calm plainness beyond courage.

I said, "A chap didn't mean to add to your cares."

Edin said, "There will be questions about your sudden leaving."

"No need for any plain answers.  My compliments must go to Vandis, and a plea to pardon my rudery.  Cara, if she will, would be best to carry those.  It could also be understood, not in such words spoken, it is because of some insult concerning Col that I've made myself scarce."

"That uncouthness of Daf's?  The two are now drinking together at the king's table."

"Not that," I agreed.  "It would be believed if Tam of Cumba were thought to be the one. It was Tamson Col beat in the short staves." Edin, I saw, was too young for those lingerings, and I had to recall to him Caif's betrothal to Tam when Col was fathered.  Knowing Tam's temper, not many would doubt the smouldering grudge could flame out anew.

Edin's lower lip was jutting.  "You can't ride for Lunn with such a little gawd."

"I'll be safe among Mynas," I said, grateful for friendship. "Your proper charge, if you are willing, is Col."

After we settled more details, Edin got to his feet. "Who was this Donal?  Is Col's fathering more than has been let on?"

"Who is Evan, to say yes or no?  Time holds the answer."

"Then we must keep Col whole, while time is making up its mind."


As for Col, he always loved games.  He wouldn't believe himself in danger, but glee soon had him planning how he would borrow old clothes and a low hat such as Mynas wore, and leave by the stable gate amongst lesser servants and the baggage.  Thus while those of name were finishing their farewells, he would be out on the road with the scawts; no need for him to pass by the broad front steps, where King Vandis and Forn would doubtless be, waving ta-ta.  For all the journey he would stay poorly clad, and even if soldiers of Raug came for a look he could be unnoticed.

When I told Col he would stay with Edin, not go with Follen, when the companies divided, a sly look came into his face. He was thinking of war, and I warned him how I had instructed Edin to put him under guard if needed.

"Why do they do as you say, kings' sons and even kings?"

"Edin is a good friend."

"Well, but Neal, too, and he is not anyone's friend, except for Neal's benefit," Col said with acumen.  "Kennet and Follen wait for your word, and so does Alma."

He meant, of course, why? in a land where only warriorship was coming to count. It wasn't a question a chap had really pondered. "I don't give orders," I said. "They know I've often guessed well. Also I crave not a sausage of my own, lands, wealth, rule. Fellows can be trusted when they desire no more than they have."

"Or when they've got all they could ever desire."

"Isn't that the same?"

"Not always. A chap might believe he had no yens, till he saw or heard of something he hadn't known about."

This way of dispute was Marten to the life, though I thought it had been put in Col's noggin by the sight of all the bright girls in their finery. He did next ask, "Must I stay all the time with the Suvram rebels? I have my effects at Seeyow."

"They can be brought," I promised. "But you will come to Seeyow again, and often."

"And Sevenin? That is not a great ride from where Edin is."

"Sometimes, but not alone; only when armed cumnies are going that way. Kennet and Cara would make you welcome, I'm sure."

This was slight teasing, but Col looked shyer than I had seen him, and was without words. In mercy I added, "And Robin too, I don't doubt." At that he became more himself, but I was with the frequent question of how much should be told about Col. There were no worries about envy with either Kennet or Cara, but as was, neither would think Col high enough for their daughter. Supposed royal descent on the side of his father, a Myna, as recounted to me by the head of a dauwas' guild, would hardly do much to alter them. It was soon, foolishly soon, to be thinking about wiving, but (see how scheming gets life of its own?) Robin's bloodlines would be a good alliance for Col, all the better if it came about not by dismal policy, but liking on both sides.

Beyond, there was how much Col himself should be told. That was to ask what I was about, whether I was trying to make a king, or only watching to see if one appeared. Should I tell him there was a prophecy might fit him, and cleverly used might make him king of all Brittan? Prophecies were for nitwits, but now I knew a chap would gladly use them to thwart Forn. Col might prevent a Brittan gripped forever in the stifling hand of Vandene beliefs, and wondering whether he would ever make a good king was like letting some bozo drown because if saved he might not be able to afford new shoes. Yes, yes, but while in the end I would be willing to have anyone a king, my stableboy, his dog, if the people could be made to hail him and cast off Raug, I still loved Col enough not to make him into a mere tool or emblem. Besides, I purposed what was just; foretells (all the more if disbelieved) should be given fair trial, not nudged. Best of all would be if Col, knowing not a fig, out of merit and by choice freely made, could become kingworthy. To tell him there were those who could be made to see him as one foretold would murken the pureness of those choices. Fact was fulfillment of such a destiny seemed so far, and so far out of reach that for Col to be told could change nothing real. Nothing, except Col.

How I lived then, except I didn't war, was of my time and

rank. I could stay in the saddle as long as need asked, not minding a drenching if it came, and sleep in a tent if no better lodging showed up. Before that headlong ride for Lunn I wouldn't have called me soft, not yet having learnt things I later knew better than majority, that to ride with clothes clammily soaked to the body is no glee without a servant waiting at ride's end with warmed towels and dry garments. Likewise with a tent when no pack animal has brought blankets and a straw-stuffed mattress, and when, if sleep has ever been captured, waking must be met with no fire lit, no hot drink ready. Nowadays a chap bears hardship better, and if not enjoy cold and wet, hunger and sore sleep for themselves, can take pleasure in their enduring. To have learnt wit and tactics to give myself a small snug place in a world of storm or bitter cold is worthy of pride. But that first hard journey was hard indeed, and if I wasn't heard to grouse it was because Wott didn't, and neither did Shan, nor Raneth, the youth my other gawd. This was spring, not winter, and I bally well wasn't going to be outdone for — I don't know what. Something I don't give a farting for when it comes to weapons.

Another of the old machine-roads is the usual way and the best start for Lunn. We took other, less-travelled ways known to Wott. Though we were in hurry, and these ways, because rougher and less straight, took longer, I yearned to keep encounters as few as possible. There wasn't hope of making the whole journey unobserved, but to cause doubt if Vandennis had questions to ask. I had chosen Raneth as second of my soldiers for the same reason; his looks were boyish, and any report describing my cumny that got back to Vandennis could easily leave Forn befogged whether or not Col was with me.

Once the Tren was crossed we were riding in lands part of Raug for only a few years, and off the main road a chap could easily have met Forn's challenge to find signs of unhappiness. Lumping together of small farms had torn out lots of hedgerow, and left small houses empty and crumbling, places where families had lived to farm plots they called theirs. Some no doubt had fled south when Raug came, while of the men lots would now be with Forn's large new armies, but on a hill I soon saw a big manor-house, old but with new parts built on, in a clump of lesser buildings, barns, stables and a row of poor dwellings. Those who, under Vandis, had title to the swollen farms would prefer their workers to be near at hand; the women would be used for servants.

Too, when our way took us past a muddy hamlet, we were struck by how wary its people were, watching us from indoors. There were several such, each with its own Vandene meeting-place near, an empty plot with an arch made in copy of Stonedge raised on a mound. On the third day of our journey young Raneth remarked that though there were no beggars, such as might be seen (and heard) even in streets of Pormarch or Caer, we had passed no place without people who were less than whole. By this year all over Brittan there were former soldiers who had left warring after losing a hand, an arm, a leg, or sight, and the old might be lame and twisted anywhere, but Raneth, seeing children and youths with the signs of hot branding, said it was hard to believe Raug had such a lot more thieves than elsewhere.

"And wives who spread themselves abroad," he added, glimpsing yet another young woman showing marks of heated iron.

"Only Raug," I told him, "has the Adda-priests to teach awe of the Viztas, and the Mykas to help them." (These were the ones who went with the priests and did as they said, the men who carried out the torturings and maimings. Their nickname was from the sign of the True Myke sewn in red on their shirts; this, as I've said, is a short rod, thicker at one end. Guys not of Raug, especially rival soldiers, called them instead the Cockas. Not to their faces, unless to begin a fight.)

Like all my gawd Raneth had been picked because, as Marten said long before, he shrugged over the beliefs of others. He had to have Wott's voice added to mine before truly believing this went on. Then he sought to know why the lords of Raug cared what the poor and those of no power had for belief. I didn't have an answer, but told him this would be all Brittan, if Raug's plans won.

The small cumnies of soldiers met were far from grim, exchanging with us greetings of the Peace (and that, like the paring of moon we saw rise before dark, was dwindling away), but they were ordinary fighters, not those Mykas we feared but didn't see. Wott did not become pals with my chaps, and was mostly wordless, but his squeezed mouth when there was a delay, as when Raneth broke a stirrup, told me he was afraid we would come too late. Yet he allowed, when I asked, Thea, though very ill, might yet be able to recover. For me, it was clean out of the way she could die; I needed her guidance about Col, and what he should be told about himself.

The border with Suvram for the past few years (it would be changed at midsummer, when Erril's newest gift to Raug was taken) was a little river, easily waded, but we were glad to get there. Foolishly glad, because whenever they liked Raug's armed men crossed as we did, without challenge; no soldiers of Suvram were there. Shan asked me in disgust if this place wasn't called Wellgard?

Now we were already at the fringes of the wilderness, with Lunn itself only hours away, but afternoon was nearly gone. Even Wott wouldn't go by night in such small numbers to where the rival Myna clans kept their warrens and warred over them. We steered instead a little west, to reach where, if plans held, servants, baggage and more of my gawd would join with me again in two or three days. This was a place I had been before, the house of Frant, a cousin of my wife's, on the side not royal. He couldn't turn me away, having no rank, if good wealth. Frant kept four heavy waggons busy bringing cut stone from the wreck of Lunn, and paid workers to clean away the crumbling mortar. He had masons who knew how to smooth and newly square damaged blocks, and did trade with lords or those who built for them. Once sized and matched the building stone could be sold for ten (or more) times what Frant paid the Mynas who dug out the stone and loaded his waggons. Lunn has been for ages our chiefest quarry, but according to Frant there still lies stone to do us for another thousand years. Marten says, and rightly I think, the ruins of old cities have kept our own masons stupid; few bother to learn the trueing of stone when the skills of the past can be lifted so easily. The best places for old building stuff were one of the chief issues the rival Myna clans fought over.

Frant, a large, soft guy with a large wife and two soft sons, had gained fat and lost hair since last I saw him. He welcomed me with lots of fussing, although trying to show no surprise at the meanness of my company (or, for that matter, that it included Wott; Frant dealt every day with Mynas, but not in his house). He was eager for news from the gathering at Vandennis, and when I told him by midsummer where we were would be a part of the Kingdom of Raug was quick to insist it made little difference; the Vandenes had always dealt fairly with him, and he could be one himself. He was sure his business would be left in peace. I saw that might be true for a time; Vandenes had to build, and Frant had an eye for the choosing and matching of stones, and knew how to haggle with the Mynas. In the end, he might not be needed. Plainly, if Vandis reached triumph as ruler of All Brittan, finishing fights with all his enemies, he would have forces to manage subduing of the old cities, even Lunn, by night as well as day. Edlin I had tried that, but with less than half his heart, at a time when bulk soldiers went home at harvest time. But while Great Edlin (so I guess) was put out at having to deal with the Mynas for the riches of the ruins, and knew no one could truly rule this land till he reigned over these desolations, he never cared what the Mynas believed, and didn't have fierce armies practiced in killing for belief, as Vandis had.

Very early, the four of us were in the saddle again, led by Wott, who steered eastward to strike parts claimed by his clan's allies, the Grey Cats. At that time, even by day the territory of a rival clan was no place for any Myna. We stayed below the crest of long, low hills, but at last wheeled to climb slopes patched with furze and thorn. All at once we were looking down into the vast waste of Lunn, a giddying sight, and eerie now in the low slant of silver sun.  The tumbled mounds of debris, the ragged standing walls, broken stumps of buildings, sent long shadows across the wide desolation, a grey disorder and deadness splotched with clumps of trees, thickets of bush, swathes of dull nettle and straggled weed.  It was more than enough to give a chap the willies, and Shan mumbled holy stuff.  In places, early cooking fires were putting up thin wavers of blue smoke.  Down near the river, called Tem, its loops gleaming under streaks of mist, there were (and still are) the shards of great towers, each with one side bright in the early light.  Not castles and never dwellings for people, these towers, much higher once and mostly wrecked by fires, are dismaller than any old tombstone, their ancient purpose a mystery.  Now they stand only for loss, and sadness the splendour to raise such wonders couldn't after all come out on top against time and breakage of things.

From here, because Wott said so, he and I were to go on afoot, whilst Shan and Raneth went back with the horses to Frant. Shan, however, has always thought of me as a bit gormless, not really safe on my own, and we had quite a tiff before he agreed he wouldn't follow me at a distance, and wouldn't come searching for me next day.  He was still put out, and when he rode off with Raneth, leading the two empty horses, the back of his thick neck was still showing offence.

Without Wott I would have been lost in about five minutes in the bewilderment, once we came down from the overlooking height.  In countryside a chappie astray can go on till he strikes a path: it may not lead where he aims to go, but all paths lead somewhere.  Lunn is more like being at sea, sailing, as I imagine it, among a thousand, thousand islands, and every channel a path that might be taken. We could seldom see more than a little way ahead, being among mounds, thickets of brush, head-high stands of nettles, or suddenly in a gritty dell, or a close way between dark brick walls crumbling like stale bread. The sun was well up in a sky now rippled with grey when we started a steep descent, on more pleasant ground with no dregs of buildings, where there were dense clumps of young trees, and open stretches of deep grass. We saw one or two drably clothed women out for firewood or mushrooms, but no animals were grazed here, and I didn't glimpse any dwellings.

By the foot of this long slope the waste began again. Nearing the end of grass, Wott stopped, and made a shrill whistle, fingers to lips. At first nothing happened, but the third time he whistled there was the same in answer, not far off to our left. From among tall, tattered weed a few bozos, perhaps six, appeared. Wott asked me to wait, and went to them. There were handclaspings and then talk, with Wott gesturing back to where I stood, feeling like a prize ass. Shan would've been sure, with the gloomy pleasure of blokes who foretell ruin, that my capture and ransom was being chewed over.

Not true — but here, I mustn't break my given word. It may be said these were Mynas of the Grey Cat clan, but before I knew much more than that I was being asked to swear an oath to keep every secret. At first a fellow was inclined to be lordly, but after all, dammit, I was on their bally ground, and I did need their help. That oath still binds me; my judgement says it no longer matters, but a chap can't decide on his own to put aside such a word, so (if I may make a joke on solemn affairs) I won't now let their cat out of its bag. I may say the Grey Cat leader was (and still is) a hard and able chappie named Shay, good for a friend, cruel for enemy. The way he led me, he said, had never been seen before by anyone not a Myna. How it is reached can't be told, but there's no secret a lot of it was deep below ground. Betimes we were in the wide tunnels that must have belonged to what I had only ever half-believed, the trains that sped under ancient London. Tunnels, I was told, had often been clogged, and cleared again by years of work; water trickled and there was slime underfoot, and in places earth had burst through to block the way. In the poor light of one sputtering brand it seemed to me the tunnels had been made of rings, so to be in them is like the belly of a worm made in segments. Lesser tunnels, some more crudely made by Mynas, got us round the worst blockages, and the several places where the main way had flooded. In these windings, and at the points where the large tunnels divided, the Grey Cats never seemed to be in doubt about the way.

Yet in the dark air filled with wet and rotted smells, my feet often slipping, it seemed a very long journey, and my step became the wearied tread of a bloke who has lost hope of arriving anywhere, ever. We began the long climb out at last, and when we reached wide daylight I saw by the sky, still clouding, it wasn't much past noon.

Then (leaving out more journeying) we came very near the river, where Shay and his followers left us; this now was the little realm of the Brown Hares, exiled northerners. It was a place I knew, near where what must have been the highest of all the old bridges across the Tem had been; what is left of its big square towers still stand on either side of the river, and a boat passing there must be careful to steer away from the shoals that can only be fallen parts of the bridge. Beyond was (and is) a massy building everyone knows, by reputation if not sight. We call it the Castle of Lunn, but I now know its older name, and can't see why I shouldn't use it; the Tower.

It had a very bad name with us — I mean to say, its fame was a nasty one. That it was a Myna stronghold was no secret; even Edlin I, at the height of his power, when he forced the Mynas to let people from the north pass through the wilderness of Lunn to get to the gatherings at Gridge (which wasn't very far downstream from here, on the other side of the river), hadn't been able to take away the Tower. That is, if he ever had a real crack at it. Everyone called it a place of bad luck, and it was said though a giant hoard of gold and gems was hidden deep inside, there were still places even a Myna wouldn't search. Lots of tales tell about silly asses who went there after treasure and were never seen again; you're not supposed to be able to honour the Viztas and yet believe in ghosts (this is much more true for a Vandene), but that didn't stop people from saying the Tower was haunted. Lots of different ghosts are mentioned, but scariest of all, the creature called Amblin (I can't tell if this has aught to do with the ghost of Old *Hamlet* in the play by William Shakespeare), whose head does grow beneath its shoulder. Just to see Amblin is sure death.

We went there. Of course I have no time for wind and fury tales told by an idiot, but even if it was only a place like other places it wasn't welcoming, and if you ask a sensible reason for fear, I am not a Myna, and as far as I knew only Mynas ever came out of there alive.

Parts had fallen down, and it was hard to see, with all the

broken walls and heaps of rubble, what its plan once was. There is a big round tower up on a hill, with squarer parts below, and we approached up a causeway slope, partly of broken stones, lots of which had tumbled down into what could once have been its moat, though a lot of digging and carting would be needed to clear it again. We passed under a propped-up arch like a short tunnel, crossed cobbles and went under another arched doorway into another courtyard. Dark Mynas, most with bows, were lurking all over the place, but they must have known Wott, and no one tried to halt (or shoot) us.

I thought we were making for the big round tower, but beyond a third dark arch Wott turned through a doorway, into the dim inside. It was a large hall, and a chap could see it had once been very la-dee-dah, with lots of carved wood and stone, and a floor of many kinds of stone in different colours. But a good part of the ceiling had come down so long ago moss was growing on the piles of broken stuff, and I could see plenty of birds made this a hiding place. One, a big raven, was perched against the light coming through one of the holes high up on the wall, and launched itself, spreading strong wings, as we came nearer.

Wott picked our way to a corner where rough building had made a house within a house. The doorway was hung with a coarse curtain, and there a face appeared. It was the seer attacked by the youths at Bris, Wott's mother. She was glad to see her son again, and then reached a hand to touch my face. Without any words she led me through a common room for eating and sleeping to an inner place, again curtained. It had a low bed, and not much else. A simple oil lamp was burning quietly. On the bed was Thea. At first I thought she was dead. Her face was stretched down almost to the bone, a skull with Thea's features, much worse for commemorating what was ruined. The lips were tight, and the forehead when I touched it as dry as aged paper. Not loud, Wott's mother called. Thea's eyes came open, large as ever, larger, because of how the skin had drawn back. The old light had gone, and I guessed pain had put it out.

It wasn't really sleep she came from, more a kind of practice for dying, chosen for the sake of peace. Returning, it seemed to me at first she hated her world, all pain. More quickly than I can write or you can read she went from nothing to suffering to rotten temper. Then her eyes went like a candle lighted, that sputters, dwindles near away, and then steadies small. Knowing me, she nearly smiled. Her pleasure was, I think, she had won her fight to be alive when I came.

She opened her mouth to speak, and had to clear her throat in a whisper. Then, "There are worlds to tell, Lord Evan." It was a little voice, but kept firm.

My job here is to tell a story of rule, not to display my own sorrow. From my first view of Thea I gave up any thought she might be no more than grievously ill, and she might yet get well. Here I only say I was with her two nights and parts of three days, and watching her life seep away was like a bleeding of my own. I loved Wott's mother for the care she brought, and also a dark-haired, bright-faced young girl, who helped when the other had to sleep. A chap hated himself for more than one reason, for being bored when Thea had to rest from talking, and there was bugger all to do but sit crampedly and watch her duel with hurt, for wishing, more than once, I hadn't come or had come too late. And mainly for my uselessness, for having no power to do a bally thing but watch.

Something too much of this. What I have to tell is what Thea had to tell, without lingering over how her voice smalled away and she would lie gasping for mastery over pain. Nor the other interruptions, some of them not pleasant. They would disgust me to hear told, though then I had no such feeling. Words about wounds and nasty smells and spillings of the body, it seems to me, are often worse to put up with than those themselves, when seen and felt. Besides, though a chap was never formed to be kind in the way a few women and even fewer men can be, where self gets forgotten, I did have pity to give me a hand, as well as a part that could see what happened with a cold interest, as if to store it all away for future use not foreseen. There was also admiration; Thea was losing her struggle, but fixed purpose kept her from straying into despair. That's not right: she was the other side of despair. What a chap means is, she kept going.

First (because, she said, it might change what she had to tell me), she questioned to hear about the big do at Vandennis. I spoke about Col, his triumph in the games, his sunstruck entry to the feast. Thea could only weakly show how she was pleased, and at once made me tell what I was doing to keep the boy safe. But she brushed away the news about Raug's new gain of territory at Suvram's expense, and reminded me how long ago she had called dealings with princes a waste of me. "You see now how with all your cleverness the realms have shrunk."

"But Vandis, robed and with a Myke, a small one, didn't call himself High King."

"Not yet, not in name. Your Forn knows the time. He still has the Rod."

And I still was a bald gooseberry if I could see why, if so, Forn was waiting. The answer to that was Thea's long tale, long in the years it talked about, but in the telling too. She needed lots of rests.

Thea, I hope, would forgive how I have to mangle the story. Again I have to say the words I use aren't like hers, and sometimes change things without meaning to, by trying to guess the right words. I've had a bit of help, because where Thea talked about the far ancient past, it was often a lot like what Tulsingham says, but then again, not. The names Thea used were mostly near enough to Tulsingham's that I can use his spellings, which must once have been thought the right ones. Still, much more of a botheration is a way of thinking to which Tulsingham was avowed foe. Given a choice I would be with him, but this is Thea's tale, not mine. Parts might have been made up by her, or else (as she said) belonged to lore told and retold since tales first began. All of it has magics I can't put my belief in. Yet I can't tell you over and over again this is only what she said, so have to put it down as best I can, and let the reader decide.

The proper name for the True Myke was the Bronze Rod. Bronze, Thea said, was the name of an ancient metal, first made at a place called Kish, countless years ago. On purpose, that is to say; at that time unworked ores were still in the earth, and those for the two metals, red for the sun, white for the moon, were found in the same places. Those ancient smiths soon found the blend was tougher than copper alone, yet easier to work, just as a man may be stronger in union with a woman, herself gentle — or a god with a goddess, Thea said.

(Now I knew its composition, I could have told Thea we

too have this stuff sometimes, alloy is the word, I think, with a different name. It is made by accident when old things with tin and copper are melted at once, but the Seeyow smiths, and a few in other places, do it on purpose when they can. The tin is soft as a metal, but hard to come by. Bronze is better than iron for some purports, and doesn't need a big, very hot furnace, like the hardened iron that is steel. But knowing the old name I at last knew why an old book called a farmer *sun-bronzed*.)

That first ancient forging brought together different powers: a priest of the Sun ordered it, priestesses of the Moon oversaw; its earth was of the Earth, and it was formed in fire and quenched in water, and so the Rod they forged shared in all the forces of the world. It beats me how, but you don't make fun of what an old friend refuses the easing of death to tell.

The Rod went to a city called Erech, where Gilgamesh was king (none of this is in Brittan; all these places are far away, and now lost). He was very strong and won lots of wars, but he was all wet, Thea said, when he believed the Rod could help him or anyone else to rule. Its power was to turn the world towards the dreams and wishes of those who had been part of its making. That was a balance (or it might be a muddle) of differences, but it could, after a long time, be upset. When the sun, the moon and the earth all were to each other as they were at the first forging, the New Year of the Moon (which the priestesses had chosen), there was renewal, and the Rod took on the desires of its then owner, or whoever could grasp it just at the moment of rebirth.

This didn't mean, as was thought at first, the Rod was altered for every year of the sun. In Kish and Erech, Thea said, there were men like Marten, great measurers and counters, though at first not nearly as careful. For a long time the blithering asses thought the sun year to be four equal seasons of ninety days. At the same time, the priestesses, who didn't have much outward say in ruling, counted a year as twelve moons from new to new, and the day of the Rod's forging, year's noon, was when the new moon was opposite the setting of the year's highest sun. But the next new year of the moon-women was about two weeks sooner by sun-time, and the next two weeks before that. Under Gilgamesh, who had Sun for his emblem, those priests became more powerful. In time they made their year right, and so gave everyone the proper days for sowing and reaping and whatever else they were bound to do each year. But the priestesses kept to their old year, even though its start slipped back by sun time and by the seasons, so it wasn't much use for practical uses. Once in a generation the new year of the moon came back near where it was when the Bronze Rod was forged; near, but not near enough. It wasn't till more than five centuries had gone by it once more fell exactly at year's noon. Then, with sun, moon and earth all as they had been, the Rod was reborn.

By that time the world was altogether changed, but what the Bronze Rod did, Thea said, was still known among women keeping to the ways of the moon-priestesses, who schemed to turn it towards their desires for the future. But because of what they were, though they had put thoughts into the making of the Rod, they had no more power to change it. They held to the Old Beliefs, which we no longer understand, they having been wrongly explained as often as there were chaps to do the explaining. Thea here still had a passion burning small but bright; the Old Beliefs, she said, easier to explain than hold faithful to, sought to be ally with, not to alter, what was true in nature, to make the world of people marry to the world that is, not remake to fit our greed. No less than the followers of the sun-gods, with their mannish need to change what was displeasing, the Old Believers had dreams of the world that might be, and yet to give those dreams force would need treason against belief, and so it turned out the priestesses of the moon had put heaps of their love into making a wonder they could never command. Their part was to be and to speak. Others gave the Rod its direction.

From the first, like Gilgamesh himself, fellows had gone on believing what never was so, the Rod would give great power to its owner. Still very long ago, but now in a time when the Rod was already ancient, a priestess of the moon gave it to her husband, king in a place called Macedon, just at the time of its renewal. That king's dream was to bring all the world under his rule, by force and skill of his captaincy, but holding the Bronze Rod didn't stop him being murdered and supplanted by his son. That son very soon made the vastest empire yet known, but then he too suddenly pegged out, and the dreams of his father went on with the Rod to new owners (this story of Macedon is also in Tulsingham's book, but he says a madwoman, not a priestess, was Phillip's wife and Alexander's mother. Thea, I think, would've said to this, for the men of Macedon, any moon-seer was a loony; Phillip was sun-struck). After, a place called Carthage rose and fell, and then Rome, where the rulers, silly blighters, seldom died in their beds. So Phillip's dream of a world made one by swords marched on till its five-and-a-half centuries were done, and again the Rod was reborn. This time, in what must have been a jumble of warring wishes, so there came a time with the great cities and roads falling to ruin, and the forgetting of big parts of what had been known, among senseless superstitions that never ceased to quarrel. A time much like ours, it would be easy to say, but different, I think; Tulsingham says the learning of Greece and Rome was never wholly lost, because of monks and Arabs, and we haven't got any of those. Well, Thea believed when the Bronze Rod had no sole owner at the time of its renewing, the desires it took on were those of the tribe, the clan, the people it was then among. But of course, there was always a mixture of dreams, if never again as balanced as at its birth. One chappie by himself always has muddles of desires, and when we call someone greedy or ambitious, generous or timid, strong or smarmy, we don't mean he is just that one thing. This the Rod was a mirror for, and it was those holders who were masterfulest (meaning those most mastered by a single aim) who made the Rod's power plainest.

As when later the old idea of one rule for the world fused together with the Jesus Christ belief, and the Rod, never caring who lived or died, made use of a Charlemagne, of geezers called popes who tried to be kings over kings, and led great bloody wars called Crusades. When that five centuries was passed, a new desire to know became mixed up with a greed for owning, and strong, separate countries fought each other for what they had, and for ownership of great lands newly found. These rivals had new weapons, but though villainous, they weren't yet the horrible ones found in our own story of Noble.

Even before my first close view of Lunn's ruins, I had decided it must have been those giant, bursting fires that had put the kibosh on the world of machines. Thea said, no, no matter how it seemed. Slow ruinings, such as rust, fraying, wear, disease, the loss of interest, could in the end match fire's appetite. Fire came, but not all at once.

The next rebirth for the Rod (now we seem to be up to Tulsingham's time) was for Thea the worst of all, farthest yet from what the Old Beliefs had tried to say. In the past, though destroyers had come, there was always a part left of what the moon gave, and the earth was womb for. Now they all strove to forget their birth, and there was no one to keep rein on anyone's dream of a jolly old world where there was no age, no pain, no death or distance, no cold in winter or heat in summer, no dirt or sweat or end to whoopee. It was by being so skilled, Thea said, at seeming to remake everything, people left themselves witless to live in the world that was still there, never changed, bound to return. A bit at a time their made world clogged up and failed; law, money, belief, their spiffing machines, knowledge, the rule itself. Time, which they tried to banish, did the rest.

The Rod by now had long been in Brittan, but it wasn't for grim years that it at last came to the family we call the House of Regions. Lots of us have believed, and Adda-priests have killed and tortured lots for not believing, the True Myke, which was the Bronze Rod, was given to the first King Colin, from the hands of the Viztas, in the Year of Leaving. Now Thea told me it was really a woman, an Old Believer, and she had given it knowing it would do nothing yet, its next rebirth being two hundred years away. That, the last, had been at a time when all was at rock bottom, and the nicest anyone could dream of was a roof that didn't leak, a bit of food, and to live long enough to eat it; there were no kingdoms then, only hungry clans, or bands of fighters, who would war over a dead rabbit.  But this woman, Thea said, who had great foresight, purposely retold the old lie the Rod gave power to its possessor.  It might even have been her who began the story it came from the Viztas, knowing that would make its magic be believed.  Often, Thea said, when the Old Believers had to make use of sun-men, they had to choose not what was good, but what might be less evil: sometimes they needed swords and greed as tools.  (Here, a chap has to say, still loving Thea, I find weakness, because Forn of Raug could've said exactly the same: everyone who does nasty stuff says it is for the sake of huge good happenings in the future.)

Well, it worked as the woman hoped, and Colin (the first of several so named), thinking the Bronze Rod strengthened him, could make order in the name of the Viztas.  I can't retell here the whole history, known to all us later royals, of the House of Stewards, and how it divided into two rival lines, the Colinids and the Gavinids, and how after long and horrible wars, Tobin the Peacemaker brought the two lines back together.  A date every princeling learns is YL 199, when Tobin's wife, the Gavinid queen Maud, died, and Tobin became teacher to the young king in the other line, Colin VI (only Colin V to the Gavinids).  By Thea's tale Tobin then had the Rod in his keeping, and that was the year of its last renewal.  I think he must have been half dotty by that time, when he was in his eighties (he lived to be 92).  Thea said it may well be he never showed the Rod to his new master, Colin VI, and he walled it up in a secret place at his own castle.

Now we come to nearer matters.  If the female line given for Donal the Myna was true, then he, hence Col, descended direct from that Colin, rightful owner of the Bronze Rod.  On his mother's side, though a bit less straightly, Col was in the line of Maud, or so his great-grandfather had maintained. In either case he might make a good lawful claim on the Rod, if it appeared again.

So far with Thea's long story, as well as where her own troubles interrupted her, I haven't mentioned the places where I asked for this or that to be made clearer, or wondered if parts had been left out. For by far the big part I hadn't had a dicky-bird to say, because I didn't believe a bit of it. Even with a well friend who goes waffling on about ghosts or the omens in clouds (I remember Worrel, in love, doing that, once long ago), a chap can't say all a load of codswallop, not if the friend really believes in it. All a chappie can do is listen and get numb, the more so when the friend's using up her last breath on it. But when we came to Col's title to this Bronze Rod, I said, "Law doesn't count, not if the boy's descent could be proven a thousand times. Right without power is nothing."

"Worse than nothing," Thea agreed. "Death. But if one had the power to seize it, his right would help him keep it."

Tobin's own dwelling, Thea said, had been the same one I had just come from, now called Vandennis. In new wars following the fall of the Regions, it became empty, and years after came into the hands of the Moorhen clan of the Mynas. At some time, they had found the Bronze Rod where Tobin had hidden it hundreds of years before, inside a thick wall. Being Mynas, they knew what it must be, but it was only within my own lifetime rumours of its finding had gone amongst other clans of the Mynas. Donal, Col's father, claimed it. But the Moorhens and the Brown Hares had sullen old grudges, and besides, by this time the

Moorhens were being harried by the Vandenes, having all at once found themselves within the borders of Raug. When (in exchange, as it was said, for being left alone by the Adda-priests) they ceded the castle to Forn, the bigger prize, the Bronze Rod, went with it. Amongst other Mynas the Moorhens' name was now mud, not only for this, but for having, so it was thought, given precious old secrets to Forn.

"But you, Master Evan, are the only man, Myna or other, in two thousand years and more to hear the whole story of the Bronze Rod."

"For what?" I said, not really believing that, though I knew she did. "Forn, you say, has this Rod, and so he can bring it out and give it to Vandis, calling it the True Myke, whenever it suits him."

Thea, propping her head up, smiled weakly. "Ah, but Forn believes the old lie it gives power, if grasped at the right moment. He knows that moment is coming. I hoped to live till then, but I can't. It is seven more years, seven years and a few weeks, seven years at midsummer. Then your sister's husband will give, he thinks, that power to his king. Or seize it for himself, who can know? No difference; the Rod will be among Vandenes, and take on their harsh wishes for the world."

"A rod of bronze will start to believe as Vandenes do?" It was my only slip into scorn through all this long telling. Thea was too ill for her old anger. "Belief is fog. You are clever enough, I thought, to have worked out the Vandenes first fool themselves, like anyone who over-believes. They think they yearn to make others share their faith, but their true dream is power, power at the worst. That old king in Macedon desired glory, and the world doing as he said, but these conquerors wish to order thoughts. If Forn has his way, seven years from now the world's dream will be to have no differences, no arguments, no need for thought, no reason for hope."

"For the next five centuries and a half," I said, trying to be good.

"Or for ever. After such a time, will any other hope still be alive?"

"I don't know," I said. "I can't tell how long things last."

None of Thea's brains had left her; she guessed my thoughts at once. If her story was true, the Rod had been forged more than five thousand years ago (here, for once, I write *thousand* meaning that, ten hundreds of years), yet everywhere we looked we could see the rusting away and wearing away of metal made when smithing was the best it ever was; Forn might have a rod of bronze, but how could it be the same one?

She had answers. This bronze had been made with knowledge afterwards lost, and after its forging it had been wrapped and kept in cloths woven and dipped for that purpose by the priestesses of the moon. In itself plain, the Rod, when brought to Erech, was stored in a box or chest of marvellous stonework. That was lost long ago, but the Rod had always been kept in coddling caskets, wooden or golden, once, when it was in the East, in a box of ivory (from the teeth of a huge animal, no longer known), and again in a coffer of green stone harder than our grey granite from the wild north. Seldom had the Rod been carried or left out in the light and air, partly because the priestesses had made up a story even its rightful owner might be maddened or blinded, or lose his manhood, if he held it, or even looked at it too much. This, Thea said, was a lie, but had helped preserve the Rod. Those Mynas who knew about the Rod believed any bloke would die of unveiling it, except at the time of its renewal.

"And Forn," to bring us back to now, "will unveil it, you say at Gridge, in seven years time." That's where he would be at midsummer.

"At Gridge, or here. Here is where the High King is to be proclaimed."

"At Lunn?" We had a saying, *when the king's in Lunn*, meaning, who can tell when?

"Here," impatiently. "In this place, where the kings long before the House of Stewards kept their crowns. Vandis, if you let it happen."

"If I do?"

Thea grunted annoyance I was such a dud. "You have the right king in your keeping. You know foretells. Use them."

"I have kings for friends," I said, perhaps the silliest bleated out in all the time I knew Thea. "They hold together as allies against Raug, but I don't know they would fight Vandis only to place another king over them."

"You are done with kings, my lord. They've seen your king come from the shaddas, as you said he would."

"That was chance." I recalled there was a woman, not twenty paces from us, who said chance was the craft of dreaming, but I wouldn't let Thea dub me with powers of a prophet.

"You could contrive further chances."

A chappie was utterly amazed. Fencing with Thea about how hard it would be to put Col over, in my heart I had gone back to wondering if it could be faked, not saying so because it might offend her.  But she was there before me.  "To prevent Vandis, no superstition is too hare-brained for me to make use of."

"Toys, still toys?"  Thea said.

Here, I remember, the young girl, slender with large eyes, pushed her head past the rough curtain to find if there was anything Thea needed, and brought a bowl of broth in case she changed mind.  It was that deep valley past midnight, and Wott's mother was taking sleep.

"If the Bronze Rod is what you say," I began again, "I couldn't call metal so old and revered a toy.  But you know me, Thea, and even for you I can't believe in magics."

"You believe in the magic of blood.  You believe your own born right to be a lord.  No one can see that.  On a field of battle, your blood would flow the same as a farmer's."

"Sooner," with a laugh.

"You believe in birth, knowing born kings as weak as Edlin in Suvram, as dopey as Yew of Gwyn, knowing men of no birth who would make better rulers."

"We need a way to know our kings, or we would do nothing but squabble over the rule.  Wise people could choose their rulers, but if they're not wise they will choose worse rulers than anyone born and brought up to be a king."

"Well," Thea allowed, "We all must believe in more than we see, otherwise we become like the toymakers who gave us this ruin, sending their machines faster and faster between monstrous cities all the same, and never asking why.  Whether or not you believe what I've told you, you must be its prophet, and take the tale of the Bronze Rod to those who can make it true.  You must become a Tela.  Couldn't Col's story be the tale of Arfra the

Great?"

I was going to smile, then for the first time really saw the size of the strait (so we may say) between Seeyow and the rest of Brittan. We who could read print were more different than a chap could hold in his brain; others knew some history, but we could tell history from legend. For most, even lords, surely the lowborn, there was no sure separation. Yew, as an instance, or my sister, could have listened to all Thea had told me, and whether she meant these things had really happened, or whether it was just an old tale was no question. I don't mean to say we don't know truth from lies for what happened an hour ago, or yesterday, but till I could read Tulsingham and tell it was different from William Shakespeare and other made-up stories, the unseen otherwhere, either in far places or distant times, was like a dream, where nothing was true and anything might be. So it still is for tons of us, and most particularly concerning the tales about Arfra the Great, always told as if they were happening now. A chap doesn't say, "Then Arfra went to his wife," but "Now Arfra goes to his wife," and that's because no one is sure if it is a tale of what once happened, or what is still to happen. It's the same, really, with Tobin the Peacemaker, except giving a date makes it realler for us princes. There will be better places to tell more about Arfra, but for now I'll just say he is a great hero who, if real, once saved, or was one day to save, Brittan from all its ills. To me it seems we've tangled up two separate stories, because in Tulsingham's book there's no Arfra, but two names, one of a real king, the other of a myth. A chappie could go bonkers trying to pick them apart, but *Arfra* is how you would spell the name we say. Whoever tells the story, Arfra has a childhood where it is not known he's a prince, and he above all is the king who comes from the shaddas.

Thea, very weak by now, watched longingly till she saw the understanding in my face. "Those kings of yours will fight on because there is no choice for them, not because they can hope to win against Raug. They can give you seven years for the making of a king. The Mynas don't need telling, and, except for the Moorhens, can help you. The people will choose their Arfra, if you can teach them."

"Or deceive them."

"Where is deceit, if they believe, and belief makes it all come true?"

That was bang on. Tulsingham, rightly, is very hard on prophesying, but he doesn't allow foretells may come true by being believed. To be fair, we can't be sure that wasn't part of it from the start. If a seer, say, tells a farmer he is to have terrific crops, and because of that he becomes a better grower, that is not cheating; she didn't say his crops would make themselves, or think, hearing her, he would go to bed and wait for the prophecy to fill itself full. Heaps of guys, looking for a way to escape Vandene rule, would try to make it come true, once they heard there was a king like an Arfra, waiting in the shaddas.

"But Forn won't meekly give up the Bronze Rod." It was one knot among hundreds.

"Tam of Cumba wouldn't willingly have given up Caif, but Col had to have his lineage."

"If Forn believes as you say about the Bronze Rod, it must be guarded better than Caif ever was. It might have picked an easier place to be than the castle at Vandennis."

Thea didn't answer this direct. She lay back, fighting

against enemies, including, I think, the wish to say something stinging. In the end, she said, "Before I knew you, I chose you, in the first hour we met. Then, and all years, I thought there would be another Thea after me; I come of an old line, too, but not of blood, like yours. If you refuse, I've failed."

"Where are the Dauwas?" meaning (and Thea knew it), what would become of them after her death.

"At Bris, as always in spring. They'll go on, but I shan't live long enough to give them another Thea. Now they'll end up like other guilds, owned by those they hire to guard them."

"There is another job for you," she went on, reminded. "But this was meant, too. You have to take care of Alison, since I can't."

"Who is he?"

Thea laughed, I didn't see why. We have heaps of names ending with *son*; not as many as in old times, but the younger Tam of Cumba could be called Tamson if there was chance of muddling him with his father, and such names are commoner among common people. Since that time I've seen a poem in near Print English, even before William Shakespeare. (All print, I mean, but not quite English; a dialectic, maybe.) I can't make out much of it, except it is a love-poem about a peacheroo named Alysoun. But in my head when I first heard it I spelt the name Alison, and so it has stayed.

"Not he," Thea said. "A girl, Alison. She is here with me."

"Your daughter?"

"I don't have children. Alison has no father, but her birth is higher than you know." Thea's voice went into a drowsy chant.

"Not Thea's dauwa, Dauwa of Thea, Dauwa of Thea but a virgin..."

"How old is she?"

"Twelve, thirteen at midsummer. You've seen her, haven't you? She must go with you." Thea meant the girl who had been helping tend her. While I had supposed she must be a relative of Wott's, she seemed too silver-skinned for the child of a Myna.

"Go with me as what?"

"As Alison."

"She must have a family."

"No family has her. I gave the mother her price, five years ago."

Many women first came to the guilds as children not wanted by their mothers (and fathers, too, but oftenest mothers without husbands). Thea, however, had repute for not offering children to caitiffs whose hunger took that course, so this child could really still be virgin. But it was odd Thea made out good birth for a bought child.

I was very loth. As I tried to explain, my own household, such as it was, had no place for a girl neither infant nor servant. I hadn't lived with Rowan for years. Thea, fighting now with what must be the very lees of her strength, pressed me to promise, so she wouldn't die without a legacy. A chap offered to take this Alison to Sevenin, where Col would sometimes be, and I would often visit.

"No," flatly. "She mustn't be with Col, not yet. He would see her as child, after ogling near-women at Vandennis."

I hadn't told her that, only that there had been some peachy girls. But she could hardly say plainer she saw the girl in Col's future, the Gwynfa to his Arfra. It wasn't lame-brained as all that. The girl was little, but very pretty, and only two years younger than Col. Still, she would have to blossom very chop-chop to be a rival for Robin in Col's eyes.

"She goes with you. In Seeyow, you must teach her, when you can."

"And Marten can teach her, too," thinking Maire would be a better guardian for the girl than I.

"A little, it may be." Thea's doubt puzzled me, but she added what she thought explained it. "Alison may not take to Marten's teaching, which is now son-lore."

A chap writes what was then heard, that Marten's stuff would be better for a boy. But as I've said, our word is two things, and now that I see set out here all Thea said, and realise Thea came to the brink of calling herself a priestess of the moon, it seems she may have meant Marten's lore was too much under guidance of the *sun*.

"Promise me," she said. I did, and at once began to be haunted, not knowing how much I had sworn to, nor how any of it could be pulled off.

Those weren't Thea's last words, but it was plain now she saw her business as done. She rested, having lost the look she'd had, like a small child that carries a brimming cup in careful steps, grim not to spill any before passing it on. It was now the second evening, and I had food, the first since leaving Frant's house, but for a lump of bread Alison had brought me. In a while I watched Thea again; she was dimming, but opened her eyes now and again. Far apart, she muttered reminders: *the Mynas can help you*, and *Alison has been taught the history of the Bronze Rod*, and *Watch Forn, he is no fool*, lastly, *You, too, must pay a price.* After midnight, she woke into the clear for a moment, and said, "Find yourself a bed, Lord Evan. There is nothing left we can share."

I left, and slept a while uneasily, roused early by Wott's mother, who had a hot drink for me, and said Thea was at her last. Returning to the little space, which now smelt very sour, I found Alison kneeling at the far side of the bed. Thea's head had lolled back, and her hands were flat and still.

The girl must know who was to be her guardian; I could see question in her wide eyes, as she wondered how I might differ from what Thea had told her about me. Shy myself, I gave a poor smile, and knelt so Thea was between us. Each holding one of her cooling hands, we stayed there till the shallow breathing stopped. Alison's first words to me weren't meant to accuse, but they did: "She should have died sooner. Too much hurt, too long."

Yes, but then there would not have been time for such a word. Thea's dying seemed to wake up the world; it was hardly done when Wott came with news my chaps, Shan and Raneth, were being held captive by the Grey Cat Mynas, not far from where we first met them. My gawds were pretty hot under the collar about it, but Shay was treating them well. He kept telling them, Wott said, they were lucky to be pounced on by Grey Cats, having been found on the edge of ground claimed by the unfriendly Magpie clan. Clean contrary to his orders, Shan had been out looking for me, and even making big threats about it. They had been trapped when Shay's lot had offered to lead them to me, some hopes!

It was time to go, much as I wished to see Thea was given rites. Wott's mother (I now found she was called Asta, but that name is a tradition for those who tell fortunes with the roecards) assured me there would be proper burial. I meant to say I would soon send for Alison, but the girl, very slight in the shoulders but with a quiet manner of being sure, was ready to go with me. There were two ponies nearby that had been Thea's, one saddled. The other was loaded with bundles, and that was more relief to me than seemed due; I had been fretting (so soon!) about clothes for the girl. We can go ahead a little to say, coming out of Lunn with the animals, we were kept mainly above ground, after a winding time in a wide and much shallower tunnel. That, I suspect, was taken more to muddle my directions than to help us on our way. Collecting my two and telling them off for their disobedience, I was also reunited with my horse, which they had brought with them to share their imprisonment. They groused a bit, but had to allow they had been used gently.

But before we left the Tower, Alison, having clasped hands with Asta, had darted back into the death-room to kiss Thea's cold forehead. She was crying without sound as she groped for her cloakstrings. As for me, it was all my young manhood left behind. The sky, when we came out above ground, was layered with drifting wisps of white in front of masses of lead and purple, with brighter fringes and darker caverns, as full of doubt (if I may speak, though clumsily, as poets once did) as all times to be seen ahead of me.

## Alison

It was dim of me to feel, as I did, danger was left behind with the wreck of Lunn; there was nowhere safe in any realm, as I was soon reminded.  At Frant's house I was just in time for the arrival of my household, who had made good time from the north. The rest of the dozen armed men who had gone with me to Vandennis were there.  Following behind was another scawt, and one never asked for, twelve soldiers of Raug.  At their head it wasn't gladding to see the giantness of Syme, Worrel's killer.

It was in Frant's jumbled yard with its heaps of building stuff, sorted and not, and two of his workmen, for some mason's purpose I don't know about, seemed to be trying to burn broken blocks of soft stone, making a whitish but dirty smudge of smoke. As I rode up, Bett came scurrying to tell the news.  She is my housekeeper, mistress of what household I had, and Shan's wife, a shrewd, forthright woman, not handsome but with a lasting honesty of face.  Syme, it seemed from her gaspings, had overtaken them not far from the river-crossing by Wellgard; he wished to see me, but kept asking, Bett said, about Col; she hoped they hadn't done wrong in letting Syme and his uglies ride with them, but no one had spoiled to begin a fight.  Looking over the well-armed men of Raug, who sat very still in two tidy rows, I couldn't see what choice had been; man for man my gawd was quite outmatched.

For all Bett and the others of my household knew, Col might well have left (and still be) with me, and if I hadn't been worried for the rest of us Syme's quest might have tickled me no end. It was obvious Col's vanishing act at Vandennis must have worked, and Forn hadn't the foggiest where he was. But Noble's Peace ended while Thea lay a-dying, and as a chap whose weapons are words I am not at my best when all other hands are twitching for sword-hilts.

Still, as was owed my rank, I stood so Syme would have to come to me. He rode over slowly, with two flankers, as I had, though his looked the fiercer. The blighter was large in a way not easy to keep in mind; recollection couldn't cope with the hairy forearms, thick as more thighs. His salute was correct, though his smile lacked deference. (Differences of rank are as worthy as the power to enforce them.) It was a wide mouth, and his leathery cheeks were high and rounded, so he seemed to have a hinge above the massy, stubbled jaw. The face itself was broad like a battered bronze shield, yet Syme's eyes were no more and perhaps less than ordinary size. Set as they were in dells shadowed by thickets of eyebrow they seemed smaller, and though a steely blue, gave him the evil look of a half-wild pig. As he spoke or while listening, standing or seated on a horse, he had a habit of swaying slowly back and forth. His own soldiers kept watch on him in fear. A chap if not menaced by him might call it Syme's bad fortune to kindle such a quick loathing you wondered how his father, even his mother, hadn't killed the blister young, before his neck grew too large for their hands.

I joke now, but this was a dicey moment. Syme kept the forms of respect, explaining he had orders to look for me, and with me the boy Col, whose early disappearance from Vandennis had been much regretted, not only by the Adda-priest Lord Forn but by the new king himself. They had hoped a youth with such promise, yet without a realm to call truly his own, might spend more time at the court where he shone so. I make this softer than it was; the message was given in the best language at this fighter's command, but still rough by the measure of the Print English, I use, the more so when recited like a lesson or a learnt prayer, as Syme did.

In a smoother form of the same style and with a nice-faced condescension I answered Col would be told, when next I saw him, of the joy he had given at Vandennis, where, however, I'd left him when need came for my own hasty leaving. The piggy eyes smalled more with suspicion, and letting a grating note come into his courtesy Syme said he heard word a youth was riding with me.

This, of course, was no end pleasing to me. "A young soldier is," gesturing towards Raneth, who, if anything looked apter for brawl than even Shan. Swaying, Syme stared, then switched his gaze to Alison behind, small on her small mount. Tales made Syme a brutal raper, and though I had never heard his fancy ran to the unripe the length of his gauging of Alison started a chap wondering, till I remembered Syme had never seen Col, and wished to be certain the boy wasn't with us, masked in a dress and long dark hair. But no boy of fifteen ever had Alison's white neck and fine nose, and even Syme could see those slender shoulders hadn't won the long and short staves at Vandennis.

"You see, sir," Syme said, still see-sawing, "I was told this Col would be with you. You say, sir, he never rode with you?"

My only reply was none, but a chap had to try working out what happens when a stupid, dangerous bozo, not used to defeat, can't carry out the orders he has. Those must have reached him in the field: at a guess somewhere westward of Vandennis, and to judge by mud-spattered clothes and horses, the unrested look of both men and mounts, he had made a hard ride to catch up with the southward journey of my main household. It was likely, then, that for once a small band from Raug had crossed borders without much larger forces near behind, but even weary and in numbers no more than equal to mine, these jokers were no one's idea of a picnic. Frant had a band of armed men, a crude-looking lot, some of them now looking on from next to the house, but I couldn't count on their help if a fight came. As might happen if Syme tried to make me go back to Vandennis with him. My best chance was his orders had been exactly what he said: Forn might well not wish to start others talking about Col: Syme's use to him was in strength and lack of ruth, not the sharing of cunning plots. Then again, he would hardly be here if Forn hadn't thought Syme's special skills, brutishness and the bringing of fear, might be needed.

Above all, there was a serious question whether I could avoid fighting, try as I might: my good Shan's knuckles, shiny white where he grasped his pommel, told me events might overrule; already at Lunn he had let his own reading of duty set aside plain orders. If a fight began I'd have not an earthly of making myself into a wallflower, and would be forced to contribute my own ineptness. Shan and his chaps stood ready to guard me to the death, even if it was mine. At the same time I was irked by Syme's overbearing, and for the first time glimpsed into the hearts of those who settled affronts with stripped steel: times could arrive when not even hurt and hurting, not even death given or got, could be worse than the full sight of a chappie's own cowardice.

While my thoughts ran like a crowd of startled mice, Syme pondered massively, as a toothless hound works at tough meat. At last he swayed forward again. "You see, what I was told, my Lord Evan — " he began, and was stopped by the clatter and jangle of fresh arrivings.

They were approximatively twenty fighters of Suvram, swords out, and their leader was a fellow I knew, another minor relative of my wife's. Nace is near my age, lean with a sharp beak of nose, a rasping voice and a reputation for temper. His aim as he rode up was Syme, and he recognised me late. But whilst the salute and greeting for me were comically aside from his real business, they did stop a fight beginning before any words could be exchanged.

Nace had seen Syme's cumny from afar just after they crossed the border, and had come after them. Now, showing no fear of Syme's size or ugly fame, he demanded to know by whose word armed men rode here in Suvram. The question was overdue by several years (it being known Raug's soldiery went almostly where it chose to in Edlin's realm), and at the same time near too late for asking. If I was astonished to hear any man of Suvram put up a squawk, Syme's outrage could be expected. "Suvram?" he challenged. "These lands are Raug, or soon will be." A bloke sitting on a horse can't truly haunch back, set to spring, but Syme seemed to.

"You'll need to buy them with blood," Nace returned.

"Wait," I said, quite loudly. If my authority here was doubtful, my rank counted anywhere, and I thrust it in like an iron bar between two bare-teethed dogs. I told Syme, "Till midsummer, as you well know, this is still Suvram."

Then turning to Nace, I gave him first news of the borders his land would have when the Vandennis treaty took effect. Nace was too loyal to spit when he heard what his feeble ruler had done, but he was angry enough. "At midsummer," again, turning back to Syme.

He'd had time to lose some certainty. His eyes went from Suvram's blokes at his left to my lot, mostly gathered by my waggons on his right. Beyond them was the house and the small knot of Frant's watching houseguards, which Nace, as I couldn't, could bring in on our side by naming their king. Into Syme's face came the thought he had been led into a trap, and his near-glance back over his shoulder betrayed not cowardice, I believe, but the wish he had delayed to collect a larger cumny; he almost looked north to where his armies were. "The Kingdom of Raug," he said, "isn't alone in having its armed men riding here."

Nace was curt. "The Lord Evan has lands and his lady here in our realm. As a lord travelling he has, besides, right to his gawd."

"My orders — " Syme began again.

"A gawd," I broke in, "pledged not only to obey laws of realms where it rides, but to give help, where needed, in lawkeeping." Syme was a slow-thinking giant, but he could surely count twelve and forty. More than forty with Frant's rough crew added.

"But my orders — "

Again I interrupted. "Your orders are misunderstood if you mean to bring war here. In meetings at Vandennis between your lord and the Prince Erril there were no rough words, but the time of the treaty is very plain, and no lord can overlook injuries in his own realm." My suspicion was not one of us thought a farting of Erril, but a chappie couldn't say straight out, even Erril might find backbone over a case like this. But Syme got my drift all right; his mouth stretched farther into near a grin, more than ever making his face look as if it might fold. "My orders are what I've said, Lord Evan."

"So is my answer."

"This boy, Col, lord, has been in your special care, but you have no knowledge now where he might be found?"

He was calling and not-calling me liar. It told me Syme was funking a fight at these odds. Should I? was the question. "I've said," grandly.

Syme shied a bit, and I offered him his way out, with a return to courtesy. "Your king's invitation does him honour," I said, "and Col will hear about it when next I see him. At Seeyow, I expect."

"Seeyow," Syme echoed. "A strange place, I hear, sir."

"You must visit us there, and see for yourself."

"Some day," Syme said heavily, and tried to win back a bit of his frittered bully pride: "Sooner, perhaps, sir, than we now think."

"This is the end of your business here?" Nace half-asked. "My men can see yours back to the border."

"No," I said, before Syme could speak, then softened the command by adding, "Syme, I think, knows the way, and I would like talk with you." Now it was Nace who yearned to see blood splash, but his rawlooking twenty-odd were doubtful match for Syme's hard dozen, and it wasn't only Nace's skin I was thinking of. With him out of the way, Syme could come after me again.

Syme left grudgingly, saying he looked forward to our next meeting. As he wheeled his dozen, I saw in Nace's eye it would take less than a word from me to have all set upon the riders of Raug.

When I next saw Edin and recounted this, he asked why I had worked so hard to prevent battle, when I ought to have provoked it; there might never again be so good a chance of killing Worrel's killer.

My answer was, still is, I've not been a warrior; it is my habit and maybe my job to prevent bloodshed where I can. Edin was good enough not to ask whether I was windy for myself, though of course I was. No matter what Syme's orders otherwise were, he would have been told, if trouble began, to be sure I was among the dead; if I was sap enough to be so near danger, Forn was too shrewd not to have the opportunity seized. Yet stronger in my peacemaking were thoughts of what would happen to Frant and his fat family, to the over-eager Nace and his, if Syme were to be killed here, the vengeance Forn would look for. Erril, frighted, might well help.

There was also Alison, still quiet on her pony, just behind me. Not that it was likely she would be harmed in fighting itself. But once, not long before Worrel was killed, when he was wounded in a skirmish he might have got out of, Alma, as near bitter as I ever heard her, said to me Worrel's life wasn't only his to be given away.  True, but when left without their father his children still had a mother and a realm; if I were to be killed before settling what Alison was to be, she would have sod all, would be lucky if her future was no worse than bleak.  At that moment, and for other times to come, Alison didn't seem a main concern, but a niggling distraction to bend me from larger tasks. Only now, looking back, I can see how much it altered what I did, to find myself all at once responsible for this girl.  I've given this chapter her name.

As Syme's cumny rode slowly away, white but still sooty smoke drifting, the lifted nose and hot eyes of Nace put me in thought of a small dog I once saw, barking at a larger.  The big dog, a killer like Syme, was ready to tear the small one in pieces, but was whistled in by its master.  At that, the small dog began to believe his bark had caused the flight, and bristled to give chase. It was true Nace, unintended, had come to my rescue, but I at least was clear the numbers, not prowess, had the victory.

Still, I don't mean to little Nace who gave me hope, with his fine bitterness about the agreement his prince had made, and sureness there were lots others in Suvram who would sooner die on their feet than see their land so given away.  His proper place, plainly, was with Edin in the west, but his lands and family were here in the east; it was for such reasons bulk of Edin's followers were young, without ties.  Those who stayed, as Nace put it, hoped by fighting they could put heart in Saffam, but though they hated the policies that were shrinking their realm and bringing a narrow, harsh belief they didn't share, they stopped short of treason, wishing King Edlin's second son had come first instead, but not ready to make him an only son. This I found out by cautious questions, did men in general think it just that Edin was an outlaw? The answer was a shifting one, but I could hear Thea's great sigh; still giving your thoughts to the princes that are, Lord Evan? It was Nace who let me go on to princes that might be, asking about Vandennis, and about this Col sought by Syme.

By now we were taking drink with Frant and his wife, and it was my first go as Tela. Playing a Tela, I mean; no one of my rank can really be one. I said (for all I knew it might be true) Forn the Adda-priest had heard foretellings, and a dunce could see the new Vandene King feared the blossoming of a rival to his ambitions — here, I lowered my voice — to be High King of All Brittan. Some of the old prophecies, I said, seemed to be coming true.

Even later, when a far better Tela, a chap never had more greedy listeners, I became useder to what trusting belief was given to nonsense, and learnt to watch without blushing when eyes widened and breathing paused, as they did here, when I spoke of how Col had stepped from the shadda. Now, I said, belike he returned there to wait his time. Not saying more was, I think, my best touch; when Frant asked what this meant I said, "You'll hear that story from others. Everyone who was at Vandennis will be chatting about it." This might work both ways at once; to be asked would impress those returning from the great assembly that rumours had so soon spread so far.

In haste to be on my way, as afterthought, and with a light laugh, I joined, for the first time, Col with the Arfra tales, saying how odd it was Col's childhood had been on an island, taught by our own maker of magics, Marten. Young Arfra's teacher in the tales is Merdyn (so I spell it, but more is to be said about this), and he comes to Brittan from the Isles of the West. Had I offered this in the chanting voice Telas sometimes use it might have brought laughter; better to steal the joke by laughing myself, and let it linger in the brains of my hearers.

Parting from Frant's, we headed now south and west, both to skirt Lunn and to put distance between our riding and the now threatful northern border. It wasn't till we were well on our way it came to a chap what a step was taken since Vandennis, where I had puzzled over my part in Col's story. From the throngs who hope for good bread I had become the one who stirs yeast into the waiting mixture. Nor was there any way back for a chap.

Alison was beside me as we jogged steadily, now at the waggons' best pace. She said "This soldier, Syme, sir — "

"A dangerous beast."

"That I know. He is why the Dauwas don't go to Raug. When we were last there he came once, and when he came back the next day Thea told him his money was no use. Because of how he had been with the woman he chose. Syme said he could have Thea prisoned, have her hung." Alison smiled. "She said, perhaps, but not before all Raug knew his secret doings. Syme went away." None of what I write is like what she truly spoke; she had a small, clear voice, but had need of much training for her words.

"But the Dauwas don't go back to Raug."

"No, sir. Thea said no one can be more vengeful than a strong man a woman rules by his shame."

If this was more knowing than made me comfortable, in

other ways Alison was a child, a girl child, what I understood least in the world. But for that, not much was said between us; in unease I asked fatheaded questions that, answerable with a single word, did less than nothing to nourish talk: yes, she had learnt sewing; no, it wasn't among the chief joys of her life. Even as child there was hardly any need to tell her things, being so fussless; she made herself a sleeping-place when we camped, and in the morning when we were ready to start was promptly remounted, in fresh clothes, face washed and hair neatly bound.

Between, food was a sign. She neither helped prepare the food, nor waited for it to be brought to her, finding a plate and quietly eating what was given her. There, of course, was the question, where did she fit? being neither servant nor kin. Simple to say I might have had a daughter her age, fact was I hadn't, and everyone knew that. A boy would have been simpler, since a boy of any birth could be set to soldiering, where, because lessons were hard and necessary, there was small difference between how a prince and a nobody was treated. A nobody who did well could win rank of his own; most believed in Stanglin the young captain of Tobin's gawd, who had come to court as a boy, was the king's own grandson, Frick's bastard. That was no way for a girl, and Alison could find position only by finding a husband. By Thea's hinting she was to be Col's wife and queen of All Brittan, but Col, not to say Alison herself, might have other thoughts. I hoped she wouldn't aim too high; Thea's murky hints of a good birth weren't enough, so I thought, to bring young lords a-courting. Meantime the simple question of how she would spend her days hung on what she was now.

That came to surface very soon.  Riding in the direction chosen, we found ourselves on the road for my own estates.  So they still were in law, though I thought of it as the place where my wife lived.  After so much hard riding, I decided we might stay a while, at least till I could send west for news of Col, and be sure he had arrived safe.  The house was large enough that I could be there without troubling Rowan, and there was no must for us to share meals or undue talk.  A bed needs no saying.

She welcomed me, as usual, with correctness.  Rowan was hardly changed in all the years.  I remember Worrel, in that year of wivings, saying hers were looks would last a man (when a chappie's in love with an unhaveable woman, as we both were with golden Caif, or a woman likewise with a man, they always make lists of good aspects about one they can get).  Rowan's never been girlish, and wasn't now becoming matronly; the line of her bright mouth had hardened somewhat, but her eyes were still clear — not bright with the light of our courtship, but that candle blew out in her first week as my wife.  She was still slender: when they were feuding at Pormarch Alma (as I heard long after), proud of how she got back her own willow form after each childbirth, had remarked that to keep a flat belly is no great trick for a woman whose husband would rather sleep alone.  If our childlessness was gossiped (as it seemed) it would be seen as Rowan's fault, because women became wives to bear babies, yet that in turn would make my manhood doubtful, for not forcing her if she was skittish.  In gossip, all men should be lions, all women perfection.

Rowan's wifeliness did come out in the long gaze she had for Alison, the frown when, adding to the orders she had given her own housekeeper, I told Bett there'd be need for a second bedroom. I may not yet know what she was, but I wouldn't have Alison sleep with the servants. Rowan was wintry with the girl, who, not slow to feel the chill, didn't bring her own waft of summer, bobbing the faded shadow of a curtsey, and not-quite hiding a yawn with a stretched upper lip.

After she left us Rowan remarked she was a pretty child, and asked what was her family. "None, now," I said, and no word more. Rowan looked hard at me, trying to pierce the mystery.

In early morning, the weather now promising fine, I walked over dewed grass for a talk with Stee, Rowan's overseer. Mine, really; a good man. Well, all left to themselves in such posts do stealing, but Stee wasn't greedy, knowing his returns wouldn't be questioned, so long as there was gain overall, and none of the poorer farmers came near starvation. He was full of praise for the new farms in Raug, wondering whether we too couldn't knock down some hedgerows and plant huge dull fields. In an hour's talk, while I couldn't make him see Raug's example as bad, a chap did convince him I would never agree to following.

When I came back to the large house, more than ready for a spot of brekkers, I found Bett to ask where Alison was. Here was strangeness; Bett, not meeting my eyes, muttered the girl was abed. Outside, the sun was now guzzling up the heavy dew, and I hoped Alison hadn't learnt, after all, lazy ways from the Dauwas, whose habit, naturally, was to sleep late. Alison, true, had missed sleep tending the dying Thea. "She isn't sick?" I asked Bett, whose eyes were still sliding away from mine.

It came out at last. Alison was on her bed, not in it,

having been soundly birched not an hour ago, at Rowan's orders. For not paying respect, the reason was, but Bett, though she had given the beating, didn't know what form the disrespect had taken. All she could say was, the mistress (Rowan) had gone very early to where Alison slept, and come from there to the kitchens to order the punishment, and show Bett where a birch was kept. Guessing I might have other ideas, Bett said she had tried to wait till I came back, but the mistress came back and asked was it done yet, and why not?   Alison, Bett added, was both brave and stubborn, and hadn't let out a cry.

As a child I'd had my beatings, and so had my sister, often laid on by a servant, who wasn't more light-handed for not knowing what it was for, and who never heard pleas for mercy (another part of my father's contempt was I let my dislike of being thrashed be seen and heard, not proper for a warrior-to-be). But Alison was slender and fragile-seeming, and the dozen strokes she got (always, of course, thirteen) would be severe for a boy toughened by fights and bruising practice with staves. It was hard to imagine what offence might earn it. Dying Thea, I was sure, had told Alison there was naught to fear with me, and that she would be treated well.

Though for a time I was, I couldn't justly be angry with Bett, trained to obey orders, nor with her let show my anger for Rowan. Who I now went to find.

With all else, I was angered by her pretence of amazement; Rowan said she could hardly believe one of my standing and concerns would take up a slight matter like the beating of a common girl. Alison, she said, asked if she would take part in a yearly spring task, the scouring and scalding of tubs, barrels and pots left empty by winter, soon to be needed again as fruits and vegetables, coming in turn into season, were pickled and preserved — Alison, I was saying, had insolently refused.

The girl, I told Rowan, hadn't been brought here as a servant, and no matter what the misunderstanding the punishment had been far too severe, and brought with undue haste in my absence. Rowan replied she was irked by the girl's pert manner, and at the very beginning it was best to be both harsh and swift, so bad acts couldn't become bad habits. There was more, lion's share of it about my failings, about the honour that was Rowan's due but so little given, and all the while I was worrying out the puzzle Alison had refused to take part in a job all joined in. When I say, all, not my cousins or my nieces, of course, but like any of the big yearly jobs it is not beneath remoter relatives to royal blood — I myself used to give a hand with the yearly banging out of dust and grime from carpets and hangings. Had Thea put maggots of pride in Alison's head, about being Queen of All Brittan?

Quarrels between husband and wife, like fire in a field tindered by sun, don't burn out on the ground where they began, and whilst I kept coming back to the cruelty to Alison, Rowan brought in my never sending so much as a message, my riding to Vandennis without her, the well-worn wrong of my friendship with Alma, and not least how a chap did all he could to anger the Vandene Kingdom, an embarrassment to Rowan, who, like her kin said to rule at Saffam, condemned Edin as outside the law.

My retorts weren't soothing. It made no difference whether Rowan called me foolish: if her Suvram (I didn't tell her

this) was going to live as more than slave to Vandis, all that
mattered was how many swords Edin could bring together, and
everything else was babble. Still, hurt lies in what a wife says to
wound, just as true when what's said has neither justice nor sense.
Amongst the rest, when we squabbled back to our starting place,
Rowan made me gape in calling Alison "Thea's child." Shan, of
course, must have told his wife where the girl came from, and
Bett would soon have gossiped with Rowan's servants; the real
shock was in how Rowan spoke Thea's name, as if boiling down
a whole sea of bitter into one drop of venom. When I corrected,
saying Alison wasn't Thea's daughter, I seemed also to be denying
she was mine. Odd how a chappie can miss a proposition that
ought to be hitting him in the face like a bally wet cod; I had even
been thinking of the old case in Stanglin. But the actual point
was, you see, Rowan had changed from telling me what was done
to Alison was just and called-for, to saying it was a kind of
payment for my own faults.

The drab history of my married life hasn't much to do with
my real tale, and is a private business, more even than the
mourning of Thea; so far I've said little, and won't now change
that by much. All else aside it would be unfair, I having this
magic weapon of Print English, and a book which can be copied
over and over, while Rowan has no means to make herself heard.
Yet there were scandals spoken against me that year never
answered, and now as then a chap is lost to know what injury he
had done to provoke so tawdry a revenge. If sixteen years as my
wife hadn't been all Rowan had hoped, they might have been
much worse. Once it was plain the hunger there in her first kisses

was greed, not for me, but for being my wife (or wife to one of my standing), I let her alone, though lots would have thought me more a man for forcing myself upon her. Rowan was always ready to complain I didn't do as other chaps did, and never once reflected my difference meant not only long absences and strange studies, but also she could do as she chose lots of the time. I had never claimed rights, and never once struck her. Till the morning she had Alison flogged, I had never shouted at my wife.

Now, though, the air was properly poisoned. Judging that soon my servants would be bickering with Rowan's over who had been wronged, I changed mind about staying there. When I found Shan in the kitchen making a meal I told him we would leave next morning. Bett gave me a swift look and whispered in her husband's ear, then Shan, asking my pardon, suggested it would be better to wait some days before beginning a long ride. Better for the girl's sake, he said, and if there was somewhere a sly smirk under this, I didn't take it up, but agreed to delay.

Alison, when I saw her, was wan but calm, and said at once she was well enough to take a part in the scouring job.

"Why did you refuse it at first?"

"Sir, I didn't refuse. The lady said, begin now. I only said I must see if the Lord Evan has jobs for me to do."

"You shouldn't have been beaten. I am sorry you were."

"Sir, I have been beaten before. Before Thea bought me."

And must now begin to believe all the world outside Thea's was the whipping of children. I said, "You will not be again." Alison looked me full in the face, eyes unblinking; I can't say she was faintly smiling, but it was a bit like being judged by a cat. Like a cat she was too wise to give full trust, and as with a cat that was my failing, not hers.

"If you work at household tasks, it is to give help, as a girl of family might, not as a servant. When you tire you may stop without asking. I shall give orders to make it so."

"Sir, Thea taught the only way to be free of a duty started was to finish it." Still, these weren't, of course, Alison's words, but her teacher's skill with the poor words we have was now there. This last, howso, didn't sound like any Thea I had known, but then the face we turn to children is often not much like life. We come to a moment of panic, I believe, and while our brains numb our voices echo what was said to us, years before.

"But, sir..."

"You may speak." The girl had become near coy with abashment.

"Thea was sure you would teach me to read in books."

"Do you desire to?"

"If I can, sir."

This pleased me, and it was soon settled; she would scour barrels this morning, and later I would begin her with the letters. I had one or two books here in the south, but she could scarcely get so far before we left for Seeyow. Till the sounds of the letters begin to make themselves into words, teaching reading is a beastly bore, but it joyed me to think with work there could be another added to our circle of those who had learnt to read and write, thereby to speak.

As I left Alison to change herself into working clothes, she called me back. "Sir, Lord Evan, I haven't told all that was said with the Lady Rowan. The lady said I was the brat of a whore, and I..."

"Yes?"

"Sir, I said no more than what Thea taught the Dauwas to say when given scorn."

"Was it a rude thing, then? Is it scorn for scorn?"

Mouth opening to say no, Alison seriously weighed. "Sir, it is," she allowed.

To be truthful it was relief for me to know while the girl had been overpunished it hadn't been for no cause whatever. For one gain, I didn't have to go back to Rowan, say she had lied, and face being accused of taking the word of this wretch against that of my own wife. I said, "With one who has the power to hurt you, it is often wise to say less than comes to mind, as I with Syme."

For the first time there was pain in Alison's face, but she had put it there on purpose. "Sir, this I see."

At that, for the time, I left it, and left her. Only much later did I learn what Thea taught the Dauwas to say to name-callers: *Whore is a better title than Unwanted.* To give Rowan late justice, she couldn't know it wasn't invented for her alone. She must have thought it came from tales I had told Alison.

We set out again after six days, and not far from Stonedge were found by Edin with a strong cumny of forty. Having heard there were soldiers of Raug out looking for me and Col, he came to add his strength to mine. Col was staying safe-hidden in Edin's country, not willingly, having argued two full days I was like a mother bird and he ready to take part in war.

"I told him," Edin said, "I would speak to you for next year, if he kept up his weapons."

"Next year?"

"I have boys younger than Col is now, riding with their fathers. Come, Evan, no fame without danger."

Edin knew both. As warrior he was admired, and he had luck, too, the luck that goes with skill, never so far as I know having been more than bruised or scratched in all his fights.

For a time I began to wonder if it mightn't be simpler to build hopes on the true realness of Edin, rather than the unsure promise of Col. All needed to make Edin king instead of outlaw in Suvram was the death of his brother followed by that of his ga-ga father (which came first mattered, because if Erril ever became king, Edin wouldn't be his heir). There must be heaps like Nace, ready to fight Raug under a proper king. Who knew what might be done by a strong Suvram in alliance with Stanglin and the League of the West?

Edin began a Seeyow pow-wow, not knowing he was answering my thoughts. "What is called belief mazes me. Riding back from Vandennis I passed through part of the lands Erril's giving to Vandis. I thought I might find new swords there."

"Did you?"

"A few, more of them lads who'd join any side in any fight if it was a chance to bloody swords and not be hung for killing. But there are lots more Vandenes there than there were, some Adda-priests. Not of Raug, men of Suvram."

"Are you sure they haven't been sidling in from the north?"

"One, a fellow I've known all my life, he breeds horses on the north side of Tem, well west of Lunn. Once he used to agree there must have been skills before the Viztas ever were seen, but now he is a priest, and holds we were like children till taught by those who came from the sky. Did you know they have the threat, when the Viztas return, all those who aren't Vandene will be driven out to starve?"

I smiled, Edin was so indignant. "Always a Vandene weapon."

"Well, but now they're saying the time isn't far off. How does this make them stronger, how can threats change what is in a brain? You can say the sea is made of beer, but you can't make me believe it by saying all those who don't will be killed. Perhaps, after all, the sea is beer, but fear of death won't stop me tasting salt water. Yet this horsebreeder now warns me like a true Vandene, if Forn lets me off, I'll find a worse fate with the Viztas. Belief, I told him, is what seems true, not what gives me a benefit, isn't it?"

"I don't understand a bit more than you do," wondering if this meant Edin had now let go his long belief in a different sort of Vizta. "My sister became Vandene to marry, and her husband makes Vandenes by lopping fingers or scarring faces with hot iron. I used to think ordinary lives would be empty of any beliefs about what can't be seen, unless forced on them, but now I see many, perhaps main part, believe everything, different things, opposite things, all at the same time. Fear and pain, and the promise of benefit aren't used to put belief into a head, but to drive out its rivals." At that time I didn't realise, as I do now, that I was quarrelling here with Tulsingham. His book is what speaks of beliefs imposed on empty minds, but what I said to Edin can be shown every day: brains crowded with every learnt belief, roecards and Viztas, foretells that can't be altered, and charms to cause or prevent what happens... Tulsingham so much hated priesthoods he pretended the superstitions he scorned wouldn't be, except for priests, but stones were before men ever built with them. A great book, still, even if a chap now doubts some parts of it.

"Our swords will never be enough," Edin now said, shaking his head, and without knowing it echoing Thea. "Need is, a hope to fight against the fear. As in the Tale of Arfra," but that was trying to draw me out.

As he spoke, was a burst of high laughter from the two-horsed waggon where Bett and some of the young servant-girls were riding. Today Alison was with them, her pony having gone lame, and to judge by the giggles and blushes she caused was telling tales of life with the Dauwas.

I started to tell Edin about Thea, and her notion prophecies could bind everyone together against Raug. When I mentioned Mynas, Edin shook his head. "Not that I would say no to a few hundred Mynas, fighters as they can be, if ever they could be trusted. But once give them the run of our lands, and where is safety for our women or our goods? People, to be frank, mistrust this with you. Marten, well, he's mad and that is that, but Forn uses this against you. At Vandennis in private talk over and again he brought up your love for the Mynas, and even those hottest with you against Raug couldn't think of an answer."

This chilled rather than angered me; I was awfully disappointed. "Well," I said at last, "let us go down to defeat with clean hands, and the bloodline of every soldier proved."

"Meaning no offence," Edin, stiffly. "I know there are good blokes among Mynas, too."

This also was aside from the point, but I didn't say so. It

was clear as day to me that under a king they helped raise the Mynas would change from what they now were — but then, so would the kings we had, and not in ways they would choose. Still, there wasn't any beastly fraud in how I strained to keep the kings allied against Raug. That was for their own sake, whether or not an Arfra came, and to be lords still, under a High King (as I supposed them under Arfra) was better than being nothing in a Brittan ruled by Raug.

Fresh peals of giggle came from the waggon. Alison was being listened to for perhaps the first time in her life, but while she was smiling she hadn't lost her watchful look.

"Is it true the girl came to you from Thea?" Edin, doing his best to rewarm the air between us. "You, I know, thought well of her. Worrel held her in awe. A pretty girl, and will be prettier. She was with the Dauwas, then?" He chuckled. "She must make a wife who knows what pleases."

"The girl is a virgin."

"But not deaf and blind." Another ripple of laughter came from the waggon to be his ally. "Brought up among weavers, you would know lots about that craft, whether or not you'd ever had a shuttle in your hand. What are you going to do with her?"

What, indeed. "Feed her, Keep her safe, till she finds that happy husband."

It was good to come to where the great castle once had stood, now wholly ruined, and make the short crossing to Seeyow, feeling a moiety of safety in its circling coasts. Right off, it meant I could send good fighters where they would be needed. While war and plottings lasted, I resolved, I had made my last journey with such a cumbering household, too easy to find, too easy to overtake, needing too many gawds.  At Sevenin, again at Pormarch, cousins and friends had been sure I was in danger and that my dozen weren't enough, but while I had been glad to borrow larger scawt, it seemed wrong when fresh wars were surely coming.

Good, too, to be back with Marten and Maire, though with both, in different ways, I felt more distance than there once was. Marten wasn't much interested in what had happened at Vandennis.  He was aging now, beard all grey and yellowed white, eyes rimmed with red.  More careless than ever about his dress, he came to table the first night of my return in what looked like a grubby nightshirt partly tucked up above frayed and stained trousers, while the hair matted about the bald crown of his head looked untouched all spring.  There were some who now believed him really mad, no longer mad-with-a-smile, that he had crossed the border, so to say, between oddness chosen and a wandering of wits.  It was true he could forget names of people known all his life, or couldn't remember whether or not he had eaten that day, but really that was because he spent so much of his time in other worlds, of measurings and sums, watching the stars or trying to show when substances burnt, nothing was lost (I would explain that if I could; it had to do, I believe, with weighing the ash and the smoke together, but I don't know how to weigh smoke). When I gave him Thea's account of the Bronze Rod he had no time for powers and prophecies, but was keen enough with the years and months.  I still found it hard to believe ten words together of what Thea had told me, but it was interesting when

Marten, scratching away at his numbers like an old hen, told me time as kept by the priestesses of the moon would come back to its starting place after 571 of those short years, and that would be 554 years of the sun. Thea had told me for each renewing of the Rod the Old Believers, grudgingly, took 17 from their count of the years. But also, 554 years on from when Tobin the Peacemaker hid the Rod made the date for its next rebirth YL 753, or seven years from now, just as Thea said. That his reckonings gave the same date didn't surprise Marten, who only said he might have to give more time to silly-seeming lore, where true might still be found amongst all the nonsense.

Maire, who was plumpening, had moved counterwise; as Marten gave less and less of his caring to everyday, she put her roots always deeper into Seeyow and their household. When Maire failed to give full attention it was because she thought suddenly there were extra candles burning in empty rooms, or she hadn't told those in the kitchen to save firewood by baking an extra batch of bread with the joint. These errands, which most mistresses left to a housekeeper, make Maire sound miserly, but the Seeyow establishment wasn't wealthy as some or as formerly, with large outlays going to keep enough men under arms, watching the coasts. Still, that first night, Maire also gave orders for left food to be taken to a nearby dwelling where there were an ill old woman and a young one soon to give birth; it was Maire's hope the elder would live long enough for sight of her great grandchild. A chap should also put in how sad Maire was when hearing it might be long before Col came back to Seeyow. She wondered about the food in Wezram.

To Alison Maire was welcoming but less than

open-armed. At Sevenin, Cara had made up mind the proper way to treat the girl was as lesser kin, and this went so far as having Robin pass on to Alison some of the clothes she no longer wore (the gowns needed taking in, or Alison some growth before they could be useful to her). The two girls hadn't been unfriends, but had not much to say to each other. Alison had been a bit abacked, but obedient, when I told her to forgo, in better company, the talk she tickled the servants with (I've no doubt, however, Robin would've been taught lots she'd've loved to learn). On her side Robin found Alison didn't know any of the people she liked to chatter about; handsome Daf, handsome Col, the Pormarch cousins who shot so well with bows, Avanda who wore her hair tied to one side, so. Silences fell.

At Seeyow the question pressed less. Although Alison was at table with us that first evening, I no longer slept or made my living-place in that big house. Some years before I had bought from Marten another house, down the hill somewhat, a less ancient building, though stoutly made in the main. It had been a very squared place with three stairways to an upper storey, now gone, and lots of rooms, large enough for all my household, though not at first built for living in. It seems to have been a public building, and because the one original entrance arch still standing has the word *Girls* carved in its lintel, Marten, when he learnt the letters, named it the Guildhouse, by which he meant brothel, though it is hard to believe, even in old times when there were lots more people, so large a building was needed to house dauwas.

This is a poorly chosen place to have to speak about Iona. She often shared my bed there, but is no drab, niece on one side to Shan — to Bett, really, whose sister's daughter she is — and on the other, grandniece to Lydd, my old servant. He was then still in my pay, though no longer given any jobs to do; all my servants and lots of my gawds come from three or four families, intermarried almostly into one clan. There I also found girls to be with me, only one at a time, you understand, when I was living for long times without a wife. Iona was the third such, first offered to me (and taken) when she was eighteen, at the time when Rowan had left Pormarch after the quarrels with Alma. A good girl, Iona, not a beauty, but with lustrous dark hair and moist skin, even-tempered and often able to make me laugh with her mimicries or with her short, knowing comments about people. I made a start at teaching her to read Print English, but though not at all a dimwit she was soon bored by letters. All the more strange, then, when only the second or third night after my return she said words that sounded a lot like envy about my lessons with Alison. I had never spent many daylight hours with Iona, but it came clear as a week or two went by and all her mentionings were grumpy ones that Iona, to my bewilderment, saw Alison as taking away what was hers. For the moment I pretended not to notice, but as with her forerunners when they showed signs of wishing to own me, made up my decision to find a good husband for Iona. That wasn't the chief reason I cast off the others, and not in the least because I had tired of them: mainly it seemed unfair to do as lots of lords did and keep a woman for my pleasure beyond her ripest marrying years — given a dowry, such a woman could always find a husband, but I mean to say the best childbearing years. Both those who kept me company before Iona were now well married with children. It might be best, though to me sad for a time, if Iona made a start on her second and truer life. As for me, I liked Alison more and more, but couldn't see in my daytime admiring of her quickness and sense there was any duelling with what came to Iona by candlelight. As a lord I shouldn't have need to expend worry on such a consideration.

I was very restless; well-loved Seeyow seemed standing still and my time there a standing-still for me; Forn wasn't resting, Syme was somewhere riding, time itself runs like a river and to sit on the bank is to fall behind.

My mood became better when Rayman came back. Another I haven't mentioned before — not by name, that is; Rayman was the smith Forn had asked about at Vandennis, the one who had done work on old machines, though when Marten's interest in that flagged, Rayman, on his own no worker-out of puzzles, had gone on to other matters. He had first come when he was seventeen, just after the death of his father, a smith by trade. Having heard about wonders in Seeyow Rayman had come in hope of learning to outdo his father, not for pride, but because he now had a mother and twin sister to care for. His father had never earned well. It took Rayman a good month to work his way to Marten's lair; small farms often have smithing jobs to be done in return for a night's lodging and a mouth of food. Once at Seeyow, with Marten he began badly, disputing with him over the use of some ancient oblong tiles a Myna had brought. They were quite small, and marked with different numbers of spots. Marten had decided they must once have been tallies, used in place of money. Rayman was sure they were a sort of game, and even invented (or, as we later knew, recovered) the way of playing it. Which Marten had to admire, at the same time demanding to know why the tiles couldn't have been both tallies and the pieces for this game. Since then lots more sets of the tiles have been made, mostly of wood, a few with slate, and the game is played all over Brittan.

That first time, Rayman hadn't been able to stay for long, but was so eager to learn, when he left both Marten and I, each without knowing the other did, gave him small sums of money for his family, so he could come back the quicker. For eight years now that had been going on. He was now much taller than the spindly boy he had first been, and far stronger than people thought; unwarlike and with no interest in weapons beyond their forging, he was a good wrestler, and I had seen him throw tough soldiers twice his thickness. He has a long neck; that and his colouring were what made Rayman look frail, very fair with straw hair and skin that pinkens from an hour's sun. His eyes are a milky blue, and even the down on his forearms is silvery. A great one for smiles, and if his farfetched jokes were sometimes wearying, I was usually pleased to see him again.

In late winter he left to be at his twin's wedding; she had lost a first young husband in the wars, and was now making a richer second marriage. Her mother and Rayman's (not two women; she who was mother to them both) would live on the new husband's farm, southward in Marchlen.

Why, then, I asked him, shouldn't Rayman make his home here in Seeyow for good? We needed someone to teach all those just beginning to read and to count.

"I, sir?" Rayman's voice was still high-pitched. "You live, sir, and Marten lives. Why do you dress me in borrowed robes?"

(Where I can, I give his exact words, his own kind of Seeyow English).

"I shall be away a lot, Marten, as you know, has no time now for simpler learnings."

It had come to me Rayman, in his way, was now the heaviest learned bloke alive. I had read more, but knew less than he about counting and measuring. In those, Marten had gone farther and deeper, but knew lots less than yours truly about tales and histories.

"You deem me worthy, lord? I'faith, then shall I blench at this? An I do, I am a soused gurnet." From the first he had been mad on poets, above all William Shakespeare, whose words took nest easily in his round head. I remembered when he was working more at the forge, showing with quick taps of a master-smith's hammer where the heavy blows of a beefy helper should land, tip-Tong, tip-Tong, tip-Tong, with Rayman as we may say bellowing out:

*Her FA-ther LOV'D me, OFT in-VI-ted ME,*
*still QUES-tion'd ME the STO-ry OF my LIFE*
*from YEAR to YEAR,*

or some such lines. It was Rayman's mastery of that style (which, I might say, he kept only for the few who had an earthly of following it) made me wonder how much ordinary blokes could ever have understood. Lords, perhaps, and bosses and other nobs knew William Shakespeare: I suspect he pleased not the multitude, but only those of judgement. Or perhaps the general were pleased without knowing what was said: you can see that today at a fair where a conjurer or seer gathers a crowd with fine-sounding nonsense.

Alison was no end amused by Rayman. But (not to do with that) I remember when I first took him to meet her, we found her playing with a kitten, using a knotted scrap of cloth for mouse. I noticed how gently she teased; whenever she snatched away the prey she couldn't bear to see the kitten bewildered for more than a moment or two. The animal came from the last litter of a favourite stable-cat, killed since in an accident: it had struck me Alison might feel fellowship. She said, "We call this play, but he is learning to kill."

Rayman was to keep on with Alison's teaching while I was away. This absenting is an account I've debated with myself over, whether to tell lots or little about it, or leave it out entire. When I purposed to stay several weeks in the south at my wife's house, there was a reason why: Wott's mother, Asta, before we left the place of Thea's dying, had told me as a good friend, I would be welcomed for their own midsummer doings. This was a Seventh Year, she said, and a chap gathered that meant out of the ordinary. I was to meet Wott at Stonedge, on the eve of Midsummer's Eve, though the beano wasn't there but in a place often called Little Stonedge (a better name would be Rougher Stonedge, being an even less tidily raised part-circle of big stones), a strong half-day's ride to the north — yet still far nearer Rowan's house than from Seeyow. It was known the Old Believers (many blokes said the Mynas, but that was wrong: lots of each weren't the other) kept their own rites at midsummer, though all true followers of the Viztas disliked this, and the Vandenes, hating it, were sworn to put the kibosh on, if they could.

I doubted there could be rites there much longer, and resolved to take this chance of seeing one before too late. Little Stonedge, because of what Suvram had yielded at Vandennis, would become a part of Raug, just at midsummer. That made mine a perilous adventure, one I knew Neal, for instance, or Edin, would tell me to give a miss (Marten wouldn't see why a chappie would desire to watch foolish carryings-on). It wasn't a year for Gridge Meet Time, so there would be no long mid-year truce, but I was certain Raug wouldn't launch any fighting for the two days on either side of Midsummer proper, and believed with Myna help (and no faithful, clumsy attendants, as in Lunn) I could slip back into what was left of Suvram when the rites were done. It wasn't very far from the parts Edin held, and he, I knew, meant to have fighters handy in case Raug, taking possession of its new lands, failed to stop where the shameful treaty said. So what risks there still were seemed worthwhile to me, for the sake of knowing more about the Old Beliefs, so stirring to Thea.

Still, to prevent debate, I let on at Seeyow my journey was going no farther than Landin, for talk with Neal. That would be my first direction.

Maire thought it best, while I was away, if Alison slept and had her meals at the big house, but added, "She must learn to be more humble, till those of birth are more used to her." After such years it wasn't always remembered Maire herself had been no more than a tanner's daughter, but there was a grimness about her chin when she spoke of Alison, and I did recall in Col's upbringing she had been very free with the goods of her father's trade. "Alison," I warned, "is not to be beaten."

Maire began a smile before she saw I meant it. Then, "Not beaten? Not if she steals, or lies, or is rude to her betters? Children must learn, Evan. No other cure I know of drives out too much pride."

"Find one." For the only time in all the years making clear whose rank was the higher. "She is not to be beaten. I've given my word."

Maire sighed; the set mouth and upcast eyes asked unseen Viztas (in which she didn't believe) to judge this.

Alison's eyes, I remember, were hard to read when she was told I would be gone a while: she was, at a guess, fearful of being left amongst new people, yet anxious to seem untroublesomely obedient. These concerns had never been a study of mine.

Though the new southward journey was without events worth putting down, Midsummer and its rites are parts of the oddest, strongest and yet mucked-uppest recollections of all a chap's life, filled with drumming, with flamish light and deep shadow, avid faces seeming to take up every sort of outlandish look, or in fact to change shape in the leaping light from a whacking great bonfire, eyes like red coals, naked bodies breaking from deep darks to vault the flames, a flashing blade and bright crimson blood spurting down to the sticky black of below, teeth and thighs, and voices now hoarse, now shrill. And drumming, endlessly.

But, pardon, gentles all, I am not able to put in order all seen and lived through, and, having the skill it needs, would not tell half of it.

I wakened not definite whether I was hot or cold; there was dampness behind my knees and at the pits of arms, but a chill sat on my shoulders and prickled the hair of my limbs. To mention it was late morning, the day after Midsummer, is a bit misleading; I know that now, but if ever a chappie woke not knowing where or when he was, it was then. The space was small and dim, a cottage somewhat ruinous and partly rebuilt, and I had been sleeping on a type of shelf in the wall. Not alone: the stir of my half-waking woke a woman or girl next and to some extent tangled with me, and it was her unwinding brought me fully back to life. She was young, with dark hair like a furze-bush, and her bare body was far from clean, being patched with stains and soils, earth, ash, grass and maybe blood. On the flagged floor she found a sort of mantle to wrap in; standing she gave me one short, unmeaning look, then without a word went from my sight. Hidden by the bulging brick of what might be a chimney, a door opened, letting in grey light, and she was gone. It was the way a speechless animal, having finished what it is doing, eating, coupling, dropping, goes on to other concerns, needing no ceremony or leave. Her mouth, too, circled with stains, bloodstains, had put a chap in thought of — let's say a fox, having found an unguarded chicken.

But I could not pretend myself prey; in darkness, but knowing there must be blood on the lips, I kissed that mouth last night, if we can use the same word, *kiss*, for what is given in friendship, love, or cool courtesy, and the lungings and bruisings of a Midsummer do.

Under fingertips I found my own lips swollen. Washing was needed, but I was a battleground for needs: to relieve myself, to find clothes to put on, to eat (or perhaps it was the need to retch that sat on my stomach); all urgent, all asking me to do what could not be managed, move from where I was.

But only when a chappie's by himself can he keep on believing such codswallop: as soon as I knew there was still some human with me in the cottage, I was sitting up, reaching for rough weave to cover me, with my legs over the edge of the sleeping-shelf. Wott, himself part-dressed, asked how I was. There seemed to be just the two of us, but he also had a woman with him last night. Well, there'd been at least two women with at least the two of us, but my memory was unsafe about whether I coupled with more than one (a beano never sought, unlike other lords). There was memory of mouths and skins and smoke-sweaty odours, pantings and cries, but ownership was a muddle.

Wott said there were soldiers of Raug, Mykas, in the offing. A dogged morning drizzle had finished off the last of last night's big fire, and a lot of the Old Believers had gone away by now, but the Mykas had seized some they suspected of taking part in criminal rites. For once a chap was near agreement with the Vandenes: while I certainly did not aim to be made captive, a chap was not sure they were altogether wrong in condemning these frolics, or trying to stamp them out. I was not delighted for what last night showed about people's nature — about my own (only to some portion my own).

For Wott, as he made clear, Midsummer had been cat's pyjamas, and his pride at having been able to bring me to be in on it was dashed awkward for a chappie. First, I shaped to stand coldly on my rank and let him know it was all a ruddy disgrace, but that was not really in the cards; just about naked on a filthy bed, it was soppy trying to be lordly with a man who had shared what he had with me in this place. But also, he and his mother were my friends, and it was an alliance a chap aimed to keep, for my own sake as much as for policy.

Yet I could not smile and feign . Both were too practised in guessing the thoughts of those who were not Mynas, and knew too well what blokes in general would say of these doings, to mistake silences for silent compliments. They themselves... well, I have no boast of knowing what anyone thinks, besides myself (and often not even that), but surely, just beneath pride about the

Old Beliefs, there was always unease of what the daylight might see, and there can never be much distance between that and quotidian shame for its own sake.

But I struggled to understand. Granted bulk of Brittan believes the Viztas can overhear what is spoken at a Myke, how can any faiths be called ridiculous? If others believe instead all life comes from the earth, and that blood, which is life, must go back to the earth to renew it, then the ritual, at Midsummer, of killing a rabbit, a pig and a dog by cutting throats is quite sensible. Wott's mother told me the rabbit (or rabbits, really; lots more than one of each beast were killed that night) stood for increase, the pigs for plenty and dogs for thanking. Still, if things like that must be, it would seem fittinger if they were done in solemn calm, not the excitation of drums and flame, with shrieks of joyment. The next I cannot describe: the beasts, though slashed, could hardly have been dead before they were pulled apart in red-sodden handfuls. Those who could shove warm bits into their mouths thought themselves winners.

But this, Asta insisted, was not the Old Beliefs, which were a matter (so I translate her words) of healing, wooing the earth, seeing all living as one. In this, she reminded me of Forn at Vandennis, telling us the Vandenes were nothing but joy. Old Believers, I told her, had certainly done the nasties I had seen.

I can give nothing like her next words. They were a jumble, part chant, part (as I thought) nonsense. Today, if a chap had to make the best he could of it, it would be that because the sun sometimes burns too bright, and too much rain can bring flood and ruin, these surpluses do not condemn either sun or rain, which are both needed to make the crops grow. It may be this is as much my own invention as what Asta said; after years, perhaps, I think less ill of those Midsummer revels. More must be said about this, in place.

But the women, how can they be re-explained? No word comes — blokes, I mean, boast about their strength, and preen on being enough for any woman at any time, and so we do not speak of a man being raped (men, too, do not bear babes, another reason). Yet what else can it be named, when several woman, mad with fire and unstopping drums and blood, with lots of roughness, unmake a young he-virgin? Older blokes, less fearful, or more afraid to let fear be seen, had more choice and fewer scratches, but it was all as if the night and the rites had let a dark wind out of the earth's deeps, and a chap was tremendously keen, even whilst letting himself be whirled along like a dried leaf, to get back to where words and customs kept the world in place. A chap could feel the power in this caught madness, but for me it came too steep, leaving no jot of what was the best of matings, fellowship, ceremony, not to forget the soothe of laughter. Judgement was fled to brutish beasts, and I, resisting, still became one of them.

Approaching none of what is said here was spoken to my hosts, and I thanked them for letting me in on what few not of their belief had seen. This, you understand, whilst I was learning Myna ways for going from place to hiding place unseen, as cats do, steadily where cover is, and where none, quick and straight after slow considering. Wott soon had word that southward, where Edin might be found, Raug had sent lots of soldiers to mark out the new frontier, and took me to the west instead, right to the borders of Sevenin, where we parted with hope of more meetings. Wott, for one item, wished to be kept up with news about his nephew.

Col was a subject at Sevenin, too — the place, I mean, where Kennet and Cara are, which has the same name as the kingdom. A chappie managed to spiff himself up a bit, but they must've been a bit astonished when I turned up all alone with no servants or soldiers. Still they (dear Cara, especially) made me welcome, and it was super to be back where there were bed-linen and politeness.

Partly because of his long face and thick nether lip, Kennet's sometimes been taken for slow. His speech, too, is careful and a bit limping, but he had been brainy enough to keep friends for his tiny, nearly defenceless kingdom. To spot, also, that the young star of the Vandennis party was cow-eyed over Robin, Kennet's chiefest jewel. Knowing as well as anyone Col's whole history, he tried hard to find out from me if there was a secret about the lad's birth, or what was meant by talk of fulfilled foretells. Even here I still did not know how far it was wise to drop hints in royal houses. I had made mind up Kennet was no risk, but even a mild and friendly king may become less of both if he twigs a plot to rob him of power. On the other hand, Kennet was as ready as any to credit prophecies, and could be a big help making them come true, so I had to do a sort of rope-walk (one I came to know well), neither pooh-

poohing, nor scaring with overmuch eagerness. But this fit in with the course I liked better, the one with less fakery. My truest feeling was, Arfra, if he came, should come without any cheating.

The oddest Kennet said was, he had not heard Col was taught smithing. There was a story about he forged his own sword.

This was new to me, though the story, without Col, was not. In the tales, this is one of the ways Arfra is known to be king, when he makes, or I should say, remakes a sword, everyone else having failed at it. A spiffing example of how tons of us can believe two or even three warring stories at once: the sword is called Scalipal, and in other versions of the Arfra tales the young king either finds it under a stone, or else it is given him by a woman who comes from the water. How all three can be true beats me.

Kennet agreed the story was just like Arfra, and yet he had never heard it before ever Col went to Vandennis.

There was suspicion here of some tricksiness, of all what I must avoid, so I went like one who could hold butter unmelted on his tongue, saying it was often the way, when someone came all at once into light, lots of tales about him are remembered or found, that seemed not worth thinking of before.

Kennet, grimmer than he usually was, said he still remembered Col's fathering. I said nothing, and smiled.

Still at Sevenin, sharp-nosed Nace, Rowan's kinsman, found me, and was bucked to, having thought he would have to ride all the road to Seeyow. We grinned together a little, speaking of how we had outfaced Syme in the spring, and then mourned together no one of Raug could now be chased out of those same lands. But this was not Nace's business with me, and whatever that was made him uneasy.

There was reason. He came, with no written words, to speak for the Lady Rowan, on a question of lawful divorce. I should say, as not before, while plenty of laws were different from realm to realm, we still kept from the days of the Regions (it would be truer to say, we brought back) common laws to do with trade, marriage and the ownership of land. Otherwise there would be interminable muddle, since realm trades with realm, and lots of fellows, as I did, take wives and have lands in realms not their own; the Suvram lands Rowan had brought into the marriage were held by me under title from King

Edlin.

Still I was puzzled, and thought Nace must mean Rowan was asking me to divorce her.  Mine, of course, was the higher rank, and she could claim a divorce only by showing one of the wrongs allowed as grounds by the common law.  But I had not tried to kill her, put her out without clothes, taken to bedding with other blokes, or (as in one lordly case still gossiped after sixty years) to wearing women's clothes.  The real difference, not counting pride, was property: the lands where she lived were mine.

Nace became more nervous than ever.  Rowan must have meant to be discreet, choosing a messenger of such low rank (Nace is no more than a freerider) to say her case, but one nearer my own level would have come to what he had to say with less falter.  At last Nace stammered out Rowan meant to show my ways had become unnatural.

He was afraid of my anger, but for me bafflement took first place; where was her reason?  That instead of her, I had taken the boy Col with me to Vandennis?  She must know that was a legless horse.  Pressed, Nace reddened, mumbling the Lady Rowan had told him I would know what she meant.

I did not, and told him so, and also told him that after so long I was not turned into one of those bullies who treat messengers as if they made the news they carried.  At that Nace nearly smiled, and was able to say while he did not know all the story, Rowan's charges had to do with a girl, the same girl, he believed, as was with me when we stood up to Syme.  According to Rowan all the realms knew this young girl was sleeping in my bed.

Now a chap was angry.  A few weeks ago Rowan had been sure Alison was my natural daughter, and now for the sake of lands she must know I would have given her was pretending to believe this scurf from under a scullery maid's fingernails.  One more "pretending" than that, I think; this was the threat of bringing her charge in front of the court of lords that would have to be assembled if I refused to let her divorce me.  At first I was sure I would do so, mean-minded and absurd as the charge was.  Calmlier, there was more than one argument against that.  Without proof (and proof of what is not true is impossible) Rowan's charge must fail, but she knew me well enough not to fear I would have her hung for slandering of a prince, and she also knew the story of the greedy old lord and the child trained by Thea's Dauwas would become the talk of realms and part of every Tela's bag of goods, each telling adding years to my age and taking months from Alison's. My cousins and my true friends could not believe it, but still its greasy stains would stick to Alison, and might rob her of her future — I don't say the one Thea hinted, but for any husband of rank.

Rowan had been both daring and shrewd, but I also pondered what bitterness for the past and what fear for the future could bring her to an act so spiteful. It might be she had a suitor, or at least a man in regard, and was grabbing at this chance of being free and landed whilst still young and beautiful. When it came to it, only my pride was against the divorce, so long as Alison was unsmirched.

So I told Nace to tell Rowan instead, as was lawful for my higher rank, I would divorce her with her free consent (this would need her father and another male relative to agree I had used no force or trickery). She would keep the lands brought into the marriage, and the house with what was in it, except for clothes and belongings of mine. With all sternness, I added for Nace, Rowan knew the charge she had made was wholly false, and if it was heard again I would know only Rowan or he himself could have spread it, and would call on the severest punishments of the law. Nace muttered he thought, but could not be sure, he was the only fellow Rowan had told this tale to, but for certain he would never repeat it to anyone.

Larger affairs are waiting for the telling, but I'll say here that before the end of the year Rowan and I were face to face (for the last time) with witnesses; she consented to my divorcing her and I deeded her the lands in Suvram, and our eyes scarcely met; at its ending the marriage found no more meaning than in all its beginnings.

While in the south, I went to visit Col. He made a joke of what Kennet had told me, the tale of forging his own sword. "Well, it was meant as a joke. A fighter admired the hardness of my edge, and asked who made it. I told him, I myself. Truly, I helped; I pumped the bellows for Rayman." In Rayman's manner, Col chanted:

"*It IS a SWORD of SPAIN, the ICE-brook's TEM-per.* Spain was a country, like Brittan, in old times."

"So someone told me," I agreed.

"Is it true there is a girl now, Alison, at Seeyow?  That Robin said, when I was at Sevenin, and she dark-haired and pretty, and I would like her, though she is of no birth."

"Why did Robin say that?"

"Teasing," coolly, as he might have said needlework; this was a game girls did.  "Robin knows."

"What does she know?"

"That I like her, and not any other."

It seemed he missed my point; Robin's remark about birth could be taken as a warning to Col himself.  "If Sevenin can live on," I said, "Robin will be liked by lots, and is to have her own choice."

"Her father," with a dash of sour, "no matter what was vowed, will try to choose for her."  There was no need, after all, to remind him about rank.  To say his father, Donal, was great among Mynas cut small ice with people for whom all Mynas were offal.

Col's next question, then, though a stunner, came not from nowhere: "Am I to be Arfra?  You know what I mean."

I did, and had a thousand times imagined how this might come into full day, sometimes at my promptings, sometimes helped by prophecies oddly fulfilled, never just like this.  My answer was none I had made ready: "Do you think so?"

Col weighed it.  "I could be.  That, as Marten enjoys to say, may be heard in two senses.  For the ignorant, surely, I could be made to seem like Arfra.  Easily."

Plainly, it was more than the past few moments he had been chewing at this.  "Would you go for that?"

He jutted his lower lip, as if at a new question.  "The other kings, lords in their own realms, would not be so ready to cry welcome."

"In tales, not before all other hopes have been kiboshed does Arfra come again, or is to come again.  There could be a time when even the nobs might hail a king who could give them back their lands — "

"Why should he do that?"

"A high king needs lesser lords to serve him.  One law to keep the peace, and a league of kingdoms." That had always been my notion.

"If there could be a king like that, he would need the law in his own hands, and the power of life or death over the others."

"In tales, Arfra is just and merciful, giving and forgiving."

"Raug and its rulers are not so, yet they rule."

"With bitter enemies everywhere. In the end they must fail to rule All Brittan, no matter how well their soldiers fight."

"Not much failing now." Col's hand went to the hilt of the sword he'd made up, as if he was itching to be in the fight. "Great Suvram is lesser than Stanglin, now, if you do not number what is kept here, by Edin. He knows how to lead fighters."

A chappie was, it may be guessed, smiling with rue. "To my less young eyes, it would still be failing, to make Brittan one by fear, and by killing all those with different beliefs. I need hope, too."

"Marten says, to hope is a mistake. It stops true learning."

"To go as deep as Marten, you have to leave the world. Where he is, he can do without hope. But I know this, and nothing to do with what I like to believe; if people, some living under the eyes of the Addas, are going to look for signs of Arfra's coming, it won't be just King Vandis with a different name."

"Vandis," Col said in scorn. "At his investing, Forn was whispering in his ear what to say."

"There are wiser bozos than the new king," I agreed. "Still, even if you bundled into one the lineage of Vandis, Forn's cleverness and the strength of Syme, he still could never be Arfra the Great. Tyranny is not what the kings in the League of the West fight for."

"They fight for themselves. Some for the love of fighting, but mostly to keep what they have."

"True," I said, a bit put off by his way of saying it. "True, so long as you mean, not just the land and the orts they own, but what they have in their heads and their hearts. Since the borders of Suvram were redrawn, more than one has come to join Edin who could have kept his house and his lands by no more than swearing to the Vandene faith."

"I know. In a year, Edin's strength has nearly doubled. He needs more captains."

That, with a smile inside, I ignored. "Of Arfra the tales say he brings together because to serve him is freedom."

"— and will do so again," Col finished. Like all the worn Telas' phrases we were now putting into Print English, it sounded far more stirring than we were used to. "Could I be him, really?"

The twofold meaning was still there. "Not now. But there may be a time. Thea believed it; she held through your father you descend from the Stewards, and your birth was part of prophecy."

For no reason I could clearly explain I still held back the Bronze Rod business. Col's face always closed at mention of his father, but now he was bright again. "Thea had a fame herself."

Of course (it came to me), we are all superstitious if the stake is high enough. Oh, certainly, especially we of Seeyow, we might brush off what is told by a fair-time seer, about marrying well and having four children, but no guy alive can put a bored face on when a prophet others hold in awe foretells his greatness. If it were me (and with Marten I am the least superstitious person I know) I might laugh, and likely wonder, as I had for Col's sake, how such prophecies might be made use of, but buried under all the cold ashes there would still be a small red ember of interest, because such words are like flatteries, hugged no matter how false they might seem.

"Thea still has repute," I said. "Some would need to hear no word more than that she named you. For most, other signs would be needed."

"You mean, I must prove myself." Col's swift eagerness made me reach out to press his arm in affection.

"As yet, making no claim," I agreed. "As life is, perhaps the time will never come; even Thea allowed prophecies can get lost on their way. But if you are to be called from the shadows you must be ready, and you must be seen as worthy."

Col gave me a long look sideways. "All the worth of Arfra would not be enough, without Merdyn's work. I wish Marten was not called mad by so many." So he too had connected the names. If the time came, it would not be forgotten Col, like Arfra, had the teaching of a big-bearded, island-dwelling sage. I said, "But Marten, you know as well as I, can put his antic disposition on and off, and lots guess he is only mad northwest." (These words are from another of William Shakespeare's tales, and only now I see how clever a joke I made; Merdyn's name anciently was Merlin, and who better than a merlin to tell a hawk from a handsaw? Marten is also a bird's name, of a gentler sort, or else a furry beast, a chap is never sure.)

"Does Marten have any thought I could be Arfra?"

"Marten has less and less time for what might happen to realms."

"But you, not Marten, are called the Magician. More now, I expect, since Vandennis."

A chappie can be bally dim at times. It came to me at last Col's very first question, *am I to be Arfra*? had never been what he sought to know; his own resolve was made, and he knew very well he might (in one of the two senses) answer the prophecies. He was asking whether I would help make it come about.


So now it was in the open; too soon, a chappie thought. But that was both foolish and presuming in me, to think I could ready the way for an Arfra without telling him, so to keep in my own hands the deciding, whether or not he was fit. Again, if not my hands, whose? A bally daunting business, to come accidentally on the power, maybe, to work a great magic: Col I now saw, reading the signs, had given long thought or long dreaming to his chance at Arfra, but so far (I judged) his dreams had busied themselves about the ways of becoming, the glory of being Arfra, less if any about what Arfra might be for Brittan, its folk. That was my part, and like Merdyn I would have the blame if my choice was a bad one, my own blame if no one else's. Yet it was not my prophecy, nor my Brittan to teach; Col had the right to read his own destiny, and even to craft it, if he could.

"As I say," accordingly, "talk may start to stir about old prophecies moving to their harvest." And still I kept to myself, for whatever reason, the tale of the Bronze Rod.

Col's next shot was miles off. "The League of the West. They would bring forward Arfra, if it could stop Vandis."

"They would not. Not till the very end, when it might be too late. You said it yourself."

"But it might be if you told them. They follow what you say."

"Not if to make themselves lesser kings, and to bow to a boy whose story they all know very well." This was near being cruel, and Col's face went dark, but a chap had to do it, with the other fellow's dreams outrunning what was real and possible.

"If I could persuade them," I went on, "I would not. That is not how Arfra is to appear, as a war-banner waved by the princes in their fight against Raug. The League, as you say, fights all it can, to keep what it has, and could still go down to defeat shouting the name of Arfra, instead of six different kings. No, Arfra is another thing. He has to be found and known by the ordinary people, of Raug as well, not belonging to the realms and the rulers there are now, but new, so he can make a new Brittan." Late, a chap at last learnt Thea's lesson.

"He would still have the Vandenes to overthrow."

"Their priests," I corrected. "And priests are thrown down when they have no followers. Do you think the ordinary people in the farms and villages of Raug have forgotten the tale of Arfra, or stopped believing in foretells, because they call themselves Vandene? Fat chance."

Col now was proper fuddled; hearing less than asked for and much more than he desired. This, too, was a test of his metal, and I was not disappointed. He said, "If you tell me your plan, I'll try to understand."

It was a plan given heaps of thought to — or rather, a thought that like a sweat-sipping fly of a hot afternoon kept circling and coming back, no matter how much I tried to wave it away. Thea had said I was finished with princes, and must now be a Tela in Arfra's cause. It had seemed a way of speaking, but now I knew whether she meant it so or not a Tela was exactly what I must become, travelling realms to leave the thought Vandis could never be Arfra, the true Arfra would step from the shaddas when his time came.

"How could you?" frowning. "Raug is now more than half Brittan, and Forn does as he pleases there. You would be dead in a week."

"As myself. But who, away from the courts, knows my face, or could point me out, dressed in rough clothes with my beard untrimmed? As a Tela I can spread my tale, and if challenged can say it is only a tale I picked up along the way, as Telas do."

"Wouldn't it still be dangerous? Someone might know you, and even if not, you know there is not safety for anyone who travels, with the realms as they are. It sounds dangerous. And unsure. Evan, I mean, how long do you think it will take one man to travel all the tiny places of the realm with this story?"

"We've got time," but I did not tell him near seven years, much longer for him than for me. "Brittan, I fear, will have to be worse than it now is before Arfra's time comes. But there is no need to visit every corner, not if the people are as ready as seems for a tale of coming change. If all the grass in Brittan had died, and a bloke had a pocketful of seed, he would not have to go everywhere grass had been to make the lands green again. The winds are an ally, and people talk to people."

"But so slow," Col repeated with chafe in his voice. "If the League of the West believed in Arfra, then it would be talked of everywhere. An Arfra, not saying it has to be me."

"Everywhere? In all the courts, you mean." I knew he was back to thinking about Robin, yearning to have the rank to woo her. Not all of Thea's dying words had to be true, no matter where that might leave Alison. But he was being a dunce, and carefully I explained to him what a minute ago he had known: no ruler and no ruler's son, friendly as he had been, dances jigs to hear about a boy who may supplant him and his line. I said, "You are not to tell anyone about what we plan. Not friends, not Robin, no one. Except Edin, perhaps."

"So I must just wait?"

"And work. Even if there were no rivalries, even if the League of the West would welcome the coming of Arfra, I still would not try to bring it about, not yet. Merdyn, you know, is teacher and judge of Arfra, as well as his kingmaker." A bit thick, I suppose, said to someone who might come to rule over all of us, but Col had to find right words to say about how a king should rule, before a chap would say flatly, "Here is our Arfra."

Col understood me. He gave a grin, and made his own point. "You may find me worthy, but you'll be the only one, if others can say I was kept in the nest while the wars went on. I have to fight."

He was right, I sadly saw. Like all our great, Arfra is a warrior first, then a lawgiver. But I said, "Nor is anyone hailed much once dead. When you join to Edin's wars — " (Here I had to wave calming hands, as the boy sprang up with a shout.) "He'll be your teacher, and you must listen and learn, and be prudent, not just brave. Even a big gargoyle with Syme's standing, as you've heard, knows when not to fight. We now believe, Edin and I, Forn's main armies will be busy for a time, making sure of Raug's new slab of Suvram. In spring, maybe, there will be fresh trouble in Gwyn. After winter becomes over, if he likes the look of you, Edin can take you to battle." As well as the reasons given, it had come to me (sadly) Col might well be safer among soldiers than anywhere else in Brittan, till he could have a gawd of his own, bound by oaths.

"He will, he does. He teaches me, when there is time. Besides, he saw me win at Vandennis."

Crops sprout and ripen much the same, but not every season has the same measure in a lifetime; Col was grown years from the boy I had taken with me to that royal gathering. There were ways it was like that spring far ago of my first meeting with Thea — yes, because the same had been done; what happened had shown him he was not the same as others, and like me (only with me it had no name) he had been given his life's work. Both of us now had our chores, and the next day I left, riding through a strange warm drizzle to the north shore of Wezram, for the first time making my return to Seeyow by water.

To do so, the whole length of Farragwyn has to be coasted, but at that season it was less tempest-tost under the dark cliffs. It would have surprised my father no matter how clumsy with a sword, I am a good sailor; we talk as if sea-sickness is in some way unmanly. Not for any good reason; Worrel, I remember, hated boats, and even the crossing from Bris to March would pale his face. Our boats are small and not agile; knowing there were once bigger, much better crafts, even made of steel, I still doubt there ever could have been ships to carry thousands in comfort, if there were not the ancient, crumbling wharves to match the legend of their size. Some, far from the biggest, but still vast, are at the northwestern corner of Seeyow. Not where I landed, but on the small, separate island we call Little Seeyow.

This chapter is still Alison's, and I came back to another pickle, the big house dour, and Maire grim but satisfied; my orders the girl must not be whipped meant she was a prisoner in her own bedroom, and had eaten nothing but bread for several days, having been caught in the stables with a boy not thirteen. This was abacking, and Maire gave me more of the tale, not failing to repeat that without my command the girl's punishment would have been sorer, but soon done.

Filled with dark and disappointed thoughts, still in my salty clothes, I went to where Alison was. Lying on her bed, she was pale from being indoors, but calmly puzzling away at her reading, gave me a wan smile in greeting, and held out the book, thumb marking a word. It was *throughout*, I remember, and a chap said it for her and said what it meant, reminding even in mid-word *gh* might have no sound so far as we could tell, though perhaps it once had. She said, she should not have forgotten that, and was upsetter than the lapse merited.

Now I asked and she admitted she had indeed been found in the stables with Pol, the son of the carpenter, Arral, but not undressed, as I had been told. Alison's manner was too simple to be doubted when she said she had taken no garment off, and Pol kept his shirt.

For the last time, I hope, in all the bringing up of Alison, I did what others expected, and became angry. Remember, I was fresh from the Midsummer nightmare, and knew she had been brought up in or near those same lewd Old Beliefs. I had only to leave the room and order Bett to beat her; a chap did not have to see it, or hear her cries (but she had not cried out before). My own standing seemed to make it needful; Arral, the boy's father, was no servant but his own man, and it would be said I gave licence to my dauwa's brat to turn good boys into lechers, unless Alison was punished in a way any noodle could understand. I told her she seemed little sorry for what she had done, but we might soon find a way to make her so. In saying it could all at once be heard my own father's voice; my father, of all men known the one I had no aim to become.

The cat-look was back in her eyes, not reproach but near a triumph of knowingness. That reproached me; from the word go she'd had wisdom not to trust in my given word.

So, a little, I faltered. Alison, take heed, had lived a goodish spell among women whose life was coupling with men. Even so, as I threw at her, she must have been taught it was otherwise for gentles, and the boy's age made it worse; a man grown could have persuaded, even threated her, but with Pol she must have been teacher. She did not deny this.

With my made anger working up again she did say she had never spread herself for that or any other boy or bloke, and when she added she had never meant to, there came into her voice a hurt; she was miffed it could be thought of her. She spoke of Thea, who taught whilst for the Dauwas, whose lives would otherwise be much leaner, there was no shame in whoredom, there were and would always be other rules for Alison, who was to be loved by men, and have choice of who took her in honour.

Though this bemused me, it was plain as Lydd's nose (in age, Lydd's fondness for beer was beaconed on his face) the very idea she would choose to be loved by this Pol blister was an insult to her.

Still, I was not yet ready to let ire go (like drink, anger is a feeling of surging strength, and a spiffing excuse for doing hurt), and with sarcasm demanded what then she had been doing with Pol untrousered. She answered with cool patience: she had been teaching him how best to please himself when, as he whined or boasted was at least thrice a day, he became a man too soon to woo or to afford a woman.

This story has not been told before. If, soon after the happening, I had recounted it, say to one of my cousins, or to Maire herself, I know it would have seemed not much lesser crime than had been charged against Alison, because I could never have echoed the note in her voice, more what was not there than what was, no giggle or leer or hint of shame. It was what the Dauwas did, she explained, for young sprouts who hadn't their price, or who complained too long went by between one visit of the Guild and the next: to Alison it was somewhere between a game and an act of kindness, not real trade, for which money changed hands.

Here, because I had yen to, I reached out and hugged Alison, partly in relief, partly to salute such knowing innocence. All the same, it was no go, and assuring her she was not to have any more punishment, I began as I best could to explain just why.

A question we stuck on. This was Seeyow, where Alison, though as yet lacking the words and skills by which Seeyow proceeds, had already learnt no belief is taken without scrutiny. In the end a chap could do not better than to say the ways of chastity and a woman's good fame were as they were, the ways of this time. Again she asked why, and with this child-woman, bland as a five-year-old, knowing as a Thealing, I could feel the hard ground swim and slide under my feet as not since, in ladhood, Marten had first asked my reasons for keeping to the tale of the Viztas. At last I reminded that Thea, too, often said there must be somewhere a border to the asking of whys, and a sensible truce with what was. Why ferreting after why, Thea had said, left in the end no meaning in everything; too much *why* had taken the ancient world from glory to its shattering.

About to content herself, Alison all at once asked if that was not the Vandene way, to take what was without questioning. After thought and three bad starts, I decided it was quite the opposite. The Adda-priests said there was no need to ask because there was one known reason for all, but Thea said, and I was with her, we must know there are always going to be some puzzles outside explaining. Perhaps it was so (Thea, it seems, told Alison this) that the value put on a woman's chastity came from a chap's need to know he had fathered his own children, but that did not mean she could do as she bally well pleased so long as it could not get her with child, while to ask why men had that need took us into the magic of blood: all our rules about when and for whom we bared our bodies had no why in the end, except we were not dogs and were not flies, not the cannibals that each other eat, the anthropophagi, or chappies whose heads do grow beneath their shoulders.

That, perhaps because it sounded like Rayman, made Alison laugh. Then, as best she could with the few words of Print English creeping into speech much like Thea's, she asked if it might not be better, then, if a bloke could manage it, to be Vandene, and always know what was good and right and true.

Other than the voice of Thea echoed there, and it came to me there would be more to Alison. Till now she had seemed — not just an added care, since a chap had taken to her from the first, but a worry, surely, when larger concerns needed seeing to. Now I could see as she learnt more words, Alison was going to be good company, one to listen as well as talk to, in time even a friend. I told her to bathe her face, and took her to the kitchen for real food.

Maire, when she found Alison was not to have more punishment, was as sarcastic as she dared, wondering what the world would become if girls were given such licence. She asked also what was to be done about the boy, whose father was said to have thrashed him, then sent him into hiding to escape worse.

Till then I had not considered there would be general expectation of an agonied fate for Pol, and when with Alison I went back to my own littler house, I sent for the father, whose carpenter's shop was just across a scrap of wasteland from me.

Arral is small with shoulders both stooped and narrow. Deep lines run down his cheeks and out from the corners of his eyes, making him look, not like an old geezer, but an unwell child; his skin is dust grey. Bruited as a good craftsman whether turning a tool-handle or building a stair, his speech is so clotted with the accents of Gwyn that even I, who've heard that speech all my life, can miss words. Another Gwynishness is his inner fire; with his dark, gleaming eyes and laden tones he can make joining of wood seem like part of a new religion.

He was scared to be summoned so, but let his tongue canter, and before I could ask told me his son swore he never touched the lady, nor she him, swore it under threat of a second and worse beating, not that there had been any stint to the first. Arral was trying to suggest the business in the stables had been not more than childish foolery, but his insistence on the heaviness of Pol's punishment seemed to argue the other way. A chap did not even bother to point that out, having little attention left for this, now no more than an excuse for bringing Arral to my house and into my plans.

In stories kings and princes go wandering disguised as nobodies, but never explained is how they work the change. I was well known here on Seeyow, and if seen riding out in old clothes on a poor horse would soon be gossiped about. I foresaw setting out and returning lots of times over the next few years, and at one of the Stoneplain gatherings or some other a chance word, servant to servant, could be the end of me; a seeming traveller of no rank could vanish without accounting ever given.

Arral, I knew, had a brother, Will, on the mainland, an odd blighter with more trades than someone of his skills should follow. Starting in the family trade, he had taken to boat-building, and was now sometime fisherman as well, besides ferrying people and goods back and forth to Seeyow. He did not, like lots who worked that trade, live on the Strait under the shadow of the once-great castle, but a little way up the coast, a wilder part, with dark mountains rising behind. There was a village nearby, but that quarter did not teem with people, and the road which went twisting inland was a lonely one, just the job for me. Back in the days when feeling was strongest against the Brown Hares, Will had brought Mynas of that clan on their secret visits to me or to Marten. He used a lonely cove on the north shore of the island, but for me he'd have to go to Little Seeyow. Perched on cliffs there, there is a crumbling castle or house, still sound in parts, where hardly anyone would go, search me why. Besides churches, there are places all over Brittan which people shun; this place was said to be the last home of the old Counters of Seeyow, where they had been safe for a few years. When he was younger Marten had often, and especially when house affairs kept him from measurings or the stars, said he would take that building and use it for his work. He had never done so, but now, except for the few who shared my secret, it was understood the Lord Evan was going to that same place to find lonely peace for his book studies, and might at times spend a month or more there. Strange doings for ordinary blokes, but to be expected in a magician. By this time there were people who had known me for years who did not smile when they called me that.

When he heard his brother's name Arral thought (he was right, but I didn't care) I had guessed that was where his young limb had been sent, and began to explain Will needed extra hands for autumn fishing. That I quieted, telling him that so long as the egg understood this would never be a bragging tale, I meant to do no more against him. Still, it was a hold I had on the family, whose silence as well as service I needed.

For both, both brothers must also be paid. Earlier that would not have been worth saying, but all at once a chappie was on his way to becoming a figure of jokery in our stories, Lord Sixpence (we do not say the name just so, but *sixpence*, I now know, was once a small piece of money). I was giving back my wife's dower-lands in Suvram, and if six kings said Evan should be heir in Gwyn, Evan's sister had all the take from the family lands there. All that was left to me, besides small holdings on Seeyow which hardly paid their own way, were my estates in March. Fully half of those moneys went to keeping men under arms in that besieged kingdom.

It was Rayman, more and more my deputy in all, who told me with the divorce a fact I was now spending more than could be taken in. It was true, as we chewed over, I could have done with fewer to serve me, but these were not odd-jobbers hired daymeal at a fair, they were families bound through generations to mine; a chap must find small presents of money or property to who married or gave birth, settlings for those too old to work, and we judge quarrels, help name children (in more ways than one), see the dead given right burying and (some of us) weep at loss. I was not mooded to choose which must be told to find other work.

My armed cumny was otherwise; quite a few, especially the young and wifeless, were bored with jogging beside me, and would rather be with Edin, whose rebellion was adventure. Edin's renown brought him young men who gave no farting who ruled in Suvram: how much more those of my own cumny who, chosen always for not caring how others believed, must see Raug and its Adda-priests, those who forced belief on others, as enemy. By passing word to Shan that any of my fighters who wanted it were free of their oath and could join Edin, I added to Edin's strength, and helped my own cause, vis-a-vis the moolah. Rayman was no end bucked.

Another explaining left out of stories is how wandering rulers make sure of a realm left when they come back. Rayman was going to have a load to bear. He was one of very few in my confidence. Both Marten and Maire had to believe in my studies on Little Seeyow, because Marten, thinking about where the pole star was, or pondering the weight of burnt bones, could not be trusted, if he knew about my travels, not to chat in front of servants or visitors.

Between me and Maire there was now a coolness that could not be helped. Plainly we were never going to agree about Alison's upbringing, and I decided the girl would now stay at my house. Iona, by the bye, was gone and married, to a guy who would treat her well, or else (as he well understood) have no unbroken bone in his body. She was the last of my, well, the odd old word seems to have been *concubines* — and our tender parting was more paining for me because of hard tasks, the changes, the hurry there was. Now that there is time for such a word, I am too far away to find it.


Not far from me lived Sheal, a woman of fair birth, cousin in some way to Caif's mother. At the time of Col's babyhood, she was Caif's companion and ran her household in those last four desert years of Caif's life. Sheal was eldered now, less able to see to her own comfort, and when I asked her to my house to live and help instruct Alison in dress and manners, she said yes, once promised there would be no border-fighting with Maire, as in Col's case. There was more to this than different views about the training of children; Sheal had no money of her own, but believed (with fair warrant) her birth was better than Maire's. It might be Sheal was just a hair more apt than needed be to show or tell about how those of the best blood behave, a disease of poor cousins. Yet considering Alison's readiness to chatter with serving girls (for that matter, to debag a carpenter's son), I did not think a helping of Sheal's haught could do any harm, while on Sheal's side I hinted Alison's birth was better, her destiny grander than could now be seen. If Her Shealship took that to mean the girl was my own untold daughter, she was far from the only one.

The day I told Alison my plans was cold and rainy, not promising for lonely wanderings. We were at my house, and before I could begin Alison told me she had some lines to say, and proudly recited a piece Rayman had taught her, from one of William Shakespeare's plays, *I do not know one of my sex!*; a ridiculous play, but all about yet another magician on an island, and Alison did it so well it was hard to keep in consideration she understood no more than half (perhaps) of the words. Quite a bit even I don't get, except that like lots of William Shakespeare it glues itself in a chap's head. I made mind Rayman must give her other books to study. This learning was a good trick, but like fine needlework taught to one who can yet not put back a missing button. He should give her, I said then, Tulsingham, who, as well as lying less than William Shakespeare, has far more words for use every day; there are words in William Shakespeare I've known half my life and never found another place for; fardels, quietus, orisons.

Before much more was said she asked whether I was going away again, and whether it had to do with foretells and the Bronze Rod. When I told her my plan, she said suddenly she would go with me. Telas were often seen with young apprentices, and she could dress herself as a boy (that was William Shakespeare again!) and be very helpful to me.

This was plain loony. With her light bones, fine hands and plumed eyelashes Alison would never pass for a boy, certainly not for a boy who would be any safer from harm than a girl, and she knew she had another future. Yet she was near waterworks when I refused her offer.

Jogged I might not return, I made a will with Rayman. His rank was now formally raised to freerider (though he seldom used a horse), which would help him in his dealings with Sheal. He too strongly held I should have a companion with me, but his very fair, easily remembered looks could only draw attention, and he was needed here, besides. In the will we drew I asked Kennet and Cara to take Alison, but also allotted her rents of her own. I had no other heir, but there were arrangements to be made for those of my household (I recalled Worrel telling me never to provide too generously for servants in a will; those closest to you should never think a chap worth more dead than alive). That done, and a simpler version made in our own signs in case anyone thought Rayman was making it up himself, it was all ready; I would leave at middle night.

Alison, told that, was very quiet at meal, and vanished without a farewell. A chap first thought she was sulking, but I need not have worried; in an hour she came back, dressed in boy's clothes she had borrowed, and with her dark hair sheared to cheekbone length. A good girl, but the answer was still no. Nix. Negative. What Sheal might spout when she saw Alison thus was outside my imagining.

## Tellings

Landed at sickly first light with my sorry horse on empty shore to the north of the strait, I made inland by a rough, uphill, little-used way, wishing first to lose myself and so begin, as it were newborn, my Tela's life.  All that day, seeing only a few humans, I kept away from dwellings and busied roads, and for the first time since childhood felt terror at the cool hint of nightfall, going much beyond just knowing it would be cold (or cold and wet), and I had no bed to go to, no hope of fire or hot food.  It was a feeling I came to greet as an old friend, or rather as a familiar, tested foe; in late afternoon a cloud crossing the sun can bring that grab at the heart.

If this were my story I could fill chapters with my solitary journeys as a Tela, the danger and comfortlessness, long boredoms and often annoyances that were large, in their time, to me.  It was other than a chap had expected: it was less hard as feared to endure weather, rough beds (if any), and the food, mostly poor and often scant, of the common people.  It should be said I put up with more of that than any other Tela; any, at least, who knew his craft.  Real Telas called, whenever they could, at the houses of the royal and the rich (in my house, as had been in my father's, we always gave a Tela a bed for the night, and money for the road, and had them at table).  But that was no go for me, since a great house was the one place I might be known.  In amicable western lands, Lord Evan the Tela could have been made into a jape, but still it would be a gag that travelled fast, and would be the kibosh of any secret wanderings for me.  Within Raug, I could not guess what my fate would be if I were rumbled.  I would be held, no doubt, and Forn be told.  He would soon see no one at home could know where a chap was, and it was his free choice whether I lived or died.  On the whole I expected he would have me killed, brother-in-law or not, for all the botheration I had caused him and could in future.  So bread and broth and rough lodging was the utmost I ever could get for my tales, and often I had to sleep under a hedge.  This was especially true when someone poor, trying to be kind, told me the road for some big house where I would be sure of a welcome.  So as not to seem mad, I would have to be seen making for it, ofttimes leaving behind the real chance of lodging, though meaner.

How it might be if I felt doomed to a bally lifetime of no better a chap can't say; knowing if I lived I would be going back to the coddlings of Seeyow made it possible to bear hardship.  It even helped with the fear.

What I expected to be difficultest, the telling of tales to the lowly, turned out to be easy as pie for me.  Quite often, after I became practiced, it was a real tickle to be listened to, not as Lord Evan, but because of what a chap had to tell.  What was harder to put on was the rank of a Tela.  Prince passing for beggar sounds easy enough in a story, but the ones who made up the stories were not princes, never knew what it was to be one from birth.  As lords go, I am not called stuck up, but still it was hard for me, my first days as a Tela, to let a village woman tell me my news was stale, and an old cottager shout at me to speak louder, or to have to take my gloomy horse off the side of the way to let soldiers pass, all without showing how irking it was to a chap.

Telas are lots like the wandering merchants, bulk of them Mynas, who buy as well as sell; my little stock of news was at whiles added to with village stories, which I could better in telling. For a time in my first weeks, now across the borders of Raug, I was following a couple of days behind another Tela, and kept meeting with poor jokes he left behind, about the divorce of the Lord Evan. Of course, a chap had to show no offence, indeed to go them portions better. Happily, they were the usual, about the lord not knowing how, or not having what he needs, to keep his wife smiling; if any scurf about Alison had come into it I might not have been so jocose.

Tit for tat, it was all Covent Garden to a cabbage what I told would in turn be taken up by another Tela. My intention was to start people thinking of the Arfra stories, but I was cautious, at first, about joining them directly to the name of Col, who was, anyway, as yet little known to the common; there was time ahead for that, and too plain hints would give Adda-priests the chance to argue them away. Also some caitiffs might get the idea of croaking Col, to be at the safe side.

In Old Raug (by which I mean places that were Raug even when I was born) the ordinary people, when unwatched, were friendlier than expected. There, I found lots of anxiousness about their Vandene faith. If they heard a made-up story having a happy ending, without a big plug for the goodness of the Viztas, hearers would become uneasy, and more times than not someone would add a worshipful after-end. Yet to me this seemed to come from fear rather than real piety, like the dull thanks of a child scolded or scourged into manners.  No doubt that these plain people were very afraid of the Addas and their Myka gawds, and had reason to be.  But this too made them more helpful than anyone about where I risked running into soldiery on the hunt for disbelief: they were also used to the idea a chap could desire to give such things a berth without having to be any sort of criminal.

Another dodge I soon found was, even with types who believe everything, there are different kinds of belief.  It was best, I learnt, to put the Arfra tales in amongst small bits of country news too dull to doubt.  If they came after another tale of marvels, Arfra's doings were still believed, but in the same way as dragons, aeroplanes, or electricity, or the king with the golden touch, real somewhere, which no one ever expected to see.

In that first year I made four journeys.  The longest took me farther north than I had been since the time we brought poor Caif back from Cumba, and I was ten weeks gone from Seeyow, returning on a squally evening stung with snow, near the half of the year, midwinter.  It was so spiffing to see Alison again: in her life and the life of her learning ten weeks was a lot, and she was so full of grinnings to see me back, and so eager to show off what she had newly read, with Rayman or alone, it made me forget my aches.  But she also had (always) an ear greedy to devour up discourse about my travels, and we found plenty such pliant hours.

I stayed there for the worst of winter.  Marten, all at once, had descended from his tower, and in the rottenest gales would still come stumbling and flapping down the hill to my house, more beggarlike than ever I was as a Tela, his clothes lumpy and foodstained under his ragged cloak. He had been fond of Alison right off, and I believe he aimed to be sure she was not given untruths to believe; he started again where we had been thirty years ago, ranting out the old doubts and older jokes about the Viztas, more scorning than ever lives could be ordered by such silliness. Alison was large-eyed and silent at his big speeches; neither I nor Rayman ever told her what or what not to believe. Sheal, though, when she was with us, showed pain at slights to the Viztas, and I tried to give her business to do elsewhere when Marten came.

Not always clear now when considering daily things, Marten still kept his keen edge for thought. After food sometimes he and Rayman would dispute learning, and Alison sat quiet, taking in all she could, as if increase of appetite grew by what it fed on. Those words come from one of William Shakespeare's plays; when I said them to Alison, but years later, she said, "It can be so with learning, but do you think it ever could have been with the married? Or should be?" In the play it is of a man and wife, but Alison has never forgotten all the husbands who were Thea's clients. I said in answer, "I don't know what should be. Rowan, I believe, was poisoned by *should*."

(Later on, it must be mentioned, Marten put up with from Alison what he would not from anyone else, surely not Maire, a gentle concern after his health.)

Again, that is aside from my story. One night with a wind moaning outside Rayman said to Marten that if, then, old, hard devices had been done, as they both believed, unhelped by any all-wise Viztas, then surely one who could say how the stars and not-stars wound about each other in the sky (by which he meant Marten himself) could also tell how machines were made. Most, he knew, needed powers we can never bring back, but in the beginning simpler machines must have been done, since some were needed to make the later ones.

We had been talking about pulleys, as they were called. Any nit knows by circling the rope about a smooth tree, you can pull more than if you simply pull, and Marten now said there had been windings of ropes, or chains were still better, with certain patterns of wheels, by which Alison's slender arms could be strong enough to lift the end of a farm-cart. He had in a stained old book part of a drawing showing this machine, called winch, and he could think out what was not there.

Rayman said, "Nay, then. There is naught of metal a man can draw that I can't smith." This, in its way, was as much a facer as Marten's renewed taste for company; Rayman had not swung his hammer in three years. But out of this talk came the Seeyow Winch, although the famous one was not the first built. That one Marten broke, trying heavier and heavier loads, but not before he had shown with its handle turned fast by Alison it could indeed lift a cart. In making the second, stronger winch, which can still be seen where the boats dock, helping to load and unload heavy cargo, we had help from another master-smith, whose curious part in this tale will be told in its place. It must be said here, however, this first machine was the beginning for devices now coming more and more into use everywhere, like potters' wheels and spinners worked by pressing with the feet, and other tools to save sweat.

Already I've run ahead again, because the worst of winter

had passed, and I returned from another of my hidden journeys, before the first winch was finished. With Forn and his squadrons of Addas still busy in the new-ceded territories, and only Edin's cumnies doing any fighting, Raug's borders had been quiet for the first year of its new king's reign.

That could not go on; two kings, Yew of Niragwyn and Jon of Farragwyn, plainly had only short times to live. Neither of the two places, often seen as a single kingdom, could have father-to-son succession, and Forn could be trusted to make what he could of that.


This was a third year, again time for midsummer at Gridge. There, Yew of Gwyn, with not-far-distant death as plain as writing in his face, let it be known to the gathered princes he at last had chosen who was to follow him as ruler. My sister Gwynis.

Excepting Raug, the other kingdoms, led by those of the west (Neal was again present for the failing Jon) at once made plain they saw this as wrongful. For a younger sister to be advanced over an elder brother cast doubt on any law of succession; that my father had willed our lands in Gwyn to my sister did not alter what everywhere was law and custom. In a trice I was surrounded by friends naming me for a kingship they knew very well a chap had no desire for.

Beneath this, not so publicly bruited, there was, of course, the sureness the husband of Gwynis, Forn, would become the real ruler, turning Niragwyn into a mere province of Raug, one dividing Farragwyn (and Seeyow with it) from its friends in Sevenin and Marchlen. Vandis was alone in approving Yew's choice. Not even the threat of extinction (as the tale was told) could make the northern kingdoms consent, while Tobert of Stanglin told Yew his wits must have gone with his hearing (Yew had become very deaf). Reporters who were there said even the spaces between blotches on Yew's face turned purple, and he shouted any king has the right to choose his own heir, which sounds brave, but never has been true.

And Forn, Yew's blandisher for years, where was he? Careful not to be heard in any open debate, he did come privately to see me. This was usual for Gridge, but ever since the fright I had from Syme, my appetite for phony courtesies had gone, and he could not miss the saw edge on my voice when I regretted being unable to accept the invitation he sent by his captain.

Forn answered that Syme was a champion warrior, but not always the best for carrying a message. His only meaning was to say Col would always find a welcome at Vandennis, and that was still true.

This was too silly for an answer in kind. After enduring my silence, Forn said he heard the boy was not now with us at Seeyow.

"That is true," I answered. Though I did not then know it, Edin had left him in Sevenin, where the absence of Robin, here at Gridge, must have been miffing him. I told Forn he must have come for embassies more important than phony courtesies. Such rudeness was a shock to his smiling, but if I guessed right about what he sought, I knew he would not stalk off in offence.

As he did not, and he was less coiling than usual in coming to point: his wife, my sister, had been honoured by King Yew, but there were those who believed, or said they believed, that I, Evan, should have been chosen instead. This had been heard from those claiming to be my friends and allies, but not from Evan self. Forn, pulling his wisest face, said he would not think a chap would hunger to take on the cares of heirship — soon, by the looks of it (the looks of Yew, i.e.), of kingship. After all, had I not put aside regency in Marchlen just as soon as there was someone to take a chap's place? Besides, it was well known I leant, rather, to learning. Friends with my interests in regard, he said, instead of their own, might guess a chap would like far better to be a queen's brother, welcome at Caer as everywhere else, and able to go on in peace with my studies. He did not mention such choice would at the same time be amazingly convenient to his schemes.

All true, I agreed, and his self-pleased face lightened. No living could suit a chap better than to be without thought in head for wars, alliances, frontiers, rule and health of realms. Sadly, that could only be in a Brittan with peace, where no realm was threated by any other, and beliefs went untampered. Besides, as only son of Yew's only sister, I was lawful heir, like or not, in Niragwyn. True, a chap took major pleasure in learning, but as he knew, we all had duties, too.

After that were no more toyings. Forn's hiss became of annoyance, as he demanded to know my price (not a word he used, but his point could not be plainer) for telling my friends I would stand aside from my sister's naming as heir. He promised, or made hint of promising, well-loved Seeyow might be its own free realmlet, its wholeness agreed by treaty with myself as Marten's heir. Forn also reminded that by swapping undertakings with Raug, Yew had kept his realm undisturbed through all troubles. He was sure, too, my sister would wish me to have the lands my father had willed instead to her, and in the Gwyn she ruled I would be as high as anyone.

So much here could not be true or was left unsaid, a chap didn't even begin to ask; would Forn's two daughters (i.e., my nieces) not be above me in Gwyn? And what about my beliefs, when that became (as it of a surety must) another Vandene kingdom? and those of my servants and friends? Why should I believe this blighter who had sent out his killer-hound to hunt down Col, and likeliest have me bumped off on the Q.T., would now welcome a chap where his wife was (in name) ruler? Empty questions, and instead I said the whole business was rid of my hands. If Uncle Yew had taken for his heir one distantly, or in no way, related to him, though there would have been mutterings, it was likely his choice would stand. But to point so near to him, and then choose younger over elder, sister over brother, rewaked all those doubts and squabblings that long ago had strewn apart the House of Regions. Amongst rulers, I said, there was need for steady law, and if younger sisters were to be brought forward, younger brothers, perhaps, and elder sisters, surely, must have claims? This made reference not only to Edin in Suvram, but to Forn's own kingdom, where Vandis had an elder sister lots of blokes believed would make a better king than he. Forn had not begun in any mood to be pleased with me. Now he was no end vexed. Not that he moved from bribe to threat, because threat had always been there.

In those old times, he said, quarrels about the succession, more often than not, were settled by death of a claimer. Raug, with power reaching to every corner of Brittan, had no need for lessons in law. Some who thought themselves safe from Vandene justice might come to regret the chances they were given for peaceful bargains.

I shrugged, and said it was no job of mine to change the laws of succession, or the brains of other rulers, but if my sister and I, in joint statement, were to give up any claim to inherit in Gwyn, and Yew then chose another heir, more of the rulers, I believed, would accept that.

Forn, natch, enquired to know, what other? His eyes held suspicion I was setting a trap. Well, but it was more in the nature of jest, there being not an earthly he would concur to my proposition. For years, I reminded, Yew had all-but called himself ruler of both Niragwyn and Farragwyn, and why should that not go both ways? Why could Jon's heir (viz., Neal) not be Yew's also?


Edin laughed when I told him of this talk. "Why not? Forn could think of no reason, and you and he together will make Neal king of the Two Gwyns."

As he well knew, it had ended in fact without an inch of change, but with heaps more bickering. Likely as it was Forn would use soldiers as his next argument, I had ridden west for conference with Edin, to chew over how our plans might be changed by this. Edin's chief stronghold was now at Lyddan, a very ancient town, stone-built on the crown of a hill (most places there in the west had nestled in valleys or folded in tucks of the sea). Parts, anyway, of the first houses still stand there, some rebuilt, but much of the old stone had been used, too, to make defences on the slopes. It was a strong place, but Edin was wise enough not to have chosen, as animals sometimes do, a lair that could become a trap; Lyddan guards entrance to a long, slowly sloping valley leading back to the borders of Wezram, well-watered and with good crops and pasturage for large herds. It was looking out on that pretty valley in late afternoon of a long, hazed but golden summer's day that Edin and I tried to guess where Forn would next bring his main force; my sister, I offered, had never been happy when made to wait for any benefit, and the armies of Raug would not be likely to sit still and wait for Yew to die. Edin believed we should keep men and boats near Bris. If Forn struck west, we would march on Caer from the east, and if the assault came on March we would ship fighters to the coast of Farragwyn, and again march on Caer. Edin thought if Forn (pricked, he did not say, by my sister's impatience) moved too early in Gwyn, there might be the chance to give a bad bruise to King Vandis the ever-triumphant, fated overlord of All Brittan.

It tickled me to hear Edin talk so, but was all distraction; this was not my task. As if guessing my head, Edin said, "Col had better be with me. If war is coming, he has to be part of it."

When I rode on to Sevenin, for once keeping to my own robes as Lord Evan, I found Col in the fields, working with the haymakers. "It helps thick my shoulders," he explained, and indeed his chest and arms were muscling as mine never had. It seemed to me he also liked to show his (if I guess aright) *bronzed* body to the girls who helped sort the hay, picking out weeds that might harm the cattle. I recalled Worrel, more than once a haystack sire by Col's age, and did not think Col could be tricked or trapped into a worthless marriage. For one reason, he still had hopes of Robin. Whether he knew that here, as everywhere, some of the men working nearby were on guard against assassins, a chap cannot say.

When I told him he was to go back learn war warring with Edin, he threw his pitchfork high into the air, and caught it, spinning. "Now it begins," he said.

Yet for war nothing did begin that year. After touching at Seeyow I left on another long journey as Tela, and in eastern Raug was caught and questioned by a band of Mykas, who kept me in a tiny dark storeroom till joined by their Adda-priest, Raff, a short chap with straight black eyebrows and a narrow nose. Having asked all he could think of about my tales, and whether I gave all praise to the Viztas, he had me whipped for no knowable reason, then fed me and let me go. This was the hardest test yet of my temper, but a chap stayed meek, certain I would not forget this Raff. But, as Tulsingham says of an olden varlet called Savanarola, these are the madmen who rise to power when religion runs wild.

Back in Seeyow, Marten made himself ill, staying out in cold rains to play, as Maire said, with his toys (this was when the first of our winches was crashed). He coughed a lot, and was soon tired, but as winter came on we had news of another sickness, and then a death; Jon died in Landin, and Neal was king. This was harvest for the rogue's treaty we had made years before; Farragwyn was its own kingdom again, and the failing Yew could not bring it back to heel. Not without lots of help from King Vandis.

Few kings, likely, have ever been raised so quietly. It was the worst time of the year for journeys, and mossy Landin is not sung for comforts. As a witness to Jon's desires in the succession, I had to go. I went by boat and took Alison, like me a good sailor. She had been a bit dull lately, betimes grumpy (Sheal told me, and Bett my housekeeper nearly scolded me, it was her age); now her pale cheeks blossomed and her eyes got back their shine in the gales.

No one, certainly, came from Caer, where Yew still disputed Neal's right to rule, nor from Marchlen, it beats me why. It might be young Bryan, or his mother, were trying to keep peace all round, but Worrel, I know, would have been there. By boat and then horse, Edin made the far longer trek, bringing Col, all soldier now, with the small cumny of young fighters he led. They wore striped sleeves and rode small, fast horses, and because they meant to sting quickly and live to sting again, were called the Wosps. But this was the first meeting between Col and Alison.

Your guess is as good as mine what a chap ever expected. They were in that very brief time when the difference in their ages had them on opposite sides of the border between child and grown-up. Soon, Alison would catch up and in some ways pass Col, but not yet. She was small and slim; not living with other girls her age, taught (or rather untaught) by Sheal, she had none of the flirtings; and here was Col, a young warrior, a leader of loud young warriors, Edin's pride. Besides, he was in the dumps for the old reason: while Kennet had come from Sevenin, Robin had stayed back with her mother.

There was also the occasion. We had missed the funeral for Jon, and these rites were meant for happy ones, but Col, or so

I guessed, could hardly not have in thought the dead king was his grandfather, who never desired a sausage to do with him. It is, my studies tell me, and so I told Col, our common curse to bother our old noggins more with what we have not got than what we have; it was no help when I pointed out to Col some of the best blood of Suvram was among the lads in the Wosps, and that for a son of his birth to be their leader was in itself a great victory. No, he would never be king here where his mother was born. Daf, his old rival at staves, would.

Daf too had his cumny of armed youths, which now could call themselves the King's Men. Though not trained, like Col's, amongst warmakers hardened in years of revolt, they did not look any kinder, and their young captain was hard as steel. Still two years older and a half-head taller than Col, Daf had a grimmer and less open look; even in unhappiness Col's face was young and hoping. But Daf was lean as a sapling and tempered like a blade, and was soon to win his nickname, Spear. Like Col, he craved quick fame in battle. Between the Wosps and the Kings' Men there were rougher games than those where Col and Daf first met, with bruises and a few broken bones (neither of the leaders, however, was injured), and they left a sourness behind. Edin said to me, "Don't mind; they will all be friends when they have a bigger enemy to share."

Gathered, we all agreed that could not be far off. Yew, with help from Forn, was expected to try to make Neal accept his overlordship, like his tame dog Jon in the old days.

It was the afterings of a long meal, and Neal had drunk too much. As well as beer, there was red wine in stone jars, found long forgotten in what I take it were once the dungeons at Landin, cold, dripping, echoing places. The wine had not gone bad; it was the best I had tasted, and a chap thought of an old poem about a singing bird, where there is old wine. The word *Hippocrene*, used for a *draught of vintage* may well have signified wine kept for ages in the deep-delved earth.

However, Neal said a bit stumblingly, if the two Gwyns were to be one it would be with him, not Yew and his heirs, as its lord. He could not know I had mockingly proposed such to Forn, and was abashed when Kennet, at his left hand, reminded him he was part of an alliance which put forward me as heir in Niragwyn. As Thea would have been pleased to tell, when dealing with princes there are always hidden plans within plans displayed.

Neal waved at me, farther down the table, and tried to say he meant only that Yew had no more right than he to rule over both Gwyns. While his little wife, she of the blue-green eyes, started to mutter about his rest, Neal altered the topic, turning to Edin, across from me, and saying it might be good if, as spring neared, some of Edin's cumnies, and any that could be spared from Sevenin and Wezram, came to stay a while here, where attack could be expected.

I told him, too soon. Raug was raising new cumnies, and had fighters ready to help Yew, but Forn was still windy about Edin in the new lands, and so was keeping Syme in the south, with lots of their best fighters. Since what I said was usually true, no one ever asked how I knew so much about what went on in Raug; at another time Edin said, "They think it another of Seeyow's magics, no more than they look for." He, of course, was one of the tiny few in the secret of my journeys as Tela.

He was sitting now next to Alison, and had taken care to

see she was part of the feast; it pleased me to see no condescension there, but true liking.  He said, leaving Print English so others there could construe, his fighters also had to help guard Kennet's realm; if Raug took Sevenin, they could fill the river-mouth with boats, and he could then send help here only by the longest way.  Some of his best cumnies were quite near Sevenin, and could go north or south, as needed.

While Kennet said they were welcome within his borders, if Edin wished, Col opened his mouth, and decided not to speak. He desired to be among those in Sevenin, near his Robin, but he would not give himself away to Kennet.

Neal, not pie-eyed but having had some drink, waved hands and bragged he had swords of his own here, and one more come spring.  He was smiling generally towards his two sons, but he meant the younger, Osset.  Not his brother's match in height, or brain, or fine looks, but a brave, stubborn lad with a thick-lipped face like his father's, and broad shoulders for his years. He would be let go soldiering when he passed fifteen.

He shuffled his feet a mo, and said, a bit shy, he would be with Lord Edin's lot, and Col had already said he would take him as a Wosp. Well, could he be blamed? He did things well, but all of them his brother did better, swords, shooting with bows, staves, riding, even talk.  Here in Landin he would never be free of such comparisons as I've just been making.

Daf showed displeasure, but before his father could say a dicky, Kennet, his long, sad-seeming face dipping in approval, said that was good tradition; it was the ancient way, for the younger son of a great king to look for his name away from home. Turning the words he used into Print English  makes him sound wiser, but Kennet had not kept his sliver of kingdom by rubbing blokes the wrong way, and he knew how to calm disputes.

Neal, caught between waving goodbye to Osset, and being pleased as mudlarks to be set beside great kings, said it might be allowed. Daf was still a-brood.

Then, war talk flagging, Edin asked Alison if she would sing for us, which she did, very sweetly, not a song nor even in a language I knew, though the words could only be about love, and she had a way of making each bloke there have thoughts it was his own yearnings she sang. She said when I asked her, it was a song Thea had taught her, in the language, she said, spoken before the moon was chained (then or now, neither of us could say what that meant). After another swig or so, Neal's head had begun drooping, and soon he let his quiet wife lead him away to find sleep. We stood for his going, and Daf then slowly circled the head of the table. Edin had moved up to speak to Kennet about food and beds for the fighters to be kept in Sevenin, and Daf, also a thought squiffy, but still with his cat-sleekness, leant to Alison with lidded eyes to ask what other clevers Thea had taught her, a balder question in our blunt words.

I was ready to see offence, but calm Alison smiled, and said a pet saying of hers was, harder to mix greed smooth with manners than hot water with flour in a bowl. Daf frowned, unsure whether he was wounded, and Edin, whose ears were everywhere, swivelled to advise Daf not to war in words with a Seeyow daughter.

Col, still looking for chance to put his case why the Wosps should be among those in Sevenin, had not really heard, but knew there had been an exchange or two between Alison and Daf. All at once he called across to Alison, "Will you ride with me in the morning, if there is no rain?"

"Willingly, I humbly thank your lordship," Alison joked. Like him, she had dropped into our Seeyow English, which we oftenest give up among others who have not learnt it, because they find it annoying — much more than a language not at all like their own, as the meaning slithers just out of reach. Daf now was uncertain whether he was being made fun of, and he set out deliberately to be snubbish, telling his younger brother if he (Daf) had his way, Osset would not become a Wosp; the Myna's son should serve the king's son, not vice-versa.

Well, after that, and a shock, there was a right old dust-up; I cannot recall the angry and bitter ejaculations that were said and shouted, and recalling them would still lack the skill to tell about the dark hot blood of young men with their prowess yet to prove. At such a do there were, of course, no weapons worn, else we might have seen blades. Well, in a way of speaking, we did; Kennet's soft words were no use here, and it was Edin who cut short the squabble, giving a (for me) rare sight of the steel that made him such a captain; when, not loudly but with his real anger just under, he told the young to be quiet, and save their warrings for the Vandene Kingdom, I saw how easy it would be to fear him, and would not have chosen him for an enemy.

There was truce, but the party mood was broken, and the feast guttered away like a candle running out of wax. After, alone with Col still not gruntled, I tried to tell him he and Daf were nearer than he realised. The Heir in every other realm was that by birth, but Neal had come to kingship by a twisting path, and his son all the more needed to claim and reclaim his right to honours born.

Col made a grimace. "I come from the Regions in true line, or so has been said, and I don't have as much as a farm to rule. I do have the Wosps."

Of Neal, "That is more a king than Vandis can ever be. Not only because a fighter," Col went on, "He knows rule, when to promise and when to pay to get loyalty. He'll be a strong king."

In all this, even what he said about the Wosps, I could hear a question. It had to do with our last long talk, when I told him he must work at becoming Arfra; now he was asking me *is this what you meant?*

I said, "Have you thought how few care what has happened here? The ordinary people of Farragwyn might fret if the Adda-priests came to make them all Vandene, but except for that, they would shout as loud for any new king as they did for Neal."

"I think it has always been like that. If you win the soldiers, and the other lords accept you, the rule is yours."

"But not the love. Vandis has swords on his side, and enforced belief, but no strength of his own; not one bod would care if the Viztas were to take him away to the moon tomorrow."

Col laughed at my tiny joke. Then, "Love would be harder to get than obeyings."

"To earn," I said.


As happens when a thought is near lots of minds, we came back to this by a circling path. It was near time for leavings. Col and Alison were back from their riding, and she asked me to explain some detail in the making of the winch, which she had been telling Col about.

Col said, "There is part of a book at Tawn, where I read about an old war, a battle called Somme. It must be made up, I believe, just like that one about the bloke with the horn — " (as I've said, only Seeyowites wondered about such matters) " — they could never have killed in such numbers, hundreds of thousands. But I was thinking Marten, if he worked at it, could find out how they made guns and bombs. That would be one in the eye for old Forn."

"Swords and knives kill enough," Alison said.

"But the one with guns could be king over everyone, and there would be no more warring."

I said, "Till others had guns, too." It was no new thinking for me, and Neal's thought, also, for one, had gone to guns when he heard about the making of our winch.

"War should not be done," Col said, "except for some great injustice, like the Vandenes bring. Often the good are killed in wars."

"Worrel," I agreed. "And Syme is still alive."

"Then war itself can be more unjust than not fighting to make small wrongs right," Col pleased me by saying.

"Yet wars are begun," he went on, puzzling it out, "without thought. One good and strong leader could end all that, if he could have all the best fighters. Or if he knew how to make guns."

I suggested, "Or if people, even when they had less than all they hoped, still believed he was just."

"That would be after. Before coming to that, he would need strength to win a chair to sit in when he did these justices."

"A warrior, then," I agreed, though wishing for a world where it was not so. It also went against my heart to give a recipe for Arfra, who should *be* Arfra, not learn how to seem him. But I said, "If we were to have one king, he would need to be kind in victory, and a word-keeper. Because blood is believed, he must descend from kings, but he must be loved for himself, as well as feared when fear is a need. He must know how to cry tears, as well as be angry over lies or cruelty."

Alison said startlingly, "That sounds like Edin."

"Everyone honours Edin," Col swiftly agreed, and I could not tell if she had displeased him anew. "But his victories in war are what give him voice. Without swords to keep them safe, there would be no peaceful thinkers of long thoughts, like — Marten."

Yes, I knew whose name he had near used. It was, however, Alison's few words that kept my thoughts busy on the slow journey home, over a midwinter sea all at once smooth as a piece of plass. Col, as could be seen, was keeping at it with the old grey matter, but he was still only what might be, and Raug was terribly strong. Even if Thea's yarn about the rebirth of the Rod could be ignored, I still wondered whether it might be too late if we waited for Col. Not for the first time I did treason in my head, wondering again if Edin, more than a model for the boy, could himself be brought forward. Well, but the prize was all Brittan, and how thousands lived out their lives.

If a chap could not take oath Edin was our Arfra, I was bally certain Edin was better than Vandis, or any Vandene. I tried to tally which of the kings in the alliance might be turned into supporting an Edin for High King — and then, like a bird chirping over my shoulder, heard Thea's voice mocking me for coming back, yet again, to my kings and princes. There were no shaddas for Edin to come from. His birth and standing were known, and if all the western rulers with one voice called him king, he would be no more than what he nearly was now, the captain of a failing rearguard. He was lots brainier than that bloke with the horn in the old story, but not much better off, and as things went he would have the same last boast as Roland, killing off heaps of enemy before dying bravely himself. Not one single Vandene faith would be changed, not one farmer or Myna would give a farting for the younger son of a weak king of Suvram raised to be overking of our alliance. It was a pity, but we needed a marvel.

Two marvels. One I was going at with my long, ragged journeys, but there was no making the other; frogs and butterflies come unhelped from what they start as. I wondered what signs the old time heroes gave in youth, the Caesar or Napoleon Tulsingham tells about. Of course, all kiddies are wonders to their mothers, and after Alexander won the world, people would remember super-duper from his childhood. They might make parts up, but even for what was true, it was all backwards. Every child has a day or a minute of being a marvel, and Alexander's would've been nothing if he had not turned up trumps. Not many chaps think of points like that.

Again I came back from Col's maybes to what Edin was now, and to Alison's admiring. Scorning all magics, I nevertheless began trying to see if Thea's prophecies might fit Edin. She had never said exactly that Alison was meant for Col, only he must not meet her too soon. In the Arfra tales, his wife

Gwynfa also loves a younger man, Arfra's friend and subject; I asked whether I might not have it wrong, and Col was not meant to be Slantslock, the queen's lover (so we say his name, though it looks comical written down).

Then I gave myself a grin to think what twisters we all were, even us who call ourselves honest. There was no forgetting how bucked Thea had been to hear about Col at Vandennis, nor the care she'd had to explain his lineage. You can throw away stale prophecy, but not chop it up to make another dish.

We were on the deck, where it was cold but less stuffy than the house behind, at midships. Alison, I saw, had an especially good luck-disc in her lap. These are very thin, about the size of circle a large man can make by joining both thumbs and both middle fingers, and with a hole in the middle like the circle of one such thumb and finger. The Mynas have them (or had them, I don't know whether any more are to be found) to sell from time to time, and while often dull and pocky, some, like this one, are very shiny, made of a light, bright metal no longer known, and quite costly. In slanting light, rainbows seem to shimmer across them. They must once have had a use, but we like them for their prettiness, and they are thought to bring good luck: Adda-priests hate this, but even Vandenes keep them in secret.

When I asked, Alison said, "Col gave it me. When we rode, he lost temper with me, because I would not jump hedges. Afterwards, he gave me the disc, his luck-piece, to say he was sorry. I thought it was too much gift, but he said his luck would be better kept with me at Seeyow."

So, by chance, I was rebuked.

### Wars and Peace

The reader greedy for all the tales of battles and sieges, and hairbreadth scapes in the imminent deadly breach is not to find them here.  There were fights, many too many, and where valiance was great or death notable, I'll try to tell how it met us, never forgetting in this writing (as, pardon me, I did at times in the living) all this warring of princes and captains could make bugger all that lasted.  No, not so; bravery praised is lasting, and so is repute (good or cruel) won in war, and death that comes too soon may take away from us more than we can ever judge.  Only with time the plans and counterplans, the brief victories, seeming so big when near, become a senseless ruin, like the topless towers of Lunn.

The expected war did not break out promptly, though no one working in the fields or making things of wood or iron was ever far from his sword.  Yew sent messages to all the other courts to say Niragwyn did not recognise Neal's kingship, but while he marched his armies about near the border he was shy to begin real war without help from Raug, and Forn had seemingly decided Edin must first be knocked for six so that the south could be safe.  When spring came Syme sent strong forces into Edin's corner of Suvram, often with smaller cumnies for bait to bring the rebels down out of the hills.  There were fights upon fights, but

Edin would not give Syme a big battle. More than once he made fights in the moorlands with their jumbled rocks and boggy places which he knew, then while Syme's men slithered and stumbled, swooped raiders around to assault his campments, and carry off or destroy his supplies. Syme in return could not manage to find (as seemed to be one of his big purposes) any of the stocks of food and feed Edin's lot had hidden. At very onset of the campaign they drove their livestock to safety in Wezram. Syme hadn't the numbers to follow them there, overcoming all the defences there were.

In part this was because of the two far northern realms, Cumba and Umba, where the kings, Tam and Urt, were saying they would regain the lands grabbed by Raug after the Mynas' War, when Col was scarce born. Forn had to keep armies horsed up there, too; thus, when Syme in the south had not only Edin but men of Wezram against him, he could not find more fighters, and so was stopped and turned back, worse for his fame than in the numbers of his losses. Edin's plans were the biggest part of Syme's failure, but on my journeys much talk I heard was about the Wosps, now more in numbers as young sprigs of good birth went to join. It was said that, using Col's name for war-cry, they were a match in spirits for the fiercest Vandene killing for his belief. They had a way of turning up where least expected, and that (as the decrepit wife of a farmer in Marchlen told me), kept Syme's soldiers shitting themselves. Though the spreading of Col's name gladdened me, I cringed to hear it said he was without fear. That used to be said of Worrel, too, and others I could name, now dead; fear, like hunger or pain, has its purpose.

Once, near winter, when the skies were hurrying grey and the last yellow leaves hung glum on wet branches, I was back from one of my journeys, and sat thankfully by a good fire, telling Alison how Col's fame was growing. A chap could not help watching her for signs.

She said, "Daf will have to do brave deeds, now Col has gone ahead of him. In old times there were more fames than war."

The sigh in her voice put a chap in remind of something — yes, of Thea, when she used to take mickey out of my dealings with princes. For the umpteenth time I began wondering how much of Thea's beliefs Alison knew. Among Thea's last utterings was that Alison had been taught the history of the Bronze Rod, but that did not say she knew what its future was supposed to be. You can bet your bottom pound I never said a word to her about being meant, according to Thea, for Col, and about Col's own foretold destiny, as little as a chap could. For all I could tell, she might know more than I did; for reasons strongly felt but hard to explain, a chap had never questioned her about the years with Thea (nor about her, Alison's, supposed high birth).

I said, "When we need no war to save us from the dark, then we may honour the makers and Telas again."

"But you do not go to war." Meaning, I suppose, a chap was honoured, nevertheless.

The war that came — but before that still, there was Linsy, who came to Seeyow, a master-smith, knotty and raw-faced, very good at forging large pieces of metal with no weak places. He came from parts he still called Suvram, now two years within

Raug's borders, and he had fled to us so as to work without Adda-priests watching all he did to be sure it would not offend the Viztas. Since there was the smith, years ago, whose hands had been cut off by Forn's orders, Linsy's tale was good enough, but he told it too pat. Rayman and I never had a doubt he was Forn's spy. Always at Gridge, Forn had been inquisitional about Seeyow, what we might be doing there, and now word of the winch had gone about. As a Tela, a chap often made up stories about strange magics where Mad Marten ruled (this was to put over the idea there could be marvels where the Viztas had no home). Now, it was all Billingsgate to a bloater Forn had heard talk, and sent his spy. I still say Forn, though in this time his ill-fame was outrun by Ermin, who was much the more seen with the cumnies that nosed out disbelief. His commands, no doubt, still came from Forn, yet Ermin was spoken everywhere for the gusto of his cruelties.

"Forn frets," Rayman said, "about us making those same vile guns that might destroy so cowardly many a good, tall fellow in his spiffing new armies."

That sounded likely, but, "I can't see how it matters," I answered. "Spy or not, this Linsy has to do good work to keep his place. We are not making guns, and all the secrets we've got are talked about in meetings he is not to be asked to."

"Still, the certain knowledge we have no guns can aid our enemies. Also, he can see what our defences are."

"Our defences? A ninny can guess the defence of Seeyow is meeting any enemy where they land with all the swords we can gather up."

"There is still your secret, anent your long times away."

"What will being here tell him about that?"   A chap did not (and does not) know whether Marten and Maire still believed the tale of my long, single studies on Little Seeyow, but they had never told aught else. The few who knew the truth were rewarned not to blab. So notwithstanding Rayman (who was chiefly upset, it seemed, at giving true money to someone false) Linsy stayed, and in fact (as I've said) was lots of help with the second, better winch, work well worth his keep.

And war came to the two Gwyns, with Yew trying to force the plainest road from Caer to Landin.  Neal had good men there, but at first could not believe it was no trick (the reader must gather when I write of what was expected or planned or believed, these are thoughts I later learnt; sitting at Seeyow it was hard enough to get just the dope on what was happening).  I told him Raug was massing soldiers near where the northern point of Marchlen used to be; he was sure they would cross into Gwyn and come down the coast, and so he kept back a part of his own best. Thus Yew could advance, at a cost, almost to Landin, but unhelped he could not take the town or get at Neal's house.  There was a siege, and a few died just about every day without changing a lot.

Still Forn did not give straight help.  The two northern kings, true, were doing as threated, and Tam had, for the time, won back some of the land lost years ago.  In the south, too, grimly Syme was still stalking Edin.  But it may also be Forn, before joining the Gwyn war, desired Yew to have (as well as cause) losses: Raug liked weakness in friends as well as enemies.

Weather changes wars.  It had been a poor growing

summer, and rain at harvest time lessened the fighting forces for everyone, as all were needed to cut the corn before it spoiled. So winter came without much difference.

After midwinter, Col was in Seeyow for a time. I had sent to Edin asking if he could spare us fighters; Forn's big cumnies were only a day or so away, and could as easily turn right (in our direction, so to say) as left when they invaded Farragwyn. Young Osset, very loyal, came with Col, who brought a little band of the Wosps, but a larger number of men being trained. As he said, small island though Seeyow is, there yet could never be the men to prevent any landing; to line just the strait with defenders would take thousands. But against landings it was important to strike when they were new, and the invaders still trying to find their own horses and to form up in cumnies. Best, Col said, was to keep armed bands in high places, where they could watch more of the coast. It would also be good, if Forn marched, to bring as many as we could of cargo and fishing-boats over from the mainland, since an enemy that dribbled ashore, ferried in a few boats, lost any advantage in numbers it might have.

War, success in war, was already making him surer, and not only for war. His first night we outstayed all others, and when we were left alone he said, "There was a play we read when I was young, about the island and an old magician. At times I nearly believe the Adda-priests and the Vandenes are part of spell, that you could melt into air, into thin air, if you knew the right word. We shall have to call Alison Marlinda."

"Miranda."

"She is more pretty than she was, but if she gets any fuller of learning, she'll have to have Rayman for her husband." This was no more than Col's joke.  He himself often talked in ways others would call learned: once, I remember, he put a riddle in Marten's style, asking if, in realms where any belief was allowed, that meant allowing one like the Vandene, which wished to force all to the same belief.  My answer, satisfying no one entirely, was yes and no, no if a bloke could not be Vandene without giving up any idea of making more Vandenes, except by argument.

Marten said, "Let the ferrets live, if they vow not to go after another rabbit," while Col with a grin and a touch of his sword said, "I'll keep this well edged, till that day comes."

Alison sat missing nothing, except a lesson with Sheal in pretty sewing, not her chiefest delight.

Yet at Seeyow, so to speak, it was all learning.  Not for a thousand years (a real thousand, ten hundreds) had there been, anywhere in Brittan, such talk, and as Alison once said, it stopped being a thing chosen.  There were bozos all over the shop, that is (Forn, for one, and not a stupid one), who, not having our learning, also had no need to ask the questions we did; the world was explained for them because they had no words to unexplain it.  As soon as books opened for us, we knew, and could nevermore not know, how much we did not understand.  These had once been lands where all the people as there now were, I think, in all Brittan dwelt in each of a dozen or more cities, and how it was done, where their wealth and feeding came from, how they lived their days — of these books gave us only teasing peeps.  Also to think of such numbers made a chap wonder *why* they all lived.

"Nay, but 'twere to consider too curiously to ask so,"

Rayman said. "E'en as you and I, sir, they lived because they were born, and worked because they had hands." He looked down at his, leathery again, now he was back to smithing. We were beside the forge on a bright day, and he had stepped out to cool himself, and wait for Marten, who was coming to see a large new piece for the second winch. The steady tap of Linsy's small hammer came from within.

Col said, "But they had such marvels. I wish we could have the blower." This, I think, was a kind of bell, and by ringing it, a chap could talk to another chap, miles away, which sounds like Telas' tales, but they have mention in books without magics. Col also spoke about trains and cars and the rolls, aeroplanes, the wonderful wireless, which, if it ever really was, sent photographs as well as speech in an instant, and was once part of a great religion. "As we see from what the Mynas find," Col said, "what they could make they could make hundreds of times over, using their machines. Books, bricks — shoes and shirts, too, I don't doubt."

Alison asked quietly, "How could any workman love things made so?"

Col said to me, "Marten, do you think, knows more than he lets on about what drove the ancient machines? The winch, I know, is good, but it still needs hands, and I don't see how it could be driven by water, like a mill. Or how stopped if it could be driven so. There was the electric in old times, and it was there waiting to be used. And there were devices with fire, which Marten may understand."

"What Marten wishes us to know," I answered, "he tells us."

"But he is old, now," Col said.

Rayman took this up. "Aye, to this we all must come. It were shameful to have old secrets found, then lost again i'the grave."

"Besides," Col said, "it is not Marten's way to think of how a thingum might be used. He sees a riddle, and when he gets the answer, he is done with it."

There was truth in that. "Still," I said, "naught Marten finds is lost again. He keeps bags of writings, and has for all the years I've known him."

"Could they ever be read by anyone but Marten?" Col asked. "Think, Evan, what could be done if we had just one of those engines, that could outwork a hundred strong guys. Guns are the same," he added. "Fire to take the place of hands that pull a bowstring."

There it is again. I would be no end bucked to tell this tale without the haunt of guns, but it cannot be. Life is filled with tough toil that breaks bodies and twists them into frightful shapes. Even we born to be lords can see the engines used to do lifting and carrying, others for farm work or house tasks, saved lots from pain and crippling, and death too soon. There may have been machined ways of being warm in winter and cool in summer, and machines used in curing sickness. No one who was not bonkers would say no to any of these, if he could both have them and keep all the good there was without them. But bulk of what I read teaches me in all times the tools for killing have come with, often before, the ones for doing work. If there is a way to have good machines without terrible ones, I don't know it. Not their fault: tools only make real what people have for their desires, and I did not believe, with Col, guns could be used to end all war, though that might be the beginning.

But I laughed.  "It is never hard to ask questions of Marten, only to get answers small enough for swallowing."

As was, Marten, asked, said, "Rayman here can make you a cannon, which is a simple projection for such a smith.  I can make you gunpowder to put in it, if you can tell me what sulphur is, what it looks like, and where it comes from.  It's said to be yellow, and was plentiful when mountains were topped with fire."

"With a little act upon the blood, burn like the mines of sulphur," Rayman said, just to show he knew the word.  We all laughed.


Alison and Col rode together sometimes, and had lots of talk together; I was tickled to see more friendship begin, though Alison once said to me, smiling, "I could be a captain myself, if he told me as much about war as he has about Robin."

Col and his Wosps were needed more elsewhere, but he waited to see testing of the second winch.  Learning from the first, we built this one on strong iron wheels, so a team of horses could take it to where it would be useful.  It was Linsy who patiently forged special chains, giving a twist to every link.  In this way they lay flat against the pulleys, making the machine easier to work.

One more word Col said, just before, too soon, he left, comes to my thought.  Osset (for whose sake we often left off talking Seeyow English) mentioned his brother Daf, and how, since his part in harrying Yew at the siege of Landin, he had been given the name, Spear.  His new fame (Osset did not say) was growing, though still behind Col's.

Col said, "A spear is bad to have in your belly, but good in the hand, if you know how to carry it."

Was this meant to hint Col believed Daf too rash?  Osset said no dicky, and it passed without much notice at the time.  A little after, Daf was at the head of the men Neal had guarding the northern way to Landin, and when Forn sent bait in the form of a single Adda-priest with four soldiers as gawd, Daf took it, killing all five.  As well as all else I've mentioned, Forn needed an excuse to start war when Raug had no common border with Farragwyn (it may be Forn needed a reason better with King Vandis than the inheritance of Forn's wife).  Now Forn's waiting cumnies crossed the shortest part of Yew's realm, and came pouring down the narrow valley into Farragwyn.

Neal and Daf were sure these armies would go south, and they did gesture that way, but then made north and west to come against Seeyow.  With no word (as far as we could tell) from his spy, Forn, I believe, was keen to make bloody sure about the chance of guns.

For our defence, we had extra help by accident.  Daf had taken to hills, hoping to come down on the enemy's right flank as they turned for Landin.  Instead he found himself in their plain path, and they were too much for him to fight straight on.  He made a retreat, through narrow valleys which slowed the host against him, and crossed the strait to Seeyow, using up bulk of the larger boats to be found on the mainland side, then forbidding their owners to return.

Whatever thickhead commanded for Forn thought haste

importantest. He might have spent a week searching up and down the coast for enough boats, but instead sent his soldiers piecemeal across the narrows in the littler vessels they could find nearby, as they found them. Daf's losses had been little on the retreat, and his blokes were thirsty for blood; joined to our defenders they charged from place to place where the enemy landed. Through a long afternoon the killing went on, more particularly in the narrow part where the great old bridge had been; there the waters of the strait were incarnadined, and as twilight came not one live enemy had foot on Seeyow. Some of the latter boats turned back rather than face at that disembarking disadvantage Daf's fierce young riders, whose hunger for killing never lessened.

When Daf, after seeing to the making of watchfires, rode up to my house, he was soaked with blood from ankle to chest and from wrist to shoulder; his face too was smeared and his hair spattered. None of the blood was his.

If I say he was smiling, it makes him seem cruel as Syme (or Ermin). But in memory it was a quiet smile, and if there was a time when a chap saw him as another (the times were making many) who joyed in blood, when he washed himself and put on fresh clothes (they were Rayman's, the two being of a height), he was a quite civil monster, talking of losses had and given, weighing chances of a new assault, shaking his head over the enemy's folly.

Alison, willing (as she told me after) to turn a new page after their last sour encounter, brought Daf beer, and said she was glad to see him unhurt, that it was his skill, no doubt, that had kept him so. It had been my intent to send Alison with a scawt to Sevenin or perhaps Wezram for her safety. A boat had been ready all day at the far western end of Seeyow, but she had been stubborn to stay, and Daf was now sure no landing could succeed, unless tons of reinforcements came for the enemy.

When we had a meal Daf's weariness prevented him from doing much tucking in, but not from watching Alison as if afraid she would not be there if he turned away. It was no new-discovered secret that use of one weapon got the other ready (Worrel once told me that, missing war, I would never know what a real stiff was). Other times, I had found Daf a serving girl, and he knew I would've now, but there was no chance for the offer; he asked to be shown to where he could sleep a few hours, but still held eyes on Alison as if hoping she might lead him there. That was kiboshed for him when she self took leave, and Bett came at my summoning to show Daf the way.

This, I told Rayman, settled it; Alison must be sent away. We had no proper count of the armies against us, and Seeyow still might be overrun. If our friends could watch her so hotly, I asked, what could we expect of enemies?

Rayman, wrapped in words, had noticed nothing, and only went back to his nag I too should take flight, saying that Alison would not have refused if a chap had not been so set on staying. The elderly Sheal, however, had seen the same as I had. She always said (or so she now said) Alison should be somewhere more tamed than here, and where there were other girls of her age and standing.

Short of sleep myself, I soon left the table. If Alison was reading, as she often did by rushlight, I meant to tell her to be ready to leave early, without further dispute. In my house two long corridors lead away from the middle entrance, past where two sets of stairs used to go to the upper floors. A lot of rooms open off each corridor, and by Alison's door — I say door, but it must be hundreds of years since the old doors were nicked for firewood, and only a few have ever been put back; Alison's doorway, like majority, had a wool weave hanging to close it — there I found Daf.

I was jocund, and gave him he must have missed his way; he was sleeping the other end of the house. He certainly did not need to mimic confusion, and let me lead him in the right direction. Lots of armed men were about the house, in case Raug slipped invaders ashore by dark, and at the middle entrance I muttered a nonsense about feeling safer, and called gawds in from the outer door to station them where they could watch both corridors. There seemed no need for special orders; I thought their being there enough to keep Daf at home. He, you may be sure, knew very well what this was about. The darkness of his looks as we said goodnight was made of two different sulks.

Having seen him to his room, I went to my own rooms, stopping on the way to see, with a quiet glance, Alison already abed. It was only when settled I thought to wonder how Daf, among all the curtained doorways in the corridor, had found Alison's. The question soon became whether Alison had told him the way herself. What could be more to nature? a voice asked inside my head. Like William Shakespeare, like, I think, all other time, we make jokes about fathers with young daughters (and also older husbands of younger wives), their sad, silly battles to hold hunters at bay. A bit of a turn, nevertheless, to see tales about the world may have become a chap's own story. Keep Daf the same, young, strong-willed, handsome, winning warrior of good birth, and for *Alison* say instead nearly sixteen, pretty, eager for new knowings, not yet topped, but because of her childhood knowing more than most women ever will... a story I could tell to a hundred, and a hundred would say Daf came invited. The whole hundred would also say a chap did right to prevent it, as I surely had (it was all but certain I caught Daf about to go into Alison's bedroom, not having just come out; first-time maters would spend longer than he could have been there).

Well, but in part a chap disagreed with all of them. Alison, I thought, the real Alison, was not glamoured by what Daf was, and made her other choosings with a clear head. Even the prudent, true telling, can be barmy — there was time when I would have drunk up eisel or eaten a crocodile (not knowing what either is) for the sake of Caif. OK, but if Alison had appetite for Daf in her bed, where was my right to stop it, where would it be even if I had been her father? This was Seeyow, where no rules went without questioning. She might desire Daf for her husband, and if not, what? She was not mine, a precious linen I was guarding so as to give it unsoiled to Col, and the utmost to do unless I meant to treat her so and lock her away in a cupboard, was jog her of her world, and how it was with women staled. Caif's lonely ending had been sad, but I could not judge whether her short life was worse than a long one as Tam's wife would've been.

Even before I was up Daf had ridden back to the strait, where news was the night had been quiet. Alison, as soon as I saw her, told me he had come to her room in the night. She was yawning as she spoke, and yesterday morning that would have been no more than a yawn. All a chap had thoughtfully decided (what I've just written, the good sense of Seeyow) at once had to wrestle against hungry creatures gnawing inside my belly. Yet to me she still looked a girl, and I could not picture her enfolding Daf, or arched in a wild sweetness with him.

In the muddle of question and answer, happenings came out in the wrong order, and it was not till near the end I worked out that Daf had by some means returned after I showed him to his proper bed; after, as Alison said, I looked in on her and thought she was sleeping. By some means, blimey! Who would dare challenge his wanderings? It was the same with knowing which was her room. Alison said she had never told him, and pointed out Bett, like the old servant in the poem about Madeline and the sweet jellies, would have; nearly anyone would spill those beans to Daf, heir in this kingdom, hero in war. It was not even worth questioning servants or gawds.

Alison did more than answer the jackpot question; she shamed me by not thinking I would need to ask it. Daf, she told me, while eager (and full-rigged, she meant) as any guy who ever came visiting the Dauwas of Thea, was no bally raper. He wakened her as he came into her room, starting with the idea in his head she was already wooed, then believing she sought token talk for the sake of manners, then going to warmer and at last almostly wild persuasion. But she never had fear he would waive her consent, and try force.

"There is a sooth Thea taught me, and now I understand it. If a woman does not desire a man, then *no* is only lessened by reasons. Debate is ruled by men, in the realm of the sun."

From my life, I said, "With some women, betimes, *no* is

meant to start debate. The arguing against reasons is like the mock-fight of birds, or the scratching of cats before they mate. Some even are pleased by — " and I halted myself. This was not how a near-father talked.

But Alison said, "That was Thea's meaning. Giving reasons, she said, is as much as to say, try to overcome them, tell me why I should change to *yes*. But the matings of birds or cats..." She was groping.

"Your life," I said, and brought me without warning to the edge of tears, "has more purpose than nests or kittens."

"So I am taught." Alison seemed so forlorn I hugged her tight for comfort. Wiser than her age (as I was now reminded), she may have guessed why a chap broke that off, and grasped her small shoulders to move arms' length away, as if setting her in a new place. Seeing somewhat through Daf's hot eyes, thinking of how it could have been between them, had changed me with Alison. If I hugged her, it would be with a holding-back there had never been need for, and I knew there'd be no more wafting into her bedroom without a warning, or letting her come into mine dressed only in her sleeping-shirt, as now was. It was the second time a chap's life was changed overnight: two dozen years before, when Thea took me to her bed, and now, when Alison did not take Daf to hers.

Nor did she let herself be sent off. Daf, she said, had only just been proud enough not to let anger burst out. To have her removed, whether in fear of him or of the enemy (after his boast they could not now take Seeyow), would be the worst of insults.

So like the day before, boat and scawt were kept ready, but the chance they would be needed ebbed through the day, as the enemy did not come back to the assault. Many of the boats they had used yesterday had been left empty on our shore. I saw to it word came from Marten to Daf — they were, after all, cousins at a couple of removes — asking the honour of his staying at the house up the hill, and he slept there for the rest of the time he was on Seeyow. Alison had allowed she was never so likely to yield as when she saw he would accept her no, and to me it seemed foolhardy to keep sifting her in the same perilous circumstance, under the same roof.

Daf I began to like more, even as I trusted him less (putting cream where the kitten can't reach it comes not from unlike of cats, but from knowing their nature). We never once spoke about his short siege of Alison, but we circled the topic, as when he would admire her riding or riddling, and watch me against the bias to see how much I knew. It does not seem the girl Marten and I found for his bed took any edge off his yearning. He was *in yearn* with Alison, if I can make up a phrase between in love, which believes in its own rant about lifetimes, and blood-bloated, where any woman would answer need. Alison's unclear standing, I believe, helped muddle him; he had thought she might be one of the girls a prince could prod with no thought of any speaking into the Myke.

Across from us on the mainland, part of the Raug armies became defenders faced the other way, trying to seal off Seeyow, the rest, it could be guessed, going south to help deepen the siege of Landin. Daf made up mind he was now more necessary there, but when he proposed to ship across the strait in a hundred boats and mow the blighters down, I interfered for a rare time in the tactics of war, asking why he should give the enemy the same trumps he had held. They, besides, had plenty of bowmen who could have easy practice on boatloads of men and horses. There was no need; islands cannot be blockaded by land alone, and from the farther shore he could sail to anywhere on the coast of Gwyn, without loss. His bravery, I said, was in no one's doubt.

He took my advice, and at parting Alison very prettily took his two hands and kissed them. As I learnt a little after, when war paused for another Gridge, he came in good time to help his father; Landin and the valley behind were still in Neal's keeping at the truce.

That midsummer gathering did to warn me the years of Thea's foretell had worn away to three. I can remember that silly ass Tam, braying loudly in Forn's hearing he'd had less far to ride this year. It was true, but bugger all for boast; main of his way was still over lands held by Raug; we've always been too ready to see the end of all dark in lighting of a brief candle. Forn had special interest in those parts, because his family lands were out near what in my childhood was the northern border of Raug, and since giving Vandennis to the king his main dwelling had been there. To a chap's bewilderment he came to see me at Gridge, with the same threadbare feigning of brothers-in-law who could stay pals through all differences; he even brought his wife and daughters. My sister and I kissed at meeting, and eyed each other like cat and dog. My elder niece, Avanda, was ripely eighteen now, and still (or a chap should say, even more) the compeller of long gazes; word was she was all-but promised to King Vandis. Even blokes of Raug there were could be heard to say (softly) it was waste; Vandis was believed to think more of handsome young men. This a chap brings up only because it is the Vandenes who call like-to-like mating a crime against the Viztas, and the Adda-priests who let their Mykas make games of nasty punishments for any less than kings who do that. For myself, well, there is another man with the same ways I've mentioned often, and with praise, in this story.

Forn tried to woo me with a scheme where Seeyow's safety was assured, Neal keeping the title of king in Farragwyn, but both admitting Yew was their overlord, and agreeing my sister was his true heir. Having sampled failing, this was again Forn's way (and a chap said so to his face) of procuring with words what swords had failed. Still, there was also truth in what, losing smiles, he hissed back, the strength of Raug was still waxing, and it would be harder to hang onto not only kingships but lives in coming wars.

And while the league of the west kept whole, a chap could not bring in Raug's other foes. Tam was scornful of any proper alliance, asking me how many swords the western realms could send him. He knew the answer was none, but what we really itched to know was, when Tam meant any more assaults, so Neal could be ready to attack Yew when he could not look to Forn for help at Landin. Tam said he would make war in his own time.

The midsummer gathering, otherwise, was empty, with lots of public mouthings about what was the law and who had the right. Alison said, "If right goes to who has bulk swords, law ends where it began." Meaning, I believe, before laws came the weak had no hope for justice.

This Gridge (a chap reflected, as wars resumed) just went to show what was missing from the struggle against the Vandene

Kingdom. Besides what I've told about, Raug had lots of other troubles that year. Edin, of course, was still untamed, and his being where he was made unrest in all the lands Suvram had ceded. In the east, Frick made up mind there would never be a fatter chance to nick back territory Raug had burgled a few years ago, and even in parts of old Raug (I mean, that in my lifetime had always been Raug) there was bother, because the upheavals elsewhere, by interfering with farming, made for general shortage. If only there had been some one odds-on cert, a rival to dish the fierceness of the Vandene faith, if an awaited Arfra had been ready then to step from shadda. As was, mice hungry for themselves nibbled at the edges, leaving the might untouched in the middle.

Landin neared falling, then was rescued again by Daf, Edin played fox with Syme, drawing him west, so at harvest time Col's Wosps, more in number now, could go on a cheeky raid into Raug itself, carrying off a lot of food. Forn, I heard, went to Saffam to tell that fool Erril it was time he did more to bring his outlaw brother Edin to heel. Poor Erril tried, but sending Suvram blokes to fight against Edin was to give him fresh followers, not battles.

Early in winter Linsy one morning turned up missing from Seeyow. He took with him some of Marten's drawings, but left behind unfinished work: there was a new kind of lock for doors, which since has been made complete. Rayman said, "Nay, damn him for a false knave then, but I'll miss the rogue's coarse jesting." Linsy had talk even William Shakespeare would have thought bawdy.

Now Yew, in muddy weather, made a new attack on

Landin, fell from and was fallen on by his horse, broke heaps of bones, and whilst being carried back to Caer, died. So I, by the word of majority princes, was the new king in Niragwyn. Forn, however, believed other. It became his own war now, and he swiftly moved his fighters back from their threat to Landin, so as to be sure of having Caer.

So far, in more than three years of warring, Bryan of March had done little to remind of his father. Granted, Marchlen, with Raug to the east and Gwyn to the west, had more borders to guard than anyone else, but it had been pointed out to Bryan (as to his mother Alma) till we were tired with saying it that if Forn's wife ruled at Caer, Marchlen would be in a stranglehold. Now at last Bryan defied the Vandenes, refusing to let Forn march a scawt by the shortest way to fetch their claimed queen, my sister.

For the moment, with so much gone wonky for him, Forn seemed to decide to get Niragwyn well in his gripe before starting new attacks: my sister did come to Caer, but by the more roundabout northward way. Meantime, to continue the war on Neal, Syme was summoned from the south, with all his best cumnies. He tried, as guess, to slip away, leaving lesser forces to keep Edin there. This they failed to. Edin brought men by boat to Neal's aid, and Forn never guessed they were already there when he marched on Landin (it was now near midsummer), once more by the straight way. Then something made him pause; as was later plain, it was news coming from the north.

For all his loud talk last year, no one could have foreseen Tam of Cumba would act loonily as he now had, gathering up his force and striking into the heart of northern Raug, burning farms and dwellings halfway to the wilderness of Lees, another place where once a great city used to be. Nearer were Forn's own lands, nearer his heart, too, and those of other Adda-priests. As Edin said after, good allies thinking together could not have found a better way to mess Forn's plans than Tam did, fighting in his own time. Syme's cumnies, ready to sweep away Daf and come to Landin by the back door, were instead sent marching to the north; Forn himself followed with more taken from the forces facing Neal (and Edin, though they did not know that).

As King of Niragwyn I was not daft enough to take up arms myself, but I was at Landin, admiring how Edin made plans and made Neal agree to them, and anxious for Col, who, with his Wosps had purposed to shadow Syme, and was now somewhere, we believed, in Raug itself.

Edin's intent was to drive all invaders from Farragwyn, and bring a threat against Caer, which he believed, with help from Marchlen, might be captured. As it went, Caer, a strong place if well defended, fell in the blink of an eye. Edin had circled his most practiced cumnies round a flank of the main enemy mass, but while new forces came from Caer to fight him, Col, with only four hundred, captured the town and the royal seat. When Syme's army had gone on north, Col had found out the reason, and taken his band westward. Stopping in Marchlen to gain help from Bryan, he came to Caer by the least likely way, over the steep hill behind the town.

This, as I told at the beginning, and was after remembered, is the very hill where Arfra is supposed to lie sleeping with all his warriors, ready to issue forth when need is sorest (just one more muddle, because Arfra, in another account, was taken to an island in the west to be healed from his wounds). Col's lot, having left their horses on the hill's far side, came down it on foot. Bryan's help gave us a card we had lacked, numbers of fine bowmen, and the attack was altogether a surprise to the men of Raug left to guard my sister and her daughters, who were taken with the town. What first became famous was that Col, coming face to face with Avanda, his sword all blood, bowed and told her baldly her mother was not queen.

Still, Edin was a half-day's fighting away, and Col, when enemy cumnies turned to try recapturing the town, might have had quite a time holding what he had snatched. Then, like a spear out of the north, Daf came with his deadly riders and fell on the behind of that small force. He too entered Caer, and another event quickly famous was the mad quarrel he had with Col. Daf had suffered losses in the fight outside the town, and was angry with Col for, as it seemed to him, lazing about in the king's house when there was still fighting to be done. Col was hot in answer, and if Bryan (a king, you see) had not been there it might have gone to swords. I should mention that in the wondrous way gossip goes about, Col had heard about, and not liked, rumour of Daf's attempt to bed with Alison. But Osset, now Col's second, helped make an edgy truce, convincing his brother the Wosps, their horses on the other side of the hill, had no means of coming to his help.

Very many of the fighting-men of Niragwyn, all at once without their allies, refused to battle any more against Edin or Neal. So long as Yew was alive they kept their oaths to him, but lots had never liked the Vandenes, and knew if they won, Forn would be the real ruler of their land. The Red Hounds, the royal bodyguard, was first to change sides. Like my sister, I had grown up at Caer, of course, and they had no dislike against me.

So, riding to Caer with Neal and Edin, a chap gained a title I was plotting ways to be rid of as soon as could be. Not that the war was over. As we later knew, at that same time Forn was altogether crushing Tam with his allies, and Syme was hunting what was left into the north. But pish; no matter how that fight went we knew Forn, with his wife and daughters prisoners at Caer, would soon be back. He knew bloody well they would not be harmed, and I even put loose a captured Adda-priest to find Forn with a message to that effect, but that would only be salt in the wounds to his standing.

Though fooled once or twice, he had never before been foolish. What he did now may have been sign of real love for his family, but more likely of how his pride was bruised. Collecting up soldiers, not waiting for Syme who was somewhere in Cumba, Forn came back from the north in long marches through hot, dry weather, and, with no pause and no real plan, made his attack by the expectedest way, the northern road Daf had used. No matter how well trained, his lot were very weary, and once their first advance had been stopped, were terribly cut up by the bowmen, and by the quick horse Edin sent about their flanks. Forn himself, for the first time, was somewhat wounded in this battle, and nearly captured.

This victory had cost. Daf, sent on one of the longer circlings, missed the way, and for once was late to a battle. This meant, as best I can understand, Col and the Wosps were left to deal on their own with more than their numbers of the best Vandene fighters. When the Wosps, lots missing and with bulk of the rest bloodied, rode back into Caer, they were carrying a prize, the Arch banner of Forn's own gawd, but Col was not at their head.

My stomach numbed, till I saw he was riding last, holding up in his saddle the awfully wounded Osset. Helped by servants, Col carried the young man into the large room where soon I would be robed as king, and Osset died there without ever speaking. He was held in Col's arms, and Daf, himself showing signs of battle, came in just as Col shut Osset's eyes and laid him down.

Daf with his face running tears knelt next to his brother, as if to be sure he had truly died. As the two captains got to their feet with Osset lying between them, Daf slid out his sword and offered it hilt first to Col, saying from today, if Col would have him in his brother's place, he would be a Wosp (so he would have said, if he had our words). Col said no words, but nodded and turned the sword to hand it back.

This was as it should be; when there was time for stories I found out Osset, in the swirl of battle, had been caught in the midst of a whole knot of Forn's fighters, and Col had charged like a madman, hacking on all sides, trying to save the youth. Those who greatest relished telling the tale said Col's fury was enough to scare armies. His recklessness was sure plenty to affright me.

Forn's failure meant my sister, not by choice, could be at my robing as king. All the rulers of the West were there, and for the pious I had a priest. Not a Vandene, an old buffer I had known all my life (he had been the one at Worrel's funeral), who always said the Viztas were fathers and mothers to us, but desiring us to grow up, not wait like ever-infants for the Return.

It pleased superstitions a chap knew were even older that the harvest that year, gathered under deep blue skies, was super everywhere; I was not sure how a new king for Niragwyn could help the wheat in Stanglin or Wezram, but lots of people called it Evan's Harvest.  Everywhere, I should write, but the northern kingdoms, where for Forn's revenge Syme was making ruin.  We heard later he drove prisoners into barns and set fire to them, and his fighters were urged on to theft and rape.  Tam's head was brought to Vandennis (as also that gaudied trinket, the Belt of the Viztas), and his son was hiding in the wild north, but at Caer, whilst we talked about these doings and watched our borders, it was as if we had won victory worth long peace.  There was a week of cold rain after harvest, but then warm, sunny weather came back, such sweet days that except for browning leaves it might have been first summer.  The kings and princes kept finding reasons for staying at Caer and for another feast in honour of another thing and only Edin and I seemed to know there would be bitterer wars with Raug better prepared for them.  After, I called this Idiots' Summer.


"The West," Col said one day, "has never been so strong. If we can stay so, there will be second and third thoughts at Vandennis." It was early morning, before people started coming to me to ask what should be done with this dead man's estate or the house of that fled Vandene.  We were in the place where Yew had always made judgements, a bright room in that often drear house, with some good furnishings.  It was there, long ago, he had judged me fit to carry messages, if little else.  There, too, Osset had died.

"It only means," I said, "our turn comes last. The north, from what we hear, is kaput. Suvram is like a sick man, waiting to die. If Forn turns all his force on Stanglin, we can do not much to help."

"We can sting them, as we have before. My raid last year, my ride through Raug in summer, show they are not beyond hurting."

"Besides," I said, "the western realms, with a few minutes to breathe in, begin dispute among themselves. Neal seeks to have all the kings agree to outlaw the Vandene belief throughout the West."

"That comes from me."

He had spoken about this before, but a chap thought his teachings were better. "From you?"

"In talk with Daf, as a point chewed over. No one has more loathing for Vandis, and he was hot for it, before the words were out of my mouth. So long as there are Vandenes among us, there will be traitors. Those who won't change might be banished to their proper home in Raug."

It struck me, too, as just what Alma's lumpish brother Frick might say, campfire talk for dull soldiers, not words for the ruler of All Brittan. "Kennet and Cara," I answered, "say they will not have their own Mykas, riding about to see what people believe."

"Kennet. How long would his little kingdom last, without allies to guard him?"

"Bryan, too, opposes Neal on this."

"Edin is also set against it," Alison added. "A way of

making traitors, he says, not ridding ourselves of them."

Col looked sharply at her, a bit abacked she would be Edin's ear in such a business. She said, "He means, I think, those made to keep their belief in secret are the more danger. If the Addas are kept out, he says, let there be Vandenes, openly."

"Edin has weight," Col said. "Even Neal would like him as captain over all the armies in the League. As he has been, except for giving it a name. But, as you say, a year of peace, and Neal goes back to wishing to lead his own soldiers again."

"As for me," I said, not letting the other drop. "It is not a king's business to rule over what his subjects believe. As Marten would say, if lots of different thoughts are, a few are sure to be right."

"No one despises Vandene ways more than Marten."

"In talk," I said. "Seeyow talk, as called."

"And where would Seeyow, or Marten, be, if Daf had not been there last year? Rule of a kingdom in times like these, Evan, is no job for the weak or the weaponless. I don't mean you," he quickly corrected. "You are one who knows war as well as wisdom."

I dismissed his confusion. "No, I am no king here, for times of war. One of the things we should jaw about."

Alison was smiling, and when I asked why, would only say it was in remembrance of a wisdom Thea once told her. Alison's face often said more than she did; it had been her look of outrage that brought on Col's quick apology.

"Neal," Col said, "has not forgotten you once put up his name to Forn as a king over both Gwyns. As a joke, then."

"What does Neal say, about Daf becoming your man?"

Col grinned. "Kennet tells him it is proper, when I risked my life for Osset. Why?"

"Neal would be pleased if Daf became region here, and Daf would still be your man."

"Daf?" That was not the question Col would have answered.

I said, "The kingship is mine, but mine to give only if others agree." Now Alison saw there was private chinwag in the works, and asked to be excused, saying some of the young swains and flappers were going riding.

When she left Col stared after her, and I thought he must be admiring her supple grace. She was in a long frock with sleeves to the elbows, and I myself had noticed for the first time that morning her arms had stopped being of a child. But he said, "I told you you were making her too learned. She frights chaps."

"What puts wind up them is not what I gave her, not learning but her own braininess. There are blokes it doesn't scare." I was thinking of Daf, or her best listener, Edin.

"A Seeyow difference. Marten says, if sticks are full of music, no one knows till they are cut and bored for flutes. Whatever you call it, Bryan named her Evan's little witch-girl; he must have got that from his mother. Osset once asked me why she was never made to shut up. I told him, because she never speaks just for the sake of it. It is known you would never let her be beaten. Daf says, then her husband will have to do that."

"Does he?" with a milk-souring look. Though Osset was a big price to pay, the peace between Daf and Col (between Dark and Light Rival came into my head) had no end pleased me, till now.

"Young fellows say such things," Col told me. "He would woo her, if she kept to her place better."

"Her place is like yours, as high as she can climb."

"Yet Daf, you say," very swift, "might do well here at Caer."

"You," spotting his drift, "could not come from this little kingdom to be what you can be." Ever since that moment Daf had handed Col his sword I had been ridding me of any doubts, and now he heard for the first time about the Bronze Rod. A chap did not give him Thea's long yarn in total, nor spend much time with her ideas about the powers of the Rod, but told him what I believed: what we called the True Myke was really far older than any mention of the Viztas. Forn surely had it, or knew where it was, and meant to show it at the right time to make Vandis the king foretold.

"If they have the True Myke, what everyone calls the True Myke," Col said, "why not show it now?"

"Forn is afraid to have it claimed too soon. He believes in its renewal, or I think he must. It is going to be displayed in a little less than two years, and since that will be midsummer, it'll have to be at Gridge."

"Well, then? How can you stop them?"

That was just what a chap could not yet make out. "Laughter by itself may be enough. By then, the Rod will be part of Arfra's tale, not only the True Myke, but Arfra's Scalipal, so in claiming the Rod King Vandis will be saying he is the Arfra of prophecy. There are jokes even magic cannot make unfunny."

Col's face took on a light. "Then for a true Arfra to come forward, a warrior, one whose birth has been hidden, one followed for himself, who knows how to reward the faithful. Yes."

"Warriors must keep hope alive for the next two years, while I work to make that. And not more waffle about outlawing the Vandenes. The true Arfra's going to have to be the Arfra of Vandenes, as well." In point of fact, if the Adda-priests, as I expected, went on telling the Arfra tales, the Vandenes would be readiest of any.

In a new, business way, Col said, "Daf would do very well as region here. When I am Arfra, he'll follow me."

At the same time as all the plots and policies, a great mating dance went on amongst the young. There had been nothing near it since that feverish year when I, amongst the others, found a wife. Of course, it was the crops those weddings had planted that now were ripe: Worrel and Alma's children, Bryan with his sister May and next brother, Alan; Kennet and Cara's lovely Robin; even Col, in a way. Forn and Gwynis was another of those weddings, and my nieces, Avanda and plain plumpish Vera would not be left out of the beano, no matter how well my sister kept up her cold anger (every day she demanded to be sent back to her husband). There were others, too, like Daf, and the Wezram children. It was all youth; Edin was the old man among the bachelors, and he was twenty-six. Looking back, I see now under all the silly boasting about Forn's defeat there must have been knowing the goofy weather could not last; one wondrous autumn had to do for heaps of lost summers, both past and to come.

Some reserve of Alison's nature kept her at the fringe. Although Robin still spread Worrel's remembered warmth with her smiles, and the faces of both Col and Daf took on the sulky look of young bulls when they haunted after Avanda, to my eye no other eclipsed Alison's large-eyed silver and dark. She was sweet-tempered, and the learning Col fretted over did not make her aloof; it was choice, then, that stopped her from blending.

"Have you given away your kingship?" she asked me, later on the day of the talk with Col.

"Why did you smile?" I asked again.

"When Thea knew she was dying, and told me I would be with you, I asked her what sort you were. She told me lots, and about your family. When I asked if you were a king then, or would be, she said, *Not Lord Evan. He still thinks he can rule over his own life, without the trouble of ruling others.* But she was wrong, you are king." (Here, she left out at least one other judgement Thea said about a chap.)

"King," I said, "This week."

"What is the use of prophecy?"

"You know I put no faith in that."

"You serve it. You danger your life for it. When you go away, I never know if we are to see you alive again."

There was, I saw, another sense to her question. "Uses, prophecy can have uses. It may give hope. It may bring together those who agree on nothing else."

"We need not believe Thea saw all."

"No indeed." It now seemed clear Col, without a great change, would not choose Alison. If it were a condition for his being seen as Arfra? I wondered, and sent the question into exile, scared of an answer.

"Would you become Daf's wife?"

"Daf's?" she asked. "Wife?"

"At Seeyow, you said you had begun to like him."

She searched my face. "For choice, or as part of your plans?"

Because it was her good I was chasing, this sour answer nearly got me angry. "A plan to give you a bit of safety. As you say, I might be killed, and you would have no rank. A chance here for that, if I tell Neal his son can rule at Caer, with Alison for wife."

Lots of chaps, let me say, do not ask. They just tell their daughters who they are going to marry. Alison is not my daughter, but kings can order anybody about. Funnily enough, though, a chap wasn't even surprised when she started to get shirty, telling me it was never her future standing she worried over when she sat at a window, watching for me to turn up again.

Of Daf she said, "He fought for Seeyow, but has none of Seeyow in him. He would use your Tulsingham to warm his feet."

As firewood, she meant. It struck me if her husband had to have Seeyow learning, her choice was a narrow one. "A queen is not shut in one room with her husband, like a farmer's wife. You could have Sheal here with you, and Rayman, if he'll come. Daf would become king over both Gwyns, at Neal's death."

She fixed me with one of her steadiest gazes. "Do you wish me to be his wife?"

Well, I ask you. Of a course not; I did not wish her to be anyone's. My nasty journeys as Tela were warmed by the thought of Alison greeting my return, and she was all through my daily life. Would Kennet desire Robin to be gone, or even Forn, Avanda? Their daughters had been with them longer, but Alison was my apprentice and my friend; a chap needs someone trusted to air his thoughts with. While there had been the odd night with a woman, it was too long for me since Iona (who, by the bye, was soon to have the second child of her marriage), and not fair to fill that space with Alison. Companionship, I mean to say, and a safe ear. Not that any successor to Iona could replace Alison. She listened, but also considered and gave thoughts of her own.

"I aim for you to have choices," I said.

"Why must it be Daf?" Alison demanded. "Why not Edin? To rule here at Caer, I mean, as you would wish," she added. Her face was red. She was, with all her gifts, just eighteen.

"If he would agree. But he still dreams of reigning in his Suvram."

Only Alison's blush was aught new here. Edin's connection with Gwyn was slight, but all the kings in the west, except one, would rather Edin than Daf, and that one was cornered, having already said he could never repay Edin's part in saving Farragwyn. But because Daf (or his father) desired the throne of Niragwyn, I could have made marriage to Alison part of the bargain. That was not so with Edin.

Alison, without admitting she favoured Edin, understood, and part of her huffiness came back when she asked how much a fellow could esteem a marriage he had to make to get a kingdom. My mother would have told my sister (did tell her, in fact), if the offer was good, the marriage was what a wife made it, but I knew better than to try that on Alison.

The first pairing was Bryan of March with Rina of Wezram.  Her features were thick, like her speech, but she was good-natured, and a good match for Bryan.  She was his mother's second cousin, but by Alma's second marriage; they themselves had only remote relativity.  It was on the day of their betrothal I talked with Edin, just back from a few days looking after the readiness of our defences and defenders.

He said, "Would I be king here, and my heirs after me?  Or is this to be only a guardianship?"

"I desire my family lands, that's the lot.  But I believe all the kingdoms are now held in trust for the King of All Brittan, whose overlordship you and I must both bow to, when the time comes."

Edin's face was a mixture of feelings.  "In the time of my great grandfather, Edlin — "

"And mine."

"So he was.  In Saffam we grew up with the tales of his greatness, how in his day Suvram was the law, maker and breaker of kings.  When I first rebelled against my father, I thought Suvram could be great again.  Now I know that cannot be in this lifetime.  But Suvram's law would be better than Raug's."

"Do you think I would work for a law that was not?"

"Well.  If an Arfra comes, all the kings must have a say in the law, before they let themselves be unkinged."

"There is to be no unkinging.  The Arfra I see as High King, with kings for captains."

"He is growing," Edin said, filled with thoughts. "The Wosps would follow him through fire."

"Your heirs, you say. Have you thought of marrying?" (Alison, if she had been there, would have loathed me for this.)

"Not till now, as an outlaw with no lands. If you really mean to make me a king, that changes." He grinned all at once. "I could speak to Kennet. Robin told her mother she would die unmarried if she cannot have me. We must believe words like that when spoken."

Robin and Edin. Once seen it should have been plain for ages and ages. Later that day it was not altogether news to still-faced Alison, who nodded, and muttered a story about how Robin, once, had quit the meal-table and run with her skirts bunched above her knees to greet Edin.

"Poor Col. He will be angry, wish you had made him king here. But that would not have gained him Robin." (I must put in here that though Robin was a peach, and no dumbbell, it baffled me anyone with sense not to fear brain in his wife would choose her over Alison.)

"No," I said, "but *if only* is how young men lick their wounds." (This is a way of comparison; we Seeyowites understood it was not to mean they really behaved like cats.) Col had earnt admiration, and his chaps followed him smelling glory, as if it could be caught, like a pox. He might never find his way, as Edin had, to being loved, though once I thought Edin too cool; for him it had come with years. It might be, also, that the highest need to be a bit apart, hedged, as William Shakespeare says.

Col said, hearing the double news, "A king, and captain over all the armies. If the League of the West can stand, Edin will be all the Arfra they need."

This abashed me a bit, being near enough to treasons I once (more than once) thought. "If our western alliance was Brittan, or could be," I said. "But if Edin was the only king in the west, he would still have less than a quarter of the whole. Less still, if you count the Mynas."

"He has always held, choosing a wife, a man should take care," Col said. This was an intended play on the name, Caer.


My sister was not closely guarded, and when next I went to see her, she managed getting hold of a small knife. It was hidden by a cushion where she was sitting, and it was not till I came close to her Gwynis pulled out the knife. Standing up, she told me a chap had to let her return with her daughters to where Forn was, and kept making small jabbings towards me.

I was by myself. The blade was hardly longer than the palm of my hand, and when we were children I could take things away from her, grabbing her wrist. But now she was quite wild, and there was the odd chance of her sticking the rotten shiv into me. When, backing a bit, I told her to put the knife down, she only told me again a chap had to let her go.

Then Avanda came in. She was even more trusted than Gwynis. If she had asked to borrow Col's sword, or Daf's, without them even asking for what. What she did was tell her mother if she hurted Uncle Evan, they would just kill her.

Gwynis answered, not lowering her blade, to effect, those who went against the way of the Viztas knew not a jot but blood and death. In other circs this would have been an interesting glimpse of a face of Forn not shown to the general; my sister had never had any such thought for herself. As was, the pressing matter for a chap was to stop Gwynis swashing the knife about. I told her she could leave in a week; all I asked was a writing from Raug, giving up her every claim to rule here at Caer.

"Giving it up to you?" still jabbing.

"No. Who is to reign in Niragwyn is no concern for the Kingdom of Raug. Once your name is withdrawn, you are free."

"You haven't right to keep me here."

"Why not?" as the threat of the knife drooped away. "Your husband held Worrel, and bargained for land with his life."

"That was a long time ago. Worrel was a fighting man. What sort of warrior does this to his own sister?"

That annoyed me to step forward and wrest away the knife. Again, the words, translated into Print English, are politer than they really were. I said, "Gwynis, you are wife of my longest enemy. Have you ever once told him what he must not do to his wife's brother?"

"All Forn does is only for the true belief."

"Good. Then you are tickled to be wife to the hatedest bounder in all of Brittan. When you see children with faces scarred, you know they were branded in good cause."

For an instant Gwynis was going to deny such could happen. Then she said, "Those are not done by Forn."

"No, by cumnies led by Ermin, Forn's own right hand."

"If there were no lies, or the wicked stopped fighting against truth, there would be no need for strictness, and we could all be pleased. I was never happy before I became Vandene."

That was not my recollection. One of those cases where William Shakespeare can teach more than even Tulsingham; there are times in his plays where he shows something would not need to be said if it were true.  This was like that, and understanding came my sister had not been jolly for simply ages.  It was bally embarrassing for me.  I mean, what was a chap supposed to do?  She was nagging at me to send her back to her foul husband, not rescue her from his durance.

I said, "Leave when you're ready to."  Neal and perhaps Edin would be upset with me, but even if we got the writing wanted from Forn, he would go back on it as soon as his wife and daughters were out of captivity, saying any bloke had the licence to lie in such circumstances.

When Gwynis realised I was dropping that condition, she made out I meant to send the women and their servants on a dangerous journey without any scawt, then complained soldiers furnished by Edin would not give proper respect.  It was my last try at pleasing her.  Not able to think of aught else to grouse about, she withdrew into her bedroom sooner than face me unarmed.

I made to leave, but Avanda said she would bind my hand.  I had cut it a trifle taking the knife from Gwynis, and blood was dripping to the floor.  My niece came to me with a nanky, and had me sit down.

Ever since the end of childhood, Avanda, whether by choice of what she wears or because of her nature, has always seemed adorned instead of covered.  Now, as she bent over my hand, I felt myself (if I can put it so) inside the zone of her attracting; she was all the more dangerous for knowing it.  She had spoken perhaps overloud before, and now she said very softly without looking up she wished I could find more reasons for keeping them here at Caer.

It was not always feasts and holidays like this, I told her.

"I never said it was.  What is Col?"

This question gave me a strange feeling, as if there was a doom in it.  No matter how batty it sounds, that is not too strong; I cannot explain the darkness suddenly lurking.  I said, "Col is not for you.  He will never be Vandene."

She finished at my hand, and looked up with a wide-eyed smile.  "I do not ask for that reason.  Do you not know?  I am going to be the wife of King Vandis; my father has promised me."

"So rumour has been.  Poor girl."  A chap thought it, and said it aloud without really meaning to.  No wonder she did not yearn to leave Caer.

"Not yet, in two years' time."  Seeming to realise that sounded too much like agreeing with me, Avanda quickly added, "I shall be queen to the greatest king since fall of the Regions, the king to be of All Brittan, my father says.  He named me for this when I was born."

"Yes.  If your father has his way, there will be the same joy everywhere as now you find at Vandennis."

That quieted her for a moment, and then she said, "If the Viztas can hear my thoughts, I must irk them, at times, not meaning to.  What is it?" — noticing how sad I suddenly was.

"I was thinking of Seeyow."  Of how different my niece would have been if brought up there.

She gave a shudder, but not of real fear.  "There the anger of the Viztas will fall hardest at the Return," she said (or rather echoed). "You, and Mad Marten, and your little witch, teaching strange ways. I don't mind Alison, really. I wish I could come there and see. Could you keep me as hostage? so my father will keep peace with you?"

Avanda was more or less standing over me by now. Her face was very near mine. "Don't you like having me here?" she murmured, and kissed my mouth. A very light kiss, hardly above a brush of her lips, yet not a bit the sort of kiss a niece gives her uncle. She laughed slyly to see her magic work with me.

The upset was that among feelings shock came in a poor second, and a good part of that from a chap not being shocked, not nearly as much as he should be, or as he much as he was stirred by, yes, imaginings. Blimey. I stood, so she had no choice but to back away a bit, and held up my bound hand. "Thank you for this," I said. "As you must know, we do not use hostages. What waits ahead is nowhere near as fixed as told in the belief of the Adda-priests, but I think you too good to be thrown to Vandis. My work may also save you from that. I hope so."

For her, with what her father said, there could never be much difference between word and fact. How much she misunderstood me came out in her answer, also a question: "They say those who follow the Old Beliefs have charms against a marriage, as well as for one."

"I know bugger all about that." She did not believe me.

The last gathering (last in too many senses) was the do for my passing of the kingship to Edin, and for the three betrothals (Bryan's sister, May, had also found herself a husband, one of Edin's lot, from Suvram). It was only right the weather broke on the eve of this, and the speeches and drinkings went on with a cold rain driving down outside, beating brown leaves from the trees.

It was a celebration for what had been won, but I noted keenest and remember best how those who had not won took their losses. Neal was very quick to hail Edin, and speak of everlasting friendship between the two Gwyns; his son Daf seemed content to be sitting on one side of the bright Avanda. When Robin joined hands with Edin, Kennet's face had the wistful smile proper for a proud father, while Col scarce looked. He was at Avanda's other side. Alison, next to me, faced blankly away for just a moment, then rose to embrace Robin, and say in her ear naughties allowed by the occasion, worth a giggle and a deepened blush. When she sat, Alison asked me, no, told me to take her hand. Of course, I did, and it was very small and held very tight.

My sister was there because (she said) she had no choice, set on not showing pleasure at anything. For the first time I saw my younger niece, Vera, was beginning near comically to look like a stubby, curly-headed Forn. But Gwynis, after the last of the three betrothals had been spoken, turned on me to make my fault the weather in which she would now have to travel. In joke I said, "I had to change it. For the farmers."

### More Loss

It was one decent step towards single rule for All Brittan (though a measure, too, of our littling) that those in alliance against Raug were bothering less with what small kingdom they belonged to. When Edin of Suvram became king in Gwyn, taking wife from Sevenin, only his brother still called him rebel in his own land. The fighters in the part of Suvram he'd held had come to be a muddle of all the western lands, and whilst Edin was still maker of plans, now their real leader on the spot was Col.

Daf was proud to be called Col's Spear. He led the Wosps afield, but Wosps became the name of that personal gawd only, a part of the Brotherhood, in which membership had to be earned. Those who belonged took an oath for justice and steadfastness; a member must have given or had a wound in battle (or both, of course), and the sign of that was a star badge given by one of the captains. At first this was of cloth, but later Rayman, with helpers, made the badges of a white metal. Col remembered Daf's brother by calling it Osset's Star, and it was a great honour for the young fellows who wore it, as Col said, a spur to bravery.

Though there had been exsufflicate talk at Caer about carrying war into the heart of the Vandene Kingdom, the five kings, who not only would have to find the fighters but face consequences of any failing, overruled the hotter-headed, deciding to keep to their watchful defence. Thus, for the Alliance, war paused while Syme finished up the destroying of Cumba, killing or sending into scared exile everyone who had held land under King Tam. This was doubtless begun in a mood of vengeance, or of a warning to other enemies, but was later seen to furnish lands that could be divvied up for the Addas and those who led soldiers of Raug, the Mykas in particular.

Still, such acts, killings of the unarmed, the surrendered and the innocent, wrecking of houses, rapes, were the new spirit of warfare — or as I might say, an old spirit come back to haunt us. It seems war, over and again, gets and loses rules for what may or may not be done. As disputes lengthen in time, real vengeances, rumours of what awfulness the enemy has done or means to do, despair for a losing cause, all make war crueller than when it started, until at last (as is said happened when the House of Regions fell) not a bean remains of what fighting began for, no kingdom or kindness, law or settled life. As the Idiots' Summer littled in brains, soon becoming like a bright recollection of faraway youth, so many wicked deeds were done on all sides, there were times a chap could very near believe a Raug triumph, even, and even a Vandene peace, would be better. All that could be said for the Alliance was it did not go warring, like Raug, against those it already ruled. Yet whilst the Adda-priests went on rooting out disbelief and rival belief, after Cumba the Kingdom of Raug hardly bothered with the pretence its invadings were to help Vandenes outside its borders. By adopted prophecy or nude force of arms, Vandis meant to rule all Brittan.

And time was paring away.  On my secret travels again, there was now no need for me to begin at the beginning when telling any of the Arfra tales; the Adda-priests, as foreseen, were reminding everywhere Brittan once had, and was to have again, such a king.  They did not, or dare not, name Vandis as Arfra, but more and more hearers of my tales were now ready with their own about how the Arfra would be known: a woman comes from the sea, they told me, and leads the king to where he alone can take Scalipal from the stone.  Scalipal, so I was informed, was another name of the True Myke.

Still trying to think of a way to seize the Bronze Rod, these choices among rival versions might be hints to me of what Forn intended when the Rod was brought to light; for myself I was cautious but stubborn in telling bits of the legend where King Vandis could be no more like the Arfra than I to Hercules; the hidden childhood and coming from the shaddas, Arfra's fame as warrior and how he is loved by the people...  All this was part of the story before ever I laid hands on it, and so, while it might be dicey if ever a chap came face to face with an Adda-priest, none of them could debate away what I said, not without giving up the Arfra business altogether.  But more than once a chap could read in the iffy looks of my hearers they had been told to watch out for Telas outside the Vandene faith, and to take what was said with a big helping of salt (if that can mean what I think it did, a seasoning of doubt).

Now the Vandene Kingdom, notwithstanding Caer, was strutting again.  Forn told Urt of Umba, helpless with his old ally Tam gone, he must accept Vandis as his overking, and with that, the Vandene belief for his smalled kingdom, which otherwise would be treated like Cumba. Poor Urt looked wistfully to the western allies, and the kings of Gwyn and Wezram together told Vandis it wasn't right, but Urt knew we could not lessen ourselves trying to send help far to the north, and Forn, as triumph neared for him, was more pitiless than ever. Except for its name, another kingdom vanished. To show what a maze Forn is to explain, I ought to mention after my sister's return to him, at the very time his soldiers were murdering Cumba, Forn sent a short letter to thank a chap for treating his family with gentleness, and for taking taken time, in the midst of war, to let him know of their safety. The selfsame messenger brought threats; Raug's vow never to accept Edin as proper king at Caer.

Tobin of Stanglin was now last of Raug's enemies with no friendly neighbour, a tougher bird than Urt, but bleak for his future. So far Forn asked what seemed like only a little there, small bits of land, claiming Raug's right to draw the borders. But what he aimed for, as Tobin grimly knew, and his son Frick irately spat, here the eastward bank of a river, there the whole of a fenny patch, was capture of Stanglin's defences without bleeding for them. The kings in the League of the West promised to fight for this ally, but made long faces at each other when it came to asking how. Raids, Col said, to make Forn keep more of his fighters in the west; but Edin shook his head in doubt, knowing Raug had the soldiers to fight on all sides at once.

Still before any real winter came, Syme once again leading, Raug threw much strength against Stanglin, forcing a big fight rather than the little hedge and ditch businesses the easterners were best at. Tobin fought and lost the battle, and then Stanglin, under threat of gutting, became another Umba, a subject kingdom. Frick, always the iron warrior, not willing to be part of his father's submission, boated his way to March with two dozen of his toughest fighters.

They were welcome there, but when kings and captains quietly gathered at Pormarch, I saw once more how soon we would go to warring amongst ourselves, but for the shared threat of Raug. In private with me, Bryan was very het over Frick's little cumny, who acted, he complained, as if this was their own land. Loud-voiced Frick, it was true, seemed to think his sister Alma still ruled March (or should), and not her son.

These were worrisome niggles, not chief business. With, all at once, only the League of the West left to be against Raug, there were signs some rulers might think of keeping a portion of their realms as Erril of Suvram had, by making friends with the wolf. Edin argued hotly against this, pointing out the great realm of Suvram was now just a dead rabbit waiting to be picked up by the hunter, but it was Col who spoke best to hearts, saying proudly the Brotherhood would kill and go on killing fighters of Raug and its allies, as they had sworn, till Raug was fed up, or they themselves were all killed, no matter what kings did. He said everywhere were lords like Frick, who might not be able to hold their kingdoms, but would never be a part of letting in the Adda-priests and the Mykas, or of forcing belief on their people. In this, Edin had shown them all the way, and kings' sons like Frick and his own friend Daf had been eager to follow.

This was terrific. Alison, quiet and nearly invisible, was

at that meeting, and after she spoke what was in my thought when she said it was the first time she had seen Col could truly fill prophecy, indeed (as she quaintly phrased it) that he was perilous. This was no more than to echo what Col and I had agreed when we saw the power of a charm as simple as Osset's Badge to make men braver; it is a danger, indeed, that there are such magics, and evil can use them as well as good. Just look at the Vandenes, and how gleefully they killed for their beliefs. Col's speech caused those there to reswear the oath we had taken at Vandennis, over five years ago, never to give in to Raug. The meeting had come about without much warning, so no one was there for Wezram or for Sevenin, and it was sad Frick had to renew the oath for lost Stanglin; still it was a stirring moment.

After, was lots of discussion about where Raug's next blow could be expected. Edin led in this; he was against spreading out the fighters we had, anxious to prevent the alliance from being cut into Umba-sized portions Raug could swallow one at a time. Col objected this meant staying on the defensive.

"If we sit stone still and wait," he said, "Forn can choose his next victim at ease."

"What is our oath for?" Edin said. "No matter where he strikes, his next victim is all of us."

The worst soon followed. At the time of first buddings (not yet the spring, a time without a name, when icy rains or even snow may yet come) I was again travelling as a Tela, and crossed into middle Raug by a way a chap had often used, a small track in mainly unpeopled parts where, a few years back, I would still have been in Marchlen. Half an hour along, the track meets a bigger way, near a town with soldiers in it, but I always turned off into scrawny woods before that.

This time, when I was scarce a good bowshot inside Raug (the border was now marked with the Arch sign of the Viztas, done in wood) soldiers came to meet me, not (I was glad to see) Mykas, about ten mounted fighters, mostly with bows slung at their backs. It would be well to mention here Wott's remark (though a chap has not yet told that) about the soldiers of Raug no longer keeping such neat rows was on the mark, but then lots of the newer cumnnies, among them more archers than before, used horses only for riding to battle, and did fighting on foot.

These had not the scars nor hard faces of seasoned warriors; they were mainly boys, and from south of where we were, to judge by voices. Their leader grabbed the bridle of my poor steed, and asked, did I not know a Tela now needed leave to ride in Raug? He said any found wandering without that was to be seized and given to Adda-priests for questions.

Silly chump a chappie had been, I saw that sooner or later this had to be; when enough people who heard my Arfra tales had asked their priests about the differences. No doubt Forn himself would like to find the Tela who made Arfra so much unlike King Vandis. If I could get out of the present bally mess, I could from now on travel as a poor small trader in dyes or some such, except it was my Tela's cap that brought people to listen to my stories.

The turnip who had halted me told me if they had found me as I came to the border, they would have told me the new law and let a chap turn back. Those were their orders. It was a hard thought for our speech, where to say what might have been if something had been other takes lots of extra making-clear words.

It sounded like a sort of offer. Probably, I thought, the guy did not fancy to go about with a prisoner (a tattered one, no glory) trying to find a priest, or a cumny of Mykas to give me to. I offered that if he told he found me by the Arch, I would never say different.

Calling their leader "Trev," one of the others and then two more said he should let me go, sobe I would first come back to their campment, and tell them some stories. Trev, no dumbbell but not used to wielding rank, put it to me doubtfully, and I said, in style a farmer's man would understand, that it seemed fair deal.

So I went with them, not much like a captive, though knowing I would have to keep them affable. Their draggled and dirty campment was just over a hill. The cumny was about fifty, though part were out looking for food, some perhaps on patrol. It was odd to find them out in the open, camped in a collection of tents and shelters made from branches, but I soon heard every house in or near the town was already filled with soldiers. This was not far from where the armies had massed when they rode against Seeyow, but these seemed to be on their way southward.

About two dozen gathered to hear my news and any tales. For once I thought best to keep off Arfra, and did well, sitting by a smoky fire, with a story about Mad Marten getting him drunk and going to bed with the pigs (in truth he had stayed up too late with some measuring questions, gone out for a breath of air, and fallen asleep in the stables). None of my hearers seemed to be passioned Vandenes, and one lad asked me if it was true there would be a King of All Brittan before long. Someone else said yes, it would be their own King Vandis, but the first sprig was doubtful, asking how there could be an Arfra who had never drawn a sword, much less blooded one.

This caused a chill silencing. Trev, the leader who had first accosted me, warned the hinfant phenomenon he would soon be under the Captain Syme, and there would be Mykas to hear all that was said, as well as more strictness about rules. The men seemed not much to fancy that lark, but a little, sharp-faced bird said no one was going to notice a few clowns, when so many were gathering under Syme. Then Trev tried to cheer his lot up, telling them they would surely be in Bris for that year's May-fair.

The news they did not know they were giving made me anxious to be on my way. Pressed for words about Arfra, I told the shortest (and the least touchy) tale I knew, about letting the cakes get burnt because of watching a spider. Even so, the rusty-haired young doubter said, trying for it all clear, that the woman who chides Arfra does not know him for high king. Another bloke said, "Nah, ees stiw in shaddas."

At such times everyone looks at the Tela, but a chap stayed mum. If I had shown agreement, meaning Arfra could not ever be King Vandis, it might have made Trev change mind and follow his exact orders. After more small news my listeners fed me meat, half burnt, half raw, and the young, doubting one even gave me a small coin. Then I was ridden back to the border, and a smiling farewell was said, Trev by now filled with self-praise, telling me four or five times how lucky I had been to find his soldiers, rather than others he could tell about. Silly beezer.

After humble gratitude a chappie shambled away back along the track, and as soon as certain the soldiers could not see me, kicked as much haste out of my poor nag as he could give.

Near where this way struck the main road south I knew would be armed men of Niragwyn, and I would have to tell them who I was. It was a pity to let out my secret, but I had to have a better horse for a swift ride to Caer with my news. Edin was certain still to be there.

The young captain I found half knew me, recognised no Tela but a mad one would use my manner, and in the end agreed when I said he could send men, or come with me himself to Caer; if I was not Lord Evan they would have me safe. With only a couple of hours' rest, then, I got to Edin with my tale; by what a chap had heard from Trevor's lot, it was certain Raug meant to strike at Sevenin, and soon.

This, because it would cut the alliance in two, Edin had guessed, and had kept a good part of his fighters well to the south. Now, taking his own gawd, he would go there himself. As he warned Robin (who was fretting about her parents), not much of Sevenin could be held against a very strong attack, but Bris and its stream, with a stripe of the shore of the great river-mouth there, might be made too costly for the enemy to take, and as with Landin a siege might be turned against the besiegers. This was as cheering as talk could be at that time, filled with hopes but without false dreams, and I gave back words of the same sort, all the while feeling absolutely foul. It was at last plain to me what I always held was at this instant coming to pass; this was a hopeless struggle if we could fight only with arms and armies; bravery and spilt blood meant nothing. It was guilt a chappie felt, as if I was putting them up to all this warring, pretending a victory was in the cards. What's more, after all my travels sowing seeds, there was no plain view of any harvest; it could still be all I had done was help King Vandis rule as Arfra of prophecy.

Yet now, nearing two years after, notwithstanding all the dyings, a chappie has no clue what else he could have done. As Col had said, they fought for themselves. It was this, or else grovel to Raug and the Adda-priests (in Umba, rumour said, more than forty landowners and merchants who asked their king not to outlaw beliefs other than the Vandene had been taken by the Mykas, tortured and killed in vile ways, with King Urt powerless).

Still I remember Edin saying farewell to his wife, and how they seemed to me the model for young marriage, very loving. Either was the other's all, as an old poet says — but my sentiment is a liar, because if we think back a few weeks more, I can hear Edin saying in private to me, "A fellow needs two wives, or none." Edin had not long asked after my ward, and having the tenderness shared with Robin, missed (I guess) the Seeyow talk and open friendship he'd had with Alison. Robin was joy, but there were more sides to Edin. His one wife, perhaps, having soon found she would ever be watching him ride away, or watching for him to ride back, might have said a woman needs a whole husband, not half. Yet (if a chap is allowed to say this) it was these constant partings that was keeping the gilt on their gingerbread, more lovers than man and wife.

And still after two years my heart goes cold just to write down the news that came behind twelve days of rumours and guesses: Col had killed Syme, but Edin was dead.

It was not till the midsummer days, fighting having paused, when Daf came to Seeyow bringing Robin's mother, Cara, that I heard more fully what had happened.  But I'll tell it here.

Daf's account was long, filled with muddling battles, and told without the help of a language fit for the task.  What I write here is made simpler, with its imperfections eked out by my later talks with Col; even so there are parts never clear to a chappie, untrained in warfare as I am.

Edin came down through Marchlen, giving orders for men to make the crossing from Pormarch to near Bris, but he himself with his gawd crossed into Sevenin farther to the north.  As well as the name of the kingdom, also the place where the ruler lives; Edin came down to Sevenin the town in time to help Kennet and Cara escape, a strong attack having routed the defenders.

As said, Edin meant to hold at least a part of the ruins of Old Bris and the lands behind.  His plans to then defeat the enemy there were pinned on two lots of reinforcements; a force larger than had ridden with him being collected in March, and vitalest of all, Col's Brotherhood.  Edin had sent messages to Col, and expected him soon.

Meanwhile, the ones who had crossed from Pormarch were already being driven back by the main forces of Raug, coming down the river-valley from south and east of Bris.  Edin's lot checked the enemy at Old Bris itself, and acted as rearguard for those who retreated southward, in the direction from which it was expected Col's advance would come.  Kennet, Cara and their household went with those.

Daf and Col both believed Edin had meant to hold the enemy at and among the ruins of Old Bris.  In any case he soon lost any choice when he was cut off from the channel landing, and all-but surrounded there.  At about the same time as Col, riding with the Brotherhood and allies, began encountering both retreating friends and pursuing enemy, a message reached him from Edin, asking for speed. This was not only to save Edin, who now was outnumbered more than ten to one, but to seize the opportunity of taking the enemy in flank.

Already fighting, not sure what strength of enemy was between him and the straight way to Bris, Col left Daf in command of the main force (enlarged, now by those who had retreated from Bris), and took the best cumnies of the Brotherhood on a dash first east and then north to where the small river was bridged, half a day upstream from where the city had been. He found the bridge lightly held. Crossing and turning west, the Brotherhood was in a trice amongst heavily armed enemy, Syme's personal cumny. Taken by surprise, they were never able to turn and form up. The giant Syme rallied his fighters, but Col, as one of his captains said, cut his way through, fought man to man with Syme, and hacked the palooka down like a big oak. It may be (Col himself was quick to say) twenty years of fame and rule by reputation had left the great bruiser out of practice for actual fighting; be that as it may his fall bucked up Col's fellows as much as it dismayed those of Raug. Syme's head, carried on a sword, went with Col into Bris, and nothing would stand in his way. As a matter of fact, as afterwards was clear, large parts of the enemy forces had already been sent across the small river to meet Daf's dangerous advance, now very near. These, finding themselves all at once in danger from two sides, slid away to the southeast, and after fighting among the ruins, Col was in possession of Old Bris, and drove thence to the channel landing, still using Syme's head as a bleeding banner.

For the time, he had a win, a costly one. Too late for Edin, whose defence, by keeping lots of enemy clustered at Bris, had made the victory possible. But he had been driven, through three days, into a smalling circle, and at last was trapped and killed in that large old building where I had gone with Worrel, and first met Thea. So it now had memories of the three best friends a chap had known, generous warriors, losses without hope of any amends.

Edin's death was mourned everywhere in the West, but Col's feat was spoken of much the more, especially among common people. All three were names to them, but Syme's was the nightmare of whole lifetimes, and by killing him Col became his own legend. So to speak, it also took him outside any choosing of mine.

This, as I've said, a chap learnt later. Before that, when we had bare certainty Edin was dead, I went back to Seeyow, taking Robin with me, and sending word to Neal he would have to govern defence of both Gwyns for time being. The island, more than ever, had become a place of refuge, and on the journey there Robin told me she would have Edin's baby. Robin's coming there was like Caif over again, twenty years on, but Robin had the solace Alison could and did give; they would spend lots of time together, remembering the best of Edin.

But I had, for the first time, a hot quarrel with Alison, when, still knowing less than fully how the wars were going, a chappie said he would put on ragged clothes again, and go back to wandering. She was white-faced and tight as I had never seen her, and questioned to know how I could think so, with such lots of danger, Edin just dead, and so many, like Robin, who needed comfort from my being there.

"My journeys are in the same cause Edin gave life for."

"Col's kingship?" she returned (we were by ourselves, of course). "The price is already too high, and if — " The girl never finished, her eyes wet for sudden memory of being pals with Edin. Of loving him, I could've said.

A chap lectured her, with all softness, on the difference between the chance of Col's rule for itself, and to save All Brittan from Vandene victory, rule of the Adda-priests. For a mo Alison simmered down, then, boiled up again when I like a bally ass mentioned my will in Rayman's keeping. Well, I desired her to know she would still have a place if I got knocked off. It was natural of her to fear a life becoming lonelier, but others, as a chap said, had lost near friends in these long wars, and they could be honoured only by warring on, all in ways we could, till what the end would be.

"As you say, Master." Alison, not having called me that for years, and never with that sting. It was, a chap reflected, all the harder for her, helping to comfort the young widow of the man she had picked for herself. Still, when came time to leave for Little Seeyow, I still had hopes she would make peace and give her hug goodbye. But she was with Robin.

In vanishings when I judged the priests or their Mykas were starting to look for me, the Mynas had been big help. So long as I stayed clear of the Moorhens and their few friends, I could always mention the name of Donal or of Wott with profit. Though no one ever used my name, it's pretty sure lots knew just who I was, and I had often been given a meal and a bed as well as a hiding place; sometimes they told me where Mykas were riding, or put me on a little-used path to keep away from towns and travelled roads.

This time when I could feel the breath of the Addas on my neck (it was now real spring), I was towards the eastern part of Raug, and made up mind to slip away into Stanglin, where there were fenny hiding-places. In an old town called Eel, not long ago taken back by Raug, there was a little May-fair going on. When I went to booths run by Mynas and asked if anyone knew Wott of Lunn, I was taken into the back part, and suddenly was looking at the thick-browed face of Asta, sitting at a table sorting her roecards ready for telling fates. She was welcoming, but hardly said more than six words before she had a boy lead me not far, to where we came to a hill, at first seeming a natural mound. Then, under tufts of weed and grass I made out squared stones, and the high arches with pointed tops churches often have for windows.

A long way ago in this tale, a chap promised to tell part of what is known about churches. That's not what we call them, but from Tulsingham, and other words, I know these churches were a part of the Jesus Christ belief, used for meetings and (Tulsingham says) for rituals more suited to the ignorant savage than to civilised men. But we have a different tale. The common belief is that long ago, when the Viztas were new and we still like children, they hoped to please their teachers by building them lofty houses, using the skills they had now been taught. For a hundred years, the story is, the builders who had learnt craftiest kept working in secret, but when the Viztas, who did not need houses, saw how foolishly we used what they instructed, they were much peeved, and would never go inside any of the houses.

I've heard a priest say this was what brought about the Leaving, when the Viztas saw we would always be silly asses. Still, one version goes on to tell that for years and hundreds of years the churches were kept mended, swept and cleansed by hopefuls who believed the Viztas might change their hearts; blokes and women would meet there, bringing fresh flowers, and chant and sing to the Viztas, hoping they would take their gift one fine day. The Vandenes say it was the Vandene faith, after Noble and the Mighty had buggered off, that brought the end of the watch. All this is codswallop, but truth is, a lot of good building is left to stand empty, for fear of past hauntings. They're everywhere.

This was one of the larger (these used to have still another name). Above the entrance, where the crack and sliding of stone had made a steep slope, a small tree had rooted itself, and lower down daffodils were still in golden bloom. Once within, it was both more and less like a building; shafts of light came down through big gaps, and I could see tall pillars of stone, and a stone floor, still sound in parts. Though the sides stooped darkly away in falls and rubble, the middle part was very lofty. It must have all been put up, block by block, but I could dream it had been scooped out from within, cut from solid rock, a huge made cavern done with long craft and patience, a miracle of rare device. Yet everything was doubt; an archway might be only a gap, and in small light the planed walls were so stained with moist and mould, so crusted with moss and lichens, they seemed cliffs. From above in the lower places strands of leafless bramble, loops of what might be honeysuckle that would never flower, swaying tangles of white roots brushed at face and shoulders. Rat feet were scuttling somewhere, and with a loud flurry of wings a bird high above was dark for a blink against a leaf-fringed hole to the sky. There I met Wott himself, and had a peep of how strong the Mynas, made one, might be for allies: for private chat with me Wott left a secret gathering of what must be leaders, young and older, but all with the look of uncrushable fighters.

He did not seem startled to see me, having had word of a Tela in these parts (this was not our first such encounter). It was odd to me that before aught else, he asked about Alison; he had known her well, but Col was his nephew. I told him what a chap could, then asked for his news. He came from the north, and had seen soldiers, soldiers, soldiers. A smith, he said, could keep himself just making stirrup-irons for all Raug was putting in the saddle, not to speak of weapons. Being majoritily new recruits, he added, their lines were no longer as straight when they rode together. This a chap had already heard from Col, who believed losses among Forn's fighters meant their big new armies would be that much less well trained. It was a hope to clutch at, but Syme's best cumnies, fighting in Cumba, had suffered small loss.

Wott waxed proud to hear what Col said was listened to as weighty now, but he did not say so, and stuck to talk of smiths, saying Linsy who had been with us at Seeyow was Forn's man, now, in the north. The Hares old kin, the Marsh Otters, said he was making one of those lifting machines. That, as I answered, was all to the good; when we made it, we hoped our winch would be copied everywhere. There was no need for Forn to have wasted a spy on that. Still, a chap stuffed this away in his bag of news.

Wott had word, also, from the south; Frant, the dealer in stone, was a Vandene now. When a chap mentioned he was cousin of my wife, Wott looked glum, and seemed ready to clam up, till I explained (or tried to) that the blighter was neither kin nor ally of mine. That satisfied Wott, although to this day it may be told among Mynas I got rid of my first wife because her cousin became Vandene.

The Mynas of Lunn now had to cross the border to take their stone to Frant, but Wott told Frant had visits from Addas — from Forn himself, last winter. The Mynas believed this might mean Raug aimed to possess Lunn, and was questioning Frant about ways of the Mynas there. Much good might it do Forn; according to Wott, Mynas of every clan had been lying to Frant for thirty years, as to his father before. He knew less reliable about Lunn's hidden ways than even I.

I queried whether, if Raug tried to subdue the wilderness of Lunn, the Mynas would forget their clan rivalries and fight as allies. Wott made a gesture to ask why need ask. Only a clan like the Moorhens, he hooted (may their cocks rot), would be on the wrong side — and there were no Moorhens at Lunn.

Again I iterated my question: would all true Mynas fight together to help one of their own become great. This brought back the same shyness there had been before in his mentioning Col. Slowly, a chappie began to see why. Knowing what general people thought of Mynas, Wott (and others) feared claiming Col as partly theirs would hurt his chances. I pointed that if an Arfra was to come from the shaddas, he would be King of All Brittan, king for the Mynas, too. He would need their help, and would not deny his fathering. Seeing Col never discussed his father, this was pretty froward of me, but a chappie was beginning to see what a chump he had been. I'd always expected help from the

Mynas, but never asked how much help, or why, other than Col's connections, Marten's friendships and mine, it should be forthcoming. Somewhere I've read of a secret advantage called *ace in the hole*, and that's what the Mynas could be for us, our aces hidden in holes, weapons Forn could not consider in his plans.

That meant, as a chap now expounded, the Mynas would have King's Law; if one not a Myna stole from, or hurted, or killed a Myna, he would answer for it as if he had harmed one of his own. Mynas would now own their houses, hold land, like any other. (It was always hard to keep in brain that where the Mynas were was never theirs, except others lacked the force or thought it not worthwhile to drive them out: even Lunn they held by fear, not law. I knew what I said would go straight to the gathered Myna leaders here.)

Wott, his manner still very mild, showed some doubts, aware the lords there were now might be slow to agreeing. For the first time I spoke in open about the weakness of the kings (except Vandis); without help not to be found for themselves, I confided, the lords there were now could not keep their kingdoms. When Arfra came, they would bow to him, and thank him for the rooves above their heads. The King's Law, Arfra's Law, would be law. I myself was facing for the first time how bullying a King of All Brittan would have to be: Col, not sentimental like me, had seen it years ago, while still a boy; *the power of life or death over the others*, he had said, and by golly it came to that. Still, landholding Mynas were a lot to ask; Col himself might be taken by surprise. In first speaking about Mynas in this tale, a chappie said what we are all taught, what Mynas themselves said, that they think sowing seed and harvesting crops all wet, no jobs for proper guys. I would now say instead they learnt to call these unmanly because they never had lands to farm.

Wott made a small humming noise, and avowed Mynas would fight for an Arfra like that, especially if they knew he was their Arfra. His (can a chap say?) closed, unhoping face put me in mind of Alison, when I first asked her to trust a chappie's word.

This was not the whole of our talk by a long shot, but Col, when next I saw him, said, "Yes, the Mynas should have the good of King's Law — if they have leaders who can promise their obedience. As it is in the Brotherhood, loyalty goes both to and from."

This was at Seeyow. Cara was there, too, and Daf, who brought her. So for a time was Kennet. He soon went back to Wezram, where fighters mustered and trained, still untouched by Raug.

Sevenin was gone, except for a small patch in the north and the foothold at Bris, but Raug was not pressing any new attacks; the death of Syme, blokes said (hoped, rather), made them timid to take on fighters led by Col. It was late summer when Col came to Seeyow, and the first duty he did was go to Robin, by now big-bellied, and try to put in words (as Alison, who was there, told me) his sorrow he had been too late at Bris to save Edin.

Considering how long Col had wished for Robin, and how young they still both were, some (Rayman, to name one) expected them to go beyond shared bewailings. Rank would no longer have been in the way; widows in general have their choosing, and Robin's father, moreover, was king without his kingdom. Whilst Col, if no king (yet), was at 21 the famousest warrior alive, and seemed it in every step he took. No one, I think, can say whether the glory of feats performed is really there, surrounding the famed; whether it shines from inside, or is in the watching eye of admiration — whether, mayhap, a hero becomes a mirror for our praise and our awe. In mere rank, too, Col had succeeded Edin as undoubted war-captain of the West. But he behaved with Robin (this might have been otherwise if Edin's small son had come earlier or later) just as a fellow would with a sister bereaved, and to Alison as if he saw her for the first time.

She was, be it noted, lovely in a new way. I doubt how much taller she truly was, but because of a change in bearing and the set of her chin we no longer thought of her as very small; she always had an agile body, but there was now no kitten in her gracefulness. It was a proper treat to watch her, not unmixed joy for me, knowing, seeing in how she was courted by the young warriors, I would not have her much longer. Saying *have*, I don't mean she was ever an ort a chap owned, or should own, but whilst they call me Magician, and Rowan once said I had no blood, only ink in my veins, Evan is just another poor blighter, and Alison was woven into my life. It should be told, when I came back from my trip, our quarrel might never have been, but that she allowed herself, maybe, more tears than ever before when she came to hug me home. Yet "nothing was changed" must always be a lie for any with the power to say it: words that in themselves make what they deny.

Col's new admiring came after a renewal from Daf, not

like his former urgent try at putting her to bed; for some reason he now treated her as one of his own standing (and that, unless marriage is in the cards, means trying to get to the same place by longer and politer roads). Alison, with me, wondered that two years of warring could make for better manners: a courteous Daf, she said, was what lots of girls dream, still a panther, but one with a collar.

Soon, Col and Daf disagreed, but not over Alison, and not with the bitterness of their younger quarrels. It was about the best way to guard Seeyow. Quite likely, Daf would not dispute any other war business with his famed boss, but Daf, remember, had very well run the former defence. Col for the bulk part liked Daf's measures, such as the high barrier of poles and iron bars (found among the piles of stuff in Marten's courtyard) to impede landing along much of the narrows; and the one disagreement was at last settled in Col's favour: the fishers and traders keeping boats at and near the strait on the mainland side were compelled (Daf had to do that, using his father's powers) to bring those crafts over to the island. This was a hardship for them, and really meant to have any living they had to move their homes, but Col was firm, pointing out if the yokels waited, as Daf urged, till there was imminent peril, a sudden attack by Raug could capture all the boats they needed. After this, Daf was gone. The kings had made me Guardian for Niragwyn, with an heir still growing inside Robin, but at my suggestion Daf would run things at Caer while a warrior was the greatest need for rule.

All I have been telling has place, but seems slight to me, next to the talk we had when Col first came. It was just after his seeing Robin, and we also spoke of Edin, calling to thought days in this very place when young Col had learnt from his tall friend. Rayman was with us, and said, "He was likely to have proved most royally; realms and islands were as plates dropt from his pockets." Col looked with cocked eyebrows, but he knew that was Rayman's way; in him simple words of his own would have been less true in feeling than this.

I praised Col's killing of Syme, Worrel's avenging at last, adding, "and so you have killed your giant." One of Arfra's early feats — a real giant, you understand: by "real" I mean, gigantic, after the way of tales, not that real giants ever were.

Col said calmly, "I am Arfra now, all but Scalipal, and that (turning, touching his hilt, to Rayman) could be this sword we made together."

Here happened a response beyond my explaining. Rayman, a proper son of Seeyow, knowing like any of us (of Seeyow, that is) the frontier between tales and truth, certainly not forgetting Col knew next to damn all about smithcraft, said, "*As is foretold.*" His long, light-lashed face was more filled of devotion than can be imagined.

Then Col gave me a quick, private, half-smiling glance, asking me to admit what a piece of cake it was. He said, "Evan, time to proclaim Arfra. Raug is checked for a bit, but they are winning; Arfra must come from the shadows while there is still aught left to save."

"Not yet."

"I am not asking." Col was cool as blocks of monumental alabaster. "Or if I am, only to ask if you still would have a part in this. But for a name, I am there now. Have I told you how I ended the bickering in March? I told Frick he and his gawd could come with the Brotherhood, and I gave him Osset's Star."

"He accepted?" Frick was war-tried, nearer my age than Col's, not easily flattered.

"He took his oath that minute," Col said. "Then Bryan, too, hungered to join us. I told him Marchlen needed its king, but gave him his Star. His two brothers will be with us."

Rayman said, "There are lads on Seeyow who would give all they ever hope for, only to wear that Star. One asked yesterday when the Lord Col would come; a son of the carpenter, a strong, good-looking youth."

This, I recognised, would be Peet, the younger brother of Pol, the boy given kinky lessons by Alison when she was newly here. Col said, "Have him come and let me see him. We've got lots of lads of no family willing to work towards their place in the Brotherhood."

Turning back to me he said, "It is like this everywhere I go. You once told me I had to learn my trade, Evan, and I told you warring was part of it. The master is always the last to see his apprentice is full-grown; I am grateful to you, but with you or without, I am going to take my tide at the flood."

"May it lead on to fortune," Rayman said, pleased at the words Col had found.


There was truth, right enough, in what Col said. In my schemes for bringing him forward, a chappie now saw, there had always been one silliness. If only I (or someone else, come to that) was to judge whether he was ready to be Arfra, that time could never come, because anyone worthy would not wait to be told: I could not have an obedient pupil and the fitting ruler of All

Brittan in one person. It should, ergo, rejoice me he was now at the point of giving me the kiss-off.

So, in part, it did. There were still places where we would disagree, where Col, I thought, would say my wish for ruthfulness applied to worlds of dreams, not real ruling. But again, he was the one to rule, and though I might offer advice, it would be nitwitted to expect him to do just as I would. Still, a chap did expect to be something to him.

None of this was any of the reason why he could not declare himself Arfra now. I said, "Col, I've worked for lots of years to prepare this."

"I've kept at it, too." Here, he was ironic.

"You have not had easy tasks," I agreed. "All the more reason for patience now."

"There is not more time for patience."

"What will happen if you step out now, tomorrow, and call yourself Arfra? What will you have that you have not now?"

"What will happen if I wait? Now, I've got armies, and kings looking for someone to save them. This time next year, quite likely we may be no more than a few outlaw bands, hiding in the hills from the Vandenes. It must be now, or soon."

I kept to my path. "Then you'll have every follower you've got now, and not one sausage more. The worse part is, you'll have every single enemy you've got now, not a sword or a bow less. You won't even gain the Mynas, whose time for the appearance of Arfra is the same as the Vandenes have been teaching for years, three seasons from now, at Midsummer. All you need is the same patience your mother had when you were born." A chap meant, it was the same amount of time.

"How can chances be made better by weakening ourselves? If we kill five enemy and lose two of our own, that's a lost fight."

"And will be, whether you are called Col or Arfra, unless your naming comes at the right time. Next year, at Midsummer, all Brittan will be ready, and Forn means to unveil the Bronze Rod so everyone can see. We know who his Arfra is, but I see plenty of doubters. I've listened to birds in the armies of Raug; there must be Mykas and Adda-priests who know in their hearts Vandis could never be the foretell. Certes, the Mynas do, and they are ready to work for the proper Arfra. But if, at that moment, with everyone watching, a man stands out, in all ways nearer prophecy than Vandis, to claim the Rod, even true Vandene believers will be shaken. There are soldiers of Raug, captains, even, among them, who could not do battle against him."

"Why would that not be true now?" Col questioned. "Spots that are called Raug are only so because they are forced to be. We have held out against Raug partly because they have to spend their armed men watching for rebellions."

His face was lit with eagerness. I did not think I could explain any better, and was bally sure I was not going to say it all again. "Well," I said, getting up as if to leave, although this talk was in the room most mine of any, where I do reading and writing. "You have my advice. To me it seems time is the key. Your friends will follow you, now or any time, and if you won't wait, a chap will do what he can. But where shall I begin, when Forn tells his blokes, *our enemies, in their desperateness, have put up a false Arfra, as could be foreguessed, with the time of the true Arfra drawing so near*?"

"Wait, Evan," Col said. "What is it they say the Bronze Rod does? The Old Believers, not the Vandenes."

No ruddy joke, to win a debate and then see what's been chewed over turn from words to real. Telling Col again what Thea had taught about the Rod, I knew his question meant he would take my advice, and wondered what I might have caused. Suppose Col, who nowadays followed danger like its lover, was killed before next summer? or Forn won everywhere, and we were all dead or prisoners? Even if we held out so long, how could Forn be stopped from raising Vandis?

Till now Col had left all that up to me. Now, naturally, he sought to hear what plans I had to overturn Forn's. He had, as he said, a right to know, and on the day before he left Seeyow I told him all I could see for myself. The Rod, I believed, was either at Vandennis, or with Forn in his northern place. Both were being watched by our Mynas. It was odds on Forn meant to unveil this sign at Gridge, since that was where we would all be at midsummer.

Col protested, "If there is war everywhere next year — "

"There will be Gridge Time, or Vandis will declare Noble's Peace." I was quite sure. Forn purposed the right of Vandis to rule All Brittan put outside any doubt. It struck me, also, with all his shrewdness, he was still what Tulsingham calls a pawn to superstition. He was too clever to swallow, in his own conviction, Vandis could ever be Arfra, but I was sure he believed in the power of the Rod, and that it must be claimed at its due time.

"A thing that was held by Alexander," Col said, dark eyes

glowing. "That Caesar and Achilles thought could make them win. Such magics seem less silly when they've been believed so long."

"You've kept away from your books too much," I chid. "Achilles is only in a tale."

"When I am king, I'll have you and Rayman to remember suchlike facts for me," with a quick laugh. "And Alison. There is part in this for Alison to do, I guess. Lots of people already think she has powers. Is she my Gwynfa?"

This was startling in its baldness, and seemed to me the oddest question, from one who, a week ago had told me, and rightly, he was no longer my apprentice: of all, surely a chap who is his own should pick his own wife.

"Well, Thea all-but chose Alison for you, and I've thought it might turn out. What do you think? What does she?"

"Do you ever know what she thinks?" with near-annoyance. "Besides, picking a queen is not like picking just a wife. If I am to be the king we talk about, Arfra need not marry a woman because he likes her talk or the shape of her bum. He can have that, freely." Seeing a chappie's startlement, he amended: "I mean, as rule, not my feeling about Alison."

"What about loving?"

"The King of All Brittan can have that, too, without marrying. Arfra and Gwynfa in the tales are only like ordinary lovers because ordinary people tell the tales, and listen to them. It would be different, really. You know the king Tulsingham says changed a realm's belief by accident? He hindered himself with one wrong wife after another. Choosing a queen is policy, like everything Arfra must do — and all you've done with me, since

I was a boy."

That accused, but I was moved to sorrow, not guilt. Laying a hand on Col's hard shoulder, I said, "Policy did not make your fate, only the chances for it to unfold. You know I disbelieve in fate: you are still free to choose your ends."

Col frowned for a moment, then grinned all at once. "What chances have you made for Alison, then?"

This came back to plans. The Adda-priests had been telling the tale, not of Arfra forging Scalipal, but of a woman coming from the water to bring it to him, or him to it. If, as I hoped, there was any way of grabbing prophecy for ourselves, Alison would be that woman.

"And give the Rod to me," Col said, thinking. "How can we ever get it away from Forn? It must be guarded with armies." His eyes opened very wide. "Break the Gridge truce?"

It first seemed this must be a poor joke. Then I saw how sensible blokes might maintain for sake of saving all blokes from everlasting Vandene rule, no uncouthness went too far. "Could the reign of Arfra, the oath-keeper, begin with a dodge like that?"

"I say no," carefully. "But you've astonished me before now."

With or without the truce, I told on, it would be too late once the Rod got to Gridge. Still, I did not see Forn bringing it there himself, or guarded by big cumnies of soldiers. There had to be a magic to its appearing, and he would surely try to bring it south in secret, then perhaps have it brought from the sea by some Myna woman, from the Moorhen clan, likeliest.

"How from the sea?" Col wondered. "The sea is a long way from Gridge, a good day's ride."

"I am not in his thoughts. But Marten says when he was a child it was still the rule, on midsummer's eve, to go down to the river, where it widens, not more than an hour beyond Gridge, and watch the midsummer sunrise from where, according to tales, the Viztas first came ashore." This custom, I knew, had been brought from Stoneplain, where the Beakrock, half a day south, is also said to be where the Viztas landed.

"This is all guessing."

"I have not always guessed badly. If Forn leads everyone down to the shore, and has Vandis waiting at waterside, and instead of his woman Alison comes from the sea with the Rod for you, then there will be Adda-priests kneeling to you as Arfra of prophecy."

Col pictured it in his brain. He shook his head. "If you can get the Bronze Rod away from Forn, you deserve to be called the Magician, What help do you need for this?"

With all the doubts I still had, this was a delighting question. Not long before he would've asked much more about my schemes (more than a chap could've told him, or knew myself), and before that would simply have left it all to me. Now his trust was not a child's, but that of a big leader, who knows he must leave parts for others to do. I told him there would be help from Mynas, but there might be a time when I would need a few good fighters who would find a way to do what I asked, not expecting me to be a warrior myself. Chiefly, his job was to stay alive.

"You could find easier, for anyone making war on Raug," he said. "If the worst comes, All Brittan by next Gridge may be nothing but Raug, with Seeyow, bits of of Wezram, and a few outlaw bands to annoy it. Evan, where are your plans if Forn decides he has no need to bring out the Rod?"

Sometimes, jolting from sleep in the lonely black before dawn, I had panic doubts that went beyond that. How was I so sure there was a Bronze Rod, now or ever? The word of a dying mistress of dauwas? Who would not say a chappie must have a screw loose, to tailor so much of his life and what hopes he had to that, and to words from men and women noone else of my rank would trust with a horse, with a loaf of bread? A story could be made up where Thea had been paid by Forn, or simply off her onion. Sane, if she believed every word she said, that was no proof of rightness. The Adda-priests saved me; if they had not been so busy foretelling Arfra, I could've made the cold sweats last into full daylight.

"What?" I told Col, "and have to wait five hundred and fifty-four more years for his next chance? He may not expect to live so long."

Again I told him, with his reputation won, he no longer needed to be at the front of every fight. He said, "How can I order others to do what they know I do best?"

"They know there is no other whose death would sink us all. More than brave deeds, you owe Brittan your living on."

The king-to-be (as now I say) gave me a long, earnest look. "You are for me, Evan," as if the thought was new. "With men, even with Daf, I hear them say so, and wonder what they ambition for themselves — oh, I've got Daf's loyalty, I know that, but only lowly blokes are happy with serving, and I cannot have real friends if I come to be Arfra; friends share, and that is not for sharing."

As before, when he spoke about Alison, I was sadded (and still am) Col saw so clearly, so soon, how kingship would divide him from others. "Gaining it can be shared, and keeping it."

He nodded. "You are the — what did they call the fellows who planned big buildings, and saw them built? There is one called Robin, in Tulsingham's book. Wren, not Robin."

"An architect." A mysterious, complicated word.

"You are the architect, the architect of Arfra."

Good heaven, but he had found it, the way of making himself gladly served. Even the Magician's chest could puff in prideful gratitude.

She had been quiet in mood since Col's leaving, and now was time for me to go: my meetings with Wott were too big a part of my schemes to be left to an off-chance; I would see him by arrangement at Caer.

After circling chat, she, very calm, said, "Is your plan I should be Col's Gwynfa? We see he is to be our Arfra."

"Have you had a marriage offer?" A daft question. It was plain Col must have made mind up after our talk.

"Two," she said, with a laugh. "But the other, no doubt, would stand back, if he knew Col was bidding for me."

That must be Daf, but there was a bite here, some scorn of mannish dreams, as if she was saying no rival loyalty could ever turn her aside from the one she set heart on.

"And do you hope for Col?"

"I wish him all good. I'll marry him, if you say it is needed to fill out his legend. If you say I should."

This, on face of it, was pretty cool for her, and (as it suddenly seemed) cruel to me. Why must it all be put on Evan?

"You know," I said, "Above all, I've always desired you to be happy."

"Not quite all," she (too aptly) amended. "When I was still little Thea taught we were happy if we might be, but could not be happy going against what we knew to be — " Alison had a thought, but no simple way to say it. She made a fluttering gesture. "Thea called it our service."

Service to what? was, of course, what crossed a chap's thought. My last chinwag with Wott had left a chappie a bit uncomfortable about whether I had made allies of Mynas and Old Believers, or they found a use for me. But the difference, in point of fact, was only the words you used for it, and my work had been cut out for me more than half a lifetime ago, when I had come on an Adda-priest spouting his piece in where was then Marchlen. What might be best beats me, but I knew what was bad, and stopping the Vandenes came before everything.

Or so a chappie had thought. When dying Thea said about me, too, paying a price, I thought she must've meant, oh, not having time to be a small king on my own account, perhaps my risky travellings as a Tela, giving up my own comforts, Seeyow studies, even my married life. So she might, but what about these two accusings, quite different but so much the same, that the price I must pay was other people's choice, the lives of those I yearned to love best?

I was blur-eyed when I told Alison, "I must ask you, if it can be swung, to help with making Col a king. Beyond that, you must choose for yourself."

"Oh," Alison said.

## The Last Spring

It was a winter of no good news, steady defeat. Our hopes had been for an early winter and a hard one, to give us some rest. It had never come, and Raug never paused in its warring all through the mild, rainy weeks after harvest was in, or the dryer weather, still mild, of the short days.

Forn had found way to keep the West from gathering its fighters, by making attacks in two or more places at the same time; when the Brotherhood sped to help Marchlen, threatenings came to Caer or in the south. The northern strip of Sevenin was soon kaput, forcing Col to give up the dear-bought foothold at Bris. This also bared Pormarch to attack, and though, replete with ace bowmen, its taking was hard, arrows ran short at last, and Bryan's chaps had to bust out of encirclement by night. Bryan with his Nettle-Greens was soon helping Neal in defence of Landin, and too was his mother, Alma, whose bow had croaked tens or hundreds of enemy, depending on whose tale.

With Marchlen overrun, Caer was jeopardistic, with fierce fights not so much for the town as the roads it needed to live.

If, when spring dawned, Raug had failed to make true about Col's worst forebodings, it was only by a bit, and that only because Forn let himself be drawn aside from putting all strength against the League. Just as we despaired, Raug paused. An army which once more had seemed about to attack Seeyow melted away like Assyrians in a poem, and in other places the enemy numbers shrank; they just guarded the ground newly won.

I heard of big cumnies marching north, but it was quite a time before we had real news of what Forn was up to now. It was spoken there had been an uprise in conquered Umba; how true this was, and how much of an uprise if so, could never be fixed. Not enough, you can wager much, for the vasty forces Raug brought to quell it. This puzzle was riddled when Forn made it loudly known King Vandis in person had led in these fights. There were huffing tales of battles fought and prisoners taken; poor King Urt was brought back to Vandennis bound. It needed least brain to see the big armies used were so as there could be no risk to Vandis; even so a chap heard when a band of his own lot, riding back from a search, were for a sec mistaken for armed enemies, Vandis hid amongst carts carrying his supplies.

Perhaps wicked to admit, on balance I was heartened. This silly do (silly for everyone but the poor Umba blokes) could have no sense, but for trying, so late in the day, to give Vandis some cobbled reputation as a leader for war. For me there were no more doubts about his proclaiming as Arfra; it was coming.

This still meant vanishment of another kingdom, and at about the same time King Tobin, who had lived in deep shame since the Adda-priests and their Mykas (as his forced treaty with Raug allowed) had brought fear and pain to his realm of Stanglin, died — some said, did himself in. Frick was the heir, but he was riding in the south with Col, and without quick hope of gaining his inheritance.

A bit more about Frick: you know he's Alma's brother, a burly beezer who had been fighting for more than half his life; he has his scars, and his left hand is two fingers short. In a luckier time he'd've won, long ago, heaps of honour for his prowess, but warring for his land with no ally near enough to give help, all his wins added up to great loss. It was the bitter taste of being a strong soldier for a hopeless cause that led, I believe, to his quarrelsomeness when he found his refuge in Marchlen. The king there, his nephew Bryan, he thought of as boy, and, judge O ye gods, Frick thought not much of having his ideas for tactics debated by those with far lesser years or battles than he had lived through. Even when a stripling, he thought fighters listened too much to me.

Nevertheless, after the killing of Syme (a famed deed Frick himself would have given all he owned or hoped to to bring off) Col was a hero for him. Joining the Brotherhood, Frick soon, with his own small gawd, became Col's doughtiest captain (Daf was away in Gwyn). From early days, fighting for his own Stanglin, he had been known as unforgiving, and now he was accumulating a reputation for cruelness that made some call him Col's own Syme. That was too much to speak, of course. Col said, when asked if Frick might not be too harsh in treatment of captives and so forth, it was high time our side had a warrior to spread a bit of funk.

Thus, of kings, when new grass sprang and the pale ferns began to unwrap selves, only two were living in their own houses (of the Alliance, I mean to say; outside it, Vandis was at Vandennis, and the ga-ga Edlin II still doddled at Saffam); Neal, brawling bitterly over the country about Landin, and Follen at Tawn in Wezram, still intact, its approaches guarded by Col and the Brotherhood. Seeyow, too, remained a safer place, Daf having lots of tough fighters waylaying the narrow valleys and the coast road that led there. Practically everywhere else, so long as they kept away from thick woods and other places to hide bows, the soldiers of Raug could ride at will. It was mainly by water the sieged fragments of the Alliance kept in touch, and even there was becoming no piece of cake, with Raug building more and more boats, causing anxious watches on our too-long shores.

The coming of flowers, no sign of hope this year, only jogged me how short time was shrinking down. I needed talk with Wott. As several times before, we had agreed to see each other near Caer, but Caer (Caer of my childhood!) was now in Vandene hands. A chap supposed Wott would make his way to Seeyow, but ten days after our planned meeting, I was still watching for him, and wondering where to ride if I put on my old clothes again and went out to find him.

Before a chappie could do, in worry, truly muttonheaded deeds, Daf came across from the mainland, bringing with him a Myna, new to me, a small, hollow-chested young rodent, with the kind of sharp, evading face that helps people go on believing all the bad stories about his people's dishonesty and cunning. I don't say that is just, just a fact.

He had news of, and from, Wott, who had not even begun the journey for Caer. He was in Suvram, tending his mother, Asta, who, a month ago, had been beaten and hurt by Myka soldiers, for telling her roecards in Vandene territories (I easily remembered the screaming youths who attacked her in Bris when we first met; such bonkers bullies were now keepers, not breakers, of the law).

The young Myna, named Sil, also had riddles for me, said crookedly so only I could know what they meant. That was all very well, but they did not do; all my hopes needed the Mynas, and of Mynas only Wott could scheme with me.

I asked his messenger if he could lead me to him, amd he said, if anyone could be led anywhere. It was a big journey, and the soldiers were everywhere now. Reading one of his fears, a chap told him I would not be dressed as he saw me now.

"You can't go with this bozo. This is a trick of Forn's." Daf was leaner than ever, but hard as iron, his face weathered, with the keen, waverless eyes and set mouth of an untiring warrior.

"No," I said. "Sil has the Brown Hare tattoo. These are our best allies, and the best hope of making Col a king." A chap no longer saw any reason not to speak this openly.

Daf had slipped into Seeyow English (He had learnt some from Col, and Alison had taught him a little more, when he came now and again for day or so, and a bath and decent meal) to say, "Swords cannot do that. Betimes, I thought they could. Now we need magics."


Where Wott was could be more easily reached from the south coast, and I decided to go by water; a longer journey in distance, but much the less risky. Nor, as I told Alison, need it take more time; by road we would have to take meandering ways to stay out of sight. Besides, with practiced sailors who knew the coast waters, a boat could press on by night as well as day, without need for rest. She was dead against my going by any route, not changed when a chap told her unless I could make schemes with the Mynas, there did not seem an earthly of preventing the triumph of Vandis and the Vandenes. Alison — but as a chappie thinks back, this was not the best of times for companionship. Marten was nearing proof (he said) that even the straightest line is really rounded, Maire was becoming fat and scant of breath, Rayman flowed with fine words from William Shakespeare about anointing of kings, and all, even Robin with her new son, even blest Alison, seemed to talk at me from behind a curtain or inside a bally cloud. Whichever pleases you, it was made by the long fierceness of my ponderings, and there was bugger all quite real for me except how, less than a hundred days from this, Col could hold the Bronze Rod.

Sil and I, with poor horses (I had put on my raggy clothes again, thinking if I kept my head down I might pass for another Myna), were put ashore in chilly morning, at a quiet place not far east of that other point where the Viztas were said to have landed, the Beakstone. From here we could make inland, avoiding Saffam and most travelled roads: though this was Suvram and still its own kingdom (ha ha), we were only a little safer from Adda-priests than in the heart of Raug.

Here, I was the guide; this was a fresh direction for Sil, and we were in country I knew quite well, not far from the lands I had given back to my wife (Rowan, I haven't mentioned, had married again, and had children of five and three). When, about noon, we had to cross the main road west from Saffam, we rode close by a small farmhouse, where an old woman was at the door, trying to guess whether the sun would find a way through the rolling clouds. As no Myna would be likely to, I nodded a greeting. She pushed her face forward like a shortsighted cat, and her pale, cheesy eyes showed sudden interest. "Master Evan," she said.

Strewth, I would never have known her, and how she recognised me after two dozen years is outside explaining, especially dressed as I was. Though now I consider, that might have helped; she often saw me as a kid grubbed and untidy from play. She was Jinny, the family servant who looked after me, then my sister, when we were small (a woman like this, in one of William Shakespeare's plays, is called a Nurse, but that word was also used for a kind of healer, so I stay in a little doubt). When my sister married, Jinny had gone with her; I never knew Jinny young, and if she was less than fifty all those years ago, it was not by many. I did remember she had come in the first place (like my mother's mother) from Suvram, and had now come back to live there with family for her last years.

I tell all this in a lump here because then, almost before there was time to marvel about Jinny, she made a much bigger surprise. Turning her head across a bent shoulder, she called out my presence to one unseen. Next second, there was the startled face of Avanda. Her instant question was the reason for my verminy clothes (In our cruder language it was much more blunt).

Well, pardon a chap, but it seemed to me, as turned out to be true, her being there needed quite as much explaining. Here, a real Tela might draw out the tale to the crawling way it came clear to me, but big doings still have to be told. In the farmhouse (Sil had to wait outside) there was a boy infant being cared for by a young woman, a sort of cousin to Jinny. He was carried in to grab at Avanda's reached arms, and she said it was my grand-nephew, Mord.  Now there was a facer.

Mord, a name in some way dark, not one I had heard.  The baby's blue-green eyes fixed on me for a little, and his mother laughed.  His mother, I say, not able to depict a chappie's bewilderment at the notion.  Avanda was not married, in secret or otherwise; she was still promised to the King of the Vandenes, who (or anyone else) she begged me must never know about Mord.

Well, a chap thought we could do a good trade in kept secrets, if only we each knew who was to be kept in the dark about what.  Forn, it was revealed, knew about Mord.  My sister had been the one to have him sent far away to the old servant's house, so the king (Vandis, that is) could not have a dream he existed (if that sounds like a Tela's tale of wonders, so I mean it to).  All at once, a chappie had a new and strangely upsetting thought, and I asked the age of the baby.

Avanda, you may be sure, had to go first through the everlasting mother's game of doing as if Mord himself could give the answer, but in the end she told me: just half and a half of that; he would be one year old at midsummer.

Three-quarters (Print English can say it better); and three-quarters of a year before that was a year-and-a-half, time of that dizzy dream of victory when the League of the West captured Caer, and the Idiot's Summer began.

Keeping any accusing out of my voice I asked who was the father, and my niece said with a sly, sideways look, lots had wished to know that.  But for Mord, we were alone, the others having found tasks to take them thence.

So, frighted for the answer, a chap asked whether it was

Col, and felt a strange chill on my heart. Avanda, in her mode, chose to prattle instead of reply, saying how famous Col was now, how all young fighters of Raug would give treasures to kill him, and take his fame, how livid her father would be if she had done the main event with his enemy, the bozo who pipped his Syme. Naming that captain, she made the face of one given a really off egg.

This, no answer, looked like being all I would get. The toothless wonder, still so young he could remind of anyone, had a less fair look to him than his mother, though not the dark eyes so striking in Col, with his light hair. There seemed no strong reason Mord couldn't be Col's; that was most I could say.

What this might mean in future would've been bugger all to fret over, if Avanda had truly given away the offspring, as Forn believed, but here she was, doting like a dimwit. This was the first she had seen of her scion, she told me, since the start of winter. Having been sent to stay at Saffam by her father (who neither knew nor itched to know what had become of little Mord), she had taken this chance, riding out with no scawt. That she had been let do this was explained a short time later.

The puzzle of what she was doing at Saffam was not one to take my attention, though as I discovered, the answer was quite a jackpot for importance. We came to it sideways. Avanda, with some of her remembered teasing, trying with quick fingers to pick loose threads from my coat, reminded that at Caer a chap had vowed help stop her marrying the king. Her father, she vouchsafed, said Evan had done more than whole armies to prevent his plans, but if someone did not thwart this one, come Midsummer Avanda would be queen. It was hard to swallow she did not desire that, but above all she wished not to be wife to Vandis. Lots of fillies must've said, through years, they would not wed some gargoyle, not for all Brittan; a chap's niece is the only one a chap ever knew truly offered the choice, and, crikey, she meant it.

Naturally, a chap asked if she was to be hitched at Gridge (as I suspected), and she said, no, it would be at Lunn, soon after. This held a fresh mystery: from my last meeting with Wott I knew soldiers of Raug had come there. They first tried, through Frant, the dealer in stone, to make treaties with the Mynas, but when that fell through, lots more came, enough so they could trumpet they had captured Lunn. But by Wott's story, they kept to close circles at night; there had been some little warring, any small number of Vandene fighters daft enough to be out of sight of more were odds on not to be seen again; in the dark or venturing into dark places no number could call itself safe. But mainly the Mynas, having counted how many enemy were nearby, were content, for now, to let Raug believe the wilderness was all-but tamed. It was at Lunn, Avanda attested, that King Vandis was to claim rule of All Brittan, though he would first be known at Gridge.

When I asked her knowledge about the Woman who was to come from the Sea, Avanda laughed. She was to be the Woman. That was why she was here in the south.

How could that be? Everyone knew whose daughter the girl was, and promised wife to Vandis, but when I put that to Avanda she said (as far as I could twig it, from the words she had) her father believed that made it better, as when a tree always barren suddenly had fruit to show. A dubious thesis, but Forn might be bang on; such believings were his line of work far more than ever mine.

When, trying to get all the plan, I asked what she had to do, it was very much what a chap might have guessed, except if you had given me all the women in Brittan to choose from, I would never have taken Avanda (if I were king, I mean, and not her uncle). She was to take boat from Saffam so as to come sailing out of the sunrise, on Midsummer's Day, step ashore, and point to King Vandis.

Just point, she said, and I asked if she was to have a thingamabob to hand the royal twerp, a weapon or a Rod. My drift was ill-disguised, and my niece put at once fingers to the small wooden effigy at her throat, and said I must mean the True Myke. That, she said, was to be at Gridge, under one of the fallen stones. Her last job would be to point which one, and as there were crowds of them, she was fretful she would point to the wrong one. Then the king would say, or her father proclaim for him, anyone who did not think Vandis was proper King of All Brittan could try to take Scalipal, which was the True Myke, from under that stone.

This all would've sounded barmier than it did, except lately a chap had been hearing a change; it used to be said Arfra's sword is stuck in a stone, but now people, when they recited the tale, were saying *under* a stone. Forn must've instructed his Addas so.

Avanda giggled, and said it was to be a big stone twenty strong men could never lift, but Vandis was going to do it by himself. She knew he was not terrifically strong, so there must be a trick to it. There was, certes; a Seeyow trick, called winch.

My scorning laugh made Avanda eager, she taking it to mean someone from Seeyow would know how to take the True Myke, and she not have to marry Vandis. That was leaping too far, but a chappie's brain was going nineteen to every twelve, trying to see what could be cooked up out of this windfall of inside info, and, while cautioning her against too much trust in magic, a chap did say that if I could work my will she would not be there, and neither would the Rod, Scalipal, the True Myke, however she liked to name it. It was sadding to see all the silliness my niece described would seem terrifically meaningful to believers who witnessed it, more than good enough to be called a fulfillment (though in ways not dreamt) of Arfra's tale: a woman, a stone, and a rod to call Scalipal — which, at the same time, Forn believed gave power, and almost everyone else would take for the True Myke of the Viztas. It was as if all our follies were coming together at once, and yet follies twisted to my purpose were just the job for putting Col in the saddle. Avanda confessed she had thought of being lost between Saffam and the landing, but knew never be forgiven by her father, or by Vandis, who would have her flogged to death, or minced.

She said that as a cool cert; family ways as passioned belief made them. At the same time, I had, for the first time in simply ages, a kind thought for my sister, who had seen to the baby's care, and even half of one for Forn: here was a mewling thing that could've kiboshed the work of a lifetime; he might not mind what became of Mord, but he had not, as possible, had the child killed at birth.

As for saving Avanda (not to say All Brittan) from Forn's plans, a chappie was still working it out, but I told her if schemes went well, it could be made to seem she had been captured by Raug's enemies. Still, I had to say if, notwithstanding all a chap could do, Vandis still pulled it off, my own chances of staying alive, let alone protecting her, were worth no old rope.

In a much less grumpy way she is lots like her mother, believing what she thinks to: she made up mind a chap had ancient magics on his side, and my warnings were just part of the mystery, like a fairground conjurer.

Well, I would have to get in touch with Avanda after making schemes with Wott. When I asked her if she could come back again to this place there was a replay of her vain, teasing manner (as if I were asking for greasy purposes of my own). Yes, she said, she had a friend who some days was boss of her gawd and scawt. He had been so today, and she would meet him later so as to come back to Saffam with her gawd. She told me learnedly (it was just like Marten bringing out a sooth now discovered about movements of the stars), young fellows were easy to lead by their hopes, whether or not those stood an earthly of ever being real.

Not only young ones, I said. She looked hard to see if a chap meant more than that, but I went on to say there would be a message for her here about what she was to do, either from me, or a bloke named Wott, who, I warned, was a Myna, but a friend. Wide-eyed, pretending it was naught unusual, she said she had no dislike for Mynas; she heard Col was so by birth. This was also to resume teasing my guesses about the siring of her baby, a mystery that would have closed my resumed ride in darkness, if I had not had schemes for Midsummer to chew on.

Whim made Vandene cruelty so much the worse. For Wott's mother, it was not possible to guess, from week to week, whether the Vandenes would welcome or forbid the sort of crafts she did, but the roecards had been her living for bulk of her lifetime. When taken by the Myka soldiers, she had been working her way westward from Lunn, meaning to reach Bris for the May-fair. She was mending now, though her nose would never be straight again, and she had lost a thumb, crushed by the Mykas, and cut off when it began to rot, by one of the healers the Mynas have. A nicer side of the Old Beliefs: because they know about herbs, barks and earths against pain and to stop bleeding, Mynas have much better luck than anyone else with such loppings, which done properly could save lots of lives when war-wounds go smelly.

I listened to her tale, more hours after leaving Avanda. We were in what was left of an old building, near halfway between Saffam and Stoneplain, but well off the travelled way. Wott, ergo, had quite fresh news of Lunn, where yet more soldiers of Raug had come. They, and workers they guarded, were doing works hard to understand, unless, as Wott thought (or at first pretended to), it was meant for King Vandis to have a new house at Lunn. Not new-built, but there had been lots of clearing away in the small territory of the Brown Hares, most near the place where Thea had died, and I first found Alison.

Half-prepared for this by what Avanda had told me (which I had not yet let on to Wott), I remarked that Thea, when she was dying, had said it was there the next High King would be proclaimed.

This earned me, as rarely, one of Wott's dark, Myna looks. He was stunned, I believe, by how much Thea had trusted me, one of the blood of the princes. Powers concerning that place must be important if Forn was willing to hold it using up soldiers who otherwise might have brought last defeat to our alliance in the west, but when I asked Wott if there was a foretell Forn might have learned, my Myna friend studied his own hands, not to give me the discourtesy of avoiding an answer. All he would impart in the end was that a woman would know.

"Thea would have told me."

"All respect, sir, I think Thea did tell all you were meant to hear. It's not one of the foretells meant to help us do the proper things." Wott was changing into a species of priest as a chap watched: "If the true Arfra is with us now, and made king as he should be, in Lunn, we'll know. If not he can never rule over the Old Believers, and his line must soon end, as was seen with the Regions. But this goes back to ages before them, before Viztas were ever heard of. It's a kept secret, sir, so its power can't be stolen by the worthless, like this Vandene king. But now we think Forn must've heard it from the Moorhens, when they gave him the castle, Vandennis, as called."

I could not remember ever hearing Wott mention the Moorhens without adding words of despising. This was my first hint they might be changing sides again. But that was important, because they had been in Forn's trust. Too much that was crucial was being kept from me.

"This is bad. Forn has Mynas' secrets I have not."

"Forn!" Wott said sneerfully. "He plays in our stories, too; my mother has him in the roecards, Lord of Lies."

"His lies can make a king at Lunn," I warned. With, so to speak, one eye, a chappie could see the funny side. There was a time when I kept Col in the dark, so that fulfillment of prophecies could not be counterfeited, and now Wott was doing the same trick to me, and for the same reason: the real Arfra would need no telling.

It was time to remind Wott who was the Magician, and my chat with Avanda gave me a chance. "The machine, the winch, that Forn had his smith copy from Seeyow; it is going to be brought south, pulled by lots of horses — "

"It has been," Wott said, and I saw the magic work with him.

"Then it must now be near Gridge, but somewhat hidden." Now Wott was properly flummoxed, knowing a chap could not have gone anywhere near Gridge to see for self. He agreed the winch was amongst trees between the place of the midsummer rites and the river. That was still part of the realm of Suvram, but might as well be Raug, for all Erril would ever do about it.

I seized on the new standing my good guess had given me, saying, "If the Bronze Rod is to be kept from King Vandis at the coming hour of its rebirth, only I can bring together all needed."

"Mynas," with knowing slyness, "might steal the Rod before it can be brought to Lunn. We know it's still in the north, but not at Vandennis."

That quelled one of a chap's fears; how they knew would have to wait. I said, "Not enough. If Mynas get hold of the Rod, to give to who they aim for king, he'll be king of the Mynas and sod all more. I can raise a King our small kings will bow to, and lots of Vandenes, even Vandis himself, perhaps. The same one you would choose, and he'll be your king, too. But to do this I need all the help and all the knowledge the Mynas can give."

Well, Wott gave plenty. The Rod, or the coffer it was kept in, had been seen just days ago in a guarded room with no windows, by one of the Moorhen Mynas Forn had brought with him from Vandennis to be servants at his own big house near Lees. It was more than a year, I now learnt, since the Moorhens had turned on Forn. "He believes he bought them for all time," Wott said grimly. "But he broke given word, and made them promise to take to the Vandene faith, after vowing their beliefs would not be tinkered with. Forn has hostages, but Mynas are not ruled by that. We call them as dead as soon as taken."

It was a startlement a man of the long-grudging Mynas was so much more ready than I would be to trust the treble-dealing Moorhens. Wott said the Moorhens had been talking about somehow pinching the Bronze Rod and handing it over to other Mynas, who could bring it to Col; that, indeed, would've been the last plan, if I had not made it to this meeting with Wott.

If it could be pulled off, the Rod stolen and pursuit evaded (there was wild, rocky country nearby Forn's house, and after that, ruins of old cities, best cover for Mynas), it seemed at first the best we could hope. But it would have to be done soon, before the Rod started its journey to Gridge, and that, as a chap pointed out to Wott, would give Forn heaps of time to change tales.

He could, as an instance, have his smith, Linsy, brew up a chunk of bronze that could be shown as Scalipal and the True Myke, meanwhile putting out such a phony had been forged in Seeyow. Wherever there was doubt which was real, Raug's power of swords would carry the debate.

Wott shook head. "The Bronze Rod, we say, makes itself known. Anyone who sees it can feel its power."

If a chappie had doubts, he was not going to blab them: it was just such beliefs could make Col into Arfra. "But it would be far the better if the Rod could be taken without Forn's knowing."

"How could that be?"

By no means feeling as sure as I sounded, I told him. The Rod... well, pish, the plan should not be said twice, and is better told when we came to try it. A hard and tangled scheme, and Wott said he would have to go north himself, to see it done as properly as may be. This I could not let, and told him he had to think of good men who would follow my orders, and send messages by his Myna ways. He was needed here in the south, where he could stay to see his mother better, and just before midsummer, steal my niece as she started by boat for Gridge.

"Steal your niece, Lord?" From Wott's wonder, he might've been thinking about his half-brother, abducing Caif, and all that had caused, Col not the least.

It's not quite true I then made my way westward to have talk with Col; it would've been softheaded to try, when that way was filled with Raug's armies, and with the few men Erril still kept in the field against his brother's successors. Instead, my boat (where I could change back to proper clothes) took me coasting all the way to Wezram, and I rode east to find Col. Fighting there had ebbed as the Brotherhood and the Wezram lot stayed on guard; Forn, with his day nearing, may have thought it not worth the big losses there would be to overcome these strongest of his remnant foes. His best lots were at Lunn, too.

Col when found was with Frick, scoffing rough bread and white cheese at a house in one of the guarded hill places Edin had made stronger. He looked a hard and hardy warfarer, used to all weathers, and greeted me eagerly. News about Seeyow and the south I gave him at once, but disagreement was bred when he asked for more of what plans were made for midsummer, because I was firm there were parts for no other ears, and he told me there was no word could not be spoken before Frick. Granted Col's curiosity, it was a battle a chap could not lose, and in the end Frick himself made surly surrender, muttering his warring had more use for muscle than magics.

Col, when he had gone, said, "It is wrong to show mistrust of one so loyal. He would cut a path through Vandene meat for me from here to Vandennis."

"People call me Magician."

"Not everyone says it with love, Evan."

"I do not mourn that." Saying this, I found it true. "It is a weapon, a tool for making wonder. Unloved, a conjurer is despised only if he shows or lets slip how his tricks are worked. Then wretches stop gaping, to say how stupid it is, and wonder how any bally goose could be taken in by such simple frauds."

"I never said you were unloved. You know all the good pals you've got, everywhere free. Only, some fighters, like Frick, desire war plainer, without whisperings and plots."

Now I began to get shirty. "Look how Frick's plain warring saved his own home, Stanglin," scorchfully. "Like Sevenin, and Caer, and Pormarch. How much more plain warring till Forn has Landin, and Tawn, and Seeyow, too? A chappie must truly be a dolt, to spend his life as I do, when Raug can be humbled, any time we choose, by plain warring."

"No, no, Frick knows as well as I do we can't do it by swords. He knows there is need of strategies. But no guy brave and loyal likes schemes behind his back."

"Poor Frick." We were unspeaking for a little time, and then, cooling, I began to explain. If Col was going to become Arfra at midsummer, it might, for all I knew, be prophecy come true, but it was also going to mean a conjurer's trick to trump the one Forn was preparing for his king. The fewer who knew how the trick was done, the more to be flabbergasted by sooth.

Col got it in one, and even went beyond my thought, saying a king had to be free to reward true service, but those who knew the trick of his kinging might expect wealth and high rank just for keeping the secret. "I don't mean you, Evan," he added. "You, I know, work for the good, with reward or without."

I nodded thanks, but a chap took note Col was not dazzled by his own talk of Frick's staunchness: loyalty might be given price.

Leaving quiet, till more time to ponder, the news about Avanda and her small Mord, I told what was learnt about the fallen stone at Gridge, and the copy of our Seeyow winch — and now, after all, I have to write down some of what had been worked out with Wott, as it was then told to Col. To begin with, it seemed to me Forn, with the same conjurer's needs as us, would aim to have the Bronze Rod brought south for its hiding at Gridge, not as part of a bright and glorious ruddy procession, or even densely guarded by big cumnies of fighters, who would be sure to talk about it. Meaning it to be found at Gridge as by magic meant the Rod would travel quietly and as smally guarded as he dared.

If, as Wott so astoundingly believed, we could rely on the Moorhen Mynas at Forn's house, we might find out when that was, and with quite small numbers waylay the riding, and pinch the Rod.

"But the Rod can travel inside Raug lands all the way from Lees almost to Gridge," Col said.

"With help from Mynas, we can slip a raiding cumny, which must anyway be small, to hidden places inside Raug."

"Why is that better than stealing it from the place it now is, as in my uncle's plan?" Col demanded (it was abacking to have him all at once claim his connection with Wott).

"This. We must try to make off with the Rod, and let the Vandenes believe they've still got it." As described, the Bronze Rod was kept in a chest, and wrapped in cloths. We would assail the riding with one band, and they would damage the scawt, and then flee, drawing off as many as could be of the other soldiers. Our second lot would then kill any left to guard the Rod (in a waggon, as a chap supposed), take the Rod from its coffer, and leave something else of the same size and shape, wrapped in cloths, in its place. Also nick all with any value they could find, then do a bunk, so when the scawt came back from pursuit, they would think it had been an ordinary robbery, and be bucked beyond words to discover the Rod unstolen.

"They would take off the wrappings to be sure."

I shook my head. "It is believed, remember, if you look at the Rod except at the proper time, you go blind, go barmy, or lose your manhood. Would you, believing so?"

"When it gets to Gridge, then," Col persisted. "Forn would not put it under a stone without making sure it's the real Bronze Rod."

If one ever was, a chap thought. But I said, "Forn, unless my guess is all wet, will not be near Gridge for the Rod's hiding. He must come to the gathering by side of King Vandis. He cannot have anyone to say, of course it was there, just where he hid it." This year, Forn and Evan were in the same trade, and a chap could know his brain.

"He could go there early. We know from Wott the Rod was likeliest still there in the north two weeks ago or more, but that is nothing to say it is still there now. It could be journeying south at this moment."

What he said next gave me a proper chill: my plan could be tried, but if it failed, the only dodge left would be to do the unsayable, march armies to Gridge, seize the winch and use it to purloin and claim the Rod in front of everyone.

"Break the peace of Gridge Meet Time?" I said.

"Superstition," Col said. "A truce decreed by the Viztas. You have taught me to disprize beliefs like that."

"But not the good that comes from them," wondering how a chap could have gone misunderstood for such years. "If I pity those birds who keep their word only for fear of Viztas or gods or ghosts, or who would pinch what is not theirs, or do in any blokes who got in their way unless they had superstition to stop them, that does not mean I'm all for oathbreaking, larceny and murder."

"As a last measure. Better that than leaving All Brittan to be ruled over by Vandis."

"Don't you get it?" I said. "Just having the Rod is no

earthly, if everyone knows you swiped it; it becomes just a trophy in the war we are fighting now, and losing." For what seemed a hundredth time I patiently explained how Col, famed warrior in the League of the West, had, as we spoke, every bod he could ever have as follower. To get an inch farther than captain over a failing cause, he must have the Rod come to him as a marvel to change hearts, steal the readiness the Adda-priests had made.

"You've said for years you would do anything to prevent All Brittan ruled by the Vandenes. What about if Vandis was killed at Gridge, and Forn?"

"Anything," looking coldly to see if he could mean this, "Except help bring about a Brittan ruled by treachery and word-breaking."

"Why must it be ruled by?" he said, making this more like one of Marten's discussions about chances hardly real. "Awful, yes, to break the truce, but if one fell deed can prevent a whole age of badness, is it sage to be so prim?"

"To begin the reign of Arfra the Good with doing a murder even Forn would not, even Syme would not have," I said. "And kicking it off so would mean an everlasting watch against being ended the same way. You would could command nobody's loyalty, except with soldiers and spying."

Col laughed suddenly, very much the boy of Seeyow. "Evan, there's not going to be any offing at Gridge."

"If there is, you had better off me as well," I warned, but a chappie let himself grin to answer Col's laugh.


"Can you blame me for thinking bloody fancies, when you tell me our last chance is this plan you give, not even knowing where the Bronze Rod is now, or whether we can be in time to snatch it?"

Not even to mention all the other chances. Col was right to doubt, but I was sure Forn would not prefer to leave such a precious ort stuck under a fallen stone for longer than had to be; he would surely have it brought to Gridge no more than a few days before midsummer. Past that, I had to trust the plan, because I could think up none better. Forn's own scheme was a loony one, and loonily would it be answered.

I told Col he would hear from me before leaving for Gridge, and if we failed to pinch the Rod I would try to get word to him. At Gridge, he must be ready to step, as before, from the shadows, and could look for guidance to me, or to Alison.

"Alison?" he questioned.

"She is the Woman to Come from the Sea."

While I was away from Seeyow, Maire, having shown few signs of illness, had died. We never wholly remade friendship after differing about Alison's bringing-up, but still she would be missed. The more by Marten. The first night we had our meal together. His mood was not changed, and he never mentioned his long wife, but began a talk about America.

None of us could ever agree (I've never made up my one brain) if America was real, or a made-up tale. It comes in Tulsingham, who has no time for fancies, and yet, as explained, there and other places, with its high mountains and plains that stretch the width of six Brittans, its millions of people, endless stores of food and made things, skyscratching buildings and huge wealth, it seems more a boozer's dream of what might be than any real country.

Now Marten was saying he had worked out just how far across the sea America was. If the story about Columbus (a sailor who went there) was true, our best boats could get there in twenty-eight days steady sailing, starting at the tip of Wezram. Rayman reminded in that spot the usual winds came from the west, and Marten said there might be ways of changing winds and making them blow where we listed, using fires.

Over years he had said many other utterings that sounded strange and came out as sense in the end, so a chappie was not right away onto the truth; Rayman started asking how this wind-changer would work. Marten said only what a spiffing wheeze it would be for seafarers, because they could alter the wind again when they aimed to come home. Next sec he was saying whilst dogs might learn to read, they could not be taught writing, because they would never be able to hold pens. A heavy, hurting silence came to the rest of us.

The next day I began moving my household, Rayman, Sheal and my servants, as well as Alison, up to the big house on the hill. For one point, though our Seeyow gawd, the Peacocks, now came mostly to me for orders, they would still be oathed to obey Marten, and it was anybody's guess what garbage he might tell them now. Too, he himself (as Alison said) needed care from those who loved him. It may be said here that since then he has not become better, nor yet much worse. On good days, he is the Marten of old, like a kettle boiling over with well-thought ideas. He mixes one person's name with another, even so.

Betimes, telling Alison about my travels, a chappie had said less than he might've about dangers (she never heard how the Adda, Raff, had me whipped), and come to that about hunger and cold, but I never kept her from any news to do with plans and policies. But, look here, talking to the lady who, if we did not all end as slaves of Raug, might well be Col's wife and queen, a chappie could not simply blurt about Avanda's baby, and her hints about its fathering. It just wasn't on.

But I did not a bit enjoy choosing what parts to tell Alison, my trustedest other ears. In the end it was just that "I had learnt" the part Forn meant his daughter to have at Gridge, and with Wott I had "made an arrangement" to have her, as she desired, go astray.

Now Wott, when first speaking of what Lunn, and the Tower there, had to do with making a High King, had said a woman would know. Seeing his mother was nearby, and one other woman (then a girl) had been close in Thea's thoughts, he might as well have said, *Ask Alison*!

So, "What do you know about the King being raised in Lunn, not Gridge?"

Alison gave a long look, then clapped her hands like a gleeful tot. "Thea said you must ask me that one day."

"And what could you tell me, when that day came?"

"She said I must make up my own head. I wish you would take the Bronze Rod for yourself, and be High King."

Not sure whether that was play, or nonsense, or whether Alison, without knowing, was setting me one of those tests you find in old stories, a chap ignored it. "Forn believes more concerning Lunn; the Bronze Rod is to be at Gridge, but his fighters are hemming the Tower."

"Everyone knows it." Alison meant the saying I mentioned before, when the king is in Lunn. Blokes who could not even tell where Lunn was might say that, parting from somebody and not knowing when they would meet again. But it was not for the sake of a phrase spoken without thought that Forn had hundreds of soldiers there.

"In a way it is," Alison said. "Lots who never think of the Lunn that is know in ancient times the king was there. There our king is to get his crown."

"His *crown*?" She said it quite plainly, but a chappie was almost just as abacked as when Col mused on murdering Vandis in the truce time. A *crown* — well, as more becomes written, a chap has come to see this book of mine cannot be made known in this lifetime, and as with old books for us, there may be need to explain beliefs, in case they alter. From those old books I know no one, once, saw wrong in putting on a crown; the word was even used as another way of saying a king or a queen, or the rule of a monarch, or even the armies of the king.

When that changed can now not be said, but with us crown is the worst of omens. Tulsingham names such a fear a *tabu*, but I am not sure that was not a comical word: they had horrors that seem funny to us, like about wearing or not wearing hats in different places, and Tulsingham himself calls them "absurd and meaningless tabus." Our pious say crowns belong to the Viztas, and it caused lots of argy-bargy when, years ago, it was heard Edlin I, the great Edlin, was going to have a crown made for himself. He had to lie (according to my grandfather), saying he wished to have a crown ready for the Return, to give to the Viztas. Even that was bally presumptuous.

Alison said, "Only a true King of All Brittan would dare put on the crown."

Well, but would Forn dare putting it on Vandis's head? Only, I thought, if he could show it answered to a foretell. "The Moorhens," I said to Alison, "were Forn's pets for years, and other Mynas think he learnt secrets from them."

"There is an old crown," she said, as if talking about blinking spoons or such. "Hidden not far from where Thea died. Ancient kings wore it."

"Hidden? The men of Raug have been doing clearing and building. They might have found it."

She said, "Linsy, or any smith, could make a crown and Forn could say it's the old one."

"If that one is still hidden, could you find it?"

"Yes, if Wott's Mynas let me go there."

So, if we dared, we could crown Col as Arfra, in Lunn. If, so to say, the Bronze Rod could be kept from Vandis, if Col was already hailed. It could only be what an old writer calls ice on the cake, an ornament to what is already made.

"All the Old Believers," Alison said, "Know Arfra is to find a way to his crown."

## The Sea

When a chap saw Alison beside —

Fie! Patience, Lord Evan; better to tell first how we came to be there, at sea, sailing south for the midsummer gathering.

The Mynas were needed everywhere, hiding me, guiding soldiers by most hidden ways through the heart of the Vandene Kingdom. Because what the Mynas had not, good fighters on quick horses, were needed, sixteen of Daf's best fellows went. Daf in person for leader had not been in my plan, but Col's Spear could not be said no to, and it was true he would be extra useful. For one, it would be his job to begin the half-heart attack meant to tempt away the Rod's scawt; he understood retreat was a needed part of our scheme, and could be trusted not to change mind at the last sec, puff up with pride, and stand to fight, as another, more rash or ignorant wearer of Osset's Star might have. Also, no matter what his private opinion of Mynas, he had sense to haul in harness with them. He had not heard all the story of the Bronze Rod, but knew it was very top in importance to Col.

Since my talk to Wott, latest news had been, Forn and my sister, with many Adda-priests and Mykas, had ridden to Vandennis, so as to accompany King Vandis to the Gridge gathering. The Bronze Rod, Moorhen spies swore blue, was still where it had been.

All very well, but that news was days old when we got it, and (as Daf told me) there was more than a chance the treasure had already begun its trip whilst we were gathering ourselves and meeting with our Myna guides.

But what I still clung to was that such a treasure would never be stuck under a fallen stone for longer than had to be; surely it must be brought to Gridge as near as could be before midsummer.

Daf was picking up arts other than warring: thinking a chap meant to be with his men throughout, he gravely warned if all else came off exactly as hoped, yet we would be kiboshed if I was killed or too badly wounded to travel. What he thought (and it was likeliest true) was that I would only get in the way of well-trained fighters, but he need not have fretted; I had my own journey to make, across the breadth of Brittan, readying all those whose help was needed. (It may be said that not less amazing than our new trust in the Moorhens was that this time of ripened prophecy had made all the Myna clans leave off their everyday feuding.) By boats, I went north with Daf's lot to landing on a lonely coast and a meeting with men of Wott's choosing, and then we parted. Truth told, I was not joyed to leave working of a complicated plan to others, and Daf's sharp, final *Yes, yes, Evan, we understand* was hint a chappie was explaining too often.

By unstraight journeys, everywhere finding ordinary people very het about what the Gridge gathering would bring, I made way to Eel, that same place on Stanglin's old borders where I found Wott the year before, and to the same big ruined church. There for long days, treated well by other Mynas, I stayed, all the time fretful about how Daf was doing; hoping, too, Alison had arrived safe at the hidden anchorage off the big eastern bay called Wash.

Just as with my very first journey *incognito*, she had yearned to come with me, but whilst nowhere was truly safe now from soldiers of Raug, it was less danger to her to go with the boat, which was needed. It was the new, larger craft of Will, the carpenter's brother, room for men and horses, needing six or more to work it, and it had to make a whacking trip, south from Seeyow, all the length of our southern coast, then north again round the big eastward bulge of Stanglin the bay called Wash helps make (its other edge is the River Tem where it spreads to the sea).

Sheal, who knew next to bugger all about any plans, had said a girl of birth, unmarried like Alison, could not be sent on such a journey with only sailors, soldiers and a servant. She would say the same knowing the whole next age of Brittan might turn on Alison being in the right place; the female was past sixty now, and had not left Seeyow for years, but said she must sail with Alison.

There was no need; Rayman would be there, and Alison would be safe with him, and have old Shan with a few of his best men for gawd. Besides, she was sailing into tales of legend: the Woman Who Comes from the Sea is in none of Sheal's rules. At parting, I was, it seems we both were, Alison and I, set on keeping deep feelings out of sight. Seven years (nearly to the day) as her guardian were ending for a chap, and there was no more than a hug, a quick press of hands, and wishes back and forth for safe arrivings.

By my sixth day at Eel (the thirteenth since parting from Daf) time was shrinking dreadfully, if Alison and I were to get to Gridge (as we must) on Midsummer morning. All a chap could think of, now, was the shortcomings of our plans, the big number of places where they could go wonky. Forn might after all put safety above secrecy, and wall the southward journey of the Rod inside a scawt of hundreds (this fear came closer to truth than some others). If that was so, the big risk for Daf became sure death: he would never come back without trying an attack, however the odds.

Or Forn might be sitting in Vandennis, laughing we believed all the news brought us by his Moorhens; surely any blokes who come back to what they've once betrayed can as easily be treble-crossers? Or, if they meant us well, their eyes could still have wool pulled over; what if Forn had been keeping careful guard on a decoy, with the real Rod never having left Vandennis?

As my reprimand, it was two men and a woman of the Moorhen clan who found me at Eel, that sixth day, and passed to me a wrapped bundle they handled with pious respect. It was, or so they believed, the Bronze Rod, given them two days north and west of here, by bowmen who had been in the fight, and who no longer were closely chased.

It took a chappie's speech away that neither those fighters (it seemed) nor the ones who brought it me (this is certain) had ever been bold enough to have a butcher's to see what was inside all the linen bindings. It might have given offence to their beliefs if I had done that on the spot, and all the while I was hearing their tales and holding the bundle with proper reverence, my fingers were mad to undo the wrappings. It could still be a rotten fake, planted by Forn.

Not so, and Wott was right: the Bronze Rod proclaimed itself. It was not large, the length of a chap's forearm. When I found a private spot I unwound the bandages (as they were like); the first plain linen, and inside, a tighter winding. The stuff, stained in brown and yellow, had an oily feel, though no oil came away on my hands.

Simple, thick as my wrist at the big end, as a broomstick at the other, the Rod was a dilly, dark, smooth and with a hushed gleam. Here and there, to jog a chap if Thea's history was true I was holding the ancientest made device of Man, were little pits like tiny blue-green pocks, but there was no other mar. Easy to see why its power had been believed; there was a mystery to its plainness, as if it was smug knowing it had no need for decoration. To have it here in my hands through so many mad guesses and chancy plans outdid all foretells-come-true a chap had ever heard told with big eyes and bated breath. With no one there to hear, I said, "Col will be Arfra; Arfra will be King."

Even though I did not hear for days just how the seizing of the Rod went astray from the plan, it would be silly not to tell it here. Guided by Mynas, the two lots of fighters, Daf's riders and Myna bows, made their way to a place decided, hidden, but looking on the road about two hours' ride south of Forn's big house. They had stayed unfound there through several days, waiting for word from Moorhen allies the Rod's journey was about to begin. Yet no such word had come when, in early morning, they saw on the road just the sort of riding we had expected, three carts, two of them covered, and a couple of pack-animals, all guarded by a dozen Mykas.

Daf and the Myna leaders swiftly agreed this had to be assailed, and Daf was already on the circling ride that would begin his feint when a Moorhen servant from Forn's household found the others, still lying in hiding, and told them the Bronze Rod was with this riding, but that (for the sake of more safety without drawing too much attention, one might guess) a much bigger force of soldiers was following not far behind.

But Daf had done this sort of fighting, and already knew about the larger force, from a watcher put on high ground. He changed plans a bit, attacking and retreating, but then turning to fight. His men killed half the scawt, and the rest bunked off to find their reinforcements, a cumny of about sixty just now coming into view. Daf's lot fled over the rough country there, and bulk of the enemy gave chase. The few who stayed back to guard the carts had to ride through a sparse bit of wood, where the Myna bowmen had now hidden themselves. Some of the enemy were shot down, others dragged from saddles by lurking Mynas who sprang to grab legs.

This part of the attack was not without losses, because the Vandenes had swords and bows of their own riding hidden in one of the carts. Our bows were more and better, and the Mynas were fierce; not long and all the enemy were dead. There was an Adda-priest amongst them, and when I heard, a long time after, it was that stinker Raff, the one who'd had me scourged, I've got hardly a bit of shame to say it was satisfying to know he had been killed with the rest (in old times, priests, it seems, were mainly mild bozos who went about without any weapons, so better remind that a lot of Adda-priests have also been captains in war, and a fair fight for any warrior).

At this part of the story, even in the first, far from full, account given me by the Moorhens who brought the Rod (they had not seen the battle, of course), I was told with a big grin one of the pack-animals, a donkey, also had been killed, with an arrow in its throat. At the time a chap thought, you could never tell what may tickle a Myna.

Going through the carts, never knowing when at least some who had chased Daf's lot might come back, was done in haste. The Mynas grabbed food, some clothes and weapons, and the better horses of the dead, and they overturned the cart in which there was the box of the Bronze Rod, as if peeved when they found nothing more valued there: such a spiffing chest might have had gold and jewels in it. I had given them a rusty iron bar, wrapped as Forn's turncoat servants had described the Rod (which had come very near what I now saw), to leave behind. Now we reached to that part, a chappie had no more than slight hopes the Vandenes would not find out about the swap.

Daf, according to plan, had fled west, and the waylayers now scat-tered in small lots, heading south and east. I did, and still do, not know how many if any were overtaken and captured or killed, and there was no quick news about Daf's escape. He would try to get back to the boats that had brought us north, still waiting.

If there had been any Vandene chase after the Bronze Rod, the poor sods would've found it hard to follow our winding way to the sea, often among pools and marshes, with the middle part on a flat boat driven by poles shoved into the mud under shallow water. Then, for hours, there was squelching muck underfeet, and, most of that boring time, sight of not much else but dense growth of rushes. We came out at last on a small inlet, almostly enclosed, off the great bay, and there, like a magic, was Will's boat against the opposite shore. The Myna leading me (of the Crane clan, said to be anciently related to the Moorhens, whose first country these marshes had been) gave the same sort of whistle Wott had, years ago, when he guided me through Lunn. Will showed himself on deck, and then slender Alison, shading her eyes. She waved hand, and soon a small boat with oars came to take me aboard.

When, briefly, I again uncovered the Bronze Rod for Alison to see, she was silent. With it safely wrapped again, she said, "All through the voyage here, I wondered, what could we do if Forn sent a phony, as you feared? Or if the ambush failed?"

To tell truth, a chappie never did decide on what could be done if the Bronze Rod had gone, as Forn planned, to Gridge. The appearance of Alison in place of his expected daughter would've made a muddle, and it might well have come down to a duel of magics between Forn and me.

"It must still be that. But weren't you afraid to look at it? The priestesses told scary tales to keep it from harm."

"I still have sight," shrugging. "And do not believe I'm crackers. With the other, there should be chance to find out, during the Gridge Days."

She let her long lashes come down over a sideways look. A chap cannot remember any time before when I talked to her about my own matings, and there was, with a bit of digging, a reason for it now. Our craft was crawling to the eastward on a slate-calm sea, following the long curve of the coast, in the bronze, indeed, bronze light at the end of a hot, clear day. Alison and I were out on the open deck (there were covered parts behind, in the waist, and aft, where Rayman was napping after long watches); the boat like a burnished throne glowed on the water, and Alison's dark hair was loose, ruffled by breeze, at times just enough to flick a filament or two across her lit face, when she would rake it back with a curved hand. She was in a very unfrilled blue frock with just about no sleeves, and her arms were slim and perfect.

One of the young sailors came forward (to the front part of the boat, that means) to coil one of the ropes used to tie up. It was Will's nephew, Arral's son Peet, the one who had desired to join the Brotherhood. Col had never found time for talk with him, but told he was helping Col become a king, he was very keen. He briefed us, without being asked, the wind should freshen now, with the sun going off the water; it could not be much help tonight, but seemed set to carry us well when we turned to the south. We ought to have a day and more to spare for our journey.

A chap, actually, had been thinking how likely it was, when Alison brought the Rod ashore, that if we won she would be Col-Arfra's bride, and our queen. Then, for the second time, I began to change mind about what Thea meant, seven years before, by saying Evan himself would have a price to pay.

This time, at last, a chappie got it right. I loved Alison. Well, of course a chappie loved her, but now meaning I loved her, man to woman. Your guess is as good as mine when that began: once seen it was like fact a bozo should know had always been true.

So. But seeing made a difference, and in no time I was afraid she must notice how I looked at her — how, that's to say, a chappie all at once could look nowhere else. There was newness, and no experience gone through in an odd life is stranger than seeing what is perfectly known, and seeing it for the first time: her cheekbones, as example, lightly rubbed to colour by sun and air, or her soft mouth, now pretty enough to make me watch, instead of listen to what she was saying.

"Can we really expect," she was asking, "this small bronze thing can be enough to bring down all the strength of Raug?"

"They'll bring themselves down," I answered. Alison would be with Col, for all the rest of my life. I was bringing him her, not a bit what a chap desired. That was my part, my price.

A proper thought, but I still hungered for her. Could gazing at the Bronze Rod after all have made me mad? It was the very error of the moon, the wren goes to't (the old king says), and the small gilded fly doth lecher in my sight — here I was, ridiculous, an aging bawd, for scorn to point his slow and moving finger at. Nay, but the old gargoyle's dotage doth o'erflow the measure; give me an ounce of civet (once a sort of medicine, I believe) to sweeten my imagination. Make it a double. Tulsingham says Julius Caesar, with his bald lust for Cleopatra, made himself a sorry spectacle (but I still have all my hair, here and there greyed). Something too much of this, and that's what a chap told himself then, turning head back to policies.

To Alison's question: "If Col is King of All Brittan, what

can he do with the Adda-priests?"

This was not idle; if that time came, long enemies became subjects, and Col would need to keep them so. "He could not just say, there is no more Vandene belief — unless he is minding to make the Brotherhood into new sorts of Mykas, these hunting out belief. As the king from prophecies, he can change beliefs, over years. The Vandene faith need not be cruel."

"Is this what Col knows?" Alison's eyes had never been more brightly earnest (or so lovely). "When Daf talked about outlawing all Vandenes in the western realms, Col was hot for it, till you and Edin spoke out."

"Two years ago," I said. "He is still a young fellow, but he was younger then; with more patience he could not have been such a smashing warrior. My job, and yours, is going to be curbing his haste, not so weakening his rule. Strengthening it, because he'll have more who serve him willingly." Without saying so, it seemed to me no matter how many might hail him as Arfra arrived, he would still have to fight against the worst of the Adda-priests and their followings, gathering themselves, as might be, about King Vandis. That dunce would never tamely knuckle under, having had a lifetime of being told he was the right King of All Brittan. To pick a quarrel with all Vandenes, then, would be a lame-brained way of multiplying foes.

We nattered on so, while twilight deepened to dusk, and the star Marten (when still himself) had said was no star, but a circling world like ours, came out very bright. The sea gleamed, but there would be no moon; the skies, by Thea's story, should be very near the same as they were when the Bronze Rod was first made, hundreds, thousands of years ago. Alison hugged her own pale arms, then, as if she eavesdropped my brain, reached to touch the rewrapped bundle between us. "Because of this ort, we sit planning new Brittans. Do you think Thea truly believed in what the Rod does?"

"You knew her the better," in amaze at the question. Since hearing about the crown kept at Lunn, a chap had been wondering what other secrets Alison might have held over all our years — whether, indeed, she would call herself, like Thea, an Old Believer, even a bally priestess of the moon. It was hard to think of clear-minded Alison as any such, but letting my thoughts travel back over those years, it was too easy to see (and hear, feel and smell) what bloody rites Old Believers would be keeping just now, if they had not given them up this year so as to be at Gridge instead. These visionings made an ugly fit with my own new mood about Alison, and thoughts went bolting on to the night in Seeyow when at her doorway I found Daf —

"I was a child with Thea. You were grown." Not to gloom me more, but the gulf of ages was not what a chap desired a reminder of. Soon, seeing I had no more to say about Thea (truthfully, I was in speechless battle against an enemy that had to be beaten, my misery), Alison shivered, stretched, and said she would try to sleep. In the nights waiting for me, she added, she had lain waking.

We stood together, and with half-jest ceremony hardly to be seen I passed over the bundle with the Bronze Rod. "You should have charge of this, till you come from the sea."

About to turn away, she stopped, and re-offered the parcel. "You," she said. "You should take it. As king. It should be in your hands at the rebirth."

When she said the same before, in Seeyow, I had let it be a joke. It was growing too dark for her phiz to be closely read, but if she meant this, it made no difference, nor that we now had the bally Rod, nor even having had sight of its potent gleam. Oh, yes, there was a mad mo when a chappie could see himself in charge of the world, but I was no king of old foretells, and my answer for Alison was a little laugh in my nose.

She said, "Whose work has prevented All Brittan from being the Kingdom of Raug, and kept some freedom to be saved?"

"Lots of people's," I said, not sharply. "Too many fellows now dead. My work has tried to bring us where we can make a king to make quietus to these wasting wars and multiplying cruelties."

There was still light and to spare for me to see the flash of her eyes, and know she was holding back a fierce answer. It was puzzle to me that here, at the last, she found doubts of Col (the only meaning there could be in her goofy idea I should grab the Rod for myself). Touching her arm, I said, "You'll see. Col can prove right royally."

"Kindness is better than kingliness."

"When has Col been unkind to you?"

"For Brittan," perplexed I had taken another meaning. "If true this bronze can take on the thoughts and wishes of its holder, or only if that's what's believed, gentleness is better than glory."

A chap heard the compliment, a troubling one, but all the same, believe you me, this was not a point left unconsidered. I said, "What is jolly good in a counsellor may be defect in a ruler. To rule needs harshness at times, and glory is what makes people bear that. Praise it."

Softly, near whispering, she said, "Yes," yet it seemed she was not so much agreeing as saying she would have laid odds I would say just about that.

She questioned, "Won't you sleep?"

"In a while. In Eel, waiting for news, I did lots of dozing." Somewhat true. Also, as the ones of rank, we had the covered place at midship, and I wanted Alison to settle herself before sharing that space with her, divided by no more than a hanging. Yet before she had gone, such was my greed, I nearly called her back.

Greed is not loved by anyone, but this let me forgive myself. What a chappie coveted with Alison was not all hot blood and tingling skins: for that my thought would be to follow her, not keep her on deck. Well, yes, I did yen to clamber her, so much it could seem that without, a chap might never walk in comfort again. Yet that was no more than fragment — no, not fragment; how can this be said? It was the surge of blood you get for ripeness first glimpsed, one not known, like a fresh serving girl, but here joined to a most familiar friendship, so the hungering became soldered to all the other wishes. I wished Alison to have happy life, and wished her to be with me, be there to greet my eyes and smile when I came in, hear me, as she did, with her dark head tilted just a bit, dispute with me, as she did, and understand, at times when no one else did, what was joke — even to mock me, as had happened sometimes, for mannish folly, when clever words or ideas overlarge made a chappie prideful to insist on what could not be so. I craved to go on hearing her talk, wisely or in glee, to sit in quiet or dally over meals with her. She should be with me when I rode, beside me when guests were made welcome, my love and lots of my life while it went on. One word lurks, that seldom does, but might say all I've recited: wife.

Though abacked by this, a chappie had no doubt of it, and it was in none of the cards; deciding made no difference, save to me. It made the price Thea spoke about that much dearer — or so I began believing, till a chappie saw what a conceited ass he was being. Next day was Alison's twentieth birthday (I had a spiffing present with me), and Col, perfectly, was just two years older. And if it was not to be Col and queenship, there would still be Daf, or one of a thousand other handsome, hard young warriors, and I would still have been twenty-four when Col was born.

Still, if a chap sure had the years, he let himself off the daftness; my love for Alison was more and other than old goat. In not long I could lie down to track patiently after sleep in the steady sound of her breathing.

Before another sundown we were making better way on our southward course, out of sight of land. This, Will, not knowing the tricks of this eastward side of Brittan, thought better for safety. Some sailors might funk it, as storms and rough water were famed in this sea, but the boat was a splendid one, and the breeze, westering a bit, held good without threat; the green sea was a slow roll of whiteless swells, and there would be heaps of stars to steer by.

More stars than I had ever known, so the night never got truly dark (it was, of course, the time of lingering evenings and soonest dawns). Alison again wafted off early to bed, and I again stayed only long enough for her to be asleep.

It had been a strange, chafing day with her, at times sadding, when a chappie found he had to master a new foe: anger. Now, it's all very well, as for instance when a chap is very tired, to know as fact that short temper comes from that tiredness. It still is there, and still has other causes that seem real. Same here: not Alison's fault that of a sudden, after seven years, a chap could not see her clothes pressed by wind against her body without guessing at and coveting what was under, all the time knowing that was no go; there was plenty of reason for edginess. Yet still it seemed she was taking lots of trouble to annoy me (and to upset Rayman more, when he was with us) with pricking questions, near all about Col. Damn it all, she had spent time alone with him, and by now must know him approximatively as well as I did.

But as I saw early, and Rayman, though not the meant target, could feel, these were questions not to find out, but to challenge. Why did Col permit Frick's rumoured cruelties, was he still keen on finding how to make guns, who in history, other than conquerors, did he admire? All this was like a repeated renewal of last night's short exchange: a chap had already said you could have no rule without readiness, at times, to do hurt. You can bet I did not hand her more arrows by telling about Col's fleeting idea of breaking the Gridge truce and murdering Vandis and Forn. To do so would've been unjust to Col; words uttered at moments of despair can't be held against anyone.

On Alison's side, I thought there must be at least one cold foot over being hitched, but try as I might to keep that in brain, it still came to seem she was provoking me, doubting the work of half my life. The old throat began to go tight when I answered her. Remembering back, a chap must've thought (felt, rather, without true thinking) that if, for the general good, I could do down private wishes, then, heck, so could she. I told her she should've been there when Col, at seven, told Maire, after a beating, that to have a strap did not make her right and him wrong, or at Vandennis when he came from the shadow, and when he won at staves and his winning modesty made friends with the defeated Daf. Rayman, before he went off to do some totting of accounts, added his bit, about Col being the demi-Atlas of this earth, the burgonet (which must mean a sort of peak) of men.

Alone, Alison and I talked for a time about what had to be done at Gridge, but soon she came back to Col: would he take to my plan for new laws, bringing back *jury*, an old idea we admired?

Through that day, by hairsbreadths, I kept myself from snapping, but Alison's always been a long journey away from stupid, most especially with feelings, and the undermeaning of spoken remarks. More than once or twice I caught a look of puzzlement, as if she was wondering what made a chap unlike myself (I with what should be sweet going all sour and knotted in my tripe). When goodnights came at last they were made friendly in a careful way never needed till now. On deck by myself under such lots of stars, I hankered for the journey to end before the easiness we always had together was gone past any snatching back.

Very late, I missed Alison's breathing and her small stirs. Lots of time passed, and a chap began to wonder what had become of her.  After tweaking aside a bit of the hanging between our two low beds to be sure she was truly not there, I waited for what must be another quarter hour, and at last got up to look.

Whether I would have raised the whole ship if she was not found I can't say.  People were not lost off boats in weather like this, but what if, just for example, she had found a liking to, say then, Peet, a youngster with good looks for himself, long looks for her?  Quite likely he had heard what she did for his brother (married, now) seven years back.  William Shakespeare's black chap is agonied by doubtings, but as for Alison's appetites, the delicate creature herself was in no way to be called mine.

Coming from the greater darkness, I saw her at once.  To east, the sky already showed faint yellowing, and Alison was kneeling at that left side of the deck, with something in the lap of her long white sleeping shirt.  Even before noticing the coiled wrappings at her side, I knew she must have the Bronze Rod there.

She was still as trances, and my thought (which kept me back by the covered part, not to interrupt) was that after all Alison was a priestess of Thea's heritage, doing some needed rite.  While I stood unbreathing, she stood, and I saw the soft gleam of the Rod, as she held it chin-high in both hands.  Then it was gone.  The night was so calm I heard the plop as the Bronze Rod went into the sea.  As the Bronze Rod went into the sea.

No words would come.  I did make a sound with my voice.  Alison was startled a mo, and then, knowing me, she said with much calm, "It had been long enough in the world."

It had gone; Alison really had dropped it in the deep sea. At first a chap had no room for anger; the dark fact the Rod could never be got back was all of me.

I said, tight-throated, "How?  Men died to bring that to us."

"No.  To take it from Forn, and keep it from King Vandis. That's done."

"Why did you do this?" I pled, still numb.  "Without the Rod, we can't make Col a king."

"Oh, yes.  Col still can be king, King of All Brittan, crowned in Lunn.  That is enough."

What I chiefly felt was ill, ill and weary.  So much of a chap's life had gone into fetching us to where the Rod could be nabbed for Col.  Whether Alison hated him and always had, whether she was Forn's ally and always had been, these dizzied me, and I had to say no to a dimwitted urge to go to the boat's side and stare at the water, to be sure the bloody Rod was gone.  How could it, having been kept safe through all stories of the world? It was, swiftlier, the feeling after Worrel was killed, and for years I could not arrive at Pormarch without (in the part of me where what had been always was) expecting to hear that loud voice and enjoy his big grin.

"I am sorry, Evan,"  Even in this dull light I could tell that, though she was afraid, Alison had moved nearer.  Her feet were bare.

"Sorry?" I began, and then quite truly could speak no other word about it.  If a chappie could not lie down, he would fall: sleep was all I could think.

There were no proper tales in my dreams, but they were all loss and fear of loss, and a rotten feeling that because of what I could not make happen all loved was dying.  That tumbled on through half-waking and sleep like death, and when sleep stopped, the world of dreaming at first did not.  When a chap saw Alison beside his bed, it was as if, in the dream, we won after all, because she was alive and here.  That was before memory came back of what she had done.

One way she guessed right; she was holding a cup.  My throat and tongue were dry as treetops in a hot September, wind rustling there.  I sat up, and Alison held the cup in two hands, taking a little sip before passing it to me.  It was cool beer, and a proper lifesaver.

Soon Alison took back the cup, which I had emptied.  How she put it on the floor reminded me of a blind woman I once saw feeling for her spoon, but here it was because Alison never took her eyes from mine.

Then she kissed me.  It began with her; soon we were kissing long and longer, a kiss no ninny could mistake for plain affection.  Dead sure she knew what it meant, but not ready to be so bally certain, I wrestled out of my own eagering, and spaced us again.

What else could I grab at but the drowned Rod?  "Why, Alison?"

"I love you, Evan.  I would do anything to keep from harming you."

"Not quite anything," an echo of herself.

She leant to kiss again, more lightly, but not lesser.  "You can punish me," Alison said, "in any way you decide."

Alison said, "Tomorrow, I'll tell you why, not now."

Alison said, "These might be our last days together. It's always you I'll love, even if you have me marry another man."

Alison said, "It has been such a long time; you've made me wait too long."

These words she said I write separately because of how they were, divided by our lungings. No scrap of doubt now about what we were about to do together, and to put paid to any last hesitation I might've shown, she let on I was not the first chap she had bared for, which I soon would have guessed for myself (I could, and can, also guess the name of the only other; not Col).

Not many of the old books we have (even those taking trouble to tell about the littlest happenings of private lives) describe matings, and whilst we can never know what might be in the thousands of other books lost to us, it seems old writers might've come to believe as I have, that where strong feeling is, what bodies do is the wrong place to look for all the differences love imparts; what lovers bring to bed matters more than what goes on there. So long (a chap should add) as the body does not fail — and there it can be said my two long looks at the Bronze Rod had done me no inch of harm. But no matter how extra topping acts may be because done with Alison, they can have only the same words to tell them as a hot wallow with a harlot soon forgotten, or one more try at bringing fire back to a dank marriage. Both we were fierce and tender, bold and shy, betimes near choked with wonder. When morning was quite plain outside we found a bit of food, and with the rest of the beer had a bare breakfast. After more shared journeys we fell asleep side by side.

We were wakened soon and still early by the shout of a sailor, who had seen another sail. There were windy thoughts we might have been caught by a craft from Raug, and Shan had his men stand ready, but soon we passed by a fishing boat, and swapped waves and shouts. Then the sea was empty as before.

To toddle a few steps on the deck, or to sit with Alison was again filled with that strangeness when known is also new: there was not a change between us, and it was all different. In all years of our seven it had often been said, by assorted people, I treated Alison as my equal. Those words (or the same thought said otherwise), accused by Maire, had been a verdict on my notions of rearing a child, but to Sheal it had more to do with ranks, mine exalted, Alison's unjudged. It was an amusement to Kennet, and a glad wonder to Edin. Whilst I, knowing quite well what they meant, knew it was not near true. Oh, it had never been a chap's way to tell Alison she was not old enough to understand a thing, nor to make her take my beliefs as gospel (an old kind of holy writings). Yet now, when we took up her reasons for what she had done with the Rod, and what now we were to do, it was easy to see how far from equals we had been, because now we truly were.

Last night, you see (or this morning, if she had not waked me with cool drink last night), though I might have been able to calm myself to hear her reasons, it would've been a questioning by me, a defence by her. That was quite gone. We talked together, and quietly for the main. Not to say we stayed in tame accord, but strangest of all this newness was that the work of all a chap's life, and what was to become of Brittan, did not matter half as much as being there with Alison, our loves brought out into midsummer light.

About that, she said, "I always loved you, never anyone else."

Remembering how for comfort her small hand had found mine, at the feast when Edin claimed his Robin, a chappie must've smiled a bit. But when I mentioned his name, she said, "It seemed you never would stop thinking me as a small girl. He looked at me with a challenge, but what I loved was what you gave Edin. I loved you in him."

So I was moved — and it was the same Edin, when Robin said something like that about him, who made the rule we must believe such words when spoken.

Still, I must not waffle on about what can't ever be as out of all whooping to others as to me. We (I think she was, too) were filled with each other, but bulk of the talk was not about ourselves.

Before her unexplained act, we began with what was to come. It was hard for me to see how Col, without the Bronze Rod, could still (as Alison had insisted) be king. But she said, "There is another rod, a prettier one. It goes with the crown, and Thea called it the Sep. It was of Kings of Brittan, and Queens, too, before anyone ever said a sausage about the Viztas."

"Sceptre," I said suddenly, once again putting aside funk about the crown. "That's in William Shakespeare." As had always seemed right, I said it *skepter*, but because of Thea's word I now believe it must've been said like other words of the same beginning. Our cross-blade tool for cutting is called, to write it as said, *sizz* (in some parts they say *sizzy*), and the *scissors* I read about in old books must be the same; *scent* meaning a smell, and *science* meaning learning must also be such words. But sceptre, like crown itself, was once a true emblem of being royal; a bozo king in William Shakespeare complains they've put a barren sceptre in his gripe, meaning, I take it, his kingship is not worth a brass farting.

The hiding, of which Alison was so certain, gave me more puzzle than ever. She said with the crown it would help its holder be king over Mynas and others who still kept to any part of the Old Beliefs, and if it looked as spiffing as Thea had told Alison it would be more like the True Myke than the simple Bronze Rod ever was. But where was Alison in all this? If she was ready, for the sake of Col's rule, to bring these relics out of hiding, to some degree pulling wool over lots of eyes, what did that say about her beliefs, and why had those brought her to drown the Rod itself? That had made Col's kinging much the harder.

"But it held overmuch power," she said.

"You've always said like me you hold all that to be codswallop." Sight of the Rod's untroubled gleam, true, might've been enough to make anyone think again about its powers. Yes, but Alison's dumping of it overboard, or the words she had for it, did not proclaim a move she had just thought of.

"It was in my mind," she allowed, "from when you said I might be the Woman Who Comes from the Sea. Before that, there was bugger all I could do, but I could not be the one to hand so much old trouble to Col. Last night, it was hard to make mind up to a deed so affrighting. I sat with the Rod on deck ever so long before summoning up the blood for it."

If a chap had waked sooner, or not lain waiting so long before getting up to seek her, the Rod might still be with us. But in Alison's voice I heard truth of the wrestle she'd had, and it came to me that all yesterday, when she so pested me with doubtings of Col, had been part of that struggle.

"But why?" not yet letting my heart reach to the terrors she had gone through.

Alison's explaining was like Alison, not simply told. There were parts she was very loth to speak. Thea, she reminded, had regretted that right from the beginning with the king called Gilgamesh, the powers of the Rod had been mistaken, and that had happened over and over thereafter.

"As with the one in Macedon, and his bully son. Beezers who longed after power believed the Rod gave that."

"The priesthood Thea belonged to is very old," Alison went on, picking up another strand. "I understand them, because Thea at first thought I must be one of them. After teaching me part of what they know, it was seen I would never become one. I know just one other alive." (So did I.)

"When you taught me, you once said about wars of religion, when a few think they've got onto truth others can't find, they never let it go. It may not count tuppence, but they kill and die for it. Just their private sharing of it must make them so."

"The priestesses of the moon, as Thea told me about them, were never makers of wars."

"But still they are stubborn as an Adda-priest about having truth. No one can know whether the powers of the Bronze Rod are, were, what Thea believed. Still, because she was so certain it did not bring power, she could never see what you have taught for ever so long: belief that starts false can become true just through being believed. Remember, you say the same about foretells, they can fulfill themselves."

"But not belief if belief wars with sense," I warned. "Not all the belief there could be can make horses fly." (But a chap can't really *know* even that's true.)

Alison said, "I thought of all those old conquerors who were dead sure the Rod gave them power. That is why it had been in the world long enough. Col, like them, believes killing is given a purpose by strong rule."

"Has he told you that?"

"He told you, again and again, if you listened to him as you listen to Forn, or Frick, or Neal, or anyone else. If you could hear yourself when you say what he is like."

I was abacked. "When have I ever said aught but good about Col?"

"You excuse him; he is only young, a warrior, and warriors must do nasty doings; he'll be different when he comes to power, is he no better choice than to be ruled by Adda-priests..."

"And is he not?"

"You said yourself, your bally horse would be better. If Thea, after all, was right about the Rod, is it Col's wishes for the world we desire? Col as king, to keep us from Vandene claws, yes, but not five hundred years of the mastery Col stands for."

"Col is of Seeyow." I was quite miffed. A chap knew what Alison was saying did not mean she had stopped admiring a chappie, but still it was a bit of a stunner to find so many grains of salt mixed with an admiration I had held for granted.

"He was at Seeyow," all cool. "Not of Seeyow as you mean it, as Marten has been, or Edin was, or I am, or Rayman.

But Rayman is more blind than you, looking at Col."

"Col is admired everywhere, even in Raug. If not, with the Bronze Rod or without, we could never have dreamt making him king. Bryan, Daf, Frick, king's sons all, beg to wear Osset's Star. Harder than I am, yes, but a king must be."

You can see from this last that Alison's doubtings were no utter strangers to my brain. Still, I was a long way from praising her drowning of the Rod, and she, as I say, was a bit shy to press her points, knowing Col meant lots to me. For a long time now we were silent, or tried to see how, sans Rod, her coming from the sea could, on the spot, do in Forn and his hopes. It seemed quite out of the cards Forn had been fooled by the fake left in the Rod's place, so he would be prepared for a change in plans: without the Rod his best bet would be the crowning of Vandis, if Vandis dared put on a crown, at Lunn. There he was in for surprise from gathered Mynas, but in the meantime Forn, suspecting the Rod would find its way to another would-be Arfra, must be trying to put out the Rod, after all, was neither Scalipal nor the Myke of the Viztas.

Alison smiled at that. "You think Forn truly believes, as much as Thea did, in the Bronze Rod. If so, losing the thing is just the start of his fret; he'll be waking all night in case it comes to Col."

"Which, thanks to you, it can't."

"Must we be for all Forn is against?"

A Seeyow answer, if ever there was one. To tell the honest, in Alison's act, right or wrong, it was easy to see Seeyow, to see myself. That was in her voice; she was asking me to agree that to keep the Rod from Col was nearer my own teachings than bringing it to him.

Little by little, as our talk came and ebbed, a chap began to see the lad as Arfra of legend had made me overlook or explain parts of Col in which, to be sure, he was not worse than others. Alison wisely asked, was it enough? would I in full wisdom, forgetting he was Col, wish to give unreined kingship to one no crueller than our time, no more covetous of power than others, no ruthlesser than other warriors?

But still I loved the splendour that was in Col. "Like Daf," Alison said, sounding one who makes peace with a sad fact. "He also — never mind. I hope he escaped safely."

With some (my niece, as example) this breaking off would be a game to warm curiosity, but Alison had really changed mind. It was a good time later in the day she told me, with no pleasure, Daf believed Col had let Edin be killed.

This was outside words; Col (as I said to Alison) had taken on Syme's dreadful lot, killed Syme himself, trying to reach sieged Edin.

"Daf's belief is they could've reached Edin in time, if Col had not split his forces. Without the best of the Brotherhood, Daf still came near as dammit."

"Daf, then, thinks Col made a mistake. You can hear that after any big battle; second leaders always have plans that would've worked better."

"No,"

Alison wanted to stop there, but miserably saw having gone so far she had to finish. Daf's belief was Col had made delay in charging to where Edin was, as a way of ridding his only rival, and because of Robin.

"That's loony," I said. "Col was all for Edin. Besides, he has been polite to Robin, no more, since her widowing."

"Before his renown, she was as high as he could aim," Alison said, as near sourness as she had been. "Now she serves no use to his ambitions. But do not say this is true, only that Daf fully believes it. And still he goes with a few fighters into the middle of Raug, to help that Col become a king. He may be dead, helping that Col."

Good gracious. She held up, as 'twere, the mirror, and a chap saw himself as blokes in general. All the time I had thought knowing made me apart. Tulsingham (to bring up an extreme instance) was amazed that when the rulers in Rome went bonkers they still got people to do what they ordered, and there were always some who, even when these rulers did completely dotty and truly awful horrors, went on thinking Caesar was the cat's pyjamas.

No mystery, it is easy as pie. Just look at Evan. I had given away the rule in Marchlen, and twice in Niragwyn, partly because of being too busy, but mainly because of feelings like this: I knew a ruler has to pick who lives and who not, even if he only decides what is worth warring for. At times, there comes no praise either way; it is just as easy to blame Tam, who squandered Cumber in war without hope, as to condemn poor Tobin, who did the opposite and watched his kingdom made nothing. By being Merdyn with Col for an Arfra, a chap could share glory without having any guilt.

Besides, once having chosen a ruler to admire, a bloke can give reasons for, and even praise, deeds he would call dreadful with one he resolved to dislike. Tulsingham, even, does this, with Elizabeth, who was queen in William Shakespeare's time. Tulsingham lets her off scot free for bumping off her cousin and rival, and says she was astute to get rid of her, and yet it is hard for a chap to see how Elizabeth's wisdom is different from what's called beastliness when one of those Roman rulers did the same, except Tulsingham has decided he favours Elizabeth. So it was with Daf and Col. So it might be with me.

Yet, as I told Alison, believing the crummiest that could be told about Col (and that's not saying I did), he would still be the noblest Briton of them all, when put next to that worm, that canker Forn wished to put over us. "It is a fault to fall so in love with goodness we let evil win, because we're too prim to help what is not perfect. We can still make Col king, if not — "

There a chappie stopped, feeling a proper fool. I was saying back just what she told me, and arguing for a course already begun.

This made a good time to fetch her birthday present, which, sooner than carry riskily across Raug lands, I'd had Rayman bring. It was a kind of headdress: the fine network cap I had bought off a boat from France that came to Wezram, and the green stones (these may be the emeralds I've read about) had been in my family for ages, all of my mother's that had come to me. The work of hanging them by tiny chains to the edges of the cap had been done secretly by a worker in small, precious orts ("An you call him smith," said Rayman, who brought him to Seeyow, "then must you speak of shoeing moths."), using gold I had got from Wott. We have not much gold, and what there is gets mainly measured as money.

I told Alison the headdress befit the Woman Who Comes from the Sea, and I had expected her to wear it for her wedding.

Though admiring, she did not yet put it on, but held it on both hands. "When Col hears what became of the Bronze Rod, he will not be pleased with me."

"There is no need for him to hear it. Only you and I got a good look at it. We can tell him Forn never had the Bronze Rod, just a phony anyone would twig."

Alison said, "Oh, Evan." Yes. Col as king would have his desires.

We sat looking out on the empty sea, flickering with bright, the sun high above. The breeze had kept moving into the west, and we were tilted over, longer waves, often with curls of white foam, coming with the wind. Alison, not glad, said, "I wish we could sail to behind the wind, find America. Or that island Arfra's taken to, when wounded at the last battle."

"I know." So we sat, smalling the world to the space with us in it. They called me Magician, but real magic is when, with no plans, a chap's ordinary life becomes so rich there no taste or touch, hearing or scent enough to hold it all, and what is seen sharp enough almost to give wound.

Sailors all over the shop began shouting, thudding us back into the less-real world called real. Noon, and we had raised the headland where Tem opened to the sea. Right soon would we be back amongst schemes and counterings, dicey moments and big chances, the fate of Brittan and all that. Nothing was sure, not even that I was bringing Col his bride.

## Gridge

Hookbeak sea-birds came skimming near; the east was fire, and now a sliver of brilliant sun exposed itself. Last night clouds had come heaping in from the west, and there had been drizzle; I had begun to get wind up in case no sunrise was to be. But later it was another starry night, and as dawn came there were just a few stripes of cloud.

Giving the sign to the rowers, I murmured, "It is time," to Alison, taking her hand, cool but a bit dank. She was in the lightest of gowns, full-sleeved and long in skirt, and her hair was capped with the birthday headdress. She had sucked in her bottom lip, and was holding it under her front teeth, and though the light was still scant I could see she was very wanny. The sailors with me now guessed we were half an hour's steady row from the jutting point, coarsely grassed, where (in the newer version) the feet of the Viztas, countless years ago, were said to have first touched land.

Where the Tem, still wide, has absolutely left off being sea, we had rested a day, and added a littler boat for coming to the shore on Midsummer morning, one to be rowed with two pairs of oars, which seemed more in keeping than sail with our solemn job. Besides, Will in the larger boat was unsure about the ever-shifting sandbanks hereabouts.

At anchorage, I had come near a right old dust-up with

Shay and others, bigwigs among the Mynas (there were even a clutch of Magpies, thitherto the worst enemies of the Grey Cats), who came, as plotted, to meet us. The set-up at Lunn, Shay said, was hunky-dory for us, no matter what the Vandenes thought. Forn had put still more soldiers there, but none of the silly asses were in right places, and the treasures, the Sep and the other (he would not even utter the name) were safe with his blokes.

Thinking and rethinking of next dawn, a chap had made up mind it would not do for Alison to waltz ashore without something surer to do down Forn. I required the Sep from Lunn, so she could put it in Col's hand (a chappie was not silly enough to try making the Mynas cough up the unspeakable crown). There and back in time to bring it would be a toughish trip, but the Mynas were used to night travel, and it could be done with hours to spare, if they would get weaving pronto.

Well, Shay's face darked over, and he got very mulish, muttering it was a treasure Mynas had kept a long age, and could come to the rightful holder only as per foretells. To that effect. In this he had lots of hench, and a chap did not seek to put spanners in our good alliance with the Mynas, but we had come to the very seamark of our utmost sail, and so I was a bit carbolic instructing Shay if we were to speak of foretells, the Woman Who Comes from the Sea was no dusty specimen.

Shay, backed up by Sil, the young Brown Hare who had led me to Wott in spring, retorted Mynas had, besides, their own beliefs, and it might've got sticky, if not for Alison. Shamelessly putting a priestess disposition on, a wheeze remembered from Thea, she shook them with words about how, in the raising of Arfra, the Magician from the Island makes all the running.

Crikey, she even ghasted me, putting in some high-sounding Print English stuff, half-gibberish to them, about raising spirits from the vasty deep, embarking in a sieve, rats without tails (they understood that all right) and yawning graves, such a deal of skimble-skamble stuff a chappie might've tittered, except it was doing the trick, and Alison did everything but wink at me to get me going on in the same vein.

Ergo, feeling a bit daft, a chappie gave with the portents. I said, as best I could in language they could twig, Arfra's hour had come, and any who failed him now would be in the old minestrone, and no mistake (I do not give my authentic words). The Arfra, I quoth, was of the seed of the Mynas, but if, because of deeds they did or failed doing, his flowering got nipped in the bud, the stock would wither too.  They would shrivel like frostbitten plums, and never have another sprouting.

Of course, for any guy is always a tittle or two of mystics on that score.  The first time we ever remember carrying a sudden long stave it was pretty weird, and about every bloke has known an hour, whether with tootsie, wife or strumpet, when for love or money he could not lift one.  Still, I was disused to having tough bozos quail at warnings, coming from old Evan, that old Evan would not give a farting for.  Straight up, it was a jot embarrassing so to wake superstitious dreads, not what Seeyow had always stood for — but then, if we could not make Col a king, Seeyow would not stand at all.  Such niceties asided, it worked like a dose of salts.  Grousing ceased, and Shay made tracks for Lunn.

I wrote about Mynas traipsing about by night, but of course there was not much, that time of the year.  It was late but still undark enough to make out shapes of trees, and inkblots starting to join together in the light sky, when Shay and his cumny rode back, carrying most respectfully a leathern bag with the Sep inside. Really quite a lot nicer to see than the Bronze Rod, even if more battered about: it seemed to be of both gold and silver, with a lot of good crafting, and the top end spreads out a bit like a flower.

It lay now in Alison's lap. As light bettered, the bloke at the tiller informed there were people on the shore in hundreds. Perhaps not hundreds, but I could see two gatherings, on the muddy edge itself, and on the knolls above.

Alison muttered to me, "Forn will see this is not the woman he expected, long before we get there."

"What can he do, what can he say? It is the Vandenes who had everyone ride down here to see a wonder. Can Forn now say *that is not the marvel I had cobbled*? At times to cry fraud is confession of your own cheating."

After yesterday I was certain with the manner of our coming, and all the years of foretelling that lay beneath it, no one would say it was only Alison with Evan, two we all know. Alison was known to have weird powers: if seven people each had six cherries, she knew at once and with no waggling of fingers how many cherries in all; she could recite magic-sounding rhymes, and write the signs only the sorcerers of Seeyow knew. If Forn believed (quite likely he was right) that at this time, in this place, with all ancient tales twangling in othe air, one as little cloaked in mystery as his daughter could pull off this stunt, I was ruddy certain Alison could.

If news about theft had reached Forn, he must expect the Rod to show up somewhere, and be ready to cry fake. Also, not knowing his daughter had vanished, too, he must have buried some object worth showing under a stone at Gridge for Avanda to point out. Now, with Avanda wondrously replaced by Alison, he would try (a chap thought) to take over and do the pointing lark himself.

A chap more than half wished he could be on shore as well as where he was. All the lords of Brittan raised hands to shade their eyes as they stood waiting just above the worst of the mud, but our boat came from the full flame of sun on flat water, so no one could be sure of who we were till the boat was rasping to still. Someone, Forn likeliest, had caused boards to be laid across the sticky part of the tidal shore.

Vandis, I noted, had worn his newest and snappiest, and put on the famous and gaudy Belt once Tam's; he was as slim and young of face as at his raising to kingship — in one way, younger, with a pout to his mouth seven years of doing as he bloody well pleased had given. He (or Forn) had taken care to have all the rulers nearby, whether captive like Urt, nearly so like Erril, or still in crumbling alliance against him, like Neal, Kennet, Bryan and Follen. Others of their families were with them, and all were done up as peacock-like as poss, but Col was decked, as I had advised him, weeks ago, in his plainest war-worn clothes. He was standing well to the left, almost the last of the curve of royals. Frick, big and frowning, was next to him.

I jumped from the boat, and handed Alison down. When

we crossed the short causeway of planks, the array of kings was not twelve steps away, and Vandis, his mouth open a bit, was giving Forn a daggerish look.

I said, in style I'd had lots of practice with as a Tela, "Lords of Brittan, here is the Woman Who Comes from the Sea, to give you your king. Here he is!"

In front of Col, I stood to reach for and draw his sword from its scabbard  and hold it straight above my head, saying, "This is Scalipal, forged by the king himself!" Then I handed it back to Col, hilt first. He sheathed it, and Alison, holding the Sep two-handed, came to kneel a sec in front of Col, then give it him, with the clear words, "Arfra, King of All Brittan, here is your sign."

Col too, looking, may it be said, aye, every inch a king, held the Sep aloft. Of those near him Neal (and who but Neal?) was quickest off the mark; he dropped to his knees with a shout of, "The king!" Frick was next, and the others, Kennet, Follen, Bryan with his brothers, Alma and the rest all did the same, and the shout was being taken up like an echo by the mob up on the knoll.

No matter what you think of a bloke's beliefs or how he goes about promoting them, you have to squeeze out a bit of admiration for how he plays a game gone wrong. Forn, no doubt about it, was up against the wall, and if he had been ordinary the tale could have ended there on the shore, the clamour for Col sweeping up even lots of the Vandene captains and soldiers. But with only a moment of stun, he all-but jumped forward, waving arms, crying for a wait.

He got his quiet. In it, his well-steered voice was flat after all the declaimings and acclaimings. The sword, he said was never from the Viztas (making the sign); everyone knew it was made by Rayman of Seeyow when Col was only a boy. What was more, the rod given him was not the True Myke, Scalipal, which had yet to come from the stone. Looking straight at yours sincerely, he said all a chap had done was to show us the king of Seeyow, while the forecast King of Brittan was standing here. Forn wheeled to point at the pouty Vandis.

This brought a growl like a haunched dog from Frick, and a somewhat half-hearted shout from some of the captains of Raug, answered at once by a better one from those of the Alliance.

I said, speaking more at Forn than to him, that he was the one who brought the lords here to witness the Woman Come from the Sea, as in the tales. Well, presto, here she was, making her choice. Forn (who, by the way, must be fretting over what had befallen his daughter) answered that tales also told about false claims to be Arfra. There were more tests, at Gridge and at Lunn, and then, oho (he did not speak that), we would see who was Arfra, all right.

My brain was racing like billy-o. If Forn still promoted Gridge, he must believe he had the Bronze Rod, or a passable fake, as his ace in the hole. If he had come early to Gridge to see the hiding of the Rod done properly, he likeliest would've had a squint to be sure it was the genuine article. Being a careful cove, he might well have had Linsy make a spare, to be on the safe side, and if that phony was now lying under a stone, bringing it out could still snatch King Vandis's fat from the fire: it would be my turn not to be able to cry *fraud!* without letting on the tricks I had been up to.

Well, it was one thing to know more than half of Vandis's own people were more than half convinced Col must be the one; they would go to Gridge and watch Forn do his stuff, and the harder we tried to dodge that, the more Forn could make of it. We could still end up dividing as before, the Alliance having a king but Raug with three times their swords.

Alison was watching to see what I did. So was Col, though he was hip enough to try to seem aloof, too certain of his kingship to bother with this bickering. All this weighing up had taken less than a sec, and as I had no other choice than, I agreed the King of All Brittan would welcome any test, and was glad to let everyone see who was the false Arfra. Col, to tell the honest, looked less than joyed.

Forn did not like how ready I was to agree; it was funny to see the blister caught just between triumph and doubt; I had made his daughter disappear, and set Alison in her place, and what else might I be able to swing? But like me he really had no choice but adhere to his guns, the True Myke, Scalipal, the Myke of the Viztas, was at Gridge, waiting for Arfra, this was to be the noon of its rebirth, he had the right man, and sucks to me.

Before I could answer, Alison said if that was so, we should go there and see. She was heard only by us who were nearby, and Col, who had yet to speak, kept his face quiet, so only one who had known him from childhood could see the worry there.

Forn was not smiling, either; Alison's confidence shook him more than my smoothness, an act he had seen full many a time. He said, trying to prepare just right, it was the True Myke, not a sword, that was sincerely Scalipal, and that king who chinwagged to the Viztas did not need any other weapon.

A chap could not let that breach go begging, and I said it was a good job, too, all of us having heard about the Vandene king's skill with a sword. This (though more ponderal in our tongue, like all I put down here) raised smiles; even one or two of the important Raug captains could not hold down quick smirks, and poor King Urt looked as if he would spit. Like Col, Vandis was trying to keep a distance from the dispute, but he was seething.

Then I said, gesturing to Col, the true Arfra was a fighter, a killer of giants, vanquisher of Syme, a warrior other warriors followed, the one who came from the shaddas, who with his fighters as foretold came from the Hill of Caer, and was one worthy to carry Scalipal. This as best I could in our shabby words; Oh, how I wished then Forn, at least, had some Print English, so I could do a Rayman, not only laud Col, but dislaud Vandis in a selection of William Shakespeare's ramping words, like Hotspur does Bolingbroke!

Forn, though, knew he could not win on this ground. Only Gridge could save his bacon. Noon, his noon, was still hours away.

Before that, I did make a moment to be privately next to him, and told him Avanda would not be harmed. His look was like a fish, as if a chap wasn't there, so I left him and went to be sure there were horses for Alison and me. The time was odder than a dream, caught between belief and doubt: throngs parted for me and there was white-eyed awe of Alison; when Col made tracks, every inch but one a king, he was in a circle of effulgence, observed of all observers, yet still on spec.

When we were all aboard horses, he came to ask me to hold the Sep for him. "This must not be the Bronze Rod."

"This is the Sep of the kings," I said. "The Bronze Rod is gone."

"What does that mean, gone?'

Alison broke in. "I drowned it. It was truly the Bronze Rod, but it was too perilous to put in your hands."

This was really what she believed. I'd had vaguer tales ready, but understood Alison's confounded need to be truthful. Yet it made the old sit. bally awkward.

Col stared at her. "You got it, and then got rid of it? It was mine by right, my heirloom. I am the only one to decide whether or not it was bad for me."

"Once in your hands, and deciding would have been too late. Trust me, lord."

"How can you know?" Col demanded.

"I know."

"Don't do witching with me. I knew you before."

She never flinched. "Powers come when needed. No matter if someone remembers us before we had them. Not even a king."

Phew. This, Marten ago would've said, could be heard in two ways (poor Frick, riding near, trying to fit the words he could pick out into some sort of sense, would've liked to hear it in just one). And there came to my poor, innocent noggin it was not just a hit Alison had scored in a bout with words: she was giving warning to a shrewd young fellow who never stopped calculating.

(What a chap really wished was to find a private spot, and catch her in a great hug, knowing at last how right she had been to give the Bronze Rod to the sea.)

Col gave it best thought. "You drowned it, you say? After all Evan's plannings, when you knew it could make me undoubted king? No one could do aught so foolish. If I find you've kept it for yourselves — "

"Come, Col," I said quite sternly. "You are to be Arfra, fair dinkum, and we your subjects, but if you are going to kick off in suspicion of those who've done bulk to make you king, you'll have a short reign, and a lonely one. You have to trust me now, at Gridge and when we go to Lunn, and Alison, too. When have I ever done aught except to bring you nearer this day?"

"Did you agree to getting rid of the Rod, then?"

"With suchlike powers, I have to trust Alison's word,"

He looked at her, and nodded slowly. "But that was a hoardable moment, when we saw who it was in the boat. I thought Forn would fall over." This Col said again, in language to be understood by Frick, who had been more and more sulky. Now he laughed.


Gridge, at high morning. Only those of blood were there at the middle, where the litter of felled stones was, but a big throng crowded about; I don't suppose more than sixty or so could really see what was going on, but the ones in front kept telling those behind. I found it droll amidst the soldiers on the side where Raug had its big campment a chap could see the copy of the Seeyow winch sticking up; it only added to chances for making this rite ridiculous.  Not the observance itself, which is old and solemn, but the magic Forn meant to make of it.

Lack of his daughter made for a bad beginning; she had been supposed to point at the right stone.  It was easy to find; not the greatest of the fallen slabs, and one end was propped up a bit; I could see the marks chains had left there when they'd had it up.

Forn did his best.  He started with a changed version of the Arfra legend, saying the Viztas, at the Leaving, had left behind the True Myke, also called Scalipal, where only the true King of All Brittan, Arfra of tales, could lay hands on it.  Everyone knew the story of how all the lesser kings could try, but only Arfra could take it from the stone.  Vandis stood there through all this like two of eels waiting for the liquor (an ancient expression denoting, it seems, gawpish inaction).

Here was the stone, Forn said, and the True Myke was beneath it.  He challenged anyone who could to take the True Myke.

There was no one now to help a chap decide between two risks: either Forn's lot had buried what ours left behind after the robbery, or else a passable fake for the real.  By doing nothing, we might miss grabbing away the last chance for Vandis to do down Col, or I could take Forn's challenge and end up handing Col a rusty iron bar to go with the Sep.

I could still hear Alison reminding me Forn himself believed in the Rod, and that might be my best clue.  At some time in all the years he'd had it, he must've had a quick butcher's to be sure what it was, but I did not think he would feel dead keen to risk his eyes, wits, or other parts more often than he had to.

So I said in a bored way Col-Arfra could lift the stone, Alison could, anyone, a child could, using a winch like the one I saw over there, a machine, as all knew, first done at Seeyow, where we used it for lifting heavy weights of all kinds.

This gave Forn hardly any pleasure. Now, having made the offer, he was afraid Col would ask for the winch in fact to be brought forward.

I went on to ask where was the profit? The king had his rod, and soon would have his crown. The last word caused a general mutterment, and made Forn jump as if stuck in the bum, but soon he got himself back on course. What he had to say needed Print English, and might have been like: "You try to bunkum us with your well-known Seeyow trickeries, claiming for an Arfra one whose blood is half Myna, and now you blaspheme this holiest place at its sacredest hour. Impudent upstart, the True Myke is here!" What he did say was pretty much to the same purpose.

Though my mention had spoilt its coming, the winch was now hauled into the inner ring. It was even heavier and bigger-beamed than the second one at Seeyow, but I had doubts, for all the windings of chains, Vandis could raise the stone without aid. His reliance on Forn bethought me of a child promised treats if only he is good.

Linsy was there to give the orders. He had clearly learnt from first raising of the stone; he had a crowd of the heaviest soldiers holding down the winch, standing on its platform, and more grasping the uprights on the side away from the load. Still, there were cock-ups; two chains were looped about the end of the stone, but one was too short, and at first took all the weight, so that a link pulled open, and the stone settled back bigly.

By the time another chain had been put on and everything done to the satisfaction of Linsy, Forn was taking swift glances at the sun, so near overhead. Vandis had come forth to turn the handle, but it was a long one, and the help of two crouching soldiers made this look less and less like magic. A chappie could've enjoyed the jest more not knowing Col's best supporters would start to waver if Vandis could once lay hands on something thought to be the True Myke.

This time, though slowly and with creaks in its frame, the winch did the job, raising the stone so the end was, as might be, shoulder high from the ground. Forn gave sign that was enough, and Linsy took a wedge of iron, using a heavy hammer to knock it into the teeth of the biggest chain wheel. Looking none too safe, the stone stayed, wobbling just a bit.

"See!" Forn said, pointing. In what was quite plainly a new-made hollow under where the stone had been, there was a box of dark wood. The ring of watchers drew closer, and two men lifted out the box, which had carved patterns done with good skill, and put it at the feet of Vandis where he stood, a bit puffed. Forn, beside him, quickly knelt to open the coffer, and took in his hands a wrapped bundle, much the size and shape of the Bronze Rod as I had received it. Col's eyes questioned me, and Alison looked as if she was holding breath.

"See!" Forn said again. By the shrunken shadows, it was just on noon. Forn had held out the bundle for Vandis to see, and now he started to unwind the bandages. This was, natch, no job for a king, but Vandis, for the first time showing life, grabbed the bundle, and took over the unwrapping. (I've a good idea Forn, for the good of the Vandene belief, you understand, not private ambition, intended his own hand on the Rod just at the instant of its rebirth. It is not out of all question Vandis also guessed this.)

Whilst all necks craned for first sight of the storied Rod, the outer wrappings fell away. The next layer of windings was stained, but far more deeply than those with the one I had uncovered, brown and near-black. Some few of us were near enough to pick up an odd, not nice scent. Holding the thing upright, Vandis unwound, and what he bared was absolutely not the iron bar I had given the Mynas. Not. Negative.

This was brown, and hairy, and stank. All at once I knew why a Myna had grinned telling me how one of the pack-animals had been killed by an arrow. Vandis was holding up a Mynas' joke, part of the leg of a donkey, eight summer days dead.

"Regard the emblem of Vandis!" I cried, and there was a thunderclap of laughter, first among the kings and princes nearby, but swiftly rumbling and chattering away into the bigger crowd, renewing as word of what had happened spread. Vandis let the nasty relic fall; he was looking poison at Forn, whose eyes were at me with a look he'd had before (though about lesser matters), wondering how this could've been worked.

At that instant there was a loud crash. Desiring to glimpse the cause of all the laughter, part of the blokes helping with the winch had left their posts. Without their weight as balance, the stone had fallen, toppling the winch over with it. By luck, no one was hurt, but it was fit end to Forn's magic.

### Arfra of Camlock


Fain would a chap be Tela again, and forthwith be able to finish the story, saying, "*and then Col-Arfra was crowned and hailed in Lunn, and that was the beginning of his glorious reign, told of in many other tales.*" And perhaps history was no worse when it melted down fact into the mould of a parable, teaching how grand people might be, instead of telling meaner, more disappointing truth. Tulsingham, with his yen for plain facts, likes it shown that heroes, after all, are not so unlike the run-of-the-mill us, and I began this job vowing to deliver a round, unvarnished tale, but now a chap is less sure this is the voyage he meant to do, or ought to have begun.

Only one Midsummer has come and gone since Col-Arfra was indeed crowned and hailed at Lunn. Even after the crowning, with few in the offing to dispute his right, the king, as forecast, did have killing to do. Still at Gridge, while some sort of Midsummer rites were being led by a priest (not an Adda; it was the same decent old geezer who solemnised my kinging at Caer, and later married Robin to Edin), King Vandis managed to skidaddle unnoticed. With a few of the leading Myka captains and Adda-priests (Forn not included, which I'll come to in a sec) he went north post-haste, and gathered up fighters, men who, not having seen him waving about a stinking leg from a dead donkey, might still follow him. Our own king's soldiers, led by the Brotherhood, went after him. They had help from Myna bows in one bloody battle, and after that, quite a lot of the Mykas changed sides, and Vandis got bumped off over breakfast by his own captains. Thereupon, Col-Arfra entered Vandennis, and renamed it as his royal seat.

It is good for that, being near the centre of Brittan, but in point of fact the chief place for big confabs is at Stonedge. The king moved the Midsummer meeting back there, as was of old, but is also putting up more pillars so he can roof the old middle ring over for a round meeting place, such as more tales say Arfra has.

He was married, however, in that same castle where he first came from the shadows, and the new queen also took a fresh name, Gwynda. That day was cloudy, and the great hall was filled with dim; the queen was shining enough to teach the torches to burn bright.

To tell that part in proper order, after we'd had the rites (this is back again, now, before Col-Arfra's crowning), Alison pointed out the mistake Forn had made about noon; it was year's noon when the true King of All Brittan was to be known, and that, as I well remembered Thea telling, years ago, was not ordinary midday, but when the rising curve of moon and the setting midsummer sun faced each other across the sky, eight hours or more from now. Then, we agreed, the king would receive his crown, not here but at the Tower.

Where that is can never be secret; the oaths I swore before were all for not spilling the beans about hidden Myna ways. I mean, a chap could row up the river in a bally boat, knowing he would find the Tower, round a bend or two, on the right side, just a bit back from the bank, and too big to miss. Boats were not in long supply, considering the throng that now aimed to go, and the ferrying across Tem would be a long business, but we had heaps of time and I suspected a craft would be found for Col-Arfra when he needed it. So we rested, had food, and did some nattering at the campment of the Brotherhood. To get peace for that we had to put out Col was not going to listen to anyone till after we had been to Lunn: half Brittan suddenly had big things to tell him.

But in mid-afternoon Col did see Wott, who had just made landing, the abducted Avanda still with him, caught between enjoying her part in conspiracy and funk for what her father might do. Col told her what her father *could* do had shrunk since last she saw him.

So I was told; I was not there. The first a chap heard about Avanda's turning up was when Wott found me in a nearby tent, to tell that Col, with only two gawds, had ridden off taking Avanda to find her family (Gwynis, and Vera, my younger niece had come to Gridge with Forn).

If worrisome, this surprised me less than it did Alison. Ago, she had told me Col had been hot to bed Avanda (during the Idiots' Summer at Caer), but, as Alison said, so with every fellow that was but armed. A chap was unsure Col knew about Avanda's child, Mord, but guessed he might be learning at that moment.

Still, for one who had talked like a cucumber (some sort of cold food that used to go in sandwiches) about breaking the

Midsummer truce now to trot over to the Raug campment was not less than odd. Frick heard a bit too late to have any say; he charged off to try undoing it, but by the time he brought together a cumny of the Brotherhood to go looking for their commander, Col was spotted riding back unharmed. With us again, he had not lots to say about his jaunt, except King Vandis must've scarpered in great haste, leaving behind bulk of his servants, all the carts with his clothes and comforts, and also his sourpuss sister.

For us, this led to a new set-to with Frick, who said the whole job would have been done by now, but for the Lord Evan, and his love for saving Vandene lives. He meant, I was the one who had been so aghast about breaking the truce, so letting Vandis flee.

Alison spat fire, and tiraded that without the Lord Evan, it was Frick and his kind who would have been done. If not for Lord Evan, she said, Vandis would have been holding the Bronze Rod, the True Myke. Ago, there would not have been a League of the West, nor a shadda anywhere left for a king to come from. Tough talk. I seldom heard Alison speak now except in our Print English, and was startled at the force she brought to the lesser tongue. She would never have been such a tigress, I am sure, if insulted for herself.

So Frick, in wrath, reminded she was speaking to a king, meaning himself, she a lowly girl, but Col, very lordly, interrupted to say, yes, a king without a dom, unless he decided to present it back to him. Besides, Frick was speaking to no lowling, but to the bringer of the Sep, the Woman Who Came from the Sea, to be honoured. As for saving Vandene lives, bloody hell, more than half Col's subjects were to be Vandenes, new times Frick would have to usen himself to. It was wonderful and a bit embarrassing to see how Col could make an underling of the older warrior. Col's defence of Alison — this is the main reason I bring up this brief bout — pleased me, at the same time as bringing back fears he meant her, after all, for his bride.

When we had another few ticks alone (you can bet we grabbed every one we could get, not knowing tomorrow), Alison laughed at me. "Col has not changed private mind. I am to be held in honour, not that he likes me, but because that brings Col glory."

She might aptly have said the same about my magicianing. I said, "That is wise in him."

"Oh, yes, I mean to say no other. But in dealings with kings raised by magic, we are unwise to see love in what is mere good policy."

My turn to laugh, then to seize Alison and kiss her forehead. "You know, I have spent my life hoping for and perhaps helping train a king whose brains rule over his heart."

In what a chap could see was only a sec of being grave before she started returning kisses, Alison said, "I do know. But now we are achieving this, you must not have it break your heart."

Soon after, she left with Wott, going to Lunn to have everything ready, and for me chaos was come again. Even whether Col-Arfra made her the queen was not the sum of anxiousness: Col himself had once said a king, whose marriage was just part of the ruling, could, quite aside, take what pleased him; it is ordinary guys whose choice gives up all that is not chosen. Hope, which two days ago was as far from me as treason (hope on my own account, I mean), was now messing up a chappie's careful philosophy.

Time passed, sun slid west, we rode, cutting off the loop of the river, going straighter to the place, very near opposite the Tower, where the bridge once crossed.

Ferried over, watched by many hundred eyes, we were led by Wott, making for the fat central *keep* as the word once seems to have been. We climbed to an open place in front of the very ancient, bulged walls. It had grasses, and someone, Mynas it must be, had worked hard to make them short and even as the nicest lawns of the king's house at Saffam, the latening sun striking slantwise to give it the soft look of the fur at a cat's breast. There is not any great hill, but we were high enough here to look westward across a gleaming loop of river to where the bronzing sun dipped near the dark, broken pillars of the once-crowded wilderness. East, the sky above mists of no colour was blue with light inside it, like a clear gem.

Near the big tower, straight in front, there was a stone chest, which may once have been to hold a dead body; it was much bashed about, but the top had carving, what looked like the figure of a man, armed with a sword, lying on his back. Four Mynas were standing guard.

Ten or twelve paces short of the chest, Wott halted. Col and I did the same, with all the others spreading behind, soon making a ring. Then, from a shadowed doorway, Alison came, again dressed as when we arrived from the sea at dawn. There had been chatter amongst the crowd that followed us, but that now ceased, and so did the chant, *Arfra! Arfra! Arfra!* of the Mynas, watching from high places of the walls everywhere. In the quiet, a shiny raven, wheeling down, did one hard caw.

Alison said, in her clear voice, "Here is the King of All Brittan, to get his crown." She pointed at Col, and though the word *crown* still brought murmurs, there was no challenge. Forn, with his family, I knew, had made the river-crossing before us, but he was not now to be spotted. The other Addas there were in the crowd seemed awed as anyone else.

Alison went on, "This is the time, year's noon, when old sun and young moon look in each other's faces." She gestured west, where the reddened sun was settling. She pointed east, and dashed if Thea's words had not come true; a thin pale bend of moon had ridden above the mist.

What the skies did was good as gold and silver; every other damned thing was a ruddy fraud. At Wott's wave, two, then four of the Mynas guarding the coffin thing tried to raise the big slab of lid, then complained it would not budge; it was locked (one pointed to a keyhole just below the lid, near the middle.

Alison said, "Lord Evan, where lies the king's key?" All this had been arranged earlier.

I stretched up a hand, and, lo, in the late light a key glittered as I snatched it from the sky. The crowd gasped, but this is a dead easy trick I betimes used as a Tela, learnt from a friend of Asta. He did this and other marvels at fairs. Hardest, once you know how, is remembering your wonder before, and not thinking just because it is you doing it, everyone can see how simple it is. You also learn you can be bold outside all belief; while Alison was making everyone look at the rising moon I had taken the key from my pocket in open view, and kept it hidden in my hand.

Bowing, I handed the key to Col. The Mynas had given

it a good shining, but it was a crude one; the lock it fit could not be much.  Any challenger likeliest could open it with a bent nail.

Behind Wott, Col went forward, stooped to fit the key into the hole.  It turned easily, and the Mynas surrounding the chest bent again to lift slowly the massy lid.

Alison stooped to take the crown from the stone chest, and pass it to me, two-handed (just as she had a cup of drink, not yet two nights ago).  Plainer work than the Sep, a broad round band with little crosses sticking up, and a bigger one in the middle at the front.  But the eight or ten big jewels set in the ring looked good to me, and the weight as I took it told me it was really gold: as with the other piece I was struck with wonder that a treasure with so much value as money had been kept whole and safe so long by those who have such little of their own.

Holding it up high brought end to the hush, as gasps and murmurings broke out all over the shop.  Col, the Sep held in his right hand and the crook of his other arm, had turned to see the crown, and the noise of the watchers let me say to him, without being heard by the general, "Kneel!"

He went down on one knee.  I announced, as the crown was above his head, "This is your king, and by this crown he is known!"  A chap spoke in Print English, not caring how much was understood in words, when acts were so plain to read.

Considering how a chappie's sweaty hands were shaking, it's a bloody marvel the crown went on straight.  Not a bad fit.  I gave Col a hand up, and he turned to face his people.

Wott cried, "Arfra!" and now everyone there took up the shout.  Col motioned with his left hand, and, blimey, from who noticed where, Forn, smiling his old smug smile, stepped forward at this invitation.  He flung up both hands, and in the chant of an Adda, said, "Praise the Viztas, who show us our king, Col-Arfra, ruler of All Brittan."

Then, "Who made the world that was?" — the start of the bally Evening Answers.  He got the answer, too, from more than half the crowd, but before he could go any farther Col turned and nodded to Wott, then to me, as sign we would go on as the plan was.

Even so, I was livid.  Plainly, Col had cooked this up with Forn when returning Avanda to her family, and a chap felt as if he'd been made part of Vandene rites.  Behind Col's back, as we started to process down the hill, Alison's eyes found mine.  I thought she seemed halfway to laughing.

Just as if we were alone, I could hear her chiding my ire, pointing out it was no other than pained pride, Col having made up to Forn without my advice or even knowledge.  My advice, that is, for this single here and now; a chap should instead be glad Col had followed my way (and this was my way): by pretending to think Forn's cruelties were no worse than the ways of war, and by giving the Vandenes a part they had not earnt (to say no more) in his kinging, he made peace with half his realm.  A good peace, if the Vandenes were stripped of power.  As must be so; Col knew the price of treaties, and surely it was not without something given in return Forn had got his part in these rites.  Sanely mused, outside first anger, the wonder still was Col had been able to grab at the chance King Vandis gave by leaving Forn.

"But he should have let me in on his thoughts," I said (still inside my own brain, you understand).

"He is king," the answer came.

In the same roofed place where Thea had died foretelling a king, which the Mynas (I guessed) had spiffed up no end, the king took his stand. Before anyone else, Avanda (as she still was then) came forward and knelt to Col-Arfra. All the high-ups that day had worn what finery they had with them; no one was quite as peacocked as Avanda, wearing what must be the gown in which she would have come from the sea; it was long and blue, dipping deep to the rise of her breasts, and fine craft had made the stuff shimmer. Col raised her, and kissed her hands. It was perfectly clear this was no surprise, at least to him, and now I saw (as Alison did, too) what, more than continued place in the new realm, Col had held out to Forn. It was smashing really, bringing the Vandenes in whilst giving not a sausage to their belief, by making the chief Adda-priest's daughter their queen.

Thus, in a compound of prophecy with policy, Col-Arfra came to rule All Brittan, and all the small kings there, all captains of soldiers, all heads of Myna clans swore glad oaths to obey him. When it came to my turn, he clasped me, and murmured in my ear an apology for keeping the treaty with Forn to himself. "I had no time. Today I could not stomach another wrangle with Frick, as would have been. That is a better king's man given choices already made."

"It was well done," I said. "The Mykas, no buts, must be disbanded, and there can be no more forced belief."

Col-Arfra was grinning. "So Forn understands." As he said this, Col took the hand of smile-wreathed Avanda.

"What can you tell me about Mord?" Col said, now in a

voice for her to hear, as well. "You've seen him, and never said a word. We shall have him brought here. Or go there, to Saffam at least. They are all my courts, now, aren't they?"

That was a touch of boyish glee that gladded me. Then he brought Alison to him, putting hands on her shoulders, and his proud look was as if challenging a question for his choice of Avanda over her. This also was young, in a less happy way, and had no real reason; Alison had never spoken or acted as if she counted herself as destined queen.

The place where we were was starting to look like the hall for a feast given by some rich blighter as uncaring as Marten about the rank of his guests — and one who had never heard of the warrings in the past twenty-five years; I even saw two of the Myka captains in talk with Shay of the Black Cats.

These sorts of goings-on, ordinary Raug traders at elbows with both lords and Mynas, could not last, of course, and the new realm has degree, priority and place like any other. But it does show what a mood could come, that day, from shared hailing of a single king. Avanda had not left his side (or ceased to smile) since he raised her after her oath.

Just the other day, her father came to see me here. On his way home from court, he said, but for pretty sure I was not even supposed to pretend believing that was true: to reach Seeyow needed about four times the ride than his straight way home.

That very day a chap had been pondering: if Forn had left the whole business of the Bronze Rod alone, or brought it out only for a gathering of Vandenes at Vandennis, chances were the armies of Raug could've made Vandis King of All Brittan by force. What did it matter if he was no Arfra, or if a few soon-starving bands of outlaws (as we had been on our way to being) still would not bow to him? Forn, in his way, was sold out by his own belief, forced by belief to gamble all Raug had won on a ceremony that could add not a jot that was real. Of course, he didn't know it was a gamble, and as Alison reminded, the ceremony was founded on fakery. Even so (I maintain), if Forn's beliefs had been faked he would've been content to let war do his job.

Besides the king's father-in-law, he is Prince of Raug — but it's a Raug shrunken back to roughly what it was when I was born. Forn is also still chief priest of the Vandenes, but their ambitions (and his for his belief) have smalled, too. They do not say Adda, now, and for the sake of a governable realm we pretend the cruel Vandenes all were killed with Vandis.

Well, as said, Forn came to see me one rainy day, and his chumminess was made all the funnier by the work a chap set aside to have chat with him; I had been writing about Col's covert leaving from Vandennis, and my surety Forn would've had him killed in a trice if he had guessed a coming rival to King Vandis.

Now (after a swap of family news) he sought my help in opposition to a new law. It was meant to settle all the many quarrels over lands caused by the return of territories grabbed by Raug. Frick, Neal, and others, Forn said, wished to make it so that where the before owners (so we call them, though really only tenants) were dead, or for any reason were not to be found, the lands would go back to the last true owners, the once-kings now local princes (and collectors of taxes) under the King.

This, Forn said, was unfair, because there were lots of Raug blokes who would be beggared. They had got those lands, their only living, by paying good money into the coffers of King Vandis, nabbed by the King of All Brittan after Vandis's death.

Tales of heroes never make much of taxes, though they always keep waffling on about the splendours of the kings' court, and how generous he is. But how can any king maintain his soldiers, much less any splendour, without revenues? In our world as it is the big point about being a king is what he owns. King Col-Arfra now has all lands. He says so, and no one openly disputes it. His law states the princes lease their former realms from him, and landowners from them, and so on down to the small farmers with a couple of fields.

"Why am I to lie awake over what becomes of blighters who sought profit from loss of others?" (These were the blokes who murdered so much hedgerow to make their fat new farms.)

"You stand, mostly, on the side of fairness. These men only followed what was then lawful, they had no voice in making the law, which was the king's. Lots sold their old farms to buy the new ones."

Times are when neither laughter nor tears can do the job. The king's law, in good sooth! The world doth truly know who made all policies for both the Vandis lately dead and his tubby father, and here was that man asking his longest foe to help repair a portion of the ruin his Vandene madness had wrought.

In the end I told Forn if he, as Prince of Raug, saw to it these poor creatures could buy back their old lands, I would press for repayment of what they had paid (no more) for the new ones.

He either saw that as just, or recognised the best he could get, and left next day.

A chap might've told him he would do better jawing to Rayman. Oh, certes, the Lord Evan's great power, his influence with Col-Arfra, are bywords everywhere, and when, with my young wife, I visit court, in the city and castle that used to be Vandennis, there comes feasting and flattery.

When there it is to Rayman the Lord Evan goes for the news. He no longer comes to Seeyow, and in large measure has taken my place at Col's side. He is thought to be my chap at court, but is much more the king's. Since I am king's man myself, it ought to come to the same, but in real life there is fair difference. No doubt Rayman is very able, and in discussion with Col-Arfra, he brings in pretty much the same points as I would. But where I might use them to dispute the king's choices, for Rayman is enough to have any objections heard and noted. Col-Arfra, for all his honouring of yours truly, is far comfier with that sort of tamed dispute.

Like others, Rayman, last time, was full of the latest daftness about the Heir. That he is exactly like the king himself at three is agreed by everyone who did not know Col at that age, but Rayman, one of the few who did, ought to have better memory: to my eye Mord is put together in a way utterly different from Col's early squareness.

Still, all, including the king, seem satisfied with the boy. For the Mynas, Wott is specially proud of the slight darkness to Mord's skin, saying it comes from his grandfather's side. Well, but Col's complexion and hair were always as they are now, fair as his mother's, and that darkness was (and is) only in his eyes. The odd light blue-green of Mord's eyes (there are smooth stones in Col's crown a deeper shade of the same colour) I've seen in only one other person, a woman who, by luck, seldom comes to royal gatherings, and then is so quiet hardly anyone notices much about her.

When Col told us the Queen, Gwynda (Avanda that was), is carrying, I caught myself in the same dark thoughts when I first heard her son's name, a shiver of fear. For all sakes, I hope she'll have a girl, and only girls henceforth. Thus, Mord's right to succeed could never be challenged, whereas a younger boy might store the chance for new and bitter wars, especially if Mord becomes more like — but there are truths should not be written, even in private books.

It suddenly strikes a chap I have not told what befell Daf after the raid that seized the Bronze Rod. Lots of joys came to Col-Arfra on the day-into-night of his crowning, but none, I believe, was more top-hole than when Daf, road-weary but unwounded, turned up at the Tower, late because he had gone first to Gridge.

As chanced, my eyes were on Avanda, whose eyes went wide, and she very nearly rose to her feet and went to greet him. Recollecting herself, she touched Col-Arfra's arm, and he, now seeing Daf, leapt up with a roar of welcome, brushed past Neal (who also was glad to see his son) and exchanged a big hug with his friend. Five of the fellows who had helped pinch the Rod were still with him, and soon we heard a full well-told account of that action, and of Daf's escape from pursuit. He'd had too many enemy between him and the waiting boat, so had journeyed by night till the Gridge Meet Time began. Then, no word of his raid coming south, he and his soldiers rode openly on the broadest roads, calling themselves men from the wild north, on their way to the Midsummer gathering.

That also explained why Forn's men had so trustingly buried the smelly surprise from the Mynas at Gridge. When the scawt came back, and found, to their great joy, the coffer was still there, with what looked like the Rod still inside, they must've decided to keep mum. It just shows how, though feared masters may get better service day to day, they pay for it in the end, by having mistakes hidden from them.

Since then Daf has become, as Col-Arfra hailed him that day, the Spear in the King's right hand. He led the forces against the last of King Vandis, and a bit later, in the north, against an invasion of wild men from beyond the settled realms. These had been collected and somewhat tamed and trained by Tam, Tam's son, meaning to lead them against Raug. Hearing about our change of rule Tamson tried to call off his invasion and ask Col-Arfra to make him lord over his father's old realm, but his men, already licking their lips over plunder, disagreed, did him in, and came ravaging over the border. With the Mynas now royal allies, any foe is going to find it hard to raid and hide, and Daf, with heaps of swift horsemen, soon gave the old heave-ho to all they did not kill. Since there was now no admitted heir in Cumba (A flame-haired daughter Tamson fathered with a rude woman of the far north may yet be a bother to us there), Urt of Umba became lord over both realms, biggest of all the tax-collectors.

Robin has now agreed to marry Daf. Grinning Col told us this just after the news about his own wife's state, and his glee was a world away from the glumness back when he lost Robin to Edin. But that loss was also a rebuke, not a meant one, to Col's standing, and Col-Arfra the king was only amazed it had taken Robin so long to take Daf. It needed at least the sixth asking, he said, to do the trick.

He meant Daf's looks, and the manner he learnt from Seeyow, are admired, and even if he was crude as his father, ugly as Syme, he would have his choice of women, being King's Captain and best-trusted. Shrewd Alison believes those are exactly the reasons Robin, a widow with her own voice, made Daf do so much wooing. Well, now Edin's small son can have good fostering.

The armies Daf leads, welding the Brotherhood to the best of what were the Vandene cumnies, are stronger than either or ever, but have yet no enemy to test them. Not, I should say, in Brittan.

Col-Arfra next said, "That wedding should be before Daf goes abroad, Have I said we are sending a hundred of the Brotherhood over the sea?"

"I heard it from Rayman."

It should be explained that since Col-Arfra's reign began, we've had more dealings with overseas spots; the boldest of our seamen now go across to bring back wine and some made things finer than ours, and the foreign ships come more often to our ports. Their sailors tell that the place once France is now lots and lots of petty realms, none of them bigger than our Stanglin, and those lands are rife with small wars, even more than Brittan before the king came.

One of these little lordships, whence we get good fruits and cheese, asked for Col-Arfra's help against their neighbours, in a quarrel about a river-bank, and there Daf is to go, with his hundred fighters. He and the king believe they will be more than enough to bring victory to our new ally.

"It would be better," he said, "if we could have guns by then."

My heart again went cold, but there is no stopping this; guns are coming as surely as other remade machines that could more swiftly do jobs we want done. Rayman says he now knows what all the substances are that went into gunpowder, and can find them, given time. Linsy is going to forge the strong tubes needed: a cannon is far easier than the winch we made, or so Rayman says. Using them, and the littler, portable guns they talk about, is easier still; children and silly asses will again be able to destroy great warriors and sages, as of old.

Rayman's belief, and now the king's, is that guns can save lives, by making blokes too windy to fight. "Only the royal armies can have them," Col-Arfra said.

"For a while," I answered grimly.

At the same time Col-Arfra aims to begin building large boats, more than we could ever need just for trade. He now talks often of old cities lost to us, like Paris, Calcutta and Rome, and when he says the word *empire*, it is like a ripe fruit that fills his mouth with sweet juice.

As for guns, is this, with the killing and hurt that go with it, history that must happen? If I had never learnt to read old books, and hence never taught him, could he now be so dead keen on reviving the mouldy dreams of Gilgamesh and Tiglath Pileser, Caesar and Napoleon? If, after all, Thea was right, the Bronze Rod was what held those dreams, but now the Rod lies lost under the sea where hands can never touch; not likely people could be guided by the dreams of fishes or seaweed.

This, then, ought to have been the first age since the youth of the world when people could choose their own fates. But as Alison says, and our adventure showed, if the real Bronze Rod, by any of its names, goes for a burton, men can always make or find another, and swear it is a McCoy. That need not be only bad, but all powers need wariness.

When Col was young we used to say how one good that came from having single rule was safety for travellers, and now the king says his empire could do the same for more realms, so if he purposed to a chap could go looking to see if there still are Pyramids in the place called Egypt, and discover whether America is real or fable, all without fear of war or waylaying. Not a small benefit, and true too there must be lots of chaps, scattered over the world, who possess bits of learning, have invented or re-invented useful devices, know healings, wisdoms to make crops bigger, or buildings stronger. Brought together, or just linked by the roads and writings of a world made safe, they might teach all of us to have better life, with less toil, less pain, less hunger, and so more gentleness and courtesy.

Perhaps, also, a chappie like me is too hard on this deathless hunger to rule. I, and other guys (and, it might be, more women) of my bent ask little more than to be left alone, as we would leave others alone, to spend life as pleases us, harming no one. But that cannot be: till everyone is content to let others live their own lives, this corner of the realm where I live needs the king's law to keep it safe, and behind law, threat of the king's swords. Many chaps (Frick would soon say) have too much squeam for fighting, yet claim the prizes of victory, still keeping right to say weapons they've helped forge are too cruel.

Alison has remarked I would rather be in a happy-ending tale that can stop where lovers marry or the varlet bites dust (these are just examples), and no more gets told. She wiser, knew early we could only keep our realm from the worst, not turn Vandennis into storied Camlock (she bunged the Rod into the sea, after all). But for all sorts of fellows, whether clever as Rayman or dry-eyed as Frick, the raising of our king was a happy ending that still has not left off. And Camlock is the new name Col-Arfra has given Vandennis.

Yes, but what are the changes, other than the stopping of wars, to make lots so joyed to live in the reign of Arfra of Camlock? I was tickled pink, goes without saying, when people began seeing Col could fill the bill, but when clever Rayman all at once begun serving and adding to the legend about a boy he used to show wrestling tricks, when much the same happened to that scarred and soured warrior, Frick, I kept watch to see if they would wink, or give a hidden grin; it was hard for a chap to swallow their complete belief. Too, Forn surely does not inly believe Col-Arfra speaks straight to the Viztas using the Sep, yet he now teaches his Vandenes that the king has the True Myke. It seems to me blokes conspire with themselves: desire to believe the marvel comes first, and then everything goes to show it true.

We are getting at last to a single law for All Brittan (beyond, if the empire gets off this ground). Like all laws, there is death in it.  A good king can have subjects who are greedy, ambitious, envious, quarrelsome, dangerously mad, and if there is someday to be a realm at peace where law and punishment have no use, that day is not yet (and that realm will not need a king).

We've had hangings, too, and whippings still.  The usualest crime is theft, and as the end of warring gives us better shots to feed and clothe ourselves, there ought to be less reason for hanging thieves.  But so far there are still lots of poor among those who cheer Col-Arfra at the gatherings.

Maybe a chap yearns for too much from foretold heroes, as if any king could ever rule by love freely given and deserved.  If the Arfra we've got is short of the magnificence of prophecy, at least no one is now made to follow, or say they follow, any faith: our king lets his father-in-law give praise and credit to the Viztas, but still cannot believe in private they ever were, and no one can now be punished for saying so in public.  Or for trying, Seeyow fashion, to work out how olden people might have done things unhelped by starry tutors.

The reign of Col-Arfra, then, though this is not ever after, is heaps better than what it prevented.  What is more, lots of the time a chappie is happier, and happy more often, than ever he could have thought to be, and for reasons never once imagined.  Not a realm's reasons.

My fears, that Col-Arfra, wived, might still pick Alison for concubine, have faded.  Ago, when he said young men were made scareful by the learning I had given her, it never struck a chap Col could be speaking for himself.  He would've scoffed the very idea;

nevertheless, he stays very stiffish with her, as if having to keep telling himself he is boss — whereas his wife, who was first I heard to call her the witch-girl, now natters blithely with Alison, mainly about clothes and the latest wonders of Mord's growing. She even asked, when newly hitched, for a few good man-pleasuring tricks from Thea's workshop.

Alison and I sometimes squabble, are not always each other's whole delight, and if we tried to live in poetry, where love all love of other sights controls, making one little room an everywhere, would both be bored dopey in three days. A chappie says these only to lessen his own soppiness, living as I ever am bang inside a great gratitude that can easily drown my proper judgement and earnt staidness in salty sentiment.

All at once is plain I've overpraised Tulsingham, all through this book of mine. Outgrowing him seems a lot like with Alison, only the other way round — a fellow had been out of love with Tulsingham, i.e., for a long time without noticing it, very obvious once seen. We still must thank him for heaps of facts, but he thinks it would be best to have a world run all by logic, like one of the smooth old machines, and you might as well say humans could fly if only they were birds. Tulsingham scorns all superstition, but faith in a world never seen is just as superstitious; reason becomes another religion. It now seems to me a chap has to welcome and make friends with the mysterious, not trying to kill it with explanations, loving shadow, as poets do, as well as light.

Both. Unreason too, as poets show, is not all poetry and

kindness; consider what the Old Beliefs can perform. But if that
dark bloodthirst cannot ever be logicked away, might it not be
better, Wott and his mother could say (and if not, I say it for
them), to make one special place and time when tameless needs
can be used, perhaps for a while used up, instead of shackling
them, till the chains break and let loose vast wars and rapings? A
chap offers this as might-be, not fact. Facts are nowhere near as
numerous as once I knew.

At the time of Thea's death a chap was near agreeing with
William Shakespeare's dreadful bozo when he says love is only a
lust of the blood and a permission of the will, and now it seems to
me no thesis a chap could actually prove is as certain as this fable
of my love for Alison, when I watch her reading, or she looks up,
glad to see me, or of a sudden, at a meal-table ringed with guests,
grabs for my hand with hers.

Except how to sit still, a chappie's learnt not a bit. Young,
I was praised for the unmeant killing of a poor bloke, and
renounced blades; grown up I helped to raise a king, and have
sworn off being either Tela or Magician. All too dicey, messing
about with futures.

That day of the crowning (which seldom goes out of a
chap's mind for long), when we were letting heels cool off
between noon and year's noon, Col more than once had come
back to Alison's drowning of the Rod, how I had allowed it, how
it could ever have been done. He was niggled by this, but then,
quite boyishly, he asked, "Was it because you or she thought with
the Bronze Rod I would have too much power? Do you think I

could be like those Roman itlas?"

"For myself, you know I never believed the Rod had any special powers." (a bit dodging the question, I confess). "That is all in people's brains."

"Oh? Is that all?" With a laugh, knowing how often I had taught that's just where power verily is.

He stared away, as if looking at a portrait of the future. "I'll need every scrap. The kings in the Alliance are all for me now, because I might save them from Raug, but as soon as those varlets feel safe, oaths or none, they'll go back to their old little realms and squabbles, unless I have power in their heads."

"That need not be magical. Earnt respect is power."

Col's hand was still resting on my arm. "Evan," he said. "What you have gone through to get us where we are is never forgotten, but if you make me king, you make me king. The power does not stay yours, to spoon out to me. I'll never be such a mug as to not give ear to your advice, but there will be others I listen to, and I'll have my own thoughts. And the deciding is mine. Is that understood?"

"Always, sire." (not a title we use, but it seems to have been kept just for kings, not simply another way of saying *sir*; I speak the two words with the difference there is between *fire* and *fir*). "This is just what a chap has been saying for years. But see that for me, or anyone given my job, it is not easy to recognise a time foreseen has at last arrived. No bells have rung."

This also seems like a load of flannel, written down, but at the time I was truly stirred by what Col said, and more than ready (as a chap might have said at the time) to lay down my long burden. Grand stuff. Tales have tons of it.

Later, when Col-Arfra had his crown, when he greeted Daf, and called him Prince of Brittan and the Spear in the King's right hand. Almost before the envy could jump into Frick's face, Col-Arfra was there too, telling him, "You shall be, as natural, Prince of Stanglin, where your father ruled, and equal with any chap in my Cabinet."

That was admirable, and as the King pleased each of the kings in turn by making them princes over what had been their own ruddy realms, mine met the speaking eyes of Alison, and she made a tiny shrug. We could call our long day's task done: Col-Arfra was going to be good at this lark.

Again if a chappie sounds mockish, it is of himself, because at the time there were tears of pride behind dryer, more cynic admiration. The more so when he saw our look, reading it, I believe, as wondering when our turn for reward would come. "You last," he said, just to me, "because my whole rule is yours. But Neal knows you are to have Seeyow for your own; do you take Prince of Seeyow as your title?"

Actually, a chap declined to be any more than Region here, so long as Marten is alive, and I also startled the king by saying Alison, as well, should be ranked in his Cabinet (which was not his unnudged intent). Still, all the time, quibbles and dealings, all short of humbled gratitude, seemed right miserly to my moved heart, where many memories of Col's childhood and youth jostled with present gladness.

As already, an hour before, when he stood with his crown first on. When I say he was translated (I, who journeyed to sow cunning seeds of legend, who had just done a rotten conjuring turn with the key), as if power was bright inside him, the question comes, really changed? or only by what we hunger to see? I'm a Vandene if I can tell any difference: all we see brings in what has been said and thought. Where aching hopes, treasured beliefs and famed foretells come together with a hero and dare to put a crown on him, the glory is there, let my wet eyes be witness, is really there. Arfra had come, here was a king, whence comes such another?

That is why a chap sits here on Seeyow, a Magician in retiral, a quiet country husband, with no more yens to begin changes he can guess no plain end of. I know evil when seen, but what might be good is nothing like as easy to foretell, and I am not willing to urge much more than kindness and courtesy between those near to each other. Alison once abacked me by calling Col dangerous, but so Col-Arfra is, like any who can get himself followed by other blokes not even asking the simplest selfish question, *what good is in this for me?* But us, whether we help make kings and heroes, or only give them our abject allegiance, what about us? In that big moment, sharing in the fire from Brittan's sun, none of us gave a brass farting whether the Arfra stood for gentleness or vengeance, what killings, benefits or pains, wise laws or wars with nasty weapons, his reign might mean; we were only fiercely gleed to be part of his glory. Us, the hero's confederates, are just as dangerous.

That is how seems proper to end my

Oh, one more little point about the sayings of dear Thea, only part of which came true to be recognised. I once asked Alison what she knew about her own fathering, recalling Thea had made hints about a higher birth than seemed.

Alison was between frown and giggle. "My father was, or is, a dyer, and my mother was not his wife. Thea instructed me how everyone in the kingly families valued bloodlines. She said it made for no difference in the end, because you would come to love me for myself — "

"So," I said.

" — but at the start, you would rather hear foggy half-tales."

There was no weight to this talk, but just the same it was a bit of a facer for a chappie who, from very young, has always caused wonder by his ready mixing with all ranks of people, to be so assessed by a friend. Coming now, the news certainly meant nothing to my feeling for Alison. Perhaps a chap ought to make clear this chat was before our wedding. My bride put on her lovely headdress for that.

The End

# Editor's Afterword

The narrative presented here, to which I've given the title *The Bronze Rod*, was intended as a version for the general reader. However, the unexplained disappearance of the astonishing manuscript on which it is based now makes this the *only* surviving version, and as its editor I feel compelled to make clear my emendations to the text would never have been made except in the confident belief that the original would be available for comparison. Indeed, it was intended there should be simultaneous publication of this popular edition, and, for scholars and specialists, of the complete, unaltered manuscript, perhaps in facsimile, notwithstanding the difficulty and expense involved.

The spoken language of Evan's time would seem to bear, if anything, rather less relationship to standard English than the French or Spanish of the early Middle Ages to classical Latin, in a superficially similar period where social deterioration had led to almost universal illiteracy. The few early attempts on Evan's part (soon abandoned by the author, and not reproduced in this edition) to render the speech of his own time betray a corruption beyond the capacity of our written symbols to represent with any accuracy.

But the main text, written in what the author plainly regards as an all-but extinct "classical" language, though with few unintelligible words, presented its own problems for the editor. Evan's knowledge of written English is to be derived from a more-or-less randomly preserved collection of books, mainly from the 19th and early 20th centuries (this does not preclude, of course, earlier works, reprinted during that period).

Before discussing those problems, a word may be appropriate here about the books available to Evan. His allusions to, quotations from, and paraphrases of Shakespeare are numerous, but while he speaks of the complete works, I am inclined to believe he is to possess at most a single volume from a two-volume edition of the plays; I can identify only about fifteen or so plays as sources. The actual edition he is to have might have been determinable, had I seen any need to preserve the exact spellings and punctuation of Evan's manuscript, but while such an identification would be of some scholarly interest, it is hardly of first importance, and in any event not now possible.

The echoes of and allusions to poets such as Donne, Coleridge and Keats (for example), all refer to very well-known poems, and suggest possession of a popular anthology, or parts of one, perhaps Palgrave or the Oxford book.

Prose sources are, naturally, harder to track down, though I think there are echoes of at least Fielding, Dickens and Henry James, as well as some highly vernacular twentieth-century novels. Any reader is, of course, at liberty to speculate on the identity of the modern novelist (possibly more than one) so scathingly indicted by Evan's disbelief; twentieth century fiction is far from my own field, but many authors, I believe, could be put forward as candidates for his question as to why anyone worked so hard to produce such mean-scaled, inconsequential (or, to employ our own critical dialect, "insightful") stories.

As for the Tulsingham so often referred to by Evan, he cannot at present be identified. The name occurs in no known literary reference work for the 19th century, and library catalogues have so far been unhelpful: this present publication may bring the problem to the attention of a specialist who can identify the work. At least one copy must exist (obviously, since it is to be preserved for Evan's use), quite possibly in a private library in England. Internal evidence suggests an adherent of the skeptical movement which flourished in the wake (so to speak) of Darwin's voyage on the *Beagle*, and the work was most probably privately printed.

That Evan is to take this apparent piece of late-Victorian fustian as a great literary work (his eventual rejection of Tulsingham is certainly not on stylistic grounds) can be seen as both an irony and a cogent warning to our own medievalists and even classicists: in our joy at having something, anything from an otherwise obscure period, we are far too ready to discover structural felicities and literary graces a work may not objectively possess; mere survival, no matter how miraculous, does not make a masterpiece.

But it is amusing to wonder how Evan's work might differ if his notion of history were influenced by Walter Pater, Arnold Toynbee, or H.G. Wells (or even an English translation of *Mein Kampf*!), instead of this obscure Tulsingham. It goes beyond amusement to conjecture to what extent his actions are to be influenced by this extremely limited and partisan view of history — and, by extension, how far our own endeavors begin with a faulty vision of possible futures, founded in false views of the past.

These are questions, of course, aside from the purpose of this note. Evan, when his time comes, is to be a man of striking intelligence, but even so he cannot be made aware of the problems he faces in reconstructing written English from an arbitrary ragbag of examples. When we look back across the centuries to the literature of Greece, we know, for example, that Aesop, Aeschylus and Aristophanes are writers of widely differing sensibilities, and can even teach ourselves that, with birth-dates spanning about 170 years, they are as distant from one another in time as Gibbon, Keats and Noel Coward. Yet if we wished to be fluent in "classical" Greek, these would remain among a small selection of available models, and while what we wrote might be grammatically acceptable, nothing we could do would make us recognize the incompatibility of their styles and eras, as an Athenian of 250 BC would have.

Written English, without the drag-anchor of an elitist hegemony, has changed much more rapidly: Evan, though he obviously is to "feel" a difference between one of the Romantic poets and a realistic novelist of the 1930s, will have no means to judge the incongruity of juxtaposing their styles — or, for that matter, of echoing Shakespeare and Wodehouse in a single sentence.

Even at the risk of causing some earnestly-intended passages to appear laughable, I've retained this stylistic collage as an essential peculiarity. In a few cases where an archaism is actively misleading (as, for instance, where Evan uses *fond* in its obsolete sense of "foolish," and *contemptible* to mean "scornful"), I have, for this non-specialist edition, substituted the modern equivalent. For the same reason, while allowing the author considerable latitude in the matter of coinage (usually resulting from false analogy, as when Evan makes a verb of *aback*, apparently not seeing that *affront*, his probable model, is a different part of speech), I felt such innovations as the use of *crew* to mean "wept" (cf *fly-flew*) created too great a barrier to ready understanding, and silently substituted the intended sense.

These are fairly typical editorial emendations, and at

times, when Evan's understanding of the more complex tenses, or of subject-verb agreement in extended sentences, seemed to me to be faulty, I have ventured to make corrections, as also to simplify a few of the author's more ambitious syntactical experiments, though not at the expense of failing to preserve at least a sampling of his often over-lengthy and perhaps excessively discursive sentences. It should be noted that some of what at first sight appear to be inconsistencies of tense, especially a jarring mixture of past and present, are resolved in reading the story to its end; these, of course, I've left untouched. As a minor point, while retaining the British spelling used by Evan, I've editorially adopted American conventions for punctuation and the like.

With the question of dialogue, a bolder editorial approach seemed desirable. It is here the lack of any living tradition most handicapped our author: to return to our former analogy, no matter what one's mastery of ancient Greek or classical Latin, it would be virtually impossible to find authentic equivalents in those languages for differing levels of contemporary spoken English, to represent the speech of, say, a truck-driver, a college student, and a small-town mayor. Apart from the one attempt, noted above, to record the speech of his own time, Evan was understandably reluctant to report dialogue, and when he did so was at constant pains to note the words given were not those actually spoken. Many of these disclaimers I have excised as repetitious, and I have also attempted to suggest, using contemporary usage as my guide, the difference (commented-on by the author, even as he dismisses all the speech of his own time as uncouth) between spoken language as employed by the aristocratic circles of the various courts, and by the common soldiery or ordinary folk. Going farther, I have frequently expanded into actual reported speech passages which, while appearing as rather arid summary in the original manuscript, would almost certainly have been given as dialogue, had the author possessed more confidence in his ability to make such differentiations. While it is true this process tends to make less clear-cut the gulf (evidently great) between any ordinary language of Evan's time, and what he comes to call "Print English" or "Seeyow English" (the latter seems to begin as a term of contempt, and later, like the label "Impressionist," to be adopted by its exponents) — that is, the language reconstructed, largely by Evan himself, from printed sources, and taught by him to a small, intimate circle — I have felt the gain in readability justifies a sacrifice in contrast: except through the invention of a barbaric sub-English as it might become through several generations of corruption, which in turn would be scarcely tolerable to the ordinary reader, I have no means of fully conveying this distinction. At the risk of being wearyingly repetitious I must say again that all my emendations were made in the belief the original manuscript would remain available for study. For this reason also I omitted to preserve any exact record of my editorial alterations, from which (as the wisdom of hindsight observes) much of the original might have been reconstructed.

The work betrays many signs of haste on the author's part. Evan's quotations are often from memory and often faulty, but these I have left uncorrected. Nor have I sought to impose consistency, although there are usages, sometimes only a question of *le mot juste*, which the author gets right and wrong within the space of two or three pages. Some of his vocabulary seems to depend on what he is to be reading at about the time of composition.

These oddities, and the quaint effect often produced by his hybrid usage, are not, as can too easily be assumed, the result of naïveté; the author is in fact surprisingly sophisticated in his grasp of usage. For example, clearly perceiving the word he spells *dauwa* to be a corruption of the "Print English" *daughter* (a word he adopts for the general sense), he retains the worn-down version when referring to the contemporary institution (*i.e.*, a member of a guild of prostitutes); *scawt*, *Adda*, *gawd*, *cumny* and *tela* are all words he consciously treats in the same way, "correcting" them to Print English except in reference to specific phenomena of his own time: the reference, early in Evan's manuscript, during his discussion of the Mynas, to "miners who were not our scavengers," is irrefutable evidence of a deliberate choice on the author's part.

All oddities intact, then, I make no apology for this version of Evan's tale. It might well be another editor, with access to the manuscript, and my misplaced confidence in its continued preservation, would have wished to carry the process farther, and produce a version where the inherent discords were largely expunged. But the particular style of any work is at the same time the usage of its era and personal preferences of its author, and in clarifying a text, the editor must make judgments as to what is archaism, what idiosyncracy, in an attempt to preserve not only the sense but the individuality of the writing. Besides, while the resultant gain in smoothness and unclogged readability might be considerable, I myself can see how easily an excess of editorial zeal might rob this strange story, not only of its individual texture, but in a larger sense of a valuable lesson it has to teach us.

If, indeed, we are still teachable. To the ordinary person with no more than slight background in traditional science, advanced physics seems to overlap into what formerly were domains of the occult: I am unqualified to judge whether, as it would seem to, the rarefied work of Heisenberg and other quantum-watchers gives a scientific basis for the notion of multiple available futures, making it possible for Evan's tale to belong, not inevitably to ours, but possibly to a parallel, nearly identical, universe possessing small but critical differences — whether, indeed, it might be theoretically feasible for our consciousness to switch from one world-track to another, so that any perception of either past or future could be at the same time both true and false. One hopes incurably for determinacy but also for some access to informed choice. Otherwise, as this account of coming history itself reveals, the question of our learning anything from it will quite soon be a moot one.

Bradley Skimkin, PhD.
Berkley, California
August 11, 1989.